MORTAL FAULTS

Michael Prescott

AN ONYX BOOK

ONYX
Published by New American Library, a division of
Penguin Group (USA) Inc., 375 Hudson Street,
New York, New York 10014, USA
Penguin Group (Canada), 90 Eglinton Avenue East, Suite 700, Toronto,
Ontario M4P 2Y3, Canada (a division of Pearson Penguin Canada Inc.)
Penguin Books Ltd., 80 Strand, London WC2R 0RL, England
Penguin Ireland, 25 St. Stephen's Green, Dublin 2,
Ireland (a division of Penguin Books Ltd.)
Penguin Group (Australia), 250 Camberwell Road, Camberwell, Victoria 3124,
Australia (a division of Pearson Australia Group Pty. Ltd.)
Penguin Books India Pvt. Ltd., 11 Community Centre, Panchsheel Park,
New Delhi - 110 017, India
Penguin Group (NZ), cnr Airborne and Rosedale Roads, Albany,
Auckland 1310, New Zealand (a division of Pearson New Zealand Ltd.)
Penguin Books (South Africa) (Pty.) Ltd., 24 Sturdee Avenue,
Rosebank, Johannesburg 2196, South Africa

Penguin Books Ltd., Registered Offices:
80 Strand, London WC2R 0RL, England

First published by Onyx, an imprint of New American Library,
a division of Penguin Group (USA) Inc.

First Printing, January 2006
10 9 8 7 6 5 4 3 2 1

PUBLISHER'S NOTE
This is a work of fiction. Names, characters, places, and incidents either are
the product of the author's imagination or are used fictitiously, and any resemblance to actual persons, living or dead, business establishments, events, or
locales is entirely coincidental.

The publisher does not have any control over and does not assume any
responsibility for author or third-party Web sites or their content.

What are mortals that you should raise us up,
Set your heart on us, examine us every morning,
Test us every moment? How long?
—Job 7:17–19

Prologue

The knife was how he would do it.

Sure, strangling would be better, but she was a wiry little thing, and he was afraid she'd find a way to wriggle out of his grip. If she got loose long enough to scream, one of his neighbors in the apartment building might call the police. That was how it had gone down the last time, and why he'd spent the last twenty-two months in a maximum-security state prison. He wasn't ready to go back.

Anyhow, the knife would be good enough. Poking her with the long sharp blade was almost as good as sex.

"Penny for your thoughts."

Leon blinked, glancing at the woman who sat beside him on the couch. Her face was pale in the dim lamplight. "Huh?"

"It means, what are you thinking about?"

"You, baby. How good you look. Like a movie star."

"You're sweet."

"Like candy." He slid closer to her. Country music played on the AM radio he'd bought at a pawnshop for ten bucks. Tammy Wynette, "Stand by Your Man." "Want me to give you some sugar?"

She giggled. She was too old to giggle—thirty, maybe thirty-five—but some women never grew up. They were high school girls their whole lives.

Thinking of her as a high school girl made him stiff. She noticed.

"Somebody's getting hard." Her hand brushed his crotch. "You have quite a package there."

"Baby, you got no idea." She hadn't seen his real package yet. She hadn't seen the knife. "Mind if I, uh, loosen my belt?"

"Well"—another giggle—"I wouldn't want you to be uncomfortable . . ."

His hand moved to his belt buckle, which was the handle of a concealed knife with a three-inch double-edge blade. He could draw it in less than a second, then punch the blade into her abdomen, driving it in up to the hilt, while his other hand covered her mouth to stifle her cry. And all the time he would watch her eyes, her pretty brown eyes, as the light in them faded out.

It was almost too easy. He hadn't even bought her dinner. Picked her up in a bowling alley—a goddamn *bowling* alley, for Christ's sake. He hadn't even been trying. He'd already set his sights on the schoolteacher in Reseda. Didn't know her name, but she'd caught his eye while leading a troop of kids on a field trip to the museum where he worked as a janitor. He'd staked out the school and followed her home. She had a hubby and a kid, a nice suburban life. For the past week he'd been watching her come and go, at home and at the school.

Then this bitch fell right into his lap—while he was bowling, if anyone could believe that. He ought to visit the lanes more often.

Of course, he would get to the schoolteacher soon enough. This babe was a warm-up job, a way of getting back into the swim after two years out of action. Then he would be going on to better things—once he got through with . . . with . . .

"This might sound stupid," he said, "but I don't think I ever caught your name."

"It's Abby."

"Abby. Nice." He drew the knife. "I'm Leon."

He lunged, but she wasn't there. The blade gouged the sofa cushion, ripping out foam.

She'd sprung off the couch the instant before he struck. He saw her smile, and there was something in her face that was all wrong—a coldness and a calmness, and the coiled menace of a snake.

"No need to introduce yourself, Leon," Abby said, her voice an octave lower, a throaty, slightly scratchy voice, not so girlish anymore. "I know who you are."

The flat of her hand connected with the bridge of his nose, and something crunched like a snail.

Blood on his face, waves of light pulsing across his field of vision. She'd broken his nose, damn it.

Tammy Wynette was still urging women to stand by their man. It didn't seem like Abby was listening.

Leon lurched to his feet, swiping the knife at her. She hopped to one side, evading the stroke without effort. Her leg snapped up. A leather boot caught him under the chin. He spat blood. He'd bitten his tongue—bitten part of it clean off.

The taste of blood only made him madder. "Fucking kill you," he wheezed.

"No, you won't, Leon." Her voice had a surreal gentleness that scared him. "You've had all the fun you're going to have."

Distantly it occurred to him that she wasn't just some piece of ass he'd picked up at the lanes. She was a pro. A cop or a PI or some damn thing.

He swung out again with the knife, a wild sweep of his arm that crossed nothing but air, and suddenly she was up close, delivering three or four rabbit jabs to his belly, then clapping both hands over his ears.

Pain dazzled him. He was pretty sure his eardrums had ruptured.

And he'd lost the knife. She had it now. She'd taken it from him so deftly he hadn't even noticed.

He got in a punch to her chest before she spun behind him. Her hand chopped the back of his neck. He fell to his knees, throwing a fist at her thigh in a blind effort at retaliation, and then her hands were on his face, blocking his nostrils, sealing his mouth. He couldn't breathe. Crazy bitch was smothering him.

He flailed under her, trying to get a grip on her legs or arms. No use. He needed air. His throat burned. All pride left him, and he made a low pleading noise that barely escaped his pursed lips. A mewling whimper, a sound a beaten dog would make. She ignored it.

He fought to raise his head. If he could make eye contact, she would have to let him go. If he showed her how desperate he was, how abjectly helpless . . .

His eyes rolled in his head. He saw her, leaning close. He saw her face, her eyes.

And he knew it would do no good to ask for mercy.

I

In the morning, the first thing Abby noticed was the blood. It had spattered her jeans and blouse. Funny she hadn't seen it last night, but of course she'd been tired as hell. She hadn't even removed her clothes before collapsing into bed.

Eight hours of dreamless sleep had left her newly energized. She swung out of bed and peeked through the curtains at the traffic flowing on Wilshire Boulevard, ten stories below. At eight thirty a.m., rush hour was in full swing, which was hardly surprising, since rush hour in L.A. lasted roughly twenty-three hours a day.

Her clothes were stiff and tight, like an unwanted layer of skin. She preferred to sleep naked. She'd kicked off her boots, at least. She retrieved them from the floor and found blood on them, too. How did you get bloodstains out of leather? She didn't have a clue.

The boots could wait. Right now she was feeling dirty, and not just because of the blood. She stripped, ran the shower hot, and spent a long time under the steaming spray. Her hands and forearms had caught some of the splatter, and the water running off her arms was pink at first. She watched it spiral down the drain.

She shampooed, rinsed, and repeated, then toweled herself dry and examined her fingernails. More blood under them—a rich harvest of DNA evidence for anyone who wanted to look. She scrubbed her nails clean, then studied herself in the mirror.

The damage wasn't too bad. A fist-sized bruise

under her left breast. Another contusion on her right thigh. No cuts or scrapes. None of the blood was hers.

That's how you know if you've had a good night, Abby thought. *If none of the blood is yours.*

Dressed, she decided to go out for breakfast. According to her calendar, on Thursday, August 10, she had nothing on her schedule. She'd been busy lately, too busy. She knew from experience that it wasn't smart to push herself too hard. Fatigue was her enemy. Fatigue meant slowed reflexes, and in her business even a half-second disadvantage could mean death.

As usual, the *L.A. Times* had been left in the hallway outside her door. She flipped to the "Metro" section, found the story she wanted, and took that page, leaving the rest of the paper in her condo. She donned shades for the L.A. look, then rode the elevator to the ground floor of the Wilshire Royal condominium tower, which had been her home for nearly ten years.

The guards in the lobby saluted her with a wave. She smiled back. Vince and Gerry had been here forever, long enough to have figured out that she wasn't really a software company rep as she claimed, but loyal enough to never breathe a word.

She walked out the door into the bright morning. "Morning, Miss Sinclair," the doorman said, shutting the lobby door behind her.

"Hey, Sean. You're showing a little bit." She pointed discreetly to a bulge in his jacket near his underarm. Sean, a crew-cut blond who looked like a lifeguard, carried a Colt .45 in a leather holster under his red livery.

The bulge wouldn't be noticed by most people, but Abby had an eye for that sort of thing. From experience she knew there was no good way to carry a concealed firearm. She opted to tote her Smith & Wesson .38 in her purse, in a special compartment that she could access without undoing the clasp. The purse was weighted so she could carry it by the strap without compensating for the list of the firearm. The strap itself was reinforced with wire to prevent a tearaway. Not a perfect solution, but the best she'd come up with.

Sean frowned. "Damn. Gotta get this thing tailored. Been working out, made my shoulders wider. Now the gun's printing."

"Working out?" She took a closer look. "Yeah, I see it. Better definition of the trapezius."

"Put on five pounds—all muscle."

"I'm impressed."

"You still won't go out with me, though. Right?"

"Sean, I'm pushing thirty-five. I'm too old for you."

"Don't kid yourself, Miss Sinclair. You'll never be old."

The remark could be taken as a compliment or a prognostication. The first option seemed preferable.

She walked on before he could press the point. She had nothing against Sean, but there were other priorities in her life. Besides, she was still seeing a cop named Wyatt from time to time, and one man in uniform was enough.

A short hike into Westwood Village brought her to a health food café, where she purchased a yogurt-and-granola breakfast, then sat by the window and read the newspaper story.

At approximately eleven thirty last night, a woman was heard shouting for help from a fire escape outside the apartment of Leon Trotman, age twenty-six. Police were summoned. They discovered Trotman unconscious on the floor. Once revived, he complained of having been assaulted by an unidentified female, no longer on the premises. Trotman changed from victim to suspect when police discovered a small cache of weapons in his bedroom, including several firearms. As an ex-convict, Trotman was not permitted to own guns. The parole violation would put him back in jail.

And—Abby added a silent postscript—a certain schoolteacher in Reseda wouldn't be bothered by a stalker anymore.

Things had worked out fine. But there had been a moment, just a moment. . . .

Eyes shut, she remembered holding Leon down as he struggled for air. She'd felt the frenzied shudders of his body, heard the puling noises from the back of his throat. He'd thought she was trying to kill him. And it would have been easy, wouldn't it? Easy to maintain the pressure just a little longer, keep the air out of his lungs for a few more seconds after he lost consciousness. Easy to make him die.

If he didn't deserve it, who did? He had attacked one woman, served time, and immediately reverted to form upon his release. Put him back in jail, and in a year or two he would be out again, trolling for new prey. Why not just end it now? No one would miss him. She would be saving lives. Taking one life, yes, but saving others.

She hadn't gone through with it. But the temptation had been real. And it worried her. More and more often she found herself thinking that way. At first she'd assumed it was only stress. Now she thought it was something more—the cumulative toll the job had taken on her over the past eight years. The slow shift in perspective from protector to predator. She had spent a long time in the shadows, among violent, paranoid men. Too much time, maybe.

But what was she going to do, quit? Not likely. The job was her life. There was nothing else for her. She would just have to tough it out. It was only a phase, probably. She would get over it. Anyway, she'd never acted on those thoughts. She wasn't a killer. In her whole life she'd killed just one person, and that had been pure self-defense, a kill-or-be-killed situation that any jury would have understood, if the matter had ever gone to trial.

The bottom line was, Leon had lived, and he was headed to prison, where for the time being, at least, he would be a menace only to his fellow inmates. Score one for the home team.

Abby put away the news story. She was finishing her granola-yogurt concoction when her purse rang. More accurately, the cell phone in her purse.

She hated to answer it because it was probably work. Because she was so very responsible, she answered it anyway, giving her real name because this phone, unlike some of her others, was not registered under an alias. "Abby Sinclair."

A crisp female voice said, "Please hold for Congressman Reynolds."

Congressman? She'd never had any dealings with a politico, and she wasn't sure she wanted to start now. She wasn't even certain who Reynolds was. Heck, he might be her own congressman. She had a tough time remembering any politicians below the level of, say, vice president.

A smooth, mellow voice came over the line, a good speaking voice, the kind that went down like aged whiskey and made you feel all warm inside. She didn't need to be told who was talking. He told her anyway. "Miss Sinclair, this is Jack Reynolds. It's good to talk to you."

"Likewise, umm . . ." How did you address a congressman? *Your Honor?* She settled on "sir."

"I understand you offer assistance to people who have certain difficulties."

This was vague but not inaccurate. "That's right," she said. She didn't ask how he knew about her.

"I wonder if it would be possible for you to meet with me."

"In D.C.?"

"In Newport Beach. Congress is out of session now. August recess."

"Oh." Sure, she'd known that.

"I'm back in my district to do some campaigning. My schedule is tight, but I have an opening at four. Why don't you meet me in my office?"

It didn't sound like a question. More like the casual command of a man used to getting what he wanted.

Abby didn't much care for being ordered around, and besides, she'd promised herself the day off. "I'm afraid my schedule is pretty full at the moment, too."

"This is important."

It was always important. Always life-and-death. Sometimes literally. That was why Abby hated to say no. But she was tired. She was worn out. "Maybe if you call again in a week or ten days—"

"I require your help *now,* Miss Sinclair, not a week from now. If it's a question of money, I'll double your usual fee. I'll pay it in cash, and you can decide whether to report it. How does that sound?"

"Kind of desperate. And potentially illegal. You *are* a congressman, right?"

"I was given to understand that you have no compunctions about breaking the law when it suits your purposes."

"And I guess you feel the same way."

"I'm in a difficult situation. I urgently require your assistance, and I am willing to do what it takes to obtain it."

Although the money didn't tempt her, curiosity did. She had to know what this was all about. Tired though she was, bruised like a peach, she couldn't say no.

"Okay, I give in. Four p.m. it is." So much for her vacation. "Where is your office exactly?"

"My assistant, Rebecca, can give you that information." Suddenly the congressman's warmth was gone, replaced by the curtness of a busy professional. "See you then."

Click, and Abby found herself speaking with the same crisp-voiced female who'd been first on the line. The assistant gave directions to an office building in Newport Beach, about twenty miles south of L.A.

"You wouldn't happen to know what this is about?" Abby asked Rebecca in hope of eliciting a little sisterly understanding.

"I'm afraid I have no idea. Have a nice day."

Apparently sisterhood wasn't powerful, after all.

Abby pondered the situation. It didn't make a lot

of sense. She was in the security business. Members of Congress had all the security they needed. Reynolds ought to have had no use for her services. Unless he was arranging protection for someone else—or keeping secrets that even his bodyguards weren't allowed to know.

The phone rang again. Another politician? Maybe it was the president on the line.

"Abby Sinclair," she said.

"I just saw the paper. Thank you."

It was that certain schoolteacher in Reseda, who'd been unlucky enough to catch Leon Trotman's eye.

"No problem," Abby said.

"You saved me. You saved my *life.*"

"I'm not sure that's true." Actually, she was pretty certain it was.

"He was after me. He would have killed me. And the police couldn't do anything except talk about a restraining order. As if a restraining order would stop a man like him—"

Abby had heard the same song from dozens of clients. She didn't need a reprise. "He's back where he belongs, so don't sweat it. Just get ready to write me a big whopping check when my bill comes."

"It's worth it. Whatever it costs—you're a lifesaver, Abby. Literally, a lifesaver."

Abby accepted a few more compliments of a similar nature and managed a graceful exit from the conversation. She put the phone back into her purse.

A lifesaver. Yes, that was what she was.

Not a killer. Of course not.

2

Reynolds's office was located on the sixth floor of a glass box high-rise a block inland from the Pacific Coast Highway. Abby got there early but lingered outside till four o'clock. She didn't want to seem too eager.

At four, she took the stairs to the sixth floor, working up a slight burn in the adductor muscles. It always amazed her that people paid good money for health club memberships and then rode the elevator.

Rebecca, manning the reception desk, made Abby wait in the anteroom while her boss pretended to be busy inside. Apparently he didn't want to seem too eager, either.

The walls of the anteroom were covered with pictures of Reynolds with various celebrities and power brokers. Before heading over, Abby had visited the congressman's Web site, which was cluttered with many of the same shots, along with endorsements from miscellaneous Orange County business and civic organizations.

She'd read his biography online. He came from humble beginnings in the barrios of Santa Ana and never let you forget it. Photos accompanying the bio showed the run-down apartment building in which he'd been raised, and the canning factory—now closed—where his father had worked on the assembly line. No posh private school for Jack Reynolds—his high school class photograph showed a mixture of races and ethnicities, with young Jack, his face circled, one of a minority of Anglos. Prowess on the football field had won him a scholarship to California State

University at Chico, known colloquially as Chico State. It was hundreds of miles from home, in rural northern California. He'd worked part-time throughout college, earning money for textbooks and meals, a practice he'd continued while attending law school. Returning to Santa Ana, he rose to the position of DA—"crusading DA," as the bio put it—before his first run for Congress.

Everything about the man said that he was no pampered elitist. He'd come up the hard way, and he was proud of it.

At four fifteen the intercom buzzed, Rebecca opened the door, and Abby was granted an audience with the seven-term representative of Orange County's Gold Coast.

His hairline had receded since the photo on his Web site had been taken, his temples were grayer, and he was wearing a pair of reading glasses, which he took off, perhaps self-consciously, before rising to shake her hand. A strong clasp, his palm cool and dry.

"Miss Sinclair. Have a seat."

She knew he was looking her over, sizing her up, and she gave him a moment to do it. He would see a trim, wiry woman of thirty-four—though she looked younger, or so she told herself—with brown hair in a pageboy, selected because long hair could be grabbed in a fight. She was of medium height, tall enough to fend for herself and short enough to get lost in a crowd. Her face was pale, with high cheekbones and a scattering of faint freckles. Her hazel eyes regarded the world coolly, keeping secrets.

He resumed his power position behind his desk, while she had to settle for the role of supplicant in a straight-backed armless chair.

"Pleasure to meet you," Reynolds said in his aged-whiskey voice.

"Same here," Abby said. "Nice digs."

"I maintain this office year-round. It's where I work when Congress is out of session." He leaned forward and steepled his hands—large hands, which went with his large, athletic frame. He still had the rangy build of a quarterback, and a squinty gaze set for sixty-yard passes. "As you may have realized, I have a security issue I need to deal with."

"Don't you have the Secret Service to protect you?"

"The Secret Service doesn't provide protection to members of Congress, only to the president and vice president and their families. And visiting heads of state. Basically their turf is the White House and vice president's residence."

"Not the Senate or the Capitol building?"

"That's the jurisdiction of the Capitol Hill police."

"So you're covered when you're on the job in D.C. How about when you're out of town?"

He shrugged. "I'm on my own."

In the post-9/11 world, Abby had assumed that every politico had official protection at all times. "No security at all? You serious?"

"Some members of Congress hire personal bodyguards. Security firms are available that specialize in protecting politicians. There are also retired D.C. police officers who go into the private security business. But not every congressman or senator traipses around with an armed man at his side. Personally, I've never felt the need."

"What about public events?"

"Local law enforcement generally provides protection, crowd control, security checkpoints. . . ."

"And when you're just driving around, shopping for groceries or whatever?"

"I'm by myself. Of course, most of the time I go unrecognized. Most people don't even know who their congressman is, let alone what he looks like. Believe me, I don't draw many stares."

"It still seems crazy."

"The system may be a little out-of-date. Things change slowly in Washington. You know, it wasn't that long ago that Harry Truman used to walk out of the White House with one Secret Service man and stroll down the street for a haircut."

To Abby, it seemed like plenty long ago—decades before she was born. "So the bottom line is, you're unprotected?"

"I'm hoping you'll protect me, Miss Sinclair."

"You do realize I'm not a bodyguard?"

"I'm not looking for a bodyguard. I'm looking for someone to assess a specific threat."

"In that case, you came to the right gal."

"I hear you're quite good at what you do. Of course, I guess you don't advertise your failures." This was added with a smile.

"I don't advertise at all," Abby answered mildly. "I keep a low profile."

"You run a one-woman operation—no staff, no overhead?"

"That's right."

"But you still charge like you have overhead, don't you?" Another smile.

"I don't work for free. But there are easier ways to earn a living."

"How long have you been at this?"

"Eight years."

"Background in law enforcement?"

"You mean, did I get canned because I was a cop who didn't play by the rules? No. I've never worn a badge. My background is in psychology. I have a master's degree."

"You're a shrink?"

"I'm not licensed. It's just my academic training."

"How did somebody start off in psychology and end up being a . . . ?"

"A personal security consultant? I thought it would be more interesting than sitting in an office all day listening to people's phobias. I wanted to do field-work."

"Psychological fieldwork."

"That's what my job consists of, basically."

He grunted, taking this in. "Have you always worked freelance?"

"Yes. I used to consult to security firms. I was an

off-the-books contractor. Now I work for clients directly. No middleman."

"You come highly recommended—though I probably shouldn't mention any names."

"It's best to keep my clients' names out of this. The work I do is confidential."

"So I can count on you not to talk about what you're doing for me?"

"I haven't agreed to do anything for you yet. But yes, you can count on my silence. If I ever started blabbing about my clients, I'd be out of business in a hurry."

"A woman who knows how to keep her mouth shut." Reynolds grinned. "You may be unique."

His charm, if such it was, wasn't working on her. "I like to think of myself as discreet."

"Don't take this the wrong way, but I thought you'd be younger."

"How could any woman possibly take that the wrong way?"

He didn't seem to notice her sarcasm. "Well, I guess it's good you've got some miles on you. I'm paying for experience."

"I have plenty of experience."

"I'll bet you have." He said it with a peculiar emphasis. "How many jobs have you done?"

"I stopped counting. Roughly a hundred."

"A hundred cases in eight years? You're a busy little beaver, aren't you?"

She wasn't sure she liked the "beaver" reference. "I stay active."

"These bad guys you deal with—you have to cozy up to them, right? And sometimes do more than get cozy?"

Now she grasped the subtext. She was no better than a hooker in his eyes. "I try to remain in control of the situation," she said. He could ask Leon Trotman about that.

"Anyway, I'm told you're the go-to gal when there's a dirty job to be done."

"How flattering."

"Don't misunderstand. The service you perform—it's necessary. Not always pleasant, but that's life. A lot of people don't have the stomach to do what needs to be done. They're wishful thinkers, romantics. You and I—we're realists. We know how the world works."

She disliked being included in his company. "What can I do for you, Mr. Reynolds?"

"I'm running for reelection. I've been doing a number of campaign appearances locally. A particular woman has attended nearly all of them. She stays toward the back of the crowd."

Abby shrugged. "Political supporter. Stringer for a local newspaper."

"I don't think she's either of those things. I think she's someone who was formerly in my employ."

"You recognized her?"

"I'm not sure. It's been years. And her hair is different. It could be a wig. At the outdoor events she wears sunglasses. What I'm saying is, it's hard to tell."

"But there's a resemblance to someone in your past."

"Yes."

"When did you start seeing this woman in the crowd?"

"Three, four weeks ago. I began coming home on weekends to do campaign events. Fund-raisers, rallies, town hall meetings. At the ones that are open to the public, she's almost always there."

"And does this ex-employee hold a grudge against you?"

"She may."

"Why?"

"The obvious reason. I terminated her employment. She was unhappy about that."

"What sort of employment?"

"She was our housekeeper. This was ten years ago. Back when my kids were still growing up."

Abby had seen the kids on the Web site—two of them, Jake and Janet, in their early twenties now. A decade ago they would have been about twelve years old. "Why'd you fire her?" she asked.

"She was stealing. In my bureau, I kept a spare roll of twenties. I would count the roll and find forty or sixty dollars missing. At first I thought I'd miscounted, but it kept happening."

"Did you actually catch her stealing?"

"No. And she denied it. Hell, maybe she was even telling the truth. You see, not long after she left, I had some trouble with Jake."

"You think your son was stealing the money?"

"I don't know. He got into some scrapes— shoplifting, vandalism—and it occurred to me that maybe I'd been wrong to blame Rose. It was too late then, of course."

"Rose was the housekeeper."

"Rose Moran, yes."

Abby got up and moved around the office. She had a hard time sitting still in client interviews. "It seems like a long time to hold a grudge. Even if she was falsely accused, she would've acted out whatever hostility she's feeling long before this."

"So you think it's nothing?"

"Didn't say that. I don't really know what to think." She quit pacing and faced him. "Mr. Reynolds, let me explain exactly what I do."

Her standard sales pitch was cut off by Reynolds's upraised hand. "I already know. You stalk the stalkers. That's the way you explain it, right?"

She was surprised. "The very words."

"You identify a stalker, then arrange to bump into him, get to know him. Assess the threat potential."

"You even know the lingo. I'm impressed."

"But I'm not clear on how you arrange to infiltrate their lives. Aren't these people paranoid? Aren't they suspicious of strangers?"

"Most of them are. But there are ways of getting around that. Ways of making the meeting seem accidental so they don't suspect a setup. You know how Hollywood is always looking for a cute-meet situation? They should come to me. I know a million cute meets."

"Well, I guess it's not too tough for you to meet a guy—when it *is* a guy. You just shake your moneymaker in his direction, and he comes to mama. But in this case it's a woman. Might be more of a challenge."

"I like a challenge," Abby said evenly.

"Okay. I'll have to assume you can handle it." Abby thought this was big of him. "So if you determine that the individual poses a threat, you . . . ?"

"I make sure he—or she—is taken off the streets."

"You handle these situations without any violence?"

"Most of the time."

"And the rest of the time?"

"I know a little about self-defense. If push comes to shove—I can shove hard."

"Kick ass and take names?"

"I don't take names."

Reynolds was studying her with narrowed eyes. "You're not that big, though. Some of these guys must have a hundred pounds on you."

"Size doesn't matter. Quickness is what counts."

"And if you run up against a guy who's bigger *and* quicker than you?"

"Then I guess I'd be dead. I told you there were easier ways to make a living."

Reynolds shook his head with a slow grin. "You've got some brass ovaries, don't you?"

"So I've been told." Actually she'd never heard it put quite that way before.

"And I take it you're not averse to breaking the law now and then."

She returned to her chair and leaned against it, giving him a good look. "I don't discuss those details with clients. It's better that way—for everyone concerned."

"Deniability. Sure. Officially I know nothing. Unofficially—well, let's just say a person in your line of work can't be too hung up on legalities."

"People might say the same thing about politicians,"

Abby quipped. Reynolds gave her a cool stare. Not a man who could take a joke, it seemed. "Somebody seems to have filled you in nicely about my services," she said.

"I like to be informed about the people I work with."

"You did your homework. But I'm still not sure I understand why you need me. Most of my clients come to me because the police won't listen to them. But the cops aren't going to give a U.S. congressman the brush-off."

"I'd prefer not to go through those channels."

"Why not?"

"Because if it *is* Rose who's been going to my events, I don't want the story to come out. I told you, Jake got into some trouble with the law. Nothing ever got into the media about it. If this story breaks, and people start looking into my past . . ." He sighed. "I don't want my son getting hurt. He's put all that non-sense behind him. He's straightened out."

Abby thought it likely that Reynolds was less concerned about his son's welfare than about his own image as a law-and-order type. The former "crusading DA" wasn't the sort of guy who ought to have a family member whose criminal activity had been covered up for ten years.

She didn't voice her suspicions. "I don't suppose you have a last known address for Ms. Moran."

"Her last address that I know of is when she lived at our house. She's not listed in any local directories. I checked."

"She might be listed under another name. Was she married when she was in your employ?"

"No."

"She might be married now. She could have taken her husband's name."

"Or changed her name," Reynolds said. "Obtained a new identity."

"Why would she do that? She doesn't have any sort of criminal record, does she?"

"No, no—nothing like that."

"Then there would be no reason for her to change her ID."

"Right. Of course not." He said it too hastily.

Something was wrong here, but Abby didn't press. "I can start the next time you have a public event."

"Then you can start tonight. I'm doing a town hall meeting at a high school in Laguna Hills."

"Don't believe in wasting time, do you?"

"Do you?"

"Nope. Tell me the address and I'll be there."

"My assistant—"

"Can give me that information. I know the drill. Can she also give me a photo of Rose Moran?"

"No, and neither can I. I don't have any photos of her."

"None?"

"Who takes snapshots of their housekeeper? But I can give you the next best thing. I went through the stills my media people shoot at all my campaign appearances."

He removed a glossy blowup from his desk drawer and handed it to her. It was a crowd shot. One face out of many had been circled with a red marker. A middle-aged woman with a lot of curly brown hair that could be a wig.

"Good enough," Abby said. "Now there's the little matter of my fee."

"You charge three hundred dollars a day, correct?"

The man really had done his research. "That's right."

"I said I'd double it. Six hundred dollars, every day you're on the case. Pretty good money. I hope you're worth it."

"I like to think I am."

"Everyone thinks they're worth more than they are. I expect results, Miss Sinclair. Don't think you can take me for a ride. Well"—he allowed himself a crass grin—"not that way, anyhow."

Were all politicians like this guy? The advantages of absolute monarchy had never been clearer to her.

Abby shook his hand again, with more reluctance this time.

"Nice to have met you," she lied. "And good luck with your campaign."

"I won't need it. My opponent's a hack they put up against me just to fill the slot on the ballot. Nobody challenges me in my district. Nobody serious."

"You're sure you'll win, then?"

"I always win."

He wasn't smiling when he said it. She believed him.

Whatever else he might be, Jack Reynolds was a man who did not know how to lose.

3

Abby positioned herself on a bus stop bench in Laguna Hills at six forty-five. The entrance to the high school parking lot was just down the street. From her vantage point she would see the cars rolling in and, with luck, spot Reynolds's mystery woman driving one of them.

Having had a couple of hours to kill after their meeting, she'd gone back online, using her laptop with a wireless modem, and found the address of Reynolds's campaign headquarters in Huntington Beach. The place itself was easily identifiable by the REELECT JACK REYNOLDS sign in the window and the American flag flying overhead. Inside, she asked for campaign literature and was directed to a card table stacked with brochures. She pretended to look over the material while she checked out the place.

It was a definite step down from Reynolds's Newport Beach digs. The decor consisted of folding chairs and Office Depot furniture. Campaign signs were plastered on the walls, some professionally printed, others hand-lettered, most displaying Reynolds's uninspired slogan: FOR THE PEOPLE. Abby wondered if anyone had ever run *against* the people. Bland or not, the slogan was everywhere, tacked to file cabinets, taped to windows, even worn as a campaign button on the collar of somebody's snoozing Great Dane.

Partitions had been set up to divide the room into cubbyholes and offices. Fluorescent panels glared down, some of them flickering wanly. Banks of TV sets, volume muted, were tuned to a variety of news channels. A stale odor of pizza grease hung in the room, undisturbed by the air-conditioning even though it was roaring at full blast.

A dozen or so volunteers and staffers, mostly young, worked at two different tables. One group was stuffing envelopes, while the others were cold-calling prospective voters. Most got immediate hang-ups, but they persisted, undeterred by rejection, reading from a script whenever they found someone willing to listen to the pitch.

Abby found the atmosphere—part boiler room operation, part all-night dorm room bull session—strangely invigorating. It was electoral politics at their grassrootsiest, being played out with a sweaty energy she rarely saw in L.A., where the local style was to feign ironic detachment at all times. These folks weren't poseurs. They were serious about reelecting their congressman, and they were working hard. Reynolds might think the outcome of the contest was assured, but the message hadn't reached the troops in the field.

Abby didn't like Reynolds personally and had next to no interest in politics, but for a moment she was almost tempted to sign up for campaign scut work, just to be part of the action.

Looking across the room, she saw someone who was clearly a step above the volunteers and run-of-the-mill staffers, an angular, youngish man with close-cropped hair and what looked like a permanent five o'clock shadow. He sat in the semiprivacy of a cubicle, manning the best desk in the place, with the only swivel chair in evidence, talking on a hands-free phone while studying a computer monitor and reading two newspapers at once. Half-moons of sweat rimmed the armpits of his button-down shirt; his tie was loosened, his wilted collar open, his jacket thrown over the back of his chair. He sipped compulsively from a Styrofoam coffee cup, wincing every time he swallowed. The stuff must be foul, but it was fueling his hyperactivity.

Before leaving, she asked one of the volunteers

about the man, who was evidently the big kahuna around here.

"That's Mr. Stenzel," she was told. "Kipland Stenzel. Our campaign manager. You've probably seen him on TV. He did an interview on *Prime Story* last week."

Abby had never heard of *Prime Story,* but she nodded as if the information were meaningful. She departed with a handful of campaign propaganda, which she reviewed in her car. One of the brochures included a schedule of Reynolds's public appearances, including the town hall meeting tonight.

Rose Moran, or whoever the woman was, could have picked up the schedule at any time, just by stopping at the office. Reynolds was making it too easy for her. It was tough to foil a stalker when you advertised your every move.

Then again, foiling a stalker wasn't Reynolds's job. It was hers.

She adjusted her position on the bench and thought about the congressman. His story made a rough sort of sense, but she still had the uncomfortable suspicion that he was hiding something. He'd claimed not to have a single photograph of his housekeeper—no snapshot taken at a family dinner or holiday get-together, no picture of her with the kids. Unlikely. Then there was the protective-father act. He wanted to keep his son out of the headlines. Very noble, but Reynolds didn't strike her as the noble type. He was calculating and shrewd, genial when he needed to be, but cold to the touch if you got too close.

She made her living with her intuition. Other people might rely on linear, left-brain thinking, but she'd always been more of a right-brain gal. She saw things holistically. She trusted her inner voice. And her inner voice was saying that Reynolds needed to be handled with care.

Shortly past seven, cars started arriving for the event. Abby pretended to read a copy of the *Orange County Register* in the slanting sunlight while surreptitiously checking out each vehicle as it drove in. To keep herself alert she counted the cars. With number thirty-eight, she hit the jackpot.

A white Chevrolet Malibu, not new. The brown-haired woman at the wheel. Abby saw her clearly as the car slowed to roll over the first of several speed bumps in the parking lot.

She kept her eye on the Malibu as it crept through rows of parked cars and found a space. The woman got out and headed into the high school. She went quickly, head down, shoulders hunched, as if she were walking into a strong wind—but there was no wind. She was just someone who liked to keep her head down, someone who might have something to hide. She wore a coat that was a bit too heavy for a summer evening, and Abby was glad there was a metal detector at the door.

Abby waited until the full crowd had arrived—a decent turnout, at least a hundred people. No TV news vans, though. The southern-California media were continuing their tradition of ignoring local politics, a policy that suited a community built on narcissistic self-absorption. Abby couldn't complain. She paid no attention to politics, either.

The last person to show up for the event was Reynolds himself. In the movies, politicians were always riding around in limousines, but real life was more prosaic; Reynolds drove a Ford minivan. Stenzel, she noticed, was his passenger. Abby watched them go in.

She left the bus stop and sauntered into the parking lot, holding her key ring as if she were looking for her car. Actually her car was parked around the corner. It was the Malibu that interested her.

She memorized the tag number—a California plate, no surprise. The license plate frame advertised a dealer in the San Fernando Valley, the vast smoggy basin north of the Hollywood Hills. Possibly the owner lived there. If so, she wasn't one of Reynolds's constituents.

Abby took a peek through the side window. A

schedule of Reynolds's public appearances, identical
to the one she'd taken from the campaign office, lay
on the passenger seat. Next to it was an Orange
County map book, turned to the Laguna Hills page.
Apparently the woman wasn't familiar with the area—
more evidence she lived outside Reynolds's district.

Of course, there was one easy way to find out where
she lived, and that was to follow her home.

The town hall meeting broke up just before nine.
By then, even the long summer twilight had yielded
to darkness.

Abby liked the dark. It cloaked her.

She had picked up her car and parked down the
street from the high school, where she could watch
the departing vehicles. A streetlight at the exit of the
parking lot made it easy to spot the white Malibu as
it pulled out. Abby merged with the flow of traffic
and followed.

She expected the Chevy to head for the San Diego
Freeway, and she was right. The car took the north-
bound lanes, staying well within the speed limit. Abby
hung back by several car lengths, allowing another
vehicle or two to occupy the intervening space from
time to time.

Even at a distance, the Chevy wasn't difficult to
follow. Abby had taken the precaution of breaking its
left taillight. She could hold the single taillight in view
and be sure the target hadn't been lost.

Under other circumstances she might have risked
following closer, but tonight there was the problem of
her car. When on assignment, she ordinarily drove a
beat-up Hyundai that she stored in a spare parking
space in the Wilshire Royal's underground garage.
Today, not expecting to go undercover, she'd driven
her Mazda Miata to the congressman's office. It was
a bright red, sporty little two-seater convertible, and
even with the top up it stood out more than she would
have liked.

Most drivers would never notice a car behind them,

no matter what the make or model. But something in this woman's hunched shoulders and quick, frightened stride had suggested paranoia, and paranoia had a way of making people vigilant. Abby had dealt with plenty of paranoid types. There were lots of them—lonely people, prickly, insecure, alienated. She felt their nervous glances in supermarkets. She saw their pale faces in crowds. Sometimes she feared that her own face must look like theirs in her unguarded moments. How many Leon Trotmans could she get to know before she became one of them?

The Chevy left Orange County and passed through the crowded confines of West L.A., then crossed into the San Fernando Valley, a grid of suburban streets lined with single-family homes. The Valley was an immense openness, flat, broad, sprawling to the far horizons. As was true of any large community, there were affluent sections and poorer spots. Judging by the age of the Chevy Malibu, Abby figured they weren't heading for a high-rent district.

The car kept going, into the northwest part of the Valley, which was dominated by aging industrial concerns. Finally the one working taillight began to pulse. The Chevy was taking the Mission San Fernando exit.

On surface streets it passed through San Fernando, a small city carved out of county land. Traffic was light, and Abby stayed back, keeping the single taillight barely in view. Then the car turned down a side street, and she had a decision to make. If she followed, she might be spotted, but if she continued going straight, she might lose the target.

She compromised, pulling onto the shoulder and slowing. By the time she took the corner, the Chevy was far ahead. It pulled into the driveway of a house and was illuminated by a light inside the carport. Abby killed her headlights and parked up the street, watching as the driver emerged.

She wasn't a brunette anymore. She'd taken off the wig. Her hair was a very light blond, cut short, framing a square, pale face, a face with good bone structure half hidden in too much flesh. She would have been attractive when she was younger, but she'd let herself go. Abby put her age at fifty or thereabouts, but she moved with a curious stiffness, like a very old person—or like someone in pain.

Abby started driving again and cruised past the house, noting the street number just as she'd noted the street name at the corner. Now she knew her quarry's address—903 Keystone Drive.

She made a U-turn in a cul-de-sac, then considered her options. The safest approach would be to go home, look up the address in a reverse directory, and see if the resident was Rose Moran. Then she could arrange one of those cute-meet situations she was so good at.

The problem was, she was a little hyped up after the long tail job, and she wasn't in the mood to do research. She was in the mood to get up close and personal, right now.

Could be dangerous. Worse, it could be stupid. In the past she'd rarely approached the subject without proper preparation. Lately she'd been more willing to wing it. She told herself that her experience gave her enough flexibility to improvise her way out of anything. It might be true. Or maybe she just liked the rush she got by taking a reckless chance.

She drove back down the street. A few yards from the woman's house, she killed the Mazda's engine and let the car roll to a stop by the curb.

She took a moment to study the place. A small one-story home, huddled between look-alike houses in an aging development. The car in the driveway next door was raised on cinder blocks, and a lawn mower rusted in the yard. The house on the opposite side appeared to be abandoned, its windows boarded up. Across the street was a pocket park with playground equipment—a slide, a swing set. The park was empty now.

She got out of the Mazda and walked up the front path. She was getting a funny vibe from the place. In some unaccountable way, the little house seemed draped in sadness. Maybe it was the lawn, green and close-cropped and meticulously tended, or the flower beds with their desperately cheerful arrangements of pinks and mums. Someone spent a great deal of time on appearances. Or it might be the heavy curtains covering the front windows, curtains that were stiff and faded, as if they hadn't been opened in years.

The woman who lived here was alone. She never had company. Abby was sure of it, sure in her gut, where the truest intuitions lived.

Well, she would have company now.

4

The doorbell frightened Andrea.

She had no visitors, ever. For the most part, the only sounds in her world were the ticking of the wall clock and the laughing cries of children in the park across the street. She rarely turned on the television or radio. She didn't even own a record player or tape deck. She lived in a cocoon of silence.

Now, at nearly ten o'clock at night, the doorbell had rung.

Her first impulse was to hide. Retreat to her bedroom and wait for whoever was outside her door to leave.

But then the doorbell rang a second time, and Andrea knew she had to answer. She had to know who was out there. Otherwise her imagination would torture her with a hundred possibilities. It was better to know.

Besides, she didn't have to actually *open* the door.

She crossed the living room, past the carefully nurtured plants on her end tables, plants chosen because they didn't need much sun. Once she had loved daylight, but then she had spent twelve years in darkness, and now it was only in the dark that she felt comfortable.

Bracing herself against the door, she risked a look through the peephole. The porch light was on, illuminating a woman, dark-haired, slender.

"Yes?" Andrea called out. "What is it?"

The woman frowned, perturbed at having to speak

through a closed door. "I'm sorry to bother you, ma'am. My car seems to have run out of gas."

She gestured behind her. Dimly it was possible to see a car stopped by the curb.

This could be a trick. People were always claiming to have some automotive problem, and when the homeowner opened the door . . .

She wouldn't fall for it. She would make the woman go away. "I don't have any gasoline. I'm sorry."

"I was hoping to use your phone, call Triple A."

The phone. No, that was out of the question. For the woman to use the phone, she would have to come inside the house.

"I'm afraid that's impossible," Andrea said through the door. "Don't you have a phone of your own? One of those cellular phones?"

"The battery is dead."

"Then you'll have to try one of my neighbors."

"All the lights are out. It doesn't look like anyone's awake."

"Someone must be. If they're asleep, you can wake them."

"I'd really prefer not to do that. Can't I just make a quick call? It'll only take a minute."

Yes, it would only take a minute. A minute to place a phone call—or to knock the trusting homeowner unconscious and rob her blind.

Still, the woman looked all right. Not that you could judge a person by appearances. Andrea had learned that lesson. She'd learned about the masks people wore, and what was behind the masks—not least, her own.

"Ma'am?" piped the irritating, beseeching voice.

"I'm sorry," Andrea said firmly. "I can't help you."

There. That was that. The matter was settled. She was turning away from the door when she heard the woman say, "Please."

No one had said *please* to Andrea in a long time.

She hesitated, her lips working silently, mouthing words. Then on impulse she unlatched the door and opened it a few inches, without releasing the security chain.

"You're polite," Andrea said. "I like that."

"It'll just take a minute," the woman said again.

Andrea could feel her heart clenching and unclenching in her chest, each beat a separate jolt that traveled up her breastbone into her throat. She didn't want to release the chain. She was sure she would regret it if she did.

And yet it had been so long since anyone had treated her with courtesy. And the ticking of the clock did get irksome at times, with no voices in the house.

The chain made a poor defense, anyway. The woman could have forced open the door by now, had she wanted to. One good shove would rip the chain out of its socket.

She could probably be trusted.

"All right," Andrea said, her own words surprising her. She took down the chain and opened the door before she could change her mind. "Come in."

"Thank you." The woman stepped over the threshold, and Andrea took a step back, afraid of sharing her space. "I appreciate it. Really. My name's Abby. Abby Bannister."

Andrea realized she was expected to give her own name in return. It had been a while since she'd practiced the ritual of exchanging introductions. "Andrea Lowry."

"Nice to meet you, Mrs. Lowry."

"It's Miss Lowry. Just 'Miss.' Call me Andrea." Her mouth was dry. Speech was difficult. "The phone . . . in the kitchen." She gestured vaguely.

The woman moved past her. She was alone. No accomplice had been waiting to spring through the doorway.

Andrea lingered in the living room while Abby Bannister called AAA and arranged for service. When the call was over, Abby emerged from the kitchen. It had taken longer than the promised minute, but Andrea wasn't upset about that. She was beginning to adjust to the peculiar sensation of sharing her living quarters with another human being.

"I'm sorry I was so standoffish," Andrea said. "But a person has to be careful, you know. Especially at this time of night."

"I understand."

"The car people—they're sending someone?"

"Yes. It may take some time. I'll wait outside."

"You can wait in here . . . if you like."

"I don't want to inconvenience you."

"No, really, I don't mind." The odd thing was, she didn't. Now that she'd allowed a person into her home, she suddenly dreaded the thought of being alone again. "I can fix you something to drink."

"Well, if it's not too much trouble."

"I have lemonade. Is that all right?"

"That would be fine, thank you."

Andrea got the pitcher out of the fridge and poured two tall glasses. She was distantly amazed that she could do this. She was entertaining a guest. She was a hostess.

She carried the glasses into the living room and handed one to Abby. They took seats across from each other.

"You have a very nice home," Abby said.

Andrea doubted she meant it. The house was small and old and stuffy, the curtains were always closed, and there were security bars on the windows. No mementos or knickknacks were on display, no items of a personal nature. She'd lived here for more than a year but had furnished the place with little besides essentials, and most of those had been purchased secondhand.

Andrea asked Abby where she lived. "West L.A.," Abby said. Andrea knew West L.A. It was miles away, a much pricier area, near enough to the ocean that you could feel the sea breeze.

"I envy you," Andrea said, and it was true, and not only for living in West Los Angeles. The woman was young and attractive and seemed unburdened by fear and guilt, the two inescapable constants in Andrea's own life.

They talked for a while, sipping lemonade. Andrea found it remarkable that she could be having a conversation with a stranger off the street. She barely noticed what they talked about. She was aware only of the ebb and flow of words, the casualness of it, the surprising ease. She had thought it would be impossible to talk to anyone, especially here, in her private sanctum. Yet it wasn't so hard, after all. Perhaps she'd underestimated herself, or overestimated the perils of the world.

"Would you like more lemonade?" she asked when their glasses were empty.

"Thank you, yes. It's very good."

This time Abby accompanied her into the kitchen.

"Lived here long?" Abby asked.

"A year or so," Andrea said, then wondered why the woman would have asked that question.

"Where were you before that?"

"What do you mean?"

"Just, you know, where do you hail from? Everybody in California is from somewhere else. I was raised in Arizona."

"I was born in Oregon," Andrea said softly. She took out the pitcher and carried it to the kitchen counter next to the sink.

"That's a nice part of the country," Abby said. "Of course, L.A. was probably real nice, too, way back when. You know, years ago, before all the traffic and crime."

Crime. Andrea picked up on the word. Why introduce that subject? "There's crime everyplace," she murmured. Her hand moved toward a drawer under the countertop, then shied away.

"We seem to get more than our share. So . . . you said you're not married?"

Stiffly, Andrea answered, "No."

"Me neither. I prefer it that way."

Andrea began to pour from the pitcher.

"Though I guess," Abby said, "it would be nice to have children someday."

Andrea's hand shook, and she nearly spilled the lemonade.

"I think about it sometimes," the woman went on. "The old biological clock is ticking, you know."

Andrea set down the pitcher. "I have no children." She looked at Abby, looked at her hard.

Abby gazed back, her face open and guileless. "Ever want any?"

"Why would you ask me that?"

"Just wondering."

"You ask a lot of questions."

"Making conversation, that's all."

"Making inquiries. That's what you're doing." Andrea turned back to the counter, and this time she opened the drawer. She reached inside, and her hand closed over the thing she needed. "Who are you?"

"I already said—"

Andrea turned to face her. "Who *are* you?"

This time she expected an answer.

Abby considered the gun.

It was aimed at her chest from a distance of four feet, a Colt revolver, a .38 Special, the Commando model.

She hadn't expected the gun. It had been careless of her, really. She should have been ready.

"Who?" Andrea Lowry asked for the third time.

"I told you," Abby said slowly. "My name is Abby Bannister. My car ran out of gas—"

"Don't lie to me. I can't *stand* it when they lie to me!"

"Okay." Abby kept her voice even. "I understand."

"You don't understand. Nobody does. Walk a mile in my shoes. . . . You know that expression? You're too young to know it."

"I know the expression," Abby said.

"You don't know anything. Asking questions. Marriage, children . . . you think you're so smart."

"I don't. Really." At the moment this was true.

"You're all alike. You all use the same dirty tricks, and for what? To get a few words you can print? To get a *story?*"

Reporters. That's who she was talking about.

"Now admit it." The gun hadn't wavered. "Admit who you are. Tell me the truth. Tell me right now."

"I'll tell you." Abby took a breath. "You're right. I'm a reporter. For a newspaper."

"I knew it. I always know. Which paper is it this time?"

"The *L.A. Times.*"

"You work for them?"

"I'm what they call a stringer. A freelancer."

"How did you find me?"

Abby formulated a vague but—she hoped—plausible lie. "I was working another story, and your name came up."

"My name? Why would my name enter into it?"

"I can't reveal my sources." It sounded like something a journalist would say.

Andrea gave her a sharp look. "Your sources. Oh, for God's sake. You act so ethical, and yet you gained admittance to my home under false pretenses. To *spy* on me. To write one of your damn *stories!*"

"I was going to tell you—"

"When?"

"When we'd established a rapport."

The woman snorted, a sudden sharp noise like a gunshot. Abby managed not to jump at the sound.

"Rapport. When you'd gained my trust, you mean. Fooled me into trusting you."

"I guess so."

"You people—you *disgust* me."

"Could you put down the gun now, please?"

"I ought to shoot you dead, you little bitch."

"I'm just doing my job."

"Your job. Your job is to ruin lives. People like you have been after me for twenty years. For twenty years—do you know what that's like, never to be left alone, never to have any peace?"

"I'm sorry," Abby said.

"Ought to shoot you in your lying heart," Andrea hissed, but there was no more passion in her voice, and the gun was lowering. "Your car is fine, of course."

"Yes."

"And when you used my phone to call Triple A—"

"I didn't really make the call. I faked it."

"You're quite the actress, aren't you?"

Abby didn't answer.

"Get out. Get out of my house."

"Yes, ma'am."

"You think I'm a sideshow for your readers' amusement? You think I'm a freak?"

"No, I don't."

"You do. You all do. Well, go and write about me. Go tell them I'm as crazy as they thought. Tell them I'm a psychopath. That's what you think, isn't it?"

"I didn't say that."

"Get *out*," Andrea said again.

Abby got out. She didn't look back until she was pulling away from the curb. She expected to see Andrea Lowry in the doorway or window, watching her go, but the door was closed, and the curtains remained shut.

Abby released a slow breath. "That went well," she mumbled.

She'd managed to alienate the woman she was trying to befriend. Not that alienating Andrea Lowry was hard to do. She was afraid of people—reporters in particular. Had they really been after her at some point in her life, or was that just part of some megalomaniacal drama she was acting out?

Near the freeway entrance Abby pulled into a convenience store parking lot and dictated notes into the microcassette recorder she always carried in her purse.

"Hostile . . . paranoid . . . fixated on reporters. Claims they've been harassing her for twenty years. Has a gun—Colt thirty-eight. Keeps it in a kitchen drawer near the sink. She looked like she knew how to use it. And she was wearing a wig at the town hall meeting, so whoever she is, she's afraid of being recognized. Afraid of a lot of things. And not likely to talk to me again."

That was the bottom line. Her job was to get close to this woman, gain her trust. She'd failed.

Abby didn't like failure. And she knew Jack Reynolds didn't, either.

Still, she had more facts than she'd had before. She knew the woman's name and address. Soon she would know much more.

Or maybe she wouldn't. Information on Andrea Lowry turned out to be perplexingly difficult to find.

Nestled in the workstation in her bedroom, Abby had spent an hour on her computer, hopping from one Internet database to another. A reverse directory listed Andrea as the sole resident at the Keystone Drive address. More exotic research tools supplied the woman's Social Security number, date of birth, and credit history.

She'd been at her current address for a little more than a year. Before that, she'd lived in St. Petersburg, Florida, for seven years. She'd bought the Chevy Malibu in Florida eight years ago. Her credit card accounts had been opened eight years ago also. Her driver's license had been issued in Florida at the same time.

Before that—nothing. There was a prior address on file with some credit agencies, but when Abby ran a search, it didn't check out. The address was real, but no Andrea Lowry, or Andrea anybody, had ever resided there.

Phony background information, and an identity that had appeared out of nowhere, fully formed. It looked as if somebody had reinvented herself.

Had she been Rose Moran before she was Andrea Lowry? And if so, why make the switch?

There were many imaginable reasons for a change of ID. Andrea could be on the run from someone.

Ex-boyfriend, abusive husband, even a stalker of her own. Or she might be hiding from the law.

There was another possibility. Witness protection. Andrea could have testified against somebody, then gone into hiding with the government's help. Maybe her identity had been created by the feds, who had moved her to Florida. Then for reasons of her own she had come west.

Hard theory to test, though. If Andrea had been an L.A. resident, Abby could have used one of her contacts in the LAPD to check her out. But the town of San Fernando had its own police department, and Abby had no contacts there.

Anyway, if Andrea was in witness protection, it wouldn't be in the bailiwick of local law enforcement. It was a federal program.

Well, she knew a fed. Hadn't kept in touch over the past year and a half, but now seemed like a good time to catch up.

Abby found the number in her address book, then called the special agent in charge of the FBI's Denver office.

The time was eleven p.m. in L.A., midnight in Denver. A little late for a phone call, but what the hell. Tess would be glad to hear from her.

Sure she would.

5

It was like riding a wave, a swell of motion that expanded into a long curling comber arching upward, fighting free of gravity until it hit the shore and broke apart in a crash of spangled fragments, slivers of light.

"Oh, my God," Tess said. "My God."

On top of her, Joshua Green smiled in the darkness. "Sounds like"—his speech was punctuated by hard breathing—"a religious experience."

"Definitely." Her voice was faint and hoarse.

He straddled her a moment longer, making the moment last, then rolled clear and lay at her side. "Too bad we have to keep this a secret," he said between gasps. "The women in the office might look at me differently if they heard your reports."

"And why would you care how they look at you?"

"Hey, I've got to keep my options open, in case our relationship goes south."

Tess punched him on the arm.

He grunted. "Ow. Watch it, boss."

She liked it when he called her "boss." The old-fashioned term, still in use in the FBI, was accurate, if not appropriate. As special agent in charge of the Denver office, she really was his boss. He reported to her daily in the role of ASAC—assistant special agent in charge. "I work under you," he not infrequently pointed out.

She'd been seeing Josh Green for more than a year, but their affair remained secret—or undercover, another of Josh's cheerful euphemisms. The Bureau disapproved of sexual relationships between agents of different rank, especially when one agent was the other's immediate subordinate. They could both be disciplined if they were found out. But clandestine activity was what feds were supposed to be good at, and besides, the lure of the forbidden added an extra zing to their liaisons.

"Someday your sense of humor is going to land you in trouble," she warned.

"It already did. That punch *hurt.*"

She laughed, and then somewhere in the dark a phone was ringing.

"Who would call at midnight?" she asked.

"Somebody official is my guess. It's a cell phone."

"I know. But is it mine or yours?"

"Can't tell."

"We really need to get different ring tones. One of these days you're going to answer my phone or I'm going to answer yours. . . ."

"And the cat will be out of the proverbial bag. I think it's your phone," Josh added. "It has that cheap, tinny sound."

"Thanks a lot." Unfortunately he was right.

Tess got out of bed and crossed her bedroom to the dresser. Her groping hand found her cell phone and flipped it open. Caller ID showed a 310 area code. Los Angeles. She didn't recognize the number.

"McCallum," she answered.

"Hey, Tess. How's tricks?"

"Oh, Christ." She shut her eyes, feeling the sudden onset of a migraine.

Abby's voice teased her through the receiver. "Is that any way to greet an old pal?"

Tess glanced at Josh, then carried the phone into the living room, where she hoped her end of the conversation would be out of earshot. "Sorry," she said. "But—well, actually I'm not sorry."

"You sound kind of conflicted about this."

"No, not really. Truth is, I'm remarkably sure of things. I've had a lot of time to think, Abby." She kept her voice low. "To think about the Rain Man case."

"Living in the past? Not a good idea."

Tess plowed ahead. "It was a mistake. I never should have hooked up with you. I regret it now."

"If we hadn't hooked up, another two or three women might have drowned. We saved lives, soul sister."

"I'm not your sister. What we did was wrong. I knew it at the time. I was never comfortable with it. I can't operate like you."

"Don't feel bad. We can't all be superstars. As they say at the beach, they also surf who only stand and wade."

Tess massaged her forehead. "Will you *listen* to me? I'm telling you that I cannot be dealing with you again, Abby. Not in any way, shape, or form. We can't even be having this conversation."

"And yet we are. It's just one of those paradoxes."

"I'm hanging up now."

"No, you aren't." Abby's tone hardened. "You can't act like we don't know each other. You *owe* me, Tess."

"For what?"

"A little thing called saving your butt, if you recall."

"That debt goes both ways—if *you* recall."

"I was hoping you'd forgotten that part."

"I haven't. We don't owe each other anything. We're even."

"No, we're *connected*. We're like two paired electrons that continue to influence each other over vast distances."

Tess was losing the thread of the discussion, not an uncommon occurrence when speaking with Abby. "What are you talking about?"

"Quantum entanglement. Or loyalty. Take your pick."

"It's not an issue of loyalty."

"Sure it is. Didn't you ever read about Androcles and the lion? Androcles took a thorn out of the lion's paw. Years later he was thrown to the lions in the Colosseum. And one of those lions was the very same one he'd helped. And the lion didn't care, and ate Androcles anyway."

"That isn't how the story goes."

"I saw the director's cut. Point is, that mangy lion showed no loyalty. Do *you* want to be a mangy lion, Tess?"

Tess had forgotten how truly irritating Abby could be. "You're not going to manipulate me into getting involved in another one of your cases."

"No involvement. You're in Denver. I'm in L.A. How can there be involvement?"

"Well, you didn't call just to chat."

"I need only one tiny favor."

"I can't do favors for you."

"Tess, I pulled a thorn out of your paw. That has to count for something. Anyway, it's not a big deal. I just need to know if a given individual is enrolled in the witness protection program."

"The U.S. Marshals run that program, not the FBI."

"Yeah, like you don't have access to their databases?"

She did, and Abby, of course, knew it. "I'm not going to help you," Tess said. Somehow the living room of her apartment, which had always seemed big enough until now, was suddenly too small, the walls closing in like the jaws of a trap.

"It's not a big deal, Tess. Just a little tidbit of info that no one will ever miss."

She felt her resolve failing. "I can't do it," she said again.

"You can if you *believe* you can. Some Zen wisdom there. How about it, Grasshopper?"

Tess lowered her head. The phone was hot in her hand, or maybe it was her hand that was hot. She knew she should refuse. Should end the call. But Abby was right. There *was* a debt, and a connection.

"If I try," she heard herself say tonelessly, "will you promise to leave me alone after this?"

"Sure. Until the next time I need a favor."

"Abby . . ."

"You know, for a lion who got relief from a painful foot injury, you sure are grouchy."

"That's what happens when people call me at midnight."

"Did I wake you?"

"Uh, no. Just . . . reading."

"Reading in bed?"

"Yes."

"What's his name?"

Tess blinked. "I didn't say—"

"You didn't have to. I actually *heard* your face go red with a demure Catholic-schoolgirl blush. So is it serious? You two going steady?"

"I . . . it's somebody I . . . never mind."

"You're not giving me the good dish, Tess. Is he married?"

"Of course not."

"Just asking. Younger than you?"

Tess had to smile. "Are you saying I'm old?"

"Not at all. I'm only wondering if you're robbing the cradle. You know, women reach their sexual peak at forty. Men, at eighteen. Something to think about."

"I'm not forty."

"The question is, is *he* eighteen?"

Despite herself, Tess had to laugh. "No, he's not. But he is a couple of years younger than I am."

"Good in the sack?"

"Come on, you don't expect me to answer that."

"There's that blush again."

The ridiculous thing was, Tess really was blushing. She could feel the warmth in her face. "I just can't talk about it now," she said.

"Sex between consenting adults is nothing to be embarrassed about, no matter what those prickly old nuns taught you. I mean—he *is* an adult, isn't he? Of legal age?"

"He's thirty-six. How did we get on this subject, anyway?"

"You know how it is with me. One thing leads to another. There doesn't have to be any logical progression. It's more like stream of consciousness."

"Like swimming upstream, I'd say."

"Hey, you made a funny. Good for you. This guy is loosening you up, Special Agent. Taking some of the starch out of your undies."

Tess sighed. She honestly did not know whether or not she liked Abby. She was quite sure she disapproved of her, but as for liking her . . . that was another question.

"What is it you want from me?" she asked, resigned now.

"Got a pencil?"

"Hold on." Tess found a pad and pen, and turned on a lamp. "Go."

Abby gave the name, address, Social Security number, and other particulars of a woman whose personal history extended only eight years into the past.

"Got it," Tess said when she finished scribbling. She still felt a little stupid for getting talked into this. "I assume I can reach you at the number you're calling from."

"It's my cell. Handcuffed to my wrist at all times. And, Tess—"

"You don't have to thank me."

"Wasn't gonna. I was just going to say I need the info ASAP."

"I'll do my best. There are no guarantees."

"Never are, in our line of work."

"You and I are *not* in the same line of work," Tess said, but Abby had already hung up.

Tess refolded the phone and went into the bathroom. In the glow of a night-light she ran some water from the tap and splashed her face. Her headache was stronger than before. Funny how even a brief dialogue with Abby was enough to start her head throbbing.

She looked at herself in the mirror. The face that gazed back was framed in a shoulder-length fall of strawberry-blond hair, brushed daily to smooth out its natural curls. She came from Highlands stock; her ancestors had roamed the steep hillsides, braving the winter winds, dancing reels around bonfires, surviving poverty and famine and war. She sometimes wondered if she'd stayed this long in Denver because something about chill winds and mountain slopes spoke to her ancestral instincts.

Her forebears had been hard, tough people, and she thought there was a certain toughness in her, as well—a quality not immediately apparent in her smooth skin and quiet voice, but noticeable, perhaps, in the set of her mouth and the gray depths of her eyes. Few FBI agents ever drew their weapon in the field, and fewer still ever fired it, but in her fourteen-year career she had killed three men, each of whom had been doing his best to kill her. She'd had to be tough to survive those battles, and to survive the death of the one man—*sorry, Josh*—the one man she'd ever really loved. If there was such a thing as a soul mate, Paul Voorhees had been hers, and he still was, even if six years had gone by since a serial killer named Mobius had murdered him in a Denver suburb and left the body for her to find.

Mobius had been after her, not Paul. Sometimes she almost wished she had been home that night instead of him.

She sighed. Morbid thought. She was having a lot of those lately. Did Abby really have to ask her age? Two weeks ago she'd turned thirty-nine, and lately she was feeling every one of those years. Faint creases had appeared at the corners of her eyes, and she had to work harder to keep extra weight from collecting on her hips. She didn't like it. Though still young by any reasonable standard, she was feeling old.

But at least she had Josh. He'd been good for her, even if they had to skulk around, dining in out-of-the-way restaurants and feigning disinterested professionalism on the job. And if women really did reach their sexual peak at forty, then she still had something to look forward to.

The thought made her smile, and the smile, she noticed, deepened those wrinkles near her eyes.

She left the bathroom and slipped back into bed.

"You okay?" Josh asked sleepily.

"Fine."

"Who called?"

"Trouble."

He rolled over. "Shouldn't have answered, then," he mumbled.

Tess shut her eyes. "Now you tell me."

6

Reynolds needed to relax. The town hall meeting had gone smoothly enough—no combative questions from the audience, no slipups on his part—but *she* had been there again. Tucked away at the back of the room, in a dim corner, alone, saying nothing. Watching him.

He hoped Abby Sinclair was as good as she claimed.

Keyed up, he had driven Stenzel back to the campaign headquarters to pick up his car, then parked the minivan at his office. The minivan was solely for business purposes, its maintenance and miles tax-deductible. In the parking lot he kept his real car, a blue Mustang hardtop with a three-valve V-8.

He drove the freeways. Years ago he would have ridden a Harley, with no buffer between the wind and his body, feeling the lash of air as he screamed through a tunnel of roaring noise. But a bike didn't fit his image now, and besides, he was too old for that crap.

The long drive had calmed him down. Reynolds was feeling good as he parked near the condo in Costa Mesa. He had no key to the place, so he had to buzz the intercom. "It's me," he said when she answered. She let him in without another word.

He stepped into her apartment, and she shut the door behind him. She was in a nightgown and fuzzy slippers.

"It's late," Rebecca said, peeved.

"Out driving." He said it without apology. He didn't have to explain himself to her. She was his goddamned secretary, for Christ's sake. All right, technically she

was his constituent services coordinator, the intermediary who dealt with the various real and imagined
crises in the lives of the voters in his district. She
was stationed permanently in Orange County, the only
staffer to run his office here when he was in D.C.
They saw each other whenever he was in town. Fortunately it was an election year, and he was in town
a lot.

They went into her bedroom. "Do anything tonight?" he asked, not caring, just making conversation
as he stripped off his clothes.

"Watched TV."

"Huh."

"Nothing much on. Who was that woman?"

He glanced at her. "Woman?"

"Four o'clock appointment. Sinclair."

"Personal matter."

"You can't talk about personal matters with me?"

"Oh, I can. I just figured we've got better things to
do. What do you care about her, anyway?"

"She's very attractive."

"Didn't notice."

Rebecca made a face. "Right."

"What are you, jealous?"

"Just . . . curious."

"You know what they say about curiosity and the
cat."

"No, what?"

"It killed the cat."

"What did?"

He was exasperated. "Curiosity."

She frowned. "I don't get it. What is it, a riddle?"

"It's a saying. An old saying. I guess it's from before
your time."

"Must be."

Suddenly he was feeling old. He didn't like it. It
made him angry. Made him hot.

"You're a dumb bitch," he said quietly. "You
know that?"

"Jack—"

He shut her mouth with a searing kiss. He was tired of hearing her talk. He never wanted to hear her talk. He had enough conversation in his life.

When he broke away, he had silenced her. He unbuttoned her nightgown and let it fall away. "On the bed," he ordered.

She sank onto the mattress, naked, supine, her blond hair fanning across the pillows.

"Roll over," he said. "On your belly."

"Do we have to . . . ?"

"Roll over."

She obeyed, her bare back displayed for him like a side of beef. He whacked her hard on the ass, and she gave a little yelp of pain.

"You like that, bitch?"

"Yes, Jack."

Another smack. The cheeks of her buttocks reddened.

"You like that?"

"Yes."

A stinging wallop.

"Like it?"

"Yes." Tears in her voice.

He grabbed her by the knot of hair at her nape and yanked her head back. "Say it louder."

"Yes, Jack."

"Yes, what?"

"Yes, I like it. *I like it!*" Her eyes glittered, wet.

He reached under her, cupping a breast, squeezing hard.

"You like that?"

"Yes."

He made a fist, crushing the flesh in his hand. "Like it?"

"Yes . . ."

"Louder."

But she couldn't say it louder. She was crying.

Well, if she wouldn't talk, she would scream. He

knew how to make her scream. Some of the bruises still hadn't healed from last time. Now there would be more.

And she would like it.

An hour later, he pulled into the driveway of his home in Newport Beach. He went in via the side door, disarming and rearming the alarm system, then made his way through the ground level.

The house was big, but not quite big enough to be ostentatious, decorated in a simple but elegant style that looked more costly than it was. The decor had been his wife's assignment, one of the few times in their twenty-five-year marriage when Nora had actually contributed something to the partnership besides her family's money. For the most part she was only a prop for him to lean on, an attractive prop, plumper then she once was but still curvaceous enough to draw admiring glances. She was neither shrewd nor wise, she had little imagination and limited ambition, but she did possess the cardinal virtue of loyalty. She had been faithful to him, always. He couldn't say the same about himself.

"Jack." Her voice drifted down from upstairs. "Is that you?"

"It's me."

He climbed the spiral staircase, shedding his jacket. He found Nora in bed, a book in her hand and a mildly annoyed expression on her face.

"Your meeting must have ended hours ago."

He wondered why both of the women in his life insisted on criticizing him. "I took the Mustang for a spin." He went into the bathroom and began to undress.

"Sometimes," Nora said from the bedroom, "I think you love that car more than me."

"Don't be stupid."

"How did it go? The meeting, that is?"

"The usual."

"Press coverage?"

"No."

"Good turnout, at least?"

"Not bad. What are you doing up so late? That book keeping you awake?"

"Actually, I was waiting for you."

He had removed most of his clothes by now. Distantly he wondered why he never undressed in front of his wife. He had no qualms about stripping with Rebecca in the room. "Waiting? Why? Something you need to talk about?"

"I was just . . . feeling lonely, I guess."

He ignored the obvious implication. "You have plenty of friends around here."

"Yes. I suppose I do."

He threw on pajamas and came out of the bathroom. Nora was pretending to read, her face set in a blank stare.

"Now you're mad at me," he said with a sigh.

She didn't look at him. "How long has it been since we were . . . together?"

It had been four months, but he feigned ignorance. "I'm not sure." Before she could pursue the point, he went on the offensive. "As I recall, I'm not the one who kept saying no."

Now she did look at him. "You hurt me, Jack."

"Because of what I just said? It's the truth."

"It's not what you said. I mean, you hurt me. The last time we . . . you *hurt* me."

"I got a little carried away."

"More than a little."

"It was a scratch."

"Go on and tell yourself that, if you want to."

She returned to her book, but her eyes were wet.

"Maybe I'll sleep in the guest room," he said.

She didn't answer. That was fine. He'd had enough of this conversation, anyway.

He took the pillow from his side of the bed and carried it down the hall. He was pissed off now. The drive and his recreational outing with Rebecca had cooled his jets, and now he was all tense and edgy again.

He lay in bed, eyes shut, and took himself back to Rebecca's bedroom, his hands working her over, her mouth issuing soft grunting protests that rose gradually to screams. Muffled screams, choked off by the pillow she pressed to her face so her neighbors wouldn't hear—but screams, nonetheless.

Eyes closed, he shivered with pleasure, and unaccountably he thought of Abby Sinclair.

He would like to make that bitch scream, too.

He really would.

7

Abby was a downward-facing dog, or more exactly she had arched her body into the yoga position of that name, when her cell phone rang. Her first thought was that Tess was calling with news on the witness protection thing. It was only eight o'clock in the morning, though. A little early to be hearing about that.

She pushed herself to a standing position and answered. "Abby Sinclair."

It wasn't Tess. It was Reynolds's assistant, the ice princess, Rebecca somebody or other, who'd rejected Abby's sisterly appeal. "Please hold for—"

"Congressman Reynolds," Abby finished. "I know the drill."

Evidently the congressman was too important to dial his own phone. She waited for a half minute, wondering how much she should reveal about last night's less-than-successful enterprise, until Reynolds came on the line.

Surprisingly, he didn't ask any questions. "I'll be in L.A. for lunch today at the Brayton," he said without preamble, and with none of his synthetic charm.

Abby was confused. "You're asking me to lunch?"

"No." His tone registered impatience with her stupidity. "I'm having lunch with some contributors. I'll meet you at the hotel beforehand. The Rendezvous Court, eleven thirty. Go through the lobby and the galleria, past the elevators, and you're there. Got it?"

"There's not much I can tell you so far." And there was even less she wanted to tell.

"I want any information you have."

Click, and the call was over.

Abby was beginning to seriously dislike this man. What was worse, she was beginning to distrust him.

There might be some connection between Andrea Lowry and Jack Reynolds, but she didn't think it had anything to do with housekeeping.

The Brayton Hotel was downtown. L.A.'s central library was right across the street. It had been a while since Abby had done any research there, the Internet having rendered combing the stacks largely unnecessary. But there were some items she couldn't find online. On its Web site, the *L.A. Times* archived its articles as far back as 1985, but included no photos. It was the photos that interested her. The library would have the complete editions—text and pics—on microfilm.

She decided to head downtown early.

It took her ninety minutes of scrolling through microfilm, but she found it.

An article in the *Los Angeles Times*, dated July 14, 1991, about Orange County district attorney John Reynolds. He hadn't been *Jack* then. The populist persona appeared shortly afterward, upon his entry into politics.

The story was a puff piece, a human-interest item on the DA at home. A tough man on the job, but tender with his kids, ages seven and five. There was a description of Reynolds flying a kite with the children on a windy bluff overlooking the ocean. Daddy at home making pancakes—"griddle cakes," as he charmingly called them—on Sunday morning before packing the kids off to church. His wife, Nora, speaking of her hubby's soft side.

But not to soften up the DA too much, there was also much talk of his stern dedication to the law. Asked if he had any hobbies, he answered, "I like to put people in jail." It was reported that he said it with a smile.

Buried in the story was a brief acknowledgment of

the real reason for the sudden interest in the life of a district attorney—rumors of a run for political office next year. The *Times* story was obviously a way of testing the waters, and of putting out a favorable impression of the potential candidate.

None of which mattered. All that interested Abby was the photograph accompanying the article. The Reynolds clan at home—husband, wife, kids . . . and their housekeeper, Rose Moran.

Rose was in the background of the shot, serving up a plate of hot dogs at a family dinner in the backyard. In the fuzzy black-and-white photo her face was hard to make out. Abby fiddled with the knobs that controlled magnification and focus until the woman was centered in the microfilm reader's blue crosshairs in blurry close-up. She had a sharp, thin face with narrow lips and close-set eyes.

Not Andrea Lowry. Even the passage of fifteen years could not turn this pinched bone structure into Andrea's broader, squarer face.

There was no way Reynolds could have looked at Andrea Lowry and seen Rose Moran. His story was a lie. As lies went, it was a pretty good one, but not quite good enough.

Abby hated being lied to. It really frosted her cornflakes.

She fed a coin into the slot and printed out the page with the photo. Suddenly she was no longer worried about what she would say to Jack Reynolds. She had questions for him.

And she wanted answers.

8

Tess didn't want to think about Abby. She wanted to forget she'd gotten the phone call last night. She wanted to put the whole thing out of her mind and make it go away.

This attitude sustained her during the first hour and a half of her workday, which began at eight fifteen with the weekly squad supervisors' meeting. Her self-control continued when she returned to her office. It lasted long enough to allow her to dictate two letters and review three reports on ongoing investigations, sign out some mail, and initial a variety of paperwork, transferring it from her in-box to her out-box.

None of this was very glamorous, nothing at all like a day in the life of an FBI agent in the movies, and yet she took a secret thrill in even the more mundane aspects of her job. She never took her position for granted. To be in charge of a regional field office was a major accomplishment for any agent, rarer still for an agent who was not yet forty, and almost unprecedented for an agent lacking a Y chromosome. Only fifteen percent of special agents were female, and before Tess there had been just one female SAC, whose resentful male colleagues had dubbed her Queen Bee.

There were plenty of agents who looked back fondly on the Hoover years, when women had been permitted in the Bureau only as support staff. Some of those nostalgic types were the old guard, dwindling as they hit the mandatory retirement age of fifty-seven, but most were too young to remember Hoover as anything other than an unsmiling face in one of the official portraits that hung in FBI offices everywhere. Still, they kept his traditions alive, including the casual, almost jocular misogyny that had been part of the Bureau's culture from the start.

In her days as a street agent, Tess had heard herself referred to as a skirt, a split tail, and—her personal favorite—a breast fed. She tried not to take offense. A certain amount of ribbing and rough talk was normal in law enforcement. In theory the Office of Professional Responsibility could be summoned to investigate sexually derogatory comments, but the policy was rarely enforced. No agent, female or otherwise, wanted to be known as a troublemaker who couldn't take a joke—not in an institution that valued loyalty to the team above almost any other virtue. Anyway, she was an SAC now, at one of the country's larger field offices, and nobody called her a split tail these days. At least, not to her face.

Her office was spacious and well-appointed, with the customary leather chairs and matching leather sofa, the properly intimidating desk with an American flag beside it, and a large bookcase stocked with reference volumes and the Bureau's Manual of Rules and Regulations, known as the Big Manual; but the walls were curiously bare. Tess had eschewed the collection of photos known as an I-love-me wall, in which highlights of an agent's career were illustrated for the benefit of visitors. Handshakes with the director or the president usually got the best display.

Tess had shaken her share of hands and had the photos to prove it, but they were in a cardboard box in a closet at home, not demanding attention on her wall. The only photos she had put up were a few cityscapes she liked—Miami and Phoenix, two cities where she'd been assigned earlier in her career, and Denver itself. And there was a photo of Hoover, of course. Not to display J. Edgar's picture would be the ultimate act of sedition.

At nine forty-five the willpower that had carried her through her morning routine finally failed. There was no way around it. She had to know what Abby had gotten mixed up in. If there was a federal connection, Abby might come to the attention of the Bureau and be called in for questioning. Someone would link her to the Rain Man case. The truth would come out. Tess's superiors would learn that for the past year and a half she had been covering up the participation of a civilian in a federal law enforcement action. And not just any civilian. Abby wasn't some FBI groupie; she was an unlicensed private investigator, very nearly a vigilante, exactly the sort of person who should have no input into an official investigation. The repercussions would almost certainly prove fatal to Tess's career.

Switching on her desktop computer, she used the Bureau's secure intranet to connect with the mainframe in the Hoover Building in Washington, then logged on to the federal internal computer system. The FICS was a database containing the details of every FBI investigation, while affording access to the records of other federal law enforcement agencies as well. Through the system she accessed the U.S. Marshals Service and ran a keyword search on *Andrea Lowry*.

No hits. No Andrea Lowry was listed in the WITSEC program as a real name or an alias.

She returned to the Bureau's own database and repeated the search. Nothing there, either. The FBI had never investigated any case involving Andrea Lowry— or if they had, the case was too recent to have been entered into the system.

So that was that. She had kept her promise, and it had cost her nothing. She could truthfully tell Abby that Andrea Lowry, whoever she was, had not reinvented herself with the help of the federal government.

Part of her, oddly, was disappointed. She really had wanted to help Abby. Though it was true that they'd each come to the other's rescue in Los Angeles, Abby had taken far greater risks on Tess's behalf.

But if WITSEC was a dead end, there was nothing

she could do. She would call Abby later when she was safely away from the office, and give her the news.

She had settled back to work when her intercom buzzed with word that Assistant Director Michaelson was on the line.

Michaelson ran the L.A. field office. Tess had worked with him twice—first during the Mobius case and more recently on the Rain Man. There weren't too many people in the Bureau she actively detested, but Richard Michaelson, known as "the Nose" in recognition of his most prominent facial feature, was one of the few. He was, in fact, at the top of the list.

"Richard," she said, putting on her best pretense of affability, "what can I do for you?"

"You can tell me why the hell you're interested in Andrea Lowry."

This was so unexpected she needed a moment to process it. "Andrea Lowry?"

"Cut the bullshit. I just heard from Tenth Street." The address of Bureau headquarters. "You ran a search on her."

"How could you—" She stopped herself. Her knowledge of computers was minimal, but even she knew that the system could be programmed to red-flag any unusual searches. Though why the name Andrea Lowry would trigger such a response, she had no idea.

"I didn't realize Big Brother was watching me," she said carefully.

"Why in God's name would you think she was in witness protection, anyway?"

"I was just, uh, running down a long shot."

"It's not your case. You shouldn't be running down anything. How did Lowry come to your attention?"

"I've heard things."

"From who?"

"I believe the proper question to ask is, from *whom?* I'm not at liberty to divulge my sources. Maybe you'd like to tell me who called you from Washington?"

He simmered. She was happy to let him think she knew more than she did. He might call her bluff.

"If you have any leads, solid or not, pertaining to Andrea Lowry," he said after a moment, "you'd better damn well hand them over to us. We're running the investigation. It's our project."

"I don't remember you being such a glory hog, Richard."

"Glory?" He snorted. "You think I *want* MEDEA? Goddamned thing is so hot it's radioactive."

MEDEA. The code name of the case, presumably. Usually cases had unimaginative code names, shortened to facilitate computer entry. THERMCON, for *Therm*ite *con*spiracy. UNABOM, for *un*iversity and *a*irline *bom*bings. Occasionally someone would get more creative. One name she'd always liked was CASTAWAY, a mob-related investigation aimed at putting a certain Paul Castellano away. That one had a certain charm.

And now MEDEA. Somebody had been in a mythological frame of mind when coming up with that one. Who was Medea, anyway? Some figure in Greek mythology. Tess had been given a thorough exposure to the classics in parochial school, but all she remembered about Medea was that she played a role in the story of Jason and the Golden Fleece.

"Come on, now." She tried a little fishing. "You've never been afraid of a high-profile case."

"Ordinarily that's true. But when it's political . . ."

"Politics is your specialty."

"Not this kind. One wrong move on MEDEA, and I'll be posted in Anchorage."

"I'm not trying to horn in on your territory, Richard. But from what I understand, the seventh floor is unhappy." That floor was the power center of the Hoover Building, and its very mention could inspire fear in a dedicated rung climber like Michaelson. "They seem to think you're having trouble with MEDEA. They feel you might be in over your head."

"Ridiculous. I have the situation fully under control."

"That's not the way they're reading it back East."

"Well, if they have concerns, they ought to come to me personally. You tell your friend that the L.A. field office is entirely capable of handling MEDEA on our own."

"If they felt that way, they wouldn't be talking to me."

There was a pause. "Are you saying you might be coming on board? Is that what they're telling you?"

She hadn't intended to say that, but if the threat of her direct involvement would keep him talking, she would use it. "It's a possibility."

"Oh, hell."

"Try not to sound so thrilled."

"Why would they bring *you* in? It doesn't make sense."

She thought fast. "Look at it this way. At some point MEDEA may go to trial. When it does, you'll need somebody with credibility in L.A. to testify. They seem to feel that yours truly has the most credibility of anyone. I mean, given all the favorable coverage I got on the Mobius case and the Rain Man." She didn't like bragging, but she thought he would buy this angle.

He did. "Yes. Yes, I can see how they might think that way." He sounded worried.

She tried to get on his good side, assuming he had one. "Believe me, Richard, it's not that I want to go. Or that I think I can handle things any better than you can."

"That's a lie. You always think you can handle everything better than anyone else."

Apparently his good side was a lost cause. "I don't see why you're being so territorial. It seems to me that MEDEA is big enough for both of us."

"You're saying you *want* a piece of this case? Tess, I always thought you were trying to commit career suicide, hanging out in that little cow town when you could be in the spotlight by now. This confirms it."

"Maybe I just have very poor judgment." *And Denver is not a cow town,* she added silently.

"There's no maybe about it. Look, MEDEA is a tightly held secret. There's only a handful of people who even know the case has been reactivated." *Reactivated*—she noted the word. "However you found out about it, we can't have you sniffing around and making waves."

"That's a mixed metaphor."

He sighed, a sound of undisguised exasperation. "How certain are you that you'll be assigned to MEDEA?"

"It's looking likely."

"Damn. Well, then you might as well come on in right now."

She leaned forward, uncertain she'd heard what she thought she had. "Are you inviting me on board?"

"If goddamned D.C. is going to send you anyway, I'd rather take the initiative."

Now it made sense. "And get the credit," she said with a smile, "if I come up with a way to clear the case?"

"You overestimate yourself, as usual."

She asked herself how badly she wanted to help Abby—and ensure that Abby stayed off the Bureau's radar screen. The answer was . . . almost as badly as she wanted to piss off the Nose.

"Thanks for having me on your team, Richard. I'll be there by two p.m."

"Wonderful."

"Fax me the case report. I'll read it on the plane."

"Why don't you ask your friend in Washington to fax it to you?" he asked in a sullen tone.

"Just do it."

"If you know so much, you don't even need to read the case report." He paused, and she thought she could hear the click of mental tumblers starting to fall into place. "How much *do* you know, anyway?"

The conversation was veering into a dangerous area. "Enough to know that I'll regret getting involved," she said briskly. "Fax the report, but don't bother arranging a pickup at LAX. I'll catch a cab."

She ended the call before he could say anything more, then buzzed her assistant.

"Cancel my appointments for the next two days. I'm going out of town."

9

The Brayton Hotel had been put up in 1927 and recently renovated at a cost of thirty million dollars. The establishment was not so much a hotel as a palace, an opulent monument in the heart of the city. Vaulted ceilings hung over the Spanish Renaissance lobby. Fine carpets absorbed the footsteps of liveried bellmen. The clamor of traffic and people on the streets outside was muted, safely relegated to another world, another century.

Jack Reynolds loved the Brayton. He loved any place that whispered of wealth and status. *Whispered* was the right word. It did no good to shout about these things. To shout would be vulgar. Men of real power did not shout. They didn't have to. The same was true of buildings. The Brayton was old-money, not nouveau riche. It had no need to prove itself.

He was different from the hotel in that way. He'd been proving himself all his life.

Reynolds entered the Rendezvous Court, which had once been a library and still offered the hushed atmosphere appropriate to a bookish sanctuary. At a small table in an out-of-the-way corner he ordered black coffee. Across the room he saw Kip Stenzel, reading the latest *Newsweek*. Stenzel had outfitted him with a radio transmitter the size of a deck of cards, and Reynolds now reached into his pocket and switched it on, saying quietly, "Testing."

At the far table, Stenzel discreetly tapped his earlobe. He was receiving.

It never hurt to have a second pair of ears at a

meeting. And Stenzel could be trusted to keep quiet about whatever Abby Sinclair had learned.

The coffee arrived. Reynolds took a sip and leaned back in his chair. As always when he found himself in a place like this, he couldn't resist the inrush of contrasting memories from his boyhood. The gray sludge that leaked from the tap in the kitchen sink, which the landlord refused to repair—and now the porcelain mug of Kona coffee, imported from Hawaii and fresh ground in the kitchen. The blare of police sirens—and now the Chopin étude playing on hidden speakers. The stink of urine in the stairwell—and now the hint of cinnamon from a scented candle in his table's centerpiece.

Those were superficial differences. What really mattered was the change in atmosphere, of the very air around him. Growing up, he had hardly been able to breathe—and not only because of the waves of body odor rising from the bums who slept on the stairs, or the stifling confines of the bedroom he shared with two younger brothers. Even in the open air, his lungs had been tight, frozen. He'd been choking, suffocating, every breath constricted by furious despair. At some point in his childhood he heard the expression "trapped in poverty," and he knew immediately that it named his predicament. He was trapped in the barrio. No exit. No hope.

There were three great turning points in his life. The first came at age ten, when he was ambushed after school by a trio of Mexicans. They were older and bigger than he was, and they took turns pummeling him, pounding him in the face and belly. He could still see the blur of their fists, taste his own sweat, feel the burn of nausea with each new smack in the gut.

But he wouldn't go down. He took the punishment without surrender. Once or twice he fell on one knee, but always he was back on his feet in time to accept the next blow, and the next.

Two of his attackers backed off, exhausted, leaving only the ringleader still throwing punches and screaming, "Cry!" His broad Aztec face was twisted in fury, his mouth dangling loops of spittle. "Cry, asshole! Lemme see you cry!"

Jack did not cry. He waited until the bully faltered, worn-out by the punishment he'd inflicted, and then with some unknown reserve of strength Jack launched a pile driver at the bastard's jaw. He heard a crack of bone. The Mexican collapsed, blood in his mouth, eyes wild with pain. The other two fled, shouting curses. Jack stood over his fallen aggressor, then kicked him twice in the ribs and walked away. As it turned out, the punch had broken the bully's jaw, which had to be wired up, his meals fed to him through a straw.

That day he learned his anger could serve a purpose. He could feed off its heat and use it as a weapon. It made him stronger. Other fights followed. Sometimes he was the loser. Most times he was not. But he never backed away, and he never went down easy—and when beaten, he never forgot.

The second turning point came when he was thirteen. A friend of his, who'd been rescued from a beating by Jack's intervention, invited him on what he described as "a goof." A goof, as it turned out, was a crime—the robbery of a convenience mart. Jack's job was to watch for police. He did okay, and got a small share of the money. Other goofs followed. Nothing too serious—no one ever got hurt in any major way, and he avoided arrest, though sometimes narrowly. His activities brought him new respect. He began to realize that the other kids, the ones who never broke the law, were wary of him. They feared him. He liked that.

This was his second lesson. He could scare people. And their fear, properly exploited, would make them do all kinds of useful things. They would empty their pockets for him. They would follow his orders. The girls found him dangerous and intriguing. He lost his virginity at fourteen in the girls' locker room, where a blond sophomore had brought him for a quick introduction to the mysteries of sex.

Learning to make others fear him had made him a man.

The next year, at fifteen, came the third turning point. Until then, he had known that there were other people somewhere who had money and the freedom it bought, but he'd imagined no way of joining them. Suddenly he was big enough, agile enough, to compete in sports, and he saw his way out. Years later he attended a college lecture on a corrupt Tammany Hall politico who, the professor said, responded to criticism with the unapologetic defense, "I seen my opportunities and I took 'em." The class had laughed. Reynolds hadn't. He'd understood the Tammany Hall man perfectly. A man's life was nothing but opportunities seized—or missed.

Football was Jack's opportunity. He devoted himself to it with a zealot's passion. Football became his theology, and the ratty field hemmed in by tiers of wooden benches was his church. He pumped iron and ran miles and studied playbooks.

He learned something about himself through football. He learned that he was a stubborn son of a bitch. Once he set his mind on something, he would not be denied. He aimed to win the quarterback position, to make himself the star of the team, and he succeeded.

On the gridiron he learned another lesson. There was no worse fate than failure. Nothing could ease the ache of losing, and nothing was more unacceptable than the sour taste of humiliation at the hands of a stronger or more resilient adversary. He played to win, and usually he did win, often in last-minute comebacks that kept the school talking for days.

But the real victory he aimed for was his ticket out of town. In his senior year he got it. He received a full athletic scholarship to Chico State. He was the first member of his family to attend college. His parents frankly did not know what to make of this development, whether to be pleased or appalled. His father had assumed Jack would join him at the canning factory after graduation. Instead Jack stuffed the few possessions he needed into a backpack and set off on his motorcycle to drive five hundred miles to rural northern California. Fields of crops replaced shotgun flats. The main streets were lined with variety emporiums and feed shops, not liquor stores and strip clubs.

He'd gotten out of the barrio. And he'd done it himself, owing no one, asking for no favors, waiting on no lucky breaks.

In his speeches, which were always crafted by his staffers because he was no good with words, he sometimes used the language of victimhood. It was what his constituents wanted to hear. They liked blaming their problems on the rich, the elite, the system. He talked the talk, but he didn't believe it. He wasn't a victim, because he had chosen not to be. Anyone could make the same choice. Most weren't willing to pay the tab.

He'd never been deluded enough to think he could make it as a pro on the football field. He decided on a law degree instead. The law was a means of control. Those who understood it, who could take advantage of its complexities and ambiguities, would always have an edge on those who couldn't. Control meant power. Power meant freedom. Freedom meant a permanent escape from the barrio streets.

In law school he met Nora. They were married on a spring day in a civil ceremony. His parents attended, though he wished they hadn't. They had come without dressing up, looking ridiculous in their casual clothes, and what was worse, they were unaware of any impropriety. His father drank too much and told loud, off-color stories. His mother looked at nobody and said nothing. He hadn't realized how badly he was ashamed of them. They were rubes, and they had never aspired to be anything better. Seeing this, he knew he had shaken off the barrio for good. He was a married man, and he would make his own family to replace the one he'd been born with, the one that had let him down.

Later, when he started making money, he bought

his folks a house in Tustin, a decent suburb where they could live a comfortable life as retirees, but he rarely saw them. He didn't want to be reminded of where he'd come from. Rhetoric about his log cabin origins was handy in speeches, but he didn't think of himself as having been raised in a log cabin. He saw himself as having engineered a narrow escape from hell.

To begin in the graffiti-scarred hallway of his apartment building, and to end in the halls of Congress— a long trip, a great ascent. Now he could dine at hotels like this one, meeting with important people who kowtowed to him for legislative favors; he exercised power in his every official act, and in plenty of unofficial acts, as well.

Having risen to his present height, he would never give up what he had won. Anyone who threatened his position, anyone who stood in his way, would be dealt with and removed. He had learned that lesson, too, on the football field and in the streets.

A man fought for what was his. He didn't let scruples or sentiment deter him from doing whatever had to be done.

He thought Abby Sinclair understood this policy. At least he hoped she did. He wanted to have made the right choice in hiring her. The matter was delicate and couldn't be entrusted to just anybody.

Of course, if she disappointed him, she could be dealt with, too.

The thought played along the back edges of his mind as he watched her enter the Rendezvous Court. He gave her a quick smile, which was not returned.

Abby sat at the table. Across the room, Stenzel touched his ear, adjusting his earpiece.

"I know at least three things about your stalker," Abby said, not bothering with a hello. "She's paranoid and potentially violent. She has a gun. And she's not Rose Moran."

Reynolds blinked, surprised by the rapid-fire assault. "How can you know that?"

"Because *this* is Rose Moran." She plucked a sheet of paper from her purse, unfolded it, and pushed it across the table. It was a photocopy of an old newspaper story, with a picture of Rose and his family. He stared at it for a long moment.

"Have you been checking up on me?" he asked finally.

"Yes. Apparently with good reason. There's no resemblance between your ex-housekeeper and this woman. Why did you lie to me?"

He took a breath. An accusation of lying was not something he took calmly—even when it was true. But it would do him no good to lose control.

"I didn't lie," he said quietly, keeping his temper under tight restraint. "It's been ten years, and I thought I saw a resemblance—"

She cut him off. "I can't help you if you won't tell me the truth."

"This isn't a good photo. Rose doesn't look anything like this."

"She doesn't look anything like the woman you sent me to track down, either."

It looked like she wasn't buying his bullshit. If he'd been in her position, he wouldn't have bought it, either.

"But you *did* track her down?" he asked slowly.

"Yes."

"And she's a threat?"

"She may be."

"You just said she's paranoid and violent."

"Potentially violent. Until I know who she is and what relationship she had or has with you, I can't assess the risk."

"There was no relationship," he snapped, then regretted it, because she hadn't meant it that way.

She studied him coolly. "Who is she, Jack?" He noted how she used his first name to establish trust. She thought she was clever, but he was clever, too. He might not have a degree in psychology like she did, but he knew people.

He had settled down now. That she had learned some of the truth was an unwelcome development, but not entirely unexpected. He could handle it. He could negotiate.

"I can't tell you," he said in his most reasonable voice. "I'm sorry, but that information is confidential. It really doesn't matter, though. All you need to do for me is tell me where to find this woman. I can take it from there."

Abby just stared at him. "We need to be honest with each other if we're going to work together."

"There are some things you're not allowed to know. I'm sure some of your other clients have imposed restrictions on what they could tell you."

"If they did, they didn't stay my clients for long."

"This is a special case. I occupy a sensitive position." He spread his hands in a gesture of openness. "Surely you can see my point."

"No, I can't. Everybody has secrets. I understand that. But you can't keep secrets from me. Not if you want me to continue in your employ."

"In this case, I have no choice. I'm sorry."

"I'm sorry, too." She started to get up. "You owe me for one day's work. I'll send the bill to your office."

Reynolds was surprised. Either she was a damn good bargainer, or she really was willing to quit on him.

"So that's it? You're going to walk away—even after you said this woman may be dangerous?"

"Yes, that's what I'm going to do."

"At least tell me what you found out. Her name."

"I have a feeling you know her name. Her real name, anyway. Which is more than I know."

"What does that mean?"

"She seems to have reinvented herself. Her personal history goes back only eight years."

It made sense. It explained why he hadn't been able to find her on his own. "If she's using a new identity, what is it?"

"I don't think I'll tell you that."

The anger was making a comeback. This woman wasn't being reasonable. "Why the hell not?"

"I'm beginning to think I can't trust you. About anything. Trust is very important to me."

This was the third or fourth time she'd called him a liar to his face. Most people wouldn't get away with it once. "I'm not paying any damn bill for your services unless you give me the information I'm asking for."

Abby shrugged. "Forget the bill. I'll consider this a pro bono case. Charity work."

Red light flashed across his field of vision. "Fuck you, then. I don't need you."

"Actually, I think you do." She drummed her fingers lightly on the tabletop. "This woman is going to keep attending your events. She has a schedule of all your public appearances. I saw it in her car, right next to an Orange County map book to help her find her way around. She'll continue stalking you. Maybe at some point she'll try something more."

"Then you have to stop her. That's what you do."

"I've been planning to take a vacation. This seems like an excellent time to do so. Unless you want to come clean with me and stop playing games."

He knew he should give her something, anything, just to keep her on the case, but instead he heard himself say, "You don't give me orders, you little bitch."

Abby shook her head sadly. "Not very nice. I'm leaving now." She was out of her chair, slinging the purse over her shoulder.

"Goddamn it"—Reynolds sucked in a harsh breath—"I need to know where she is."

"Next time she shows up at one of your events, ask her yourself."

She walked off, not looking back.

He hated her. He wanted to drag her into a dark hallway and squeeze the information out of her. Literally squeeze . . .

"Fucking cunt," he whispered. He picked up his coffee. The mug trembled. His hand was shaking.

Then Stenzel slid into the chair just vacated by Abby. "She's a pistol, huh?" he said in his chipper, ingratiating voice.

"She's a piece of shit," Reynolds growled. "She wouldn't give me a fucking thing."

"That's not quite true." Stenzel tapped the receiver in his ear and smiled. "She revealed more than she intended."

"Like what?"

"Like the fact that this woman has an Orange County map book and a schedule of your appearances."

"That doesn't tell us anything."

"Maybe it does. We need to be proactive, Jack. We need to think outside the box."

Reynolds honestly detested the middle-management jargon Stenzel was always spouting. "So go ahead. Tell me what I missed."

"It's not a question of missing anything. It's more like revisiting the issue from a different analysis standpoint. The woman had a schedule. Where did she get it?"

"She could have picked it up at my campaign office."

"Yes . . . or she could have had it sent to her."

Reynolds stared into the black depths of his coffee. He began to see where Stenzel was going. "She could be on our mailing list."

"It's quite possible."

"But she has a new name. She could be anybody."

"She could be anybody with an Orange County map book. And who is most likely to use a map book to get around in your district?" Stenzel answered his own question. "Someone who's from outside the district."

"Right," Reynolds said, getting it now.

"Ballpark, I'm estimating ninety-nine percent of the people on your mailing list are your constituents."

"So we look for someone who isn't."

"That's the game plan."

"And if there's more than one?"

"We look for women only. That reduces the parameters by half."

"She could be married. Could be it's her husband's name on the list."

"Your security consultant said the lady is violent and paranoid. Doesn't sound like marriage material to me."

"Okay." Reynolds was feeling slow all of a sudden. He should've put this together. He shouldn't have to rely on a simpering toady like Kip Stenzel to make the connections. "What if there's more than one woman from outside the district who's on our list?"

"Then we check them out one by one. We look for the one whose credit history goes back only eight years."

"You can do that?"

"It's a challenge, but definitely actionable. And the mailing list isn't that big. I'm not promising a quick win, but you never know. We may get lucky right away."

"Start on it," Reynolds said. "Go back to the office and start checking the list. When you find this woman, call me on my cell."

Stenzel got up. He fished a key ring out of his pocket. "I assume you're keeping the Ford."

Reynolds nodded and took the keys. "You can rent a car. Just ask the front desk. Get moving." He didn't thank Stenzel for his help. Thanks would come later, if his idea panned out.

"Will do." Stenzel hesitated a moment. "Sinclair's disloyalty makes things more complicated."

"Yes."

"I don't know why you had to outsource. I could have handled it. Just give me my marching orders, and I would have operationalized any strategy you called for."

Any strategy? Reynolds doubted it. There were some skills that weren't taught in business school.

"Get going, Kip," he said mildly. "Get on the case. Find me a solution."

"That's what I do, Jack."

He walked away, and Reynolds was left to sip his coffee, which was getting cold, and to ponder Abby Sinclair. Stenzel was right. She could be a problem. But problems could be taken care of.

He'd hired a freelancer for a reason. Sinclair flew solo. No organization, no staff, nobody keeping tabs on her. She worked outside the law—no records to worry about. If she disappeared, no one would ever know what case she'd been handling or who she'd been working for.

Probably it wouldn't come to that. But he almost hoped it would.

IO

Abby liked making a dramatic exit, but that didn't mean she actually had to leave. Sometimes it was smarter to hang around, especially when something interesting appeared to be on tap.

Sitting with Reynolds, she'd noticed his gaze move once too often to a spot across the room. On her way out she had glanced over, and what do you know? There was Kip Stenzel. Interesting that he would be here, more interesting that Reynolds evidently hadn't wanted her to know it.

Curious, she waited outside the Rendezvous Court, studying a painting and watching Reynolds at his table in the reflection on the glass. Sure enough, he was joined almost immediately by Stenzel. The two of them remained deep in conversation for several minutes before Reynolds dismissed him.

Abby ducked out of sight as Stenzel walked through the doorway. Following at a distance, she passed behind him while he spoke with a clerk at the desk. She picked up enough of their exchange to know that Stenzel was inquiring about a car rental.

Presumably Reynolds and his campaign manager had come to the Brayton together. Now Stenzel was going off on his own in a rented car. Reynolds must have other travel plans.

She couldn't follow them both. The congressman interested her more. With any luck he had used the same Ford minivan he'd driven to the town hall meeting last night.

She took the elevator to the hotel's underground

garage and wandered among the parked vehicles until she found the van, easily identifiable by the two RE-ELECT JACK REYNOLDS bumper stickers on its rump. From her purse she took out a roll of reflective tape and tore off a six-inch strip, which she attached to the bumper. In the dim light of the garage, the tape was invisible, but outside, in direct sunlight, it would throw off considerable glare. She would be able to stay well back and still see the telltale shine.

Reynolds had said he was going to lunch at noon. He ought to be through by one thirty or so. Then she would see where he went.

Tailing a client wasn't exactly standard procedure. But then, Reynolds wasn't her client anymore. In fact, inasmuch as he refused to reimburse her for her services, he had never really been her client at all.

"Should've paid me, Jack," she whispered.

By two o'clock she was starting to wonder how long it took Reynolds to chow down. She'd been sitting in her Miata, parked across the street from the hotel garage, for more than an hour.

Finally the Ford came into view, heading up the exit ramp. She keyed the ignition. When the van breezed past, she followed. Reynolds headed onto the south-bound Harbor Freeway, the 110.

The tail job was easy. Reynolds, unlike most of the people she had surveilled, wasn't paranoid. He executed no evasive maneuvers. He signaled when changing lanes, only moderately exceeded the speed limit, and gave her plenty of warning when transferring from the 110 to the 10, and from the 10 to the 405.

He was headed back to Orange County, it appeared. Going to his office or his home. Stenzel might have had a more suspicious destination in mind. She was beginning to think she'd followed the wrong man.

Just past the Huntington Beach exit, Reynolds's cell phone chirped.

"Yeah," he said, cradling the phone between his head and shoulder.

"We got her." Stenzel's voice was excited, higher than usual.

"You sure?"

"She's on the mailing list. She lives in San Fernando, fifty miles outside our district. And her paper trail only goes back eight years. What's the protocol for me now?"

"Nothing. I'll handle it from here. Just give me her address."

"It's 903 Keystone Drive."

Reynolds nodded, committing the address to memory. "I'll be a little late getting back to the office," he said. "Need to see some people. Do I have anything on for this afternoon?"

"Your schedule's open."

"Keep it that way. And, Kip—you did a good job on this. Excellent work."

"I aim to please."

Reynolds nearly ended the call, then remembered a question he'd meant to ask. "What name is she using?"

"Andrea Lowry. Does that matter?"

"No." Reynolds smiled. "No, it doesn't matter at all."

Abby was getting seriously bored by the time her quarry entered Orange County. But when the van left the freeway, heading into Santa Ana, she got interested all over again.

Reynolds, she remembered, had been raised in the Santa Ana barrios. Possibly he was indulging in a little nostalgia by venturing home again. She doubted it. He didn't seem like the sentimental type.

On TV, Orange County existed as a place of endless beaches, posh malls, and glistening marinas. And all of those things were real enough, and had earned the shoreline its nickname, the Gold Coast. But TV always oversimplified, and the reality of the county was inevitably more complex. Inland, away from the yachts and beachfront condos, there lay a massively overdeveloped patchwork of freeways, urban centers, and suburban sprawl. Hillsides, once bare, now sprouted condos, and condos on top of condos, and still more condos on top of those. Newness was the driving force here.

The wealthier areas were adult playgrounds where everything was new, glistening, beautiful, and oddly sterile. They drew in prosperity and commerce. The older districts, left behind, became home to Orange County's underclass, which was sizable and, like everything else in California, growing.

Santa Ana was one of the old sections. Its population was largely Hispanic. Here was where the bus lines brought the chambermaids who made beds in Newport Beach's luxury hotels and the gardeners who trimmed bushes outside Irvine's million-dollar homes. Santa Ana was crowded and noisy and unpolished, its crime rates were high, and it was not a place where a man like Jack Reynolds was likely to spend his leisure time.

Abby stayed two or three cars behind him, catching glimpses of the reflective tape through gaps in the traffic. The van turned down a side street. She continued straight, afraid to pull directly behind her quarry. Her red sports car would stand out, and even a driver who wasn't looking for a tail might spot it.

At the next corner she turned, then paralleled Reynolds's projected route for a few blocks before cutting over to the street he'd been traveling on. The van was nowhere in sight. It was possible she'd lost him, but there was an equal chance he'd parked somewhere along the way. She retraced the route and spotted the van in the parking lot of a motorcycle repair shop.

Reynolds wasn't at the wheel. He must have gone inside.

She cruised past the shop, a dingy square structure with off-white stucco walls that had turned consider-

ably more off-white with the passage of time. From
inside came the whir of power drills and the sputtering
cough of a faulty engine. A hand-painted banner over
the door read HARLEY SPECALISTS. She wondered why
someone would take the time to paint the sign by
hand but wouldn't check the spelling first. She also
wondered what the hell Congressman Reynolds was
doing in a cycle shop. Nothing on his Web site or in
his office had indicated a passion for motorcycles, and
she seriously doubted that he would drop by to shoot
the bull with a bunch of mechanics on a Friday afternoon, even if they did happen to be his constituents.

The situation was becoming more complicated—and
more troubling. She didn't like the fact that Reynolds
had come here so soon after their meeting, as if her
refusal to cooperate on the case had led him to take
some more drastic measure.

Such as? She didn't know, but a fair number of
bikers were known for their participation in criminal
acts. Reynolds had been willing to tiptoe along the
edge of the law by hiring her. Maybe now he'd been
prompted to cross the line entirely.

Well, she could hardly walk into the bike shop and
ask him about his plans—although her sudden appearance in that environment would boast a certain theatrical flair.

If she couldn't talk to Reynolds, whom could she
talk to?

There was one obvious choice, and that was Andrea
Lowry herself.

It was a good thing Reynolds wasn't her client, because going behind a client's back to get info on him
from his own stalker was definitely not in her usual
playbook. And of course Andrea might not tell her a
thing. They hadn't exactly hit it off last night.

The thing was, though, Andrea knew when she was
being lied to. She must have been lied to a lot. But
suppose someone were to try telling her the straight
truth. No lies, no games, just simple honesty. Would
she respond?

It was worth a shot, if for no other reason than it was the only shot Abby had left. She drove out of Santa Ana and headed north on the 405, which would take her back to L.A.

II

Ron Shanker was in the garage when he saw the Man enter the waiting room of his shop. The Man—that was how Shanker thought of him. To everyone else he was Congressman Jack Reynolds, but to him he would always be the Man.

Shanker had been talking to a pimply red-haired kid about rejetting the carbs on his Yamaha, one of those rice burners Shanker hated. But what the hell, business was business, and with the Mexicans crowding him on all sides, he needed all the business he could get. The Mexicans wouldn't come to him, of course. They knew about the war three years ago, and although a truce was now in effect, it didn't mean the two sides were friendly.

Anyway, he couldn't keep the Man waiting, especially not in the crappy little room at the front of the shop, a room whose sole amenity was an ancient coffeemaker that dripped poisonous sludge into a stained carafe. He handed off the red-haired kid to one of his mechanics, telling him to drain the gas tank before starting the tune-up because the bike had been in storage and the gas was old. Then he headed into the outer room.

"Jack, how's it hanging?" He extended a large hand and felt it gripped by the Man's crushing fist. "What brings you here?"

"Business." He said it in the unmistakable way that meant trouble.

Shanker nodded. "Let's go into my office."

He led the Man through the shop, past the Dynotest

room, where a Harley was being run through its RPM range. Around him rang the screams of power tools, mixing with the casual profanities of his three mechanics. All of them puffed cigarettes, the burning ends glowing like red eyes behind veils of smoke.

His office was down a short hall, past the stink hole washroom that had needed a good cleaning for at least six months. One wall of the hallway was decorated with cycle calendars sent to his shop by manufacturers of tools and engine parts. Most of them displayed the wrong month, having been turned to whatever page featured the best artwork—the artwork in question consisting of color photos of busty, nearly nude, creatively tattooed women draped over motorcycles.

Reynolds entered the office, and Shanker followed, careful to shut and lock the door. He noticed that the Man did him the courtesy of sitting in the visitor's chair rather than stationing himself behind the desk. They both knew he could sit anywhere he pleased.

The office was small and smelled of carpet cleaner. An air conditioner rattled in the window frame, working hard against waves of August heat.

Shanker settled into the desk chair and tried not to look scared. It was tough to do, because the Man was one sprung motherfucker. He'd known the Man for a long time, and he'd been scared of him for nearly as long. And Ron Shanker was a guy who didn't scare easy—he had the scars on his hide to prove it, battle scars from street combat.

"What can I do ya for?" he asked with a weak, shit-eating grin.

Reynolds ignored the question. "How's business?"

The inquiry took Shanker by surprise. The Man never made small talk with him.

"Picking up," Shanker said. "Not bad."

"I guess our economic policies are working."

"Yeah, sure." Shanker didn't have a clue what economic policies his congressman had voted for.

"How's the market on the streets?"

"I seen better. Coke's down, but this designer shit,

like Ecstasy, is still pretty hot. And speed. Speed is always in demand."

"Speed kills," Reynolds said with a slight smile.

Shanker got the joke. It was what they used to say when they went out riding—and having said it, they would crank their bikes into gear and bust every speed limit, flashing past stop signs, flying through red lights. Because while they knew that speed kills, they didn't believe they could die. They'd been young.

Shanker knew better now. Like the Man, he was past fifty. He'd seen people die, and he knew how real it was.

"Any trouble from the *cholos?*" Reynolds asked.

"Not as long as we stay on our turf and they stay on theirs. Fucking taco benders are basically cowards. All bullshit, no action."

"I guess you ought to know. You get to see enough of them."

"Too many. Goddamn border monkeys spit out kids as regular as taking a crap. Hey, I got a good one for you. How many Mexicans does it take to grease an axle?" He paused before delivering the punch line. "One, if you hit 'im just right."

Reynolds laughed. It was good to hear him laugh. The two of them used to laugh all the time.

"I don't think I'll be using that one in any of my speeches," Reynolds said. "So, no new hostilities?"

"Some hassles, you know. Guys going at it, trying to prove what big balls they got. Nothing major. Not since the Westminster Avenue thing." Down on Westminster three years ago, Shanker's guys had gotten into it with a crew of Mexishits. Well, actually El Salvadorans, but they were all Mexishits in the end. One of Shanker's men bought it, but the *cholos* lost four of their own, plus another who was busted up so badly he would never pick lettuce again. After that, the truce had been called.

"Well, I'm glad you're still making out. Even so, I don't suppose you'd object if I send a little extra business your way."

"I can always use more business," Shanker said cautiously.

"Right now I can use your services."

"Like what, as a for instance?"

"Like removing somebody who's become a problem."

"Okay. I can get that done."

"Now."

"When you say *now* . . ."

"I mean today. This afternoon."

"In broad daylight?"

"People die in the daytime. If your crew goes in fast and hard, they can get away before anybody knows what's happening."

"It would be better to wait until dark."

"I'm not waiting. I want this individual blipped immediately. That a problem?"

"No problem. I just wish you'd come to me sooner. It's good to do a little preliminary scouting, you know, check out the territory."

"I just got the address a half hour ago," Reynolds said, "while I was on my way here."

"Oh." Shanker thought about this. "You were already coming? What would you have done if you didn't have the address when you got here?"

"I would have waited. I put my best man on it, and I have confidence in him. I always have confidence in the people I work with. They never let me down."

He said it with an emphasis that let Shanker know how important it was not to let Jack Reynolds down.

"So where do we find this individual?" Shanker asked.

"Address in the Valley."

"Who are we dealing with here? I mean, is this a hardened target—security protection, shit like that?"

"It's a middle-aged woman. She lives alone at this address."

Reynolds took out an index card, handling it by the edges between thumb and forefinger, and pushed it across the desk. On it was written *903 KEYSTONE*

DRIVE, the address printed in capitals to make a handwriting comparison impossible. Shanker guessed that Reynolds had never touched the surface of the card. He'd left no prints.

"I can get it done," Shanker said. He didn't touch the card, either.

"What'll it cost?"

"Forget it. Gratis."

"I'll pay. What's the going rate?"

"It's just her? Just this one woman?"

"For now."

Shanker hesitated, wondering how much he should ask for. Too much, and he might make the Man angry. Too little, and he would only be cheating himself.

"Five grand," he said.

Reynolds nodded. "I'll pay in cash when the job is done. Unless you need a deposit?"

This had to be a joke. Even if it wasn't, Shanker found himself laughing. "Deposit? What, are you shitting me? No way."

He kept laughing, though there was nothing really funny about it. Except that it *was* funny—the whole routine they were going through, the scene they had acted out. They both knew Shanker would do whatever he was told, whether or not he was paid. They both knew Shanker was in no position to disappoint Jack Reynolds. And they both knew what happened to people who did disappoint him. Joe Ferris, for instance.

Joe had made the mistake of trying to blackmail the Man back when Reynolds was just getting started in the DA's office. Ferris had dirt on him—some small-time illegal shit Reynolds had done as a teenager—and he threatened Reynolds with career-killing exposure unless he received a monthly stipend, a lien on Reynolds's income. Reynolds played along, paying him off for five or six months, until Joe got careless and allowed himself to be drawn into a private rendezvous with the Man. By then he thought he'd broken Reynolds down, made him his bitch.

Jack Reynolds was no one's bitch. The next day Joe Ferris was found dead in a vacant lot, his body mutilated in awful ways, all of which predated his expiration. The police never caught the killer and, given Ferris's rap sheet, didn't make much of an effort. But Shanker knew who had done it. And he knew that before he died, Joe Ferris had given up every piece of evidence that could have been used against Reynolds. No one could have held out against the methods that had been used, the terrible ingenuity employed.

The Man was older now, but he hadn't mellowed. He'd filled out his suits a little, polished his act, but if you stripped all that away, he was still a fighter who knew only the law of the barrio—to defend your turf, accept no disrespect, and show no leniency to your enemies, ever.

"No deposit, then," Reynolds said when Shanker had gotten his laughter under control.

"I'll put my best crew on it," Shanker promised.

"Good. Let me know when it's done."

Reynolds started to rise. Shanker risked a question. "You said there was only one person—for now. Does that mean there's another one, for later?"

"Yes." Reynolds looked away. "Another woman. Younger than this one. Harder to get at. Harder to take down."

"Gimme her address," Shanker said, eager to please. "My crew'll pop her, too."

"One thing at a time. This other woman has to be approached with care. And . . ." He let his words fade away.

Shanker waited, knowing the Man would tell him if he meant to.

"And when she's taken care of, I want to be there."

"Okay . . ." Shanker drew out the two syllables in an unasked question.

"I hired her, and she quit on me. Called me a liar." Reynolds turned to him, and something in his face made Shanker almost flinch. "I don't like that."

"Okay," Shanker said again, quietly.

Reynolds looked past him into some invisible distance. "I'll be teaching her a lesson in loyalty."

"You can teach her today, if you want."

"Not today." Reynolds smiled. His voice was low, the voice of a man speaking to himself. "Abby can wait. Sometimes the waiting is half the pleasure of it. You know what I mean?"

He didn't. "Sure."

"When I need this other matter addressed, you'll be able to arrange it, I'm certain."

"Absolutely."

"And I'll pay another five grand. With a bonus if she lasts through the night."

"That's very generous." Shanker was thinking of Joe Ferris, who had lived for four to six hours according to the autopsy, though for the last hour or two he had been blind, deaf, unable to speak or move, capable only of feeling pain.

Reynolds stood. "I'll let myself out." Suddenly he was a charmer again, a neighborhood guy. "Great to see you, Ron. You haven't changed a bit."

"You, too," Shanker managed. "We gotta get together for dinner sometime."

"Count on it," the Man said, knowing as well as Shanker that there would be no dinner, which was just as well, because Shanker never had any appetite in Reynolds's presence.

The door closed after Reynolds, and Shanker sank back in his chair. He thought about the two women. The second one, especially, the one Reynolds had called Abby. She'd walked out on a business arrangement, he'd said. Insulted him, too. Insulted the Man.

That hadn't been smart. Whoever she was, this Abby didn't have a clue who she was dealing with. She would find out, though.

Just like Joe Ferris did.

12

The air over Los Angeles was a grimy sepia tone, tinting the grid work of buildings and streets below. Looking out the airplane window, Tess saw the HOLLYWOOD sign on a far hillside, the row of giant letters reduced by distance to microscopic text, a footnote to the city. She wondered why people made such a big deal about the sign. It was only the remnant of someone's advertising promotion—for a housing development called Hollywoodland, as she recalled. Denver boasted the Rocky Mountains, a wilderness of trails and fishing holes and granite peaks running with clear snowmelt. L.A. had a defunct advertisement on a hill.

All right, maybe she was overstating things. But she truly hated Los Angeles. With any luck her stay would be short and uneventful. She would find out what Abby was mixed up in, make sure she wouldn't come to the Bureau's attention, then make a graceful exit.

The problem was, she'd found that situations involving Abby rarely proceeded according to plan.

The jet touched down with a skid of tires and made its way to the arrival gate. She'd checked no baggage, choosing to bring only a carry-on case with a few items she kept in her office for overnight stays—a change of clothes, some toiletries, other odds and ends. She had worn her gun in a pancake holster under her jacket throughout the flight, an option that was not only tolerated but required when federal agents traveled by plane. In the world after September 11, a law enforcement agent with a gun was the next best thing to an air marshal.

Most of the flight had been occupied by her perusal of the MEDEA case report, faxed to her office just before she left. The first thing she'd noticed was that the case was two decades old. It had been reactivated only within the past few weeks, for reasons that fully explained the Bureau's trepidation. It was hot stuff, all right. She was almost surprised Michaelson had allowed the material to be faxed to her, even over a secure phone line.

And she now knew why the case had been dubbed MEDEA. Apparently the name was not an example of FBI creativity, after all. It had been coined by a tabloid newspaper, and the Bureau had simply picked it up. There had been considerable press coverage. Tess remembered none of it, but she hadn't been in law enforcement then. She had been a sophomore at the University of Illinois.

Back in the eighties, the Bureau's involvement in the case had been minimal, limited to a psychological evaluation of the arrestee. Even that contribution was unusual, a testimony to the widespread media interest in the crime.

The description of the current investigation was sketchy, and there was nothing about any developments within the past week. Tess figured she would be brought up to speed on those details when she was briefed at the field office.

Outside the concourse she found a taxi and directed the driver to the federal building in Westwood. The cab headed north to the San Diego Freeway. Traffic was worse than she remembered, and eventually the flow of vehicles came to a standstill. At her urging the cabbie exited at Venice Boulevard and took Sepulveda, creeping through the stop-and-go traffic. It was hot outside, the cab's air-conditioning didn't work, and Tess was rapidly developing an animus toward the City of Angels that was almost pathological. Then she saw the church.

It was on Olympic Boulevard, east of the intersection with Sepulveda. She glimpsed the spire in the sun.

She had been to that church on her last visit to L.A., taking confession there, her first confession in many years.

"Turn right," she said. Obediently the cabbie maneuvered through the clogged intersection and turned onto Olympic. She pointed at the church, and he stopped in the empty parking lot. "Just wait here. I'll be right out."

In the year and a half since the Rain Man case, she had thought of this church many times. Confession had helped her, though she hadn't felt so sure of it at the time. She felt an obligation to this place, which she intended to satisfy with a donation to the poor box.

She contributed most of the cash on her person, reminding herself to stop at an ATM and refill her wallet. Having given alms, she was ready to go, but strangely she didn't want to. Then she understood that she'd had an ulterior motive in coming here. She wanted absolution. She wanted to confess.

Forgive me, Father, for I have sinned. I broke the rules. I broke the law. I cut corners. I allowed myself to get away with behavior that I would never tolerate in a subordinate.

Something like that.

She entered the nave and walked down the central aisle. The church was empty. Her only company was a host of plaster saints and the backlit figures in the stained-glass windows, and the suffering Jesus on his cross, lifted behind the altar.

She remembered the location of the confessional. This was not the time when confession would be scheduled, but she'd gotten lucky on her last visit, and she hoped for the same luck again.

But she was disappointed. There was no priest in evidence. She really was alone.

Well, it had been worth a shot. She knelt and prayed before the altar, but it was a perfunctory prayer, and she felt nothing. She was retreating up the aisle when she saw a gray head bent low in one of the pews. An elderly woman, sitting alone. Tess hadn't noticed her before, and there had been no other vehicle in the parking lot.

The woman felt her gaze. She raised her head and looked at Tess. Her face was wet with tears.

After making eye contact, Tess couldn't walk away. She sat beside the woman. "Are you all right?"

"I come here every day," the woman answered. "I've come for the last three months."

Tess didn't ask what had happened three months ago. "Does it help?"

"I don't know. It's supposed to."

Tess touched the woman's hand. "I hope things get better." She rose to leave.

"What I want to know," the woman said softly, "is why there is so much."

Tess didn't understand. "So much . . . ?"

"Pain. How can there be so much pain, everywhere?"

It was the same question, Tess realized, that had kept her out of churches after Paul Voorhees had died.

There was nothing she could say in reply. She had never found an answer. Somehow, over time, she had lost the need for one. It was just the way things were. There was no point in trying to understand. There was only the struggle to make things better.

On impulse she leaned down and hugged the woman gently. Neither of them said anything.

"Thank you," the woman said in the tone of a blessing.

Tess nodded. She left, not looking back.

She arrived at the federal building and received a temporary ID badge from the guards in the lobby. An elevator ride brought her to the seventeenth story, where she was buzzed into the FBI suite that occupied the entire floor. The agent who greeted her was Rick Crandall, probably her only friend in the L.A. office. Though he had put on some muscle in the past year, he still looked impossibly young to be a federal agent.

Crandall had been a rookie when she met him—a first office agent, or FOA in the Bureauspeak. He was now in his second year, still at the GS-12 pay grade. The salary he was pulling down, even with overtime, wouldn't go very far in a town like L.A.

"Rick, good to see you." She thought about giving him a hug, decided against it because the receptionist was watching, and settled for a handshake instead. "How is everything with you?"

"Not bad." His voice was flat, his manner distant.

"Still managing to impress your old man?" Ralston Crandall was a deputy director at Bureau headquarters in D.C.

"I guess," he said tonelessly, not looking at her. "You can stow your suitcase behind the reception desk for now."

He key-carded the door to a hallway and led her inside. She tried again to make conversation. "Well, your father should be impressed. L.A.'s a tough gig for a new recruit."

"I'm not a new recruit anymore. I've been on the job nearly two years."

"Right, of course. I didn't mean . . ." Her apology trailed away. Crandall kept walking. She let the silence persist for a few seconds, then stopped him with a tug on his arm. "What's the matter, Rick?"

"Nothing." He pulled free of her grasp.

"I thought we were friends."

"Yeah. I thought so, too." He took a breath. "You want to know, Tess? You really want to know?"

Without waiting for an answer, he ducked into the break room, a kitchenette with a table and chairs, the air permanently infused with the aroma of coffee.

No one else was inside. Tess entered, and Crandall shut the door. He kept his voice low, but his eyes were fierce.

"Real good friends, that's what we are, right? And friends don't keep secrets, do they? They don't lie. So I guess that's why you told me all about Abby Hollister, right? Or should I say Abby Sinclair?"

Tess froze. For a moment she could think of nothing to say. Finally she asked the obvious question. "How do you know about that?"

"Because I saw her. I fucking *saw* her, in the flesh, alive. Not drowned in the storm tunnels."

"I see."

"You lied. You lied to everybody."

"I never actually said she drowned. People made the assumption—"

"Don't bullshit me. When we arrested Kolb, he said you two were working together. You denied it. But it was true, wasn't it?"

Tess gave in. She hoped to God that Crandall wasn't wearing a wire. "It was true."

"You went outside the Bureau, hooked up with some private detective?"

"She's not a PI. Not exactly."

"What is she, then?"

"A security consultant." Tess sat at the table. "You said you saw her. When?"

"Last night. Coming out of Andrea Lowry's house."

"You were surveilling the place?"

Crandall hesitated, then took a seat, also. Some of the rage had gone out of him, but she still saw the deep hurt in his face. He had looked up to her, trusted her.

"We were surveilling Lowry's vehicle, actually," he said in a more subdued voice. "We mounted a GPS tracker on her car."

Tess was familiar with the procedure. The Global Positioning System would log the vehicle's movements, saving the information to a computer file.

"She parks in a carport," Crandall went on, "so it was easy enough to get access to the vehicle. It was my job to download the data every twenty-four hours and see where she's been. When I arrived last night to do the data dump, I saw a car parked outside the house. Later I ran the tags. The car belongs to your friend. She was visiting Andrea Lowry."

"The car was registered under her real name?"

"Yes—assuming Sinclair *is* her real name. Why do you ask?"

"When she's working undercover, she usually drives a car registered to an alias."

"Maybe this time she got careless. I watched the house and saw her leave. That's when I recognized her."

Tess nodded. During the Rain Man case, Crandall had interviewed Abby at the field office. She was posing as an ordinary civilian, using the name Abby Hollister. It was Abby Hollister who was supposed to have died later, in the storm drains, though her body had never been found.

"Did she see you?" Tess asked quietly.

"No. I was hiding in the carport. But I got a good look." He paused. When she said nothing, he added, "What the hell's going on, Tess?"

"It's complicated."

"I'll bet. You knew she didn't drown."

"I knew."

"Did you help her arrange for her car to be found?" Abby's Honda, registered in her Hollister ID, had turned up in the drainage system.

Tess shook her head. "It wasn't arranged. It was . . . providential, I guess you'd say. It was just how things worked out."

"So who is she, Tess?"

"You'd be better off not knowing." She caught his mistrustful glance and added, "I mean that. Really. The less you know, the more deniability you retain."

"Deniability? I saw her. I got her tag number. I'm already deeply into this thing."

She hesitated, fearing to ask the next question. "Does anyone else know?"

"You mean, have I told Michaelson? Have I put it in my official report?" Crandall made a brief noise like a stifled laugh. "Do you think you'd be sitting here with me if I had? The ADIC would have had you in a detention cell by now."

"That's a slight exaggeration."

"No, it isn't. He's been gunning for you for years. Ever since Mobius. You managed to piss him off. Frankly, you've managed to piss off most of the personnel in this office."

"So no one knows?" She failed to keep the relief out of her voice.

"No one. I'm covering for you."

"Thank you for your discretion."

"For participating in the cover-up, you mean? Yeah, I'm real proud of myself."

"It was a difficult situation, Rick. There were trade-offs. Abby helped me, and I helped her. It was against procedure—"

"No shit."

"—but it got the job done. We stopped Kolb."

"And you took all the credit. Nice."

"I didn't care about the credit. I got out of town as soon as the case was closed. I didn't exploit it." She hated sounding defensive.

"How about Mobius? Did your secret friend help you on that one, too?"

"I didn't know her then. She had nothing to do with Mobius."

"And MEDEA? It can't be a coincidence that you're here today after she visited Andrea Lowry last night."

"No, Rick. It's not a coincidence."

"Jesus." Crandall looked away, disgusted. "You're out of control, Tess. You're off the reservation."

"If it means anything, I never wanted it to go this far."

"You know what? It doesn't mean anything. Not to me." Crandall stood up. "Come on. You've got a briefing with the case agent."

"Not with Michaelson?"

Crandall shook his head. "He's limiting his contact with you. Can't say I blame him."

That was a cheap shot. Tess didn't respond. She followed Crandall out of the break room, aware that she had lost her only ally in the building. She was now officially alone in L.A.

Except for Abby, of course. And Abby was the exception that proved the rule.

13

Crandall led her to the squad room, where rows of desks sat nearly empty, only a few agents working the phones or reviewing notes on yellow legal pads. She saw one agent going over a stack of files in the brown-and-white folders used by all Bureau offices, along with a few of the older tan folders from an earlier era. The tan ones presumably related to the original MEDEA investigation twenty years ago. On another desk Tess saw blue documents, color-coded to signify urgency.

She followed Crandall to the rear of the bull pen, where a secretary gave them permission to enter the office of the squad supervisor.

His name was Hauser, and Tess pegged him instantly as an ex-marine. He was a tall, no-nonsense hard case with a gray crew cut, and he looked to be pushing the Bureau's mandatory retirement age.

Shell-shocked after her conversation with Crandall, she expected only more hostility and mistrust. She was surprised when Hauser proved friendly.

"Agent McCallum," he said as his big hand wrapped itself around hers, "I've heard a lot about you. You have a reputation for getting things done."

"My reputation is probably a bit overblown."

"I've looked at the cases you worked—the big ones, anyway. Mobius, STORMKIL . . . you impress the hell out of me, I have to say."

"I've been lucky in L.A."

"Yeah, luck." He winked at her. "Funny how some people have all the luck, and some don't. Anyhow, we need all the help we can get. We've opened a genuine can of worms, which is a lot less fun than a barrel of monkeys."

"I read the case report. But it wasn't very detailed. How exactly did you find the woman, anyway?"

"Wasn't easy. She did a pretty good job of dry-cleaning herself. We knew she must have gone underground, and she'd probably done it eight years ago, shortly after her release. It was likely she'd used somebody who was active in the Los Angeles area, probably somebody well-known, because she wasn't a person with a lot of criminal contacts. We found a guy who matched the description serving a ten-year sentence in federal prison. Fellow by the name of Rodriguez, who used to run a little identity-swapping operation out of Studio City. Couple of our people visited him in lockup and asked whether our subject had ever been one of his clients. There was the usual bargaining—he wanted to be moved to a less life-threatening part of the facility, which we arranged—and he gave her up. Told us what name she was using now. Once we had the name, we tracked her down easily."

"But not until last week," Crandall said. "The GPS surveillance is a recent development."

Hauser looked at Tess. "How much has Crandall told you about that?"

"Just that you instituted it."

"Then he left out the most important part. Last night Andrea Lowry drove her car to a political event in Orange County hosted by none other than Congressman Jack Reynolds."

"Did she?"

"Global positioning does not lie. We know every place that car has been and what time it was there, and one of those places was the high school where Reynolds was addressing his constituents."

"She's stalking him?" Tess frowned. "That doesn't make a lot of sense, under the circumstances."

"You don't think she'd have a desire for revenge?"

"If she did, wouldn't she have taken action years ago?"

Hauser shrugged. Clearly the mysteries of human motivation were of little interest to him. "Sometimes it takes a while for a person to get up the nerve. And you know what they say, revenge is a dish best served cold."

"After twenty years I'd say it would be ice-cold."

"Well, maybe she has some other motive for going there. Maybe she's trying to renew her contact with Reynolds. Or just trying to spook him, shake him up a little. Or she wants hush money. It's campaign season, you know."

He didn't have to say more. If the updated section of the MEDEA report was accurate, Reynolds couldn't afford to have Andrea Lowry talk.

Of course, it was possible that Reynolds was innocent, his misconduct purely a fantasy in a disturbed woman's mind. The ambiguity was what made the case so radioactive. If word of the accusation got out and was later found to be baseless, there would be many kinds of hell to pay. A sitting congressman would not take kindly to the trashing of his good name.

"She may have been going to his events for weeks, even months," Crandall said. "And the poor son of a bitch probably doesn't even know it."

Reynolds knew, Tess thought. It explained Abby's involvement. Reynolds had hired her to deal with the threat of the stalker.

"So how are we playing it?" Tess asked.

"We're continuing the GPS surveillance. Full-fledged mobile surveillance would be preferable, but it's manpower intensive, and there's always the risk of detection."

"And we still make no attempt to contact her?"

"Everything we know about this woman says she's paranoid, especially where the government is concerned. We don't expect her to cooperate with any FBI agents who come knocking at her door. We need to keep our distance for now."

"How about talking to Reynolds?"

"That's a no-go, also. We're staying clear of the congressman. We haven't even initiated surveillance on him."

"Why not?"

"We're working with an insider in his organization, someone well situated to be helpful. We can't risk raising Reynolds's suspicions. It could mean exposure for our informant. Right now it's hands-off."

"If we don't contact him or her, aren't we basically waiting for one of them to make the first move?"

"Not entirely. We're making one change. We're upgrading the electronic surveillance on Lowry. Or I should say, you are."

"Me?"

"You and Agent Crandall. I'm teaming you up because you two worked together on the Rain Man. That okay with you, Crandall?"

Crandall uttered a halfhearted, "Yes, sir." The question had been a pure formality, anyway.

Tess was confused. "I assumed Michaelson had arranged some nice, boring scut work for me to do."

"The ADIC isn't running this show. This is my case, and I'm not giving you scut work. That would be a waste of your abilities, which I deem to be considerable." Hauser grinned. "The director and I don't see eye to eye on everything. He may not be happy you're here, but I am. I want some of that—shall we say—*luck* of yours coming my way. We can use it."

Suddenly Tess was almost happy she'd bluffed her way onto the squad. "I'll do my best," she promised, feeling a bit like a rookie on her first assignment.

Hauser gave her another smothering handshake. "Sounds okay to me. From what I understand, Agent McCallum, your best is very damn good indeed."

14

Rush hour was even worse than usual, and it took Abby two hours to get from Santa Ana to San Fernando. She arrived in Andrea Lowry's neighborhood at five thirty.

She cruised past the house and saw the Chevy Malibu in the carport. Andrea was home. No surprise. Clearly she wasn't the type who got out much.

Abby parked on a side street, figuring that Andrea had few if any visitors, and if the same car was parked in front of the house two days in a row, it might get noticed. At the corner she glanced up and down the block. The neighborhood was deserted except for a few children in the playground across the street.

She approached the house and went up the front walk. The door opened before she had a chance to ring the bell.

Andrea Lowry stood in the doorway. She was unarmed, and Abby was glad about that.

"*You.*" Her eyes were narrowed to slits in her broad, fleshy face. "Do you really think I'm going to give you an interview?"

"No, I don't."

"Then go away." The door began to close.

"I'm not here for an interview," Abby said. "I'm not even a reporter."

Andrea flashed a glare at her. "You already told me—"

"I lied. I'm good at that."

There was a beat of silence as Andrea took this in. "You lied? And you expect me to believe you now?"

"I'm hoping."

"You must take me for a fool."

"I was hired to locate you. I'm a sort of private investigator. Someone thinks you're stalking him. He put me on the case."

Andrea drew a slow breath. When she spoke, her voice was softer. "Who?"

"Congressman Jack Reynolds. You *are* stalking him, aren't you, Andrea?" No answer. "I need to know why."

"I'm not stalking anyone." The denial was perfunctory, without conviction.

"You're showing up at his public events. You have a list of them in your car."

"You looked in my car?"

Abby ignored the question. "Last night you wore a wig to his town hall meeting to disguise yourself. And you don't even live in his district. Something's going on."

She saw the heavy swallowing motion of Andrea's throat. "And he . . . he hired you to ask me about that?"

"He hired me to track you down and get to know you. It's what I do. Only last night it didn't go so well."

"Track me down?" There was a new look in Andrea's eyes, a look Abby knew well. Fear. "You're saying you gave him my address?"

Abby raised a placating hand. "I haven't given him anything. I don't trust him. He's not telling me the truth. I'm hoping you will."

Andrea shifted her weight uneasily. "Why should I talk to you at all?"

"Maybe I can help you."

"But you're working for him."

"Not anymore." Abby shrugged. "You going to let me in, or should I take a seat on the front steps?"

Andrea took a hesitant step back. "Come in."

Abby stepped through the doorway. She'd gotten inside. It was a start.

The living room was dimly lit by a lamp on an end table. The curtains were closed, shutting out the sun.

"You're a private detective?" Andrea asked.

"More or less."

"May I see your license?"

"Haven't got one."

"How can you do your job without a license?"

"Same way porcupines mate—very carefully."

Andrea frowned, either not getting the joke or not finding it funny. "You could be arrested."

"The least of my worries."

"Are you some kind of vigilante?"

"I've been called worse."

"You're carrying a gun, I take it."

"Yes."

"Let me see it."

Abby wasn't in the habit of showing her firearm, but she would do so if it gained the woman's trust. She opened the special compartment of her purse and produced the .38.

Andrea nodded. "Okay. Put it back. Now put the purse on the end table and leave it there."

"You want me disarmed?"

"That's right. I don't trust you. Not entirely. And I won't talk to you until you give up the gun."

Abby wasn't wild about the idea, but she did as she was told. Without the purse she felt suddenly vulnerable.

"You were armed last night," Andrea said, not asking a question.

"So were you, as I recall."

Andrea brushed off the comment. "I wouldn't have really shot you."

"That's comforting to know. Was the gun loaded?"

"Well . . . yes."

"You point a loaded gun at somebody, there's always a chance it'll go off. You should know that."

"I just wanted you out of my house." This seemed like an understatement.

Abby smiled. "Message received. I wouldn't have

come back, except I need answers." She settled on the couch. "What's with you and Reynolds? There's a history. I'm sure there is."

Andrea reluctantly took a seat, placing herself near the end table within reach of the purse—and the gun. "I knew him once. Twenty years ago."

"You haven't been stalking him for twenty years, I assume."

She looked away. The laughter of the children in the park was audible through the curtains. "I'm not—not stalking him. I only wanted to see him again."

"Get back together? Renew old ties?"

Andrea shuddered. "No, no, nothing like that. I literally wanted to *see* him. Look at him in person, hear his voice. That's all."

"Why?"

"I don't know."

"Sure you do."

"I don't. It makes no sense. There's no logic to it. From a rational standpoint, he's the last man I would ever . . . The whole thing is crazy. It's almost . . ." She let her words trail away.

"Yes?"

"Miss Bannister . . ." She frowned. "Is that your real name?"

"No, but it'll do. You can call me Abby."

"I suppose that's an alias, also."

She ducked the question. "It's a name I answer to. You were about to say something."

Andrea faced her with a searching gaze. "Do you believe in demons?"

Abby kept her voice and expression neutral. "Do you?"

"That's not an answer."

"Are you having demon problems?"

Andrea got up, embarrassed. "Now you think I'm a lunatic."

"Didn't say that."

"You think I'm saying evil spirits drove me to seek out Congressman Reynolds. But that's not it. By demons, I mean . . . dark forces inside us. They move us to do . . . inexplicable things."

Abby selected her words with care. "I believe we all have motivations we don't understand. I wouldn't think of them as demons."

"But what's a demon, if not a dark part of yourself that can take control? Possess you, make you do evil?"

Abby didn't stir. But she was beginning to wish she had held on to her gun.

"Have you been planning something evil?" she asked gently. "Something that involves the congressman?"

Andrea shook her head in violent denial. "No, not him—not anyone—not anymore. It was years ago."

"What was?"

Andrea didn't seem to hear. She paced the room, arms crossed over her chest, hands squirming fitfully.

"I only showed up at his events because I wanted to be in the same room with him. I had no intention of doing harm. Something just made me do it. Something . . ."

Abby ventured a guess. "The same thing that made you buy a gun?"

Andrea shook her head violently. "No. No, nothing like that at all. I bought the gun for self-defense. There's a lot of crime in this area."

Paranoia about crime would not be inconsistent with the woman's psychology, but somehow Abby suspected there was more to the story. "Have you ever used it?" she asked.

"That gun? No."

"But you've used another one?"

"I used—I've done—" Andrea whirled, flushed with sudden anger. "I don't have to answer these questions."

Abby sat motionless, aware that any shift in her position might be read as a threat. Her voice was low and steady, uninflected, almost hypnotizing.

"Andrea, you admit you've been seeing the congressman. You admit there's a history of some sort between the two of you. You admit you own a gun, and you seem to know how to use it. And you talk about demons that drive people to evil acts. Now, am I wrong to be a little concerned?"

The tone worked. Andrea was calmer. "I told you," she said quietly, "I have no intention of harming anyone. I've never intended . . ."

"What?" Abby asked.

"I've never intended to do any harm."

Abby nodded. "You have, though. Haven't you?"

Silence for several heartbeats. "Yes." A whisper.

"You harmed someone?"

"A long time ago."

"Twenty years?"

Andrea didn't answer, but assent was written on her face.

"Who was it, Andrea?"

Abby waited. She was pretty sure she would hear it now—whatever the secret was.

"My name"—Andrea spoke slowly, each word pulled from her with painful reluctance—"isn't Andrea Lowry. At least it hasn't always been. It used to be . . . *I* used to be Bethany Willett."

The statement hung in the room between them, heavy with a significance Abby couldn't grasp.

"So?" Abby asked finally.

Andrea blinked. "You don't know me?"

"Should I?"

A mixture of sadness and relief passed across Andrea's face. "I suppose not. You're too young. But twenty years ago I was quite a celebrity."

"Were you?"

"Why, yes." Suddenly she smiled, a cold smile empty of amusement. "I was the most evil woman in the world, or so they said."

"Why would anyone call you that?"

The words spilled out in a rush. "Because twenty

years ago I took a gun and loaded it and carried it into the nursery where my babies were asleep. Twin boys, ten months old."

She raised her head defiantly, as if inviting judgment.

"And, well, I killed them, you see. I shot them both to death."

15

Dylan Garrick guided the van into the alley behind the old lady's house, past an overflowing Dumpster. Masses of oleander bushes screened the alley from the backyards of the homes on either side. That was good. Even in daylight, it would be easy to climb the hurricane fence without being seen.

He parked the van and killed the engine.

"We're here," he announced loudly enough to rouse Bran in the back.

Funny thing about Bran. He could sleep through any fucking thing. Fall asleep on the way to his own execution, probably. Of course, in this case he was on his way to somebody else's.

Tupelo was a different story. He was always wide-awake, annoyingly so. Throughout the drive from Santa Ana he'd been twitching and itching in the passenger seat, knocking his shoes together like a restless kid, talking too much, and twiddling the radio knob, changing stations, until Dylan told him to cut it the hell out.

Pain in the ass, was Tupelo. Good with a gun, though. All that nervous energy made him quick on the trigger, and his hyperactive wariness meant he never missed a thing.

Dylan was familiar with his crew's quirks and strengths. The three of them, in their midtwenties now, had been together since they were teenagers. They'd learned their trade well. They had the experience and the moves, and each of them had proved himself a stone-cold killer more than once.

"All right," he said briskly, "looks like she's home. Her car's in the carport." This was added for Bran's benefit. He'd been snoring like a lawn mower when the van made its pass in front of the house.

"She alone in there?" Bran asked, stifling a yawn.

"Probably. No other cars out front. Curtains are all closed."

"She got cats?" Tupelo asked.

"What?"

"Cats. Lotta these little old ladies that live by themselves, they got a whole mess of cats."

Dylan shrugged. "Boss didn't say nothing about cats."

"Hope she don't got any." Tupelo shifted in his seat. "I hate cats."

"How old is this bitch, anyhow?" Bran asked.

Dylan glanced back at him. "I dunno. Like, fifty, I guess."

"Well preserved?"

"Fuck should I know? Who gives a shit?"

Bran had that dreamy look he got sometimes. "Some of these women, they're still plenty fuckable at fifty. You know, if they got, like, plastic surgery and shit."

Dylan was getting pissed. "You wanna fuck some Valley grandma with a nip-and-tuck job, you do it on your own time. Our job's to go in, get it done, and be gone."

"Still say it would be smarter to wait." That was Tupelo, his voice jumpy and high. "Nighttime is when shit like this goes down. Whack her in her sleep, she never knows what hit her."

Dylan was inclined to agree, but his orders were clear. "Boss says it's urgent. Time sensitive, is how he said it."

"This bitch has lived fifty years. She can't live another couple hours?"

"I don't ask questions when it's the boss on the phone. Neither should you. Case you forgot, we took a goddamned oath."

All three of them had sworn loyalty to their brothers. Included in their pledge was the duty to follow orders without hesitation or doubt.

"It's the mission," Dylan added. "Okay?"

"Fuck, yeah." Bran sounded sleepier than before. "Let's blip this hag and get it over with. I got things to do."

"Equipment check," Dylan said.

They ran through a checklist of their gear. Holstered to their belts were matte black Heckler & Koch MK-23 combat pistols, the six-inch barrels extended with SOS-45 silencer modules that reduced the guns' noise output by forty decibels. Each pistol was loaded with a military-style twelve-round clip holding a dozen .45 +P jacketed hollow points, with a thirteenth round chambered. The hollow points expanded on impact for maximum stopping power. Ammo pouches held spare clips.

Sheathed to each pistol belt was an Mk III combat knife, the same knife issued to Navy SEALs. It had a six-inch stainless steel blade with a nonreflective black finish. Dylan had wetted his blade with blood only once, when he'd had to take out a security guard without making any noise. He still remembered the way the guy had flopped like a landed mackerel in a pool of blood from his slit throat. It had been a hoot, seeing him kick and thrash.

All three of them wore dark blue sweatshirts and navy blue denim jeans, the pant legs tucked into their sneakers to minimize the risk of DNA transfer. Indigo provided better camouflage in the dark than jet black. Their sneakers were the same color, and the white highlights had been colored with purple felt markers so they wouldn't show up in the shadows. Their gloves—flexible Isotoners—were black, as were the ski masks they pulled over their heads.

For long-distance communication they carried walkie-talkies, but when within sight of one another, they would communicate with hand signals like SWAT commandos. Hell, they might as well have been

SWAT guys. They had the gear, the suits, the attitude. Only thing they didn't have was a badge, and they didn't need one.

Dylan carried a few extras—a penlight, a lucky penny, and a small mirror on a collapsible stalk, useful for peeking around corners. He didn't plan on using the mirror today. This was no stealth op; it was strictly wham, bam, good-bye, ma'am.

"We good to go?" Dylan asked when the checklist was complete.

"Yeah, we're good." Bran sounded bored.

"Fuck, yes." Tupelo was rubbing his gloved hands like a maniac.

Dylan nodded. "Let's get paid."

They got out of the van. Dylan felt his heart working hard. He wasn't scared. This woman posed no threat. She was nobody, just some civilian to be zippered. Another day at the office, another thousand bucks in his pocket. But any hit got his juices flowing. It was a high, like doing lines of coke—not that he did that shit anymore. He'd been clean for two years come October. High on life—that's what he was. Or on death, maybe. High on death, yeah.

His mouth was dry under the ski mask. He licked his lips. It was a warm August afternoon fragrant with oleander and honeysuckle, and a good time for a woman to die.

16

"You killed your children," Abby said slowly.

Andrea faced her. "I did."

"Why?"

"If I could answer that . . ." She broke eye contact, turning away. "I've spent twenty years trying to understand why. The psychiatrists worked on me. I think they enjoyed it. I was a challenge. But they never figured me out. The media people all had their theories, too. There was a book—I didn't read it. A book about me that was supposed to explain it all. But how could a book explain it when even I didn't know?"

Abby watched her, trying to imagine Andrea Lowry as a younger woman, a mother of small children. "You said you were famous."

Andrea released an incongruous little laugh. "I suppose *infamous* would be the right word. They called me Medea. That was the nickname they came up with, the newspaper people. You know, the woman in Greek mythology. Her husband betrayed her with another woman, so Medea killed their children. Killed them just for spite. Then she escaped in a chariot drawn by flying dragons." She gazed moodily toward the curtained window. "Medea was luckier than I've been. I've never escaped."

"What happened to you after—after you . . . ?"

"I shot myself." She said it simply, without emotion. "Put a bullet in my head. Or tried to, anyway. I actually grazed my skull just behind the ear—this ear." She pulled back a tuft of blond hair to expose a scar. "I would have bled to death, except the neighbors heard the gunshots and called nine-one-one. The police got me into surgery. The surgeon saved my life." She replaced the spill of hair with an unsteady hand. "I wish he hadn't. I should have died then."

The story was moving too fast. Abby wanted to slow it down. "Where did you get the gun you used?"

"I bought it when I first moved to California. Even back then, everyone talked about crime. I was brought up in a small town in Oregon where people kept their doors unlocked. So I was scared. I never thought—never thought I would turn out to be the criminal, myself."

"Okay," Abby said softly. "So, once you recovered from surgery . . . ?"

"The psychiatrists started in on me. Trying to get me to remember. I didn't, you see. Didn't remember any of it. That evening was a total blank. Amnesia, the product of post-traumatic stress—that's how they diagnosed it. Would have been simpler to say there are some things a person just can't stand to face. Are you thirsty?"

The unexpected question caught Abby up short. "I'm okay."

"Well, *I'm* thirsty. I haven't talked so much in a long time."

She went into the kitchen, and Abby followed, waiting while Andrea poured herself a tall glass of lemonade. The kitchen was dark and windowless. There was no sunlight in this house, and Abby now knew why.

"Anyway," Andrea said after a long swallow, "they said I'd had a psychotic break. I'd been in a fugue state. I hadn't known what I was doing. Temporary insanity. Which was true, of course. It had to be true. No rational person would have done what I did. No one who was not insane . . ."

She took another gulp of lemonade. Ice clinked in the glass. Her hand was shaking.

"But I wonder, does that absolve me of guilt? If I wasn't myself when I did it, does that mean I'm not responsible? And if I'm not, who is? Someone must be—or something. A sin of that magnitude must have a cause. And the cause must be me or something inside me, something hidden that came into the light just that one time. . . ."

"A demon," Abby said, understanding.

Andrea nodded, her eyes dark and sad. "We fool ourselves by thinking we're in control of our actions. Then something like this happens, and we realize we've never had control. There are only urges and impulses that move us, like—like currents under the sea, like a riptide, an undertow, and they drag us where we never meant to go."

Abby was beginning to wish she'd asked for some lemonade. Her mouth was dry. "Were you put on trial?"

Andrea answered with a shake of her head. "I was ruled incompetent. Remanded to the custody of a mental institution. I stayed there for twelve years." She let those words settle in the air like a sentence of doom. "And they worked with me. They got me to remember. They brought back the memory of what I did that night. Thanks to them, I can relive it whenever I like. That's what twelve years of treatment brought me. A memory I never wanted."

"Unless you remember," Abby said, "you can never move past it."

Andrea's tongue clucked. "You sound just like them. You could be a psychiatrist yourself."

"I earned a degree in that field. Never got licensed, though."

"Apparently you don't believe in licenses."

"I'm a free spirit."

"Yes, I think you are. I sensed that about you when we met. It made me envy you. I may have been a free spirit once. I can't recall. It was so long ago." She looked away. "It's a lie, anyhow—what you said."

"What's a lie?"

"That by remembering, I can move past it. I can never move past it. Remembering only etches the pain deeper. It doesn't resolve anything. It doesn't bring closure." Her tone was hollow. "There can never be closure."

"How about forgiveness?"

"Never that, either."

Abby touched Andrea's arm, a light touch, the outreach of one human being to another. "People do things in a state of psychosis that have nothing to do with their moral values or their character."

Andrea didn't withdraw from the touch, but neither did she seem comforted by it. "So I shouldn't blame myself? But I took out the gun. I loaded it. I pulled the trigger. So who gets the blame? The demon who possessed me—that's what I'd like to think. But that demon was part of me, was *in* me." Now she pulled free of Abby's hand. "And somewhere it still is."

"The doctors must have felt otherwise, or they wouldn't have released you."

Her shoulders lifted listlessly. "They said I was no longer a danger to myself or others. They let me go."

"And you weren't subject to prosecution at that point?"

"No. After I was committed, the DA's office notified the court of its intent not to prosecute. The charges were dropped. They can't be reinstated now."

The DA's office presumably meant Reynolds, but Abby didn't want to pursue that point. "So you were free and clear."

"I was out. That's all. Just . . . out. I spent six months in a halfway house. Then I was on my own. I didn't want to be anywhere near California. So I moved to Florida. It was about as far away as I could get. I rented a cheap place, and did some entry-level jobs. It was all right. I was almost happy at times. I would walk on the beach in the evening and feel . . . almost whole."

"I'm surprised you didn't stay there."

Andrea looked at her. "So am I. Really. I don't understand it myself. But last year I started to feel . . . started to feel I had to come back. Had to be in California again. I don't know why. There's nothing for me here. Nothing but memories . . . bad memories . . ."

"So here you are."

"Yes. Here I am. My parents died years ago. They left enough money for me to buy this house and pay my bills without working anymore, as long as I didn't indulge in any extravagances. Of course, I had no desire to indulge myself. I only wanted to be left alone. That's all I've ever wanted."

"And have you been? Left alone, I mean."

"Not at first. When I was in the halfway house, they would still come after me—the newspaper people, the magazine people, the TV people. They wouldn't let me be. Most of the public had forgotten by then, but those people would never forget. To them I was an open sore, and all they could do was scratch and make me bleed."

"That's why you changed your name."

Andrea smiled a little, in acknowledgment of this small victory, this successful deception. "Yes. I found a way. It was illegal, but . . . well, I suppose you know all about that kind of thing. The name you gave me was an alias. You probably have documents to back it up, don't you?"

"Yes."

"So do I. By the time I moved to Florida, I was Andrea Lowry. No one tracked me down. No one recognized me. It was . . . wonderful."

"One more reason to stay in the Sunshine State."

"You'd think so, wouldn't you? But something drew me back. Still, I've kept a low profile. No one has intruded on me or questioned my past. I did worry that the absence of any credit history would prevent me from buying this house, but I was paying cash out of the inheritance, so the seller didn't care."

"They wouldn't have cared, anyway," Abby said. "A blank credit history simply means you have no record of defaults. There are no red flags. That's all they ever look for."

"I knew you'd be an expert on it. How many identities do you have?"

Abby had actually lost count. "I've used a few," she answered vaguely.

"Do you enjoy it?"

"Excuse me?"

"Changing your identity. Becoming someone else."

"I guess I do." Oddly, she'd never thought about it before.

Andrea seemed unsurprised. "I thought I would enjoy it. I thought—this is how naive I was—I thought it would make me free. Of course it didn't."

"But the reporters couldn't find you."

"True, I was free of them. But that wasn't freedom. I was still the same person, only with a different name. I had the same memories, the same bad dreams— and the same good dreams, which were worse than nightmares, because they would never last, and I would wake up, and the children wouldn't be there after all, and it wasn't their hair I was smelling, only my pillow. . . ."

Abby almost reached out again, but stopped herself, knowing the gesture would be rejected. "You may not believe me," she said, "but I think you've suffered enough. There's a statute of limitations on any kind of pain, any kind of guilt."

Andrea's eyes were empty. "Not this kind."

Scaling the old lady's fence was no problem. There was no dog in the backyard and no indication of a security system protecting the house.

Dylan tracked down the junction box on the rear wall of the house. The phone cable, dropping down from a utility pole in the alley, was heavy and tough to cut, which was why normally he would pry open the box to work on the wiring inside. In this case he didn't have to. A pair of red and green telco wires extended out of the bottom of the box and snaked through the siding on the wall. Sloppy, leaving them exposed like that. Some phone company drone had been in a hurry when he did the installation.

Dylan unsheathed his knife and sliced the wires. Now the house had no phone service, unless the woman had a cell phone.

He pointed at Bran, wordlessly instructing him to take up a position in the yard where he could cover their avenue of escape. One thing Dylan had learned was to always keep your exit lane open.

Bran crouched beside a leafy eucalyptus and signaled that he was ready. Dylan led Tupelo to the back door. It was locked. Not a spring latch, either. Goddamned pain-in-the-ass dead bolt. But there was a glass pane in the door, which would make things easier.

"Wish I'd brought a glass cutter and some tape," Dylan whispered through his mask.

"Fuck that," Tupelo said, and with the butt of his H & K he cracked the pane into a starburst pattern.

The impact made no more noise than the snap of a twig. Still, Dylan was pissed.

"I tell you to do that?" he breathed. "You wait for my goddamned order."

Tupelo looked away, his eyes twitching in the ski mask's slits. "Just wanna get it done," he mumbled.

Dylan inspected the damage. The glass was holding together, but one stiff breeze would blow it apart. Again he wished he had some sticky tape. Could have taped over the fragments and pulled them away without a sound. As it was, he would have to push in the panel and hope the old lady wasn't listening.

"You haven't told me," Abby said, "how Reynolds fits into all this."

"No, I haven't, have I?" Andrea hesitated, then made a flick of the wrist, as if dismissing some unheard counsel of caution. "I suppose I can tell you. I—"

"Wait." Abby held up a hand.

From the rear of the house there was a soft tinkle of breaking glass.

*   *   *

The shards fell away with a touch of Dylan's gloved hand. They hit the floor with a soft metallic clatter like the jingling of bells. He stuck his arm through the hole and groped for the dead-bolt release. In a second the door was unlocked. He pushed it open and was dismayed to hear the low, prolonged squeal of unoiled hinges.

The old lady might have heard that, even if she'd missed the noise of the falling glass. They would have to move fast before she hightailed it out the front door.

He entered the rear hall, leading Tupelo, their sneakers treading soundlessly on the bare wooden floor.

Abby glanced at Andrea and saw the woman's eyes widen in fear.

"What's back there?" Abby whispered.

"Door to the backyard. There's a glass pane in the door."

Down the rear hallway came a long *screeee* of hinges. The door, opening.

A bad time to be unarmed. Abby's purse, with the gun in it, was in the living room.

But there was another gun—Andrea's. Abby pulled open the kitchen drawer and grabbed the revolver inside.

"This thing still loaded?" she whispered.

Andrea nodded.

The gun in her hand made Abby feel a little better, but not much. Getting into a shoot-out at close quarters wasn't her idea of a good time. Too many things could go wrong. And as long as she and Andrea were stuck in the kitchen, the intruder had the advantage. He could corner them and finish them off from the doorway.

Andrea had frozen. But there was no time for fear. In a tactical situation, the first thirty seconds were the most critical.

Abby grabbed Andrea by the shoulder and hustled her into the living room. The front door beckoned, but it was too far away, and besides, there might be someone else waiting outside, hoping to pick them off if they tried to flee.

And her purse—it, too, was out of reach.

She pivoted toward a side hallway and took it at a run, Andrea following. There were two doors in the hall. One was shut. Before Abby could try it, Andrea gasped, "Closet."

The other door was ajar. Abby pushed it open and led Andrea into what was obviously the master bedroom, lit by a lamp on the night table, with a closet, a bathroom, and two curtained windows that must face the backyard.

She pulled Andrea behind the bed, kneeling with her, then yanked the lamp's power cord out of the wall socket. Now the only illumination was the trickle of daylight through the curtains and the glow of a night-light in the bathroom.

There was a phone on the night table. Abby grabbed it. No dial tone. The phone line had been cut. That meant whoever had entered the house wasn't just some junkie or random thrill seeker. Not your standard home invader, either. If it had been, the intruder would be shouting orders and stomping through the house, hoping to establish control through intimidation.

This enemy was craftier, stealthier. No teenager, but someone older, more experienced, better organized. A professional assassin with notches in his gun.

Still, the odds had improved. The bed provided concealment, and her angle of view through the doorway offered decent coverage of the hall. She could fire from her improvised sniper's blind, take out the intruder while he approached.

"Who is it?" Andrea whispered. Abby shushed her.

Through the open door, she saw a shadow pass over the wall of the hallway as the intruder crept into the living room. Then more bad news—a second shadow.

Two enemies. Maybe the odds hadn't improved so much, after all.

For a few seconds at least, they would be busy in the living room. Abby thought there might be a chance to get Andrea out through the bedroom window. She risked getting to her feet to pull aside the curtains but quickly shut them again. A third man was outside, in the backyard, toting a handgun with an unnaturally extended barrel that could be a silencer.

Not good.

She resumed kneeling behind the bed. There was no way around it—she was going to have to do some shooting. She flipped open the revolver's cylinder. Fully loaded, six rounds. That wasn't much against three armed men. She would have to be opportunistic about taking her shots. Her best bet was to take out the first man who came down the hall. If she did, the other two might run.

Sudden darkness in the living room. The intruders had turned off the lights. The most logical reason was that they intended to make a move into the hall and didn't want to be backlit. Abby had expected as much. It made her job a little harder, but she could see well enough. And she knew where to look. She had the edge.

Footsteps in the hall. They were coming.

Dylan worked his way down the hall, Tupelo behind him. He was pretty sure the bitch had taken cover in the room at the far end. A sweep of the other side of the house had turned up nothing, and she hadn't had time to get out through either the front door or the door to the carport.

It ought to be easy to bag her. But something was funny. He couldn't put his finger on it, but she wasn't behaving the way a frightened woman should. She wasn't screaming or trying to climb out the window or barricading the door. It was like she was waiting for him, luring him in.

There was a chance she was armed. Maybe she kept

a gun in that room. She might be hoping to get the drop on him. If so, she'd worked out a pretty good plan. She was hidden, and he was exposed. The darkness helped him, but not a lot. Even if he hugged the wall, she would probably see his silhouette when he got close to the open door.

He would have to go in quick. When inside, he could take cover, and if she fired, he would identify her position by the muzzle flash. His own shots would be harder to pinpoint; the suppressor module eliminated the muzzle flare.

Once in the room, he would have the edge.

Abby peered into the dimness and saw a hint of movement. The man was creeping up to the bedroom's open door. Though he had pressed himself tight against the wall, he was partially exposed to her angle of view. He appeared to be in a low combat crouch, his gun held across his chest.

This was the one moment in the encounter when she had an unequivocal advantage. She could see him. He didn't know where she was. As the mobile party, he was more vulnerable to begin with, and the hall was a free-fire zone—no cover, no concealment.

She pinned him behind the revolver's front sight. A fancy shooter would try for a head shot, but the smart money was on a hit to the body. She aimed for his torso.

He was at the doorframe. In a second he would pivot inside. He would do it fast, because that was the way the pros did it. She would have only a second to fire. If she missed, he would empty his magazine in the direction of her muzzle flare. The bed might absorb some of the shots, but she wouldn't wager her life on it.

Her heart, beating fast, counted off three seconds, four.

He made his move, spinning into the doorway.

Abby fired.

She took only one shot. Either she hit the target or

she didn't. If she hit him, one shot should be enough. If she didn't, she would need the other five rounds to repel his attack.

The gunshot set her ears ringing and drowned out any sound of impact. The muzzle flash, close to her face, erased her night vision. For a moment she was deaf and blind. But she knew she'd hit him because he wasn't shooting back.

"You got him," Andrea breathed into Abby's ear. "Did you see him go down?"

"I saw him jerk like he was hit. Then he was gone. But you *got* him. I know you did."

"There are two others." Abby drew a breath and smelled gunpowder. "Don't celebrate yet."

17

Bitch had fired before he could enter, the shot forcing him back. For a bad moment Dylan thought she'd nailed him in the chest, and all he could think of was he should've worn Kevlar.

Then Tupelo was pulling him back, away from the open door, whispering, "You hit, man? You hit?"

"Dunno." His gloved hands searched the front of his shirt for blood, finding none. "Maybe not."

He'd felt the impact, but there was no blood and no pain. Sometimes a bullet wound didn't hurt, though. It just went numb. Shock or something.

"Sounded like you was hit," Tupes said.

"Yeah. Felt like it, too." Dylan stripped off one glove and felt himself with his bare hand until he was sure he was intact.

She'd missed. Somehow she'd missed. He checked his gun, and then he understood.

He'd been holding the H & K at chest level, and the bullet had struck the goddamn gun. Shit, what were the odds on that? He could feel the nick in the silencer where the shot had been deflected.

"She didn't get me," he whispered, amazed. "Banged my silencer, is all."

"Fuck, that's lucky." Tupelo was shivering with fury and fear. "Fuck."

Dylan unscrewed the suppressor module and stuck it in his pocket. He couldn't risk firing the gun if the silencer tube had been cramped or bent. A round could get stuck in there and blow up the damn gun in his hand.

He put his glove back on and took stock.

"We take up position there." He nodded at the midpoint of the hall. "Angle some shots into her hideyhole. And get Bran in on the game, too." He keyed his walkie-talkie. "She's in the last room on the southwest side. Couple windows with curtains. You know the one?"

A burst of static, and Bran's voice. "I see it."

"Take a shot or two at them windows. Bitch is armed, so watch out."

"Old lady's packing? Cool."

"Yeah." Dylan switched off the radio with a sigh. "Cool."

"Two others?" Andrea whispered, her voice cracking. "You said *two* others?"

Abby nodded. "We'll get out of this. I've been in worse jams."

This was probably true, but right now she couldn't think of any.

"Who are they? What do they want?" Andrea's questions tailed into a helpless moan. "Oh, God, this is bad. This is so bad. . . ."

"Don't lose control. Just sit tight and keep your head down."

The advice was punctuated with a crash of glass from behind them. One of the windows had been shot out.

Andrea screamed. Abby silenced her with a hand to her mouth. A cry would only pinpoint their position.

She knew that the man in the backyard had fired through the window. He wouldn't have done so unless he was in communication with the men inside. They'd told him their quarry was hiding in the bedroom. The outside man was trying to flush out the prey.

And she'd been right about the silencer. She'd heard no report from his gun.

The flying glass, absorbed by the heavy curtain, hadn't hit them, but the bullet and the glass had left gashes in the curtain, which let in more light. If the

curtain opened up too much, she and Andrea would
be exposed to view. The only saving grace was that
the shooter was unlikely to risk coming right up to
the window, where he would be vulnerable to her return fire. Most likely he would keep shooting from a
distance in an effort to panic them into flight or score
a lucky hit.

A second noiseless shot punched through the curtain and thudded into drywall across the room.

"Keep your head down," Abby whispered.

Beside her, Andrea was shaking all over. Abby had
once cradled an injured rabbit in her hands. It had
shaken the same way.

There was one good thing about the sniper fire from
the yard. As long as it continued, the two men in the
house couldn't mount another assault on the bedroom.

They could fire from the hall, though, if they chose
a position that was safely out of the sniper's range.

In time with that thought, a muzzle flash lit up the
hallway, and chunks of plaster flew off the wall near
the bed. She heard that report. No silencer on that
gun.

Hell. She was taking fire from two directions. She
had five rounds left, and no clear target. Her options
were limited. She could sit tight until a ricochet caught
her or Andrea, or she could empty the gun and then
wait for the enemy to close in for an easy kill.

There was a chance that a report of shots fired had
already been called in to the police by a neighbor, but
response time would be measured in minutes, which
might as well be hours. Anyway, the house next door
had looked empty, and the people on the other side
might not even be home during the day.

Two quick shots from the hall. One shot was silenced; the other was not. That was bad. It meant
there were two guns, which meant both men were still
in the fight. Either she hadn't hit the first one, or
the wound hadn't incapacitated him. It was still three
against one. She was outmanned and outgunned, and
all out of countermoves. She needed to regain the

advantage, and she wasn't going to do it by crouching behind a mattress with bullets cracking overhead.

Her gaze traveled to the glow of the night-light.

"What kind of stuff do you keep in your bathroom?" she asked.

Andrea didn't understand. "Stuff?"

"Hair spray? You have that?"

"Yes."

Another shot from outside. Across the room, something shattered.

"Stay put," Abby whispered. "Head down. Don't make any noise."

"You're not *leaving* me?"

"Just stay put. I've got a plan."

The distance to the bathroom was about six feet. She could crawl, but once she left the concealment of the bed she might be spotted by the enemy in the corridor. Safer to run for it. But she would have to force the two bad guys down the hall to back off for a second.

She sprang up from the bed and angled a quick shot into the hallway, wishing she could pull the trigger a few more times and lay down some decent covering fire, but unwilling to waste ammo.

Before the glare of the gun flash had faded from the room, she sprinted into the bathroom. No shots chased her.

She should have asked Andrea exactly where she kept the hair spray. In the cabinet under the sink she found it. She didn't have to read the label to know the stuff was flammable. Hairspray was a mix of hydrocarbon propellants like propane and butane, liquid while inside the canister but gaseous when released.

She yanked a towel from the rack and jetted it with hairspray until she'd thoroughly doused it, using up a good deal of the can's contents. She hoped there was enough propellant left to get the job done.

Quickly she wrapped the can in the towel, knotting the towel at both ends. Now she needed an open flame, hard to come by in a lavatory.

The sniper outside hadn't fired in a while. Abby found his silence unsettling. He might have been emboldened to sneak closer to the house. If he got a clear shot through a gap in the curtains, it was all over. She had to act fast.

On the countertop by the sink there was a comb with a rubber-coated handle and metal teeth. Abby popped the night-light out of the wall, then shoved the towel-wrapped canister alongside the outlet. She took a breath and poked the comb into the wall socket.

Short circuit. A spark sizzled out of the socket, and the towel, soaked in flammable spray, caught fire.

She dived for the bedroom door and tossed the canister and its flaming wrap into the hallway. Someone shot at her, but she was already scrambling back.

Explosion.

She flung herself facedown as noise and glare filled the hall.

Heat had ruptured the canister, and its pressurized contents had burst free in a cloud of inflammable gas, instantly ignited. A flash-bang grenade.

The effect would be brief—rapid combustion would consume the fuel immediately—but the homemade bomb ought to drive the enemy back. She was counting on that.

She spun upright and launched herself into the hall, firing three times as she vaulted the flaming debris and charged into the living room. In the ebbing glow of the fire she could see the bad guys—two men in dark blue outfits, both wearing ski masks, one of them stripping off his mask as he stumbled away. Then he and his buddy disappeared down the back hallway, but for one instant Abby had glimpsed his face.

An instant was all she needed. She would remember him.

Dylan didn't understand. There had been a flaming object thrown from the back room, then a crash of heat and noise that seemed to suck all the air out of his lungs, a pressure wave of fire, scorching him, burning his ski mask. Now he was staggering after Tupelo in full retreat, his eyes stinging and watering, his vision shot to hell, and the mask was smoking, goddamn *smoking,* as he tore it off and threw it aside.

Bitch had fucked him up somehow, maybe blinded him, scarred him—he didn't know.

Tupelo pulled him into the rear hall. They stopped running near the back door and crouched down in a huddled conference. "You okay, man?" Tupes asked.

"Can't see good."

"You was staring right at that fireball."

"Am I messed up? Did it fucking burn me?"

"No, man, you're okay. Handsome as ever."

"Still can't see worth shit."

"Give it a minute, bro. Your eyes'll come back. Then we go in again, right? We go in and get her?"

Dylan didn't have to think about it. "Yeah," he said. "We get her."

Abby couldn't count on them to stay in the rear hall for long. She ran to the end table, where she'd left her purse, snagged the strap, then ducked beside the couch. Inside was her gun, fully loaded, with two speed loaders holding six rounds apiece. And her cell phone. Those assholes had cut the landline, but she could still call for help on her cell.

First things first. She looped the purse strap around her neck. With Andrea's gun in her left hand and her own Smith & Wesson in her right, she surveyed the shadows, waiting for the bad guys to come back.

Dylan's eyesight was returning now, the purple afterimages of the fireball fading. Tupelo had been right. He was okay. A little shaken up, but nothing serious.

But what he would do to the old lady—now, that was serious. He had a major hard-on to nail her wrinkly ass.

"Okay," he said. Slowly stood up. "We finish things."

"You think she's still in there?"

"I think so. We woulda heard her if she left."

"Why would she hang around?"

"Guess she wants to see some more action. We'll give it to her."

He took a step down the hall and stopped. Behind him, there was a scatter of gunfire in the backyard.

Abby waited. Over the continuous chiming in her ears, she could hear the tattoo of her heart, the pull of breath through her open mouth.

And a new sound—gunshots.

Not in the house. Outside.

The sniper? Had he closed in on the bedroom windows? No, his gun was silenced.

She waited through a long moment. She couldn't say how long. She had lost the ability to gauge time. It seemed as if hours had passed since the first noise of the intrusion, though objectively she knew it had been only a couple of minutes.

The shooting stopped.

Silence.

Then . . . movement in the rear hall.

Someone entering. Friend or foe? The police would identify themselves. If no one spoke, she was assuming the worst.

Flicker of illumination. A flashlight.

None of these guys had been using a flash. Abby didn't think they would start now.

The glow brightened. A dark figure appeared on the threshold of the living room.

Decision time. If it was one of the bad guys, and the flashlight found her hiding place, she would be blown away before she could defend herself.

She raised the gun in her right hand. She could take the shot.

But she didn't. Something in the figure's stance and silhouette registered in her memory.

Abby set down both guns and stood up slowly, her hands lifted. She let the flashlight find her. When it did, she smiled.

"Hey, Tess," she said. "Long time no see."

18

"Anybody hit?" Dylan yelled as the van skidded out of the alley, making tracks for the freeway.

Beside him, Bran shook his head. "Tree gave me good cover."

He glanced behind him. "Tupes?"

"No holes in me. Goddamn, what the fuck happened back there?"

"I dunno, I dunno." Dylan just couldn't figure it.

"I was drawing a bead on the window," Bran said, "and all of a sudden there was somebody in the yard next door, and they was shooting."

"Get a look at 'em?" Dylan asked.

Bran shook his head. "Too much foliage."

"I didn't see 'em, neither." Tupelo hugged himself. "I was just trying to get my ass over the fence 'fore it got shot off."

"So who was it?" Dylan pressed. "Who the fuck could it be?"

"Neighbor with a gun, maybe," Bran offered.

"Or the cops," Tupelo said.

Dylan knew it wasn't the police. "Cops couldn't get there that fast. And we ain't seen a single cop car since we took off."

"So it was a neighbor," Bran said again.

"Maybe." Dylan wasn't sure. "What is it, a whole neighborhood full of gun nuts?"

"Old lady knows how to put up a fight, for sure," Tupelo said.

"Yeah. Maybe somebody shoulda given us a heads-up about that." Dylan found the freeway and took the southbound on-ramp. "Shit. Boss ain't gonna like it."

"Fuck the boss," Bran murmured. "Let him take her out. See what kind of brass balls he got."

"Boss'll understand," Tupelo said nervously from the rear.

"Hope so," Dylan murmured. He fished his cell phone out of the glove compartment and pressed number one on speed dial. "I really do."

He had his doubts.

Ron Shanker was scared.

He sat alone in his office, staring at the telephone, which less than a minute ago had conveyed a report he had not wanted to hear. Dylan and his crew had never let him down before. This was a hell of a time for them to start.

For the moment no one knew about the debacle but him and the three men he'd hired. He wished he could keep it that way. He certainly intended to keep the news from anyone else in the club.

But there was one man who had to know.

His hand was shaking as he made the call. On the second ring, the phone was picked up.

"Is it done?" Reynolds asked without preliminaries.

Shanker shut his eyes. "No. It got messed up."

There was a beat of awful silence before Reynolds asked tonelessly, "How?"

"The lady was armed. She fired at them. She barricaded herself in a room and took shots at my crew."

"She's a middle-aged woman, for Christ's sake."

"She put up a fight, Jack. Even used some kind of goddamned grenade, they told me."

"Bullshit." Shanker heard Reynolds suck in a harsh breath. "You're telling me she's still alive? Your crew ran away?"

"They were taking fire, so they had to get out."

Another stretch of silence on the line. Shanker couldn't stand that silence.

"It's bad, I know," he said, just to hear a voice, any voice, even his own.

"It's more than bad. I relied on you, Ron, and you let me down."

He tightened his grip on the phone. "I'll make it up to you."

"Damn straight you will. You get on the horn to your boys, and you send them back in."

Shanker wasn't sure he'd heard right. "Back in?"

"Tell them to finish the job."

"Jack, I don't mean any disrespect here, but I don't know how practical that's gonna be."

"Practical means getting the job done. They didn't. So they go back in and get it right."

Shanker tightened his grip on the phone. "The cops must've been called by now, Jack. I can't send my guys into a neighborhood full of squad cars."

"The police won't be there forever. They'll take a report, examine the crime scene, and go."

"And probably take the lady of the house with them for questioning. Or for protection."

"They'll question her in the house. Hopefully she'll be too shook up to tell them anything useful."

"Maybe so, but you don't think she'll stay in the house, do you? After what happened—"

"She'll stay."

"Why the hell would she?"

"Because," Reynolds said quietly, "she has no place else to go."

19

In the adrenaline rush of battle Abby hadn't had time for emotion. The feeling part of her had been sealed off and shut down, quarantined until the danger had passed. Even after the gunfight she'd felt nothing except a strangely distanced sense of surprise that she was still alive.

Seeing Tess McCallum had been no surprise at all. For some reason it had seemed logical, almost inevitable, that Tess would be there. Abby hadn't questioned it. She'd been uncharacteristically subdued, inclined to accept Tess's suggestions as if they were orders. Tess's primary suggestion had been that Abby get out of the house and out of the neighborhood, fast.

"There'll be police coming," Tess said, "and the Bureau will be here, too. You don't want to be involved in that."

"No," Abby agreed. "I don't."

"So you'd better go. I'll say Andrea fought them off alone until I showed up. I don't know how I'll explain the gun—"

"It's her gun," Abby heard herself say. "I just borrowed it."

"You didn't fire your own weapon?"

"Never had the chance."

"That'll work, then. I'll wipe the prints off. And I'll make sure Andrea keeps your name out of it."

"Okay."

"They'll have me tied up in debriefings for a good three hours. I'll try to get free by nine or nine thirty.

We can meet at that place in Santa Monica where we met last time."

"The Boiler Room."

Sirens rose in the distance. "You'd better get going," Tess said. "Not out the back. The crime scene people will be all over that area, and we don't need any extra shoe prints. There's a side door that opens into the carport."

And that was it. Abby carried her gun and her purse through the carport, then walked to her Miata. She pulled away as the sirens were closing in.

No questions asked. No protests registered. She was content to let Tess take charge.

Somewhere during the drive home to Westwood, the shock began to abate. By the time she was showering in her condo, rinsing off the smell of sweat and fear, she was starting to feel some serious rage.

Motherfuckers had tried to *kill* her.

Yeah, and Andrea, too. But Abby wasn't thinking much about Andrea Lowry—or Bethany Willett, or whatever she ought to be called.

When she toweled off, her hands were shaking. The details of her environment seemed too sharp, the colors too bright. Her head was humming. She wanted to lie down. Couldn't. Had to keep moving. She had too much energy. She felt supercharged.

She changed into new clothes, choosing the outfit without conscious thought. Her mind was on the guy she'd seen at Andrea's house, the guy who'd slipped off his singed ski mask.

Blondish hair, pale skin, narrow lips—and on his neck, a purple tattoo.

She grabbed a sheet of paper and sketched the tattoo. It was some kind of insect, probably a scorpion. The long tail with the pointed stinger was the giveaway. She folded up the picture and put it in her purse. She would need it. Later.

Before leaving the condo, she checked herself out in the full-length mirror in her bedroom. Her ensemble was borderline trashy—short skirt, tight blouse, no bra. She wondered what subliminal impulse had made her dress like a hooker. Then she thought about the scorpion tattoo, and she knew.

A man with skin art like that shouldn't be too hard to find. One thing was for sure—she would know him if she saw him again.

And she intended to see him. She intended to have closure. Exactly what closure meant in this context, she couldn't say. But she would have it.

Tonight.

20

Before they'd left, the FBI people had repaired the damage to Andrea's phone line. She almost wished they hadn't. For hours the phone had never stopped ringing. Finally she had jerked the cord out of the wall.

There was nothing she could do about the doorbell. Its incessant chiming had become the background music of her life.

She put tissue in her ears to block the sound. She retreated to the rear of her house, but some of her persecutors had made their way into the backyard and were banging on the rear door. Fortunately the broken glass panel had been boarded up, or they might have forced their way inside.

She withdrew into her bedroom. No escape. They were outside the windows, calling her name.

God, she hated them. TV people, radio people, newspaper people. Vultures, parasites, piranhas. And they were after her again. After her—even though they didn't know who she was. She imagined how it would be if they ever learned her real identity. She would be on constant display, a freak in a sideshow, twenty-four hours a day.

She paced the house, afraid even to peep through the curtains for fear that her face would be glimpsed. If they got a picture of her and put it on TV, someone might recognize her as the Medea killer. Unlikely, after all these years, but she couldn't take the chance.

They would leave eventually. She would wait them out. She was patient. She had endured twelve years in a mental institution. She could endure this.

Her mind kept running back over the events in the house, trying to find some logic in what had happened. Not the attack itself—there was a certain rough but inescapable logic to that—but its aftermath.

She remembered huddling behind the bed. Something exploded in the hall with a terrifying burst of light and noise. Moments later, when she heard an exchange of gunshots outside, she assumed Abby had retrieved her gun from her purse and was shooting it out with the intruders. Then there was silence, a long stretch of silence that scared her worse than the explosion and the gunfire. From the living room she heard low voices but could make out no words. Then the closing of a door—the door to the carport, she thought—and footsteps in the hall. A woman's voice, but not Abby's.

"Federal agent. Don't be alarmed. The assailants have gone."

It could be a trick. Andrea remained hidden.

"Ms. Lowry?" the voice asked. "I'm Special Agent McCallum, FBI."

Andrea dared to raise her head. In the dimness she saw a woman in a business suit, gun in one hand, credentials in the other.

"FBI?" Andrea asked. It didn't make sense.

Agent McCallum nodded. "I'm here to help. Other federal agents are on the way. So are the police and paramedics. Are you injured?"

"No, I don't think so. I'm all right." Andrea got up slowly, her legs unsteady. "How did you get here so fast?"

"I'll explain that later. Right now there's something we need to discuss before anyone else arrives. It involves Abby."

Andrea was baffled. "You *know* her?"

"We've worked together in the past. As you probably know, she needs to keep a low profile, which is why it's important that you not say anything about her when you're interviewed by my colleagues. No mention of her name. Okay?"

"Not say anything?"

"I can't allow her to be dragged into this. It would be bad for me and bad for her. We need you to keep the secret. Can you do that?"

"How do I explain what happened here?"

"The gun is yours, right? Say you fired it. Here, take it." Andrea accepted the revolver, vaguely aware that she had now put her fingerprints on the handle. "You grabbed the gun and took cover in here. You held off the intruders by yourself."

"And the bomb?"

"I'm not sure what that was about. I heard the noise. Do you know what Abby did?"

"She went into the bathroom. She said something about hair spray."

"Okay. She improvised a grenade out of a can of hair spray. The stuff is inflammable. That's all you have to know. Just say you did it. If they press you for details, tell them you're too shaken up to talk about it."

"That wouldn't be a lie. I am pretty shaken up."

"We can have you taken to the hospital."

Hospital. Andrea shook her head firmly. "No. No hospital."

"Just for observation. As a precaution."

"No. I'm not going there. You can't make me go there."

"Okay, okay. No one's going to make you do anything, Ms. Lowry."

More people arrived after that. The paramedics wanted to check her over, but she refused to let them touch her. She wouldn't let any medical people come near her ever again.

They left, but the house was still crowded. There were crime lab people who marked the spots where bullets had struck the walls, and took photographs and videotapes. Police and federal agents were arguing about jurisdiction, ignoring her until somehow the FBI established that they were in control of the case. Then she was taken aside by a pair of men in suits who interviewed her gently but thoroughly about what transpired. She said what Agent McCallum had told her to say. She wasn't even thinking about it. It was as if a hypnotic suggestion had been planted in her mind and she was powerless to resist.

At some point the FBI people suggested that she leave her house for the night and stay with a friend. She told them there was no one she could stay with. They suggested a hotel. She said no. She would not leave the house, not even after what had happened. The house was her refuge, the only place she felt safe. And even now, after everything that had happened, she still felt safe here, safer than anywhere else. It was irrational, but she couldn't fight it.

One of the FBI men told her there was a chance the criminals would come back.

She knew that. Still, she insisted, "I can't leave. I just can't."

She gathered that the attack was being treated as a home invasion, a failed robbery. She knew this was wrong, but said nothing.

By nine o'clock most of the law enforcement personnel had left. Agent McCallum was among the last to depart. She thanked Andrea for her cooperation, keeping her language carefully ambiguous.

"You never answered my question," Andrea said.

"Which question?"

"How did you get here so quickly?"

"I was working an unrelated case very close by. I can't give you the details. It's an ongoing investigation. I heard the gunshots and came running."

Andrea lowered her voice so only Tess could hear. "So it's just a coincidence, you knowing Abby?"

"Just a coincidence. L.A. is a smaller town than it seems."

This had to be a lie. Andrea didn't believe in coincidence. It was possible that McCallum was working with Abby, backing her up or something. Unlikely, but the alternative was that the FBI had been interested in

Andrea herself—watching her house, even. But this was a prospect too disturbing to consider.

Alone, she wandered through the house, surveying the damage. The corridor leading to her bedroom was pocked with bullet holes, the carpet charred by Abby's improvised bomb. One bedroom window had been shattered. The bedroom walls were speckled with more bullet holes. By now the bullets themselves were gone. The crime lab experts had dug them out of the walls and taken them away. The recovery of the bullets had made the holes bigger and deeper. They gaped like lunar craters.

The thought of bullets reminded her of her own gun, confiscated by the authorities for ballistics tests. She wished they hadn't taken it. She felt defenseless without it.

But there was another gun.

She had almost forgotten it. She had purchased the gun soon after buying this house, a 9mm semiautomatic pistol. The pistol had seemed like a good choice because it held more than twice as many rounds as a revolver. But when she'd taken it into the desert to practice shooting, the gun had jammed. Pistols could do that, she learned. The feeding mechanism that inserted the cartridge into the chamber could malfunction. She hadn't trusted the gun after that. She'd bought the revolver to replace it. The revolver held only six rounds, but it was dependable. When she practiced with it in the wilderness, it never failed her.

The pistol had gone into a shoe box, which was hidden in a tiny overhead crawl space that served as an attic. She pulled down the collapsible ladder and climbed into the crawl space, hunting among miscellaneous junk—a lamp that no longer worked but that she hadn't wanted to throw out, some empty vases she'd been meaning to use for flowers, old clothes she should've donated to Goodwill. After twenty minutes of searching, she found the box with the pistol in it. The gun had not been oiled in years, and she could not be sure it would work, but she had a full magazine stashed alongside it in the box, and when she attached the magazine, it clicked smoothly into place. The pistol felt small and light, almost like a toy when compared with the bulkier revolver, but holding it gave her some comfort.

She stashed it in the kitchen drawer where the revolver had been. She hoped she wouldn't need it.

But somehow she was sure she would.

21

The briefing was held in the squad room at eight thirty p.m., after three hours at Andrea Lowry's house, during which time Tess had told her story and Andrea had told hers, and nobody, it seemed, had poked any holes in either narrative. Outside the house, the media had gathered like sharks scenting blood—first one mobile news unit cruising up to the yellow ribbon at the crime scene perimeter, then a second and third, until all of L.A.'s major TV stations were represented, along with two news radio stations, the *L.A. Times,* and the *L.A. Daily News.* Eventually a police officer placated the journalists with a hurried outdoor news conference in which he described the attack as a random home invasion foiled by an armed householder. The presence of the FBI at the scene went unmentioned, and no one among the reporters had noticed it.

All of that, along with the work of a team of criminalists who had bagged and tagged every spent shell and recoverable bullet, was now over, and Hauser's squad, minus six members who had remained in Andrea's neighborhood, had reassembled in the bull pen on the seventeenth floor of the federal building, where Hauser was sketching out a geometric diagram on a whiteboard.

"We're kicking this operation into higher gear," he said briskly. "From here on, it's a three-pronged strategy. I've broken it out in boxes." He tapped the board. "First, surveillance. Whitley and Conklin are in the house next door. Davis and Palumbo are parked down the street in an undercover van. Rice and

Bowles have separate posts in other vehicles. I doubt the subject is going anywhere tonight, but as of tomorrow we'll have a minimum of three additional vehicles in the vicinity, ready to conduct clandestine mobile surveillance whenever she goes out. From now on, she never leaves our sight. I want to know where she is at all times, and who she's talking to, if anyone. Only agents who were *not* at the crime scene are eligible for surveillance duty. If you were there, she probably got a look at you, which means she may be able to ID you. We do not want her aware of our interest."

Surveillance wasn't limited to visual contact. During the search of Andrea's house, a technical agent had bugged her phone and planted a miniature camera in the living room. The transmitters' signals would reach the house next door, where the closest surveillance agents were stationed. It was all legal, the warrant obtained telephonically earlier that day.

"So we have eyes and ears on Lowry. That's our first avenue of investigation. Number two, we work the assault. Identify the assailants, learn who hired them. We're guessing it was Reynolds, but he may be working through intermediaries. Maybe he has underworld contacts, either old friends of his from when he grew up or people he met while he was a DA. Look into any possible connections between Reynolds and criminal elements, but be discreet. We don't want him to know we're on his tail. That leaves the third investigative avenue. We need to look deeper into MEDEA. We need to know what happened twenty years ago, how much of Andrea's story is true."

The meeting broke up, with Hauser reassigning Tess and Crandall to the assault case now that they were unsuitable for surveillance duty. "We've got the Santa Ana RA working it tonight," he told them, meaning the FBI's resident agency, a subsidiary branch of the regional field office. "Tomorrow you can see what they've turned up. For now, get some sleep."

Tess couldn't sleep, not yet. She had an appointment with Abby.

22

The Boiler Room was just as Tess remembered it, a not-quite-seedy diner with a retro look. She pushed past a trio of homeless people cadging coins under the neon sign, and stepped into the white Formica glare. Even the smell of cooking hamburgers was as she remembered. They smelled good, but she'd already eaten, and she had other things on her mind.

Scanning the room, she saw Abby in a booth. The booth had a view of the entrance, probably selected so Abby could see her enter. So far, however, she hadn't noticed. Intent on the plate before her, she seemed oblivious of her environment.

Abby, oblivious? That wasn't like her. She was always alert, ready for anything.

Tess approached the table. As she drew near, she saw that Abby had ordered a steak and was attacking it with what might be described as gusto. *Savagery* would be a better word. She carved the steak with furious energy, sawing it as if she wished to saw through the plate and the table.

Tess slid into the Naugahyde bench seat opposite Abby. Only then did Abby glance up.

"Hey," Abby said. She speared a chunk of beef with her fork and swallowed the red bite.

"Hi, Abby. How are you doing?"

"Fine and dandy."

"You seem a little . . . distracted."

"Just thinking."

"From the way you're tearing up that steak, they aren't pleasant thoughts."

"Hasn't been my best day."

"At least it wasn't your last one." Tess couldn't stop looking at the steak. "Aren't you supposed to be a vegetarian?"

"I eat meat. Not a lot of it. But occasionally"— Abby stabbed another forkful of beef—"occasionally I'm in the mood for something bloody."

"So I see. You, uh, you sure you're okay?"

"Why wouldn't I be?"

"There are approximately a million reasons I can think of."

"I'm fine."

"You seem kind of . . . hyper. Like you're on speed."

"I'm always that way."

"Tonight, even more so."

Abby shot her a scowling glance. "I don't do drugs."

"I know, but—"

"Look, damn it, I'm fine, all right? I'm *fine*."

Tess sat back and nodded slowly. "I assume you're wondering what brought me back to L.A."

"I'm guessing it was either the daily smog alerts or my insouciant charm."

"Try Andrea Lowry."

"Not her real name."

"I know. I looked into it for you and set off some sort of alarm bell in D.C. The case was active, but it was being kept secret. I don't like being left in the dark."

Abby grinned at her between bites. "But you also wanted to help me, at least a little."

"Maybe a little." Tess shrugged. "Very little."

"I'll take what I can get."

A waitress drifted by the table, menu in hand. Tess waved her off. "Nothing for me, thanks." The waitress shrugged and drifted on.

"Not hungry?" Abby asked.

"Ate at the office. Sometime during the fifth or sixth iteration of the shooting review."

"Got it all cleared up, I hope."

Tess shook her head. "It won't be cleared up for a while. Gunfights aren't common in the Bureau. They always draw intense interest from OPR."

"If that's anything like NPR, it would probably put me to sleep."

"It's the Office of Professional Responsibility—our equivalent of Internal Affairs. They'll be on the case, or I should say, on *my* case, for months."

"Your actions were justified."

"I know that. So do they. They'll still have me jumping through hoops. I'll be filing forms in triplicate, giving statements, and basically wasting as much of my time as they find necessary."

"You see? There are advantages to being a vigilante."

Tess gave her a sharp glance. "Is that what you are now?"

"Just making conversation. So you were interviewed and reinterviewed for hours on end."

"Yes."

"During which time you told them the whole story—with key omissions."

"Yes." Tess hadn't liked lying, but it seemed she had no choice wherever Abby was concerned.

"How'd Andrea hold up?" Abby asked.

"She didn't breathe a word about you. Actually she didn't say much of anything at all."

"Shell-shocked?"

"Possibly. But I also think she's afraid of law enforcement."

"She's afraid of everything. Paranoid."

"She has her reasons," Tess said.

Abby looked at her. "You sound like you know what they are."

"I'm on the case. I've been briefed."

"Great. Spill."

"I'm afraid I can't."

Abby carved off another slice of meat, consumed it, and set down her knife and fork. "Then let *me* tell *you.* Andrea Lowry used to be Bethany Willett. She killed her kids and got sent to the booby hatch. She was briefly famous. The press nicknamed her Medea. Now she's out of the cuckoo's nest and living under an assumed name and stalking a congressman. Only, she doesn't call it stalking. She just feels drawn to him, she says. How am I doing so far?"

"Better than you have any right to be."

"Andrea opened up to me. I have a way of getting people to do that."

"Then it looks like you don't need me at all."

"Wrongo. There are still some gaps to be filled in. Such as the exact nature of Congressman Reynolds's connection with Andrea, and how the feds got involved. And why Reynolds would want Andrea dead."

Tess put up a hand. "We don't know that Reynolds had anything to do with the attack this afternoon."

"No, I'm sure it was just a coincidence."

"We're not making any assumptions."

"Well, I am. It was him. That guy's a real son of a bitch, you know? I mean, even by the standards of a politician, and that's saying something."

"How can you be so certain it's Reynolds?"

"Instinct."

Tess was sure there was more to it, but she also knew that Abby wouldn't share without getting something in return. "I suppose," she said slowly, "if you know that much of the story, you should probably know the rest. Especially since Andrea would only tell you, anyway."

"Yes, I think she would. We were getting along pretty well until the shooting started. The attempted assassination kind of put a damper on things. By the way, I'm assuming her gun was confiscated."

"For the moment, yes. It's needed for ballistics tests."

"Leaving her defenseless."

"She's hardly defenseless. She—" Tess stopped herself.

"She's being watched around the clock by the FBI. That's what you were going to say, isn't it?"

"Well, yes."

Abby had finished her steak. She pushed a hunk of corn bread around the plate, mopping up the juice. "I'm guessing she was being watched already, or you wouldn't have made your deus ex machina arrival. What was the lookout?"

"House next door."

"The one that's boarded up?"

Tess nodded. "It's abandoned. The Bureau commandeered it early this morning."

"When did you join the stakeout detail?"

"Midafternoon."

"So you saw me walk up to Andrea's door?"

"Yes."

"Don't FBI agents usually work in pairs?"

Tess saw where she was going. "I have a partner, but luckily for you, I had the eye at the time."

"Had the eye? What is that, a magic amulet?"

"It's an expression. It means I was watching. We trade off so we don't get tired. It's standard procedure."

"So what was your partner doing while you had the eye?"

Crandall had been using the bathroom, but somehow Tess didn't want to say that. It sounded unprofessional, and there was the Bureau's reputation to consider. "Raiding the fridge."

"You even stocked the fridge? Ritzy. You didn't tell him you'd seen someone enter the house?"

"It didn't come up."

"And how would you have explained it when I walked out?"

"I figured I'd keep watching until you were gone. I was doing most of the work, anyway. He was keeping his distance."

"Slacker, huh?"

"He's just a little unhappy with me." This, Tess thought, was putting it mildly. "He has a right to be."

"So it's your fault if your partner doesn't pull his weight? Seriously, Tess, those nuns in parochial school did a number on you."

"Let's keep my educational background out of this," Tess said.

"Whatever. Where was this antisocial partner of yours while you were inside Andrea's house?"

"In the backyard, securing the scene."

"That's not so good. He should have been backing you up when you went housecleaning."

"Of course he should have. But I couldn't afford to let him see you. I told him to wait in the yard in case any more suspects tried to flee out the back. And I got thoroughly chewed out for it during the shooting review, by the way."

Abby shrugged. Clearly she didn't care about the shooting review. She didn't appear to care about Tess at all. She hadn't asked if the shoot-out in the backyard had put her in any danger. The issue apparently hadn't occurred to her.

That was a bad sign. Abby was normally somewhat self-absorbed, but not to the point of indifference when a colleague had placed herself at risk.

"So this guy didn't see me when I went out through the carport?" Abby asked.

"That's right."

"He's Sergeant Schultz, then?"

"What?"

"Your partner. He knows nothing."

Tess just barely got the reference. She had always been clueless when it came to popular culture. "As far as he's concerned, Andrea acted alone."

"Like Oswald. Cool. So are you going to tell me a bedtime story or not? I want to hear the one that begins, 'Once upon a time there was a lovely but psychologically unstable woman named Bethany. . . .'"

Tess sighed. "I'll tell you. But I may regret it."

"Think positive. You're positively going to regret it." Abby grinned, but it was a false grin, like the leer of a mask. She was trying hard to sound casual, and not quite succeeding. Maybe it had something to do with the nervous energy that was quaking in every inch of her body. "By the way," she added, "I'm assuming the three musketeers are still at large?"

"Your assailants? I'm afraid so."

"Thanks for coming to my rescue." The words were perfunctory, but Tess had been waiting for them.

"You're welcome."

"Not that I needed rescuing, of course. I already had the situation pretty well handled."

"It didn't look that way to me."

Abby pushed her plate aside. "Hey, I scared those bad boys into running away."

"They weren't running. They were regrouping. Planning another assault."

"I wish they'd tried it."

"Do you?"

"They wouldn't have outflanked me a second time. I would've had plenty of opportunities to treat them to a little street justice."

"What does that mean?" Tess asked carefully.

"They're garbage. You know what you do with garbage? You put it in bags. Nice heavy-duty bags, with zippers and everything."

"Suppose you were the one who ended up in a bag."

"It's a risk I'd be willing to take."

"That's what worries me." Tess leaned forward. "We're supposed to be on the same side, Abby. The side of law and order."

"I don't remember agreeing to that."

"Maybe you're sorry I showed up. I robbed you of your vigilante moment."

"I'll have other moments."

Tess stared at her. "What are you planning?"

"Who, me? A nice long soak in the tub, bottle of champagne, the soothing baritone of Jim Nabors on the CD player . . ." The smile on her face said that she wasn't even trying to be taken seriously.

"Let the Bureau take care of this," Tess said. "It's our case now."

"Oh, right. You're from the government, and you're here to help. By the way, since when does a home invasion fall under federal jurisdiction?"

"This was no home invasion. It was an attempted hit."

"Still not a federal crime."

"It is when a federal agent is involved. I was shot at during the performance of my official duties."

"Fair enough. Except you still haven't told me why your official duties required you to be watching Andrea's house in the first place. I mean, what's the point? It's not like you could tail her if she went for a drive. You'd need a minimum of three vehicles to do a tail job on a paranoid target in broad daylight, and there weren't that many FBI agents around."

"How do you know?"

"Because they would've come running, like you. So if you weren't there to shadow the suspect . . . oh, I get it."

"Do you?"

"You were waiting for her to leave. Not so you could follow her, but so you could break into her domicile and—what? Do a little illegal search?"

"We weren't doing anything illegal."

"Planting a bug, then. Or should I say, bugs? Plural. You wanted to know what was going on inside her house."

"Yes."

"Well, I suppose you got the opportunity to plant all the surveillance devices you wanted, once the house became a crime scene."

"I let an agent from the tech support squad handle it. We had a warrant," she added defensively.

"I'm sure you did. Kind of ironic, though, isn't it? Andrea's paranoid, thinks people are after her—and guess what? They are."

"We're not after her. We're trying to protect her."

"No, *I'm* trying to protect her. You're trying to *convict* her."

Tess bit back a sharp reply. "The truth is, we're not

sure what to make of her. Whether she's a suspect or a victim."

"Maybe a little of both," Abby suggested.

"Maybe."

"So fill in the blanks for me, girlfriend. What do you know that I don't?"

"We can get into that." Tess lowered her voice. "First I want to be reassured that you're not going to do anything drastic."

"Like what?"

"Like hunting down the intruders on your own."

Abby gave her an unblinking doe-eyed stare. "Tess, I would never do a thing like that. Why, it sounds downright dangerous."

"You're failing to convince me."

She dropped the act. "Okay, let's say I'd like to track those assholes to their lair and give them what for. How am I supposed to do it? All I know is they were three guys in ski masks and dark clothes. I'm guessing they've ditched the outfits by now, which leaves just three guys. Last time I looked, there were a lot more than three guys in the greater Los Angeles area."

"You're not holding out on me, are you?"

"Holding out what?"

"I don't know. Evidence you found at the scene, possibly."

"Did I have time to collect evidence? You were there. Was I bagging and tagging? Did you see me auditioning for the latest *CSI* spin-off? Which I hear is going to be *CSI: Fresno,* by the way."

"All right, I suppose you couldn't have picked up anything."

"I'd play vigilante if I could, but as it turns out, I have to rely on the vaunted federal boobocracy. No offense."

"We're not as inept as you seem to think."

"That's good to know. If you were, this country would be in deep shit."

"You're in a hell of a mood."

"Getting my hair parted by flying ammo has a way of doing that to me. What were they shooting, anyhow?"

"Forty-five-caliber ACP plus-Ps."

"Hot load. Serious stopping power. Get nailed with one of those, and it could ruin a girl's whole day. Luckily I found a way to even the odds."

"Three against one isn't evening the odds."

"It is when the one in question is me." Abby shrugged. "What can I say? I believe in myself."

"There's a fine line between self-esteem and self-delusion."

Abby shifted in her seat, kicking her shoes together beneath the table. "Self-delusion is a greatly underrated quality. Personally I'm in favor of it. People who have no illusions are dangerous. It's our fantasies that keep us grounded. It's our craziness that keeps us sane."

Tess shook her head. "Now I know I'm in L.A."

"Seriously, think about it. You have a couple who are married ten years, fight all the time, but always kiss and make up, because that's what lovers do. And they're in love. That's their fantasy. That's the story they tell themselves. And then one day the fantasy dies, and they realize they're not in love anymore and maybe they never were. No more illusions. No more kiss and make up. So one of them bludgeons the other one to death with a broom handle."

"They were better off lying to themselves?"

"Absolutely. Lying to ourselves is the only way most of us can get through the day."

The waitress returned with an offer of dessert. They both passed, then remained silent until she had dropped off the check and left.

"You're a strange person, Abby," Tess said finally.

"I just have a penchant for conversational detours."

"Actually, it wasn't as much of a detour as you think. Lovers who fall out of love—that's quite relevant to the present situation."

"Let me guess. Andrea Lowry and Jack Reynolds."

"She was Bethany back then."

"But they were together? They were a couple?"

"We think so."

"When?"

"Twenty years ago. I assume you know that Jack Reynolds used to be the Orange County DA. At that time, Bethany was his mistress. She got pregnant and gave birth to twin boys."

Abby shut her eyes briefly. "Reynolds's boys."

Tess nodded. "Not that he ever publicly admitted to being the father. He was already married and raising a family of his own. He was planning a run for political office. Obviously he hadn't wanted Bethany to get pregnant at all. She'd told him she was on the pill. It was a lie. She wanted to get pregnant, because she was convinced that if she bore his children, he would leave his wife for her."

"Naive."

"Extremely. Reynolds, though, was a smooth talker. He'd met Bethany in the courthouse—she was a legal secretary. He convinced her that his marriage wasn't working, that he meant to get a divorce. She fell for it. They were together for a year or so, and she began to suspect he wasn't going to hold up his end of the deal. Having children was her way of forcing his hand."

"But it didn't work out the way she planned."

"Reynolds understood that Bethany had been trying to trap him. He's not the sort of man who likes feeling trapped."

"Not many are. How old were the twins when Bethany figured out that it was over?"

"Ten months."

"She shot them," Abby said, "when they were ten months old."

"Yes. The breakup is what precipitated the double murder and the attempted suicide. Admittedly, it doesn't make a lot of sense. She's mad at him, so she takes it out on her own kids."

Abby waved off this objection. "She wasn't thinking

of them as her kids. To her, they were *his* kids—his flesh and blood. She wanted to make him suffer. She wanted to take something away from him."

"So she punishes him by killing her own children?"

"Something like that. It's what Medea did, right?"

"I think so. Whatever her intention, she ended up punishing herself. She survived her suicide attempt, but it might have been better for her if she hadn't."

"I'm missing something here. After she woke up from surgery and realized she was going to live, why didn't she tell the world about Reynolds? She could've ruined his career."

"He got to her first. As DA, he had access to her while she was in the hospital, under police protection. He must have intimidated her into silence."

"How do you intimidate somebody who's killed her kids and tried to kill herself? She had nothing left to lose."

"I don't know. But she kept quiet, so Reynolds must have managed it. He also had her declared incompetent to stand trial."

Abby nodded. "Convenient. No testimony, no embarrassing questions."

"Exactly. She was shipped off to a mental hospital. And Reynolds continued his illustrious career, which led him to Capitol Hill a few years later."

"This is all very interesting." Abby took out her purse and removed some cash, which she counted and left on the table. "But since she's not talking to the authorities, Andrea didn't give you this info. I doubt Reynolds did, either. So are we dealing with hard facts, or just supposition?"

"What we're dealing with is the story Bethany told one of her doctors while she was in the psychiatric hospital. She doesn't even know she told him. She was heavily medicated at the time."

"And how did the FBI find out about it?"

"A walk-in. Two weeks ago this doctor came to the Bureau and reported what he'd been told."

"Just two weeks ago? She's been out of the hospital

for eight years. You're saying the doc kept the secret all that time?"

"He had no idea whether or not it was true. It could have been the babbling of a delusional patient. He wasn't going to get involved in some political mess on the basis of something a patient told him in confidence and under medication."

"What changed his mind?"

"Someone called the hospital two weeks ago, making inquiries about Bethany Willett."

"What kind of inquiries?"

"He was trying to find out Bethany's current address. The doctor, who runs the hospital now, thought it might be a journalist. But when he checked the call's origin, he found it had been made from a pay phone in the Rayburn Building in Washington, D.C."

"I'm guessing Reynolds works out of Rayburn."

"He has an office there. And Congress was in session at the time. The doctor decided it was pretty good confirmation of Bethany's story. He also decided that Reynolds probably wasn't just trying to get back in touch with an old friend."

Abby smiled. "I'll bet the Bureau was none too thrilled to get hold of that information."

"We investigate everything. We're nonpolitical."

"Right."

"It was dicey," Tess admitted. "Reynolds is a powerful congressman. He's not the sort of person you can haul in for interrogation. The situation had to be handled with care. MEDEA was reactivated, and an investigative squad was set up. They located Bethany Willett under her new identity, and learned she's visited at least one of Reynolds's campaign events."

"She's visited a lot of them. She's his number one fan."

"Which is why Reynolds hired you, I assume. He was being stalked by the woman he'd broken up with twenty years ago—a woman who's already proved herself to be psychologically unstable."

"Isn't it nice how all the pieces of our story are coming together in such a rich, satisfying mosaic?"

Tess ignored her. "Now that we've tightened our surveillance, there's no way you can contact her again. If you continue your involvement in the case, you'll be seen by surveillance. Someone will remember you from the Rain Man case. And we'll both be in a lot of trouble."

"So you're saying . . . ?"

"I'd like you to walk away."

"Disappear, get lost. Is that it?"

"Yes."

"I'm hurt, Tess. You don't want us to work together, side by side? It was fun last time. You, all staid and bureaucratic, and me, your reckless, fun-loving sidekick. It was a regular buddy picture."

"I remember that movie. I'm not interested in a sequel."

"There's rarely any artistic justification for doing one," Abby conceded. "Okay, I'll back off."

Tess eyed her suspiciously. "You agreed to that a little too easily."

"Why wouldn't I agree? I don't want to be ID'd by the Bureau, either. And it's not like I have a client in this case. I quit on Reynolds even before his goons almost killed me."

"Did you tell him where to find Andrea?"

"Nope. At least not intentionally. But I must've screwed up somehow, given him more info than I realized."

Tess thought about it. "He could've had you followed."

"I would have spotted a tail. It's something else."

"Like what?"

"I don't know. He's smarter than I thought, apparently. I led him to Andrea. I just don't see how."

"Regardless of that, you're willing to leave it alone?"

"Yeah. I'll walk. It's not like I have a choice."

Abby got up. Tess remained seated, watching her. "I've been straight with you, Abby. Are you being straight with me?"

"Cross my heart. Come on, don't you trust me?"

"I don't trust anybody." Tess looked away, feeling suddenly tired. "Not even myself. And I have you to thank for it."

"Moi?"

"You got me into this clandestine stuff. You brought me to the point where I am now, where I have to lie and cover up in front of everybody, all the time."

Abby slung her purse over her shoulder. "Welcome to my world."

"I never *wanted* to be in your world. I never wanted to live your life."

"Yeah, well, I never asked you to get directly involved in this case, either."

"I was keeping secrets even before I got involved this time."

"You're a government agent. Keeping secrets is your job."

"Not when I'm keeping them from my superiors."

"That's where I'm lucky." Abby smiled. "I don't have any superiors."

"Which means you don't have anybody to keep you in line."

"My conscience keeps me in line."

"Does it?"

Abby didn't answer that. "Bye, Tess. Nice running into you again. If I'm ever in Denver, I'll look you up."

She walked away. Tess looked after her, then at the plate across the table, the bloody carvings of gristle and fat in a thin red pool.

23

Abby did not, in fact, have plans to spend the evening in a warm bath, with or without the accompaniment of Jim Nabors's dulcet baritone. She was way too keyed up for that.

She headed into Hollywood and parked outside the LAPD divisional station on Wilcox. The front of the building was an unprepossessing brick facade adorned with a banner inviting passersby to sign up for the police reserves. She wondered if the department ever got any takers.

Having left her gun in the car, she got through the metal detector without any fuss. At the front desk she asked for Sergeant Wyatt, identifying herself as Charlene, the code name they'd agreed on. The desk officer called Wyatt, got an okay, and directed her to the watch office.

She walked through a maze of corridors, past bulletin boards crowded with actual bulletins, past crowded squad rooms modernistically refurnished during the building's recent earthquake retrofitting, and finally found the office, located near the rear door of the building—convenient for the cops who parked out back in the fenced lot.

Vic Wyatt was alone in the office, which meant he could risk a kiss—a quick kiss, almost furtive. He might be afraid of someone walking in on them, or he might just be feeling a little standoffish. He got that way sometimes. He had always wanted more out of their relationship than she had been willing to give.

"You running the show tonight?" she asked. Normally a lieutenant served as watch commander, but a sergeant took the helm sometimes. It was no big stretch for Wyatt. He was due for a promotion to lieutenant any day now.

"It's all me," he said, running a hand through his sandy crew cut. "What brings you here?"

"Do I need a reason?"

"I'd say so. Showing up at the station isn't your usual MO."

She put on a pouty face. "You talk about me like I'm a criminal. I could take offense."

"You're too dangerous to be a criminal. Besides, criminals are stupid."

"Only the ones who get caught."

"They all get caught eventually."

"Spoken like a true officer of the law. Okay, what brings me here is this." She reached into her purse and removed her sketch of the tattoo, smoothing it out.

Wyatt studied it. "Very artistic. You entering a contest or something?"

"It's a tat I saw on a man's neck. I think it's a—"

"Scorpion," Wyatt said, frowning.

"Hey, you got it right on the first try. Am I a good artist or what?"

"You've definitely captured the subject. Where'd you see this guy, anyway?"

"Around."

"Around where?"

She didn't want to tell him, but she knew he would get it out of her sooner or later. "I had a little encounter this afternoon."

"What kind of encounter?"

"The kind where people are shooting at me, and I'm shooting back."

He set down the sketch and stared at her. "Are you okay?"

"Not a nick on me. It was no fun, though—as I guess you know. You been in many shoot-outs?"

He frowned at the question. He was doing a lot of

frowning all of a sudden. "I've been in zero shoot-outs."

She found this hard to believe. Wyatt had worked out of Hollywood for years, and despite expensive efforts at renovation, much of the area still wasn't safe after dark. "None?"

"I've never fired a shot in the field. I've hardly ever had to draw my piece. Which makes me no different from about ninety-eight percent of the cops in this town."

"Huh."

"I shouldn't have told you that. Now you're looking at me like I wear a skirt."

"No, I'm not." She considered it. "Maybe a little."

"Thanks. So how serious was this situation?"

"It was nothing I couldn't handle."

"That's not exactly an answer."

"Minor dustup. No big deal."

He grunted skeptically. "Which division is covering it?"

"LAPD isn't involved. It was in San Fernando."

"I can't help you there."

"You couldn't help anyway. The FBI took the case."

"The FBI? How the hell did they get involved?"

"Hey, you know the *federales,* always horning in on the action."

Wyatt stepped closer to her and put his arms around her waist. His touch was unexpectedly gentle. "These days the feds are more concerned with terrorists than street criminals. You weren't shooting it out with al-Qaeda, were you?"

"Nothing that dramatic." She was surprised at how good it felt to be embraced, how much she needed it. "They were pros, though. One of them was wearing the body art. I was hoping it might mean something to you."

"It does. It's the logo of the Scorpions."

"The Scorpions. Scary name."

"Scary guys. You *sure* you're okay?"

She slipped free of his grasp and let him study her from head to toe. "Do I look incapacitated?"

"No."

"All right, then. So who exactly are the Scorpions?"

"Biker club out of Santa Ana. They all have tats like this."

"If they're in Santa Ana, how did they come to your attention?"

"They get around. Santa Ana is where they started. They have a few satellite clubs in L.A. If you got into it in San Fernando, you're probably dealing with someone local."

Abby thought about Reynolds's trip to the barrio. "No, I don't think so. I think Orange County is a better bet. You wouldn't happen to know where in Santa Ana these gentlemen can be found?"

"I don't, but I can talk to somebody who does. If you give me a reason why I should."

"They fired bullets at my head."

"That's what concerns me."

"It concerned me, too."

"I mean, it concerns me that you might be thinking about revenge."

"What I'm thinking of is bringing these folks to justice."

"Street justice? Or the regular kind?"

"The regular kind. Trial by jury, innocent until proven guilty, Miranda warnings, the whole nine yards."

Wyatt reached out and stroked her hair thoughtfully. "I know I *ought* to believe you."

"Come on, Vic, what do you think I'm gonna do? Track down these guys and get into another pissing match?"

"I wouldn't put it past you."

"A pissing match is one contest I know I can't win. Besides, although I may be occasionally a tad reckless, I'm not suicidal."

"Not normally. But you seem pretty jazzed, Abby. Kind of . . ."

"Hopped-up? Like I'm on speed?"

Wyatt squinted at her. "Well, yeah."

"Someone else made the same observation. So I guess it must be true. I mean, not the speed part. But I *am* a little jumpy. Can you blame me?"

"Not at all. But you know, there's a reason police officers aren't sent back into the field right after a shooting incident. The aftereffects—"

"I studied psychology, Vic. I know all about post-traumatic stress."

"Then you're aware that you're showing some of the symptoms. You're on an adrenaline high. At some point you're going to come down. You could come down hard."

She took his hand. "You'll be there to break my fall."

"How can you know that?"

"You always are."

He looked away, embarrassed. "I really think you'd be better off taking some time to get yourself together. Deal with what you went through. Get it out of your system."

"Oh, hell, I'm not a newbie. I've been shot at before. And I've shot back. I killed a man once, and I didn't lose a damn bit of sleep over it."

"Maybe it would be better if you had."

She pulled her hand away. "Are you going to help me or not?"

He thought about it. "Tell me what you intend to do."

"Find this guy. Then bring in the feds."

"How are you going to tip off the FBI without involving yourself?"

"I have a contact in the Bureau."

"Then why do you need me?"

"They don't know the city like you do."

Wyatt pursed his lips. "Nice compliment."

"It's the truth."

"I know you're manipulating me."

"What makes you say that?"

"Your lips are moving."

She bristled. "Somebody woke up on the cynical side of bed."

"It's hard not to be cynical with someone who uses you."

"Look, Vic, if my being here is a problem—"

"It is. You know it is. We can't be seen together. It's risky enough for me to come to your place. The damn doorman and those guards at the desk could pick me out of a lineup with their eyes shut by now."

"How would they be able to pick you out if they had their eyes shut?"

He ignored the question. "I've taken a lot of chances for you, Abby. And, let's face it, it's pretty much a one-way street."

"I take, but I don't give. Is that what you're saying?"

"That's what *you* said."

"You're not disagreeing."

"Would I have any reason to disagree?"

"Maybe I'd just better go."

She turned away. He put a hand on her shoulder and drew her back. His voice was softer than before. "The situation must be pretty desperate if you're coming here."

"Not desperate. Just urgent."

"Subtle distinction. You promise you're not going to go off and get yourself killed?"

"That's not the plan."

"And you aren't gunning for revenge?"

"My life isn't a Charles Bronson movie. I told you what I want to do."

"Yes. You told me."

"And you don't believe it," she said flatly. Tess hadn't believed her, either. She was tired of being doubted. "Okay, I'll take off, then."

"Not till I get you that info."

She cocked her head, uncertain she'd heard right. "Yeah?"

"One of our gang guys will know about the Scorpions. Just wait here. And try to be inconspicuous."

"I always am."

He left. She paced the small office, barely aware of the chatter on the police radio. A uniformed cop stuck his head in the doorway, saw her and not Wyatt, and mumbled something about coming back later. Other than that, she was undisturbed.

She thought about what he'd said. Yeah, she was stressed. Who the hell wouldn't be? She was tense and a little hyper. So what? She'd survived a goddamned gunfight. All her senses were temporarily heightened; her mind was racing. That wasn't a bad thing. If anything, it gave her an edge.

Maybe coming to the station house had been a bad idea. She knew she shouldn't be seen with him, especially by his fellow officers. It was the kind of thing that could come back to hurt him if she was ever exposed. But she was in a hurry. She wasn't in the mood to play it safe.

He complained that she rarely told him anything about her cases. He was right. But the thing was, she was doing it to protect him. The less he knew, the better.

That was part of it, anyway. Not the whole truth. If she was being completely honest with herself, she would have to admit that she never shared more than necessary. Not with Wyatt. Not with Tess. Not with anybody. She was the original lone wolf. It had always been like that for her, but in recent years she seemed to have retreated even deeper into isolation and wariness. She had learned to trust no one, to be perpetually on guard.

It wasn't the easiest way to live. And it wasn't getting any easier. More and more often these days, she was getting that trapped feeling. It came on for no apparent reason and lingered for hours or days. Usually a dream served as a harbinger. She would dream of herself in prison—not a real prison, simply a place she couldn't escape from. It might be nice and pretty, with attractive decor and comfortable furnishings, but she couldn't leave. Sometimes the prison looked like her condo, and other times it looked like the ranch in Arizona where she'd grown up, but most of the time it was just an anonymous place, as meticulously appointed as a luxury hotel, and as impersonal.

She'd had the dream on and off for years. She was pretty sure she knew what it meant. Her symbolic imprisonment was a subconscious complaint about the life she'd chosen.

She worked alone. She'd created a job that allowed her to interact with a wide variety of people while maintaining a cautious separation from them all. Sometimes she felt trapped in the private world she'd carved out for herself.

Still, there was more to the dream than that. She had a feeling she was trapped in a deeper sense than simple emotional disconnectedness. Trapped by . . . circumstances? Fate? She wasn't sure she believed in either. Circumstances were what you made them. Fate was a myth. Or so she liked to tell herself. Maybe she was wrong. Maybe when she'd signed up for this life, she'd boarded a train that was headed down a straight stretch of rail toward a predetermined end, and now the train was moving too fast for her to jump off.

Not that she would have jumped off, anyway. She was committed. She would ride this line to the end—even if it was a dead end. What the hell. Everything was a dead end if you looked far enough ahead, wasn't it?

Besides, there was always a chance the train would jump the rails. She wasn't sure if that part of the analogy was comforting or disquieting. She supposed it depended on whether or not she survived the wreck.

The door opened, and Wyatt came in. "Their main hangout," he said without preliminaries, "is a biker bar on South Grande Avenue, name of Fast Eddie's. There's about twenty-five, thirty members in the Santa Ana club, plus a few probates—aspiring members—at any given time."

"And they all have these tattoos?"

"All the sworn members, yeah. It's part of the initiation ceremony. The tat isn't always on the neck. Sometimes it's on the biceps or the chest or wherever."

"As gangs go, are we talking major crime or penny-ante stuff?"

"Somewhere in between. They push meth and designer drugs, but they don't produce the stuff themselves. They've made efforts to legitimize themselves—graffiti cleanup, Toys for Tots, that sort of thing. But it's all bullshit. At heart they're all about drugs and violence."

"A real credit to their community."

"They're people you don't want to fool around with."

"I never fool around," Abby said quietly.

Wyatt gave her a long look. "That's what worries me."

She didn't like his inquiring stare. It was hard to know what secrets he might draw out of her. He knew her so much better than Tess did.

She broke eye contact, moving quickly to the door. "Thanks, Vic. I owe you."

He showed her an unreadable smile. "I'll put it on your tab."

24

Reynolds had spent the night in his home office, a small, private retreat on the ground floor of his house. Nora knew better than to disturb him there. He'd microwaved a frozen fettuccine dinner and forced himself to eat it, the meal washed down with more than one glass of Scotch. At ten p.m. and again at eleven, he turned on the local news to see the story of the home invasion in San Fernando. He learned nothing from the accounts except that the reporters and a few onlookers had remained outside the house late into the night. He knew that Shanker's men could do nothing until the media left.

By midnight he had to assume that the goddamned reporters were finally gone. They wouldn't linger after doing their live stand-ups for the late local news. When the TV vans left, the neighborhood curiosity seekers would leave, too. And Bethany—Andrea— would be alone.

He had no doubt she would stay in the house. She would not trust the police enough to accept their protection. And if she was as paranoid and hostile as Abby Sinclair had said, she wouldn't have any friends she could go to.

She ought to be easy prey.

He waited, nursing another Scotch. Shanker's boys would get it done this time. Hell, they might have done the job already. Andrea could be dead, even now. Or dying, her blood draining onto the floor as she lay helpless. He hoped she knew who was responsible. He wanted her to know who had killed her.

His cell phone rang. He snatched it off his desk. "Yeah."

"It's me." Shanker's voice.

"You get it done?" Reynolds licked his lips and realized the old expression was true—he *could* almost taste it.

But Shanker took a moment too long to answer. "No," he said finally. "We didn't."

"Why the fuck not?"

"She's being watched."

"What?"

"I went up there to scout the area. Figured I would do the job myself. No more delegating. I hung out in a park across from her house. Nobody noticed me. I was wearing grungy clothes, looked like a homeless guy. I waited till after the TV assholes left."

"And?"

"A little later I saw somebody go into the house next door to the target's residence. It's a house that's supposed to be unoccupied. Abandoned. Windows boarded up. But people are in there. And there's another thing. A van."

"What kind of van?"

"Cargo type, no rear windows. Got the name of a plumbing company on it. Parked down the street. It's been there all night."

"That doesn't mean anything."

"I got close enough to see some light from the front compartment. There's people inside the van. It's a stakeout, Jack."

"Who? Cops, feds?"

"I don't know. Cops, I assume. Home invasion's not a federal crime. Undercover cops are probably waiting to see if anybody comes back for a return visit."

Reynolds gripped the phone too tightly. "Fuck it. Send them in anyway."

"I can't do that. The cops—"

"Get some backup. Three, four of your guys. Go in with shotguns. Kill the fucking cops. Blow them the fuck away. With enough firepower and the element of surprise, you can do it."

There was another long silence. "I don't think that's too realistic, Jack."

"Realistic? You don't think it's fucking *realistic?* How about your ass in a concrete drum? Is that *realistic?* How about what happened to Joe Ferris?"

"I'm just trying to look at the situation as it stands. I'm already on my way back to Santa Ana. I gave it my best shot, but for tonight, it's a no-go."

"Fuck that bullshit. I don't want to *hear* it."

"Jack, what can I tell you?"

"You can tell me you got *results.* That's what the fuck I hired you for. I even gave you a second chance to make good. That's not something I would offer to just any-body. Now you're jerking me off and making excuses—"

"It's not excuses. She's under surveillance. She's a hardened target. I can't touch her."

"Goddamn it, you listen to me. I want that woman dead. Now. Tonight. I don't care what it takes—I want you to make it happen. You hear me, you dumb dog-shit cocksucker? You *hear* me?"

"I hear you, Jack. But I can't help you. Maybe in a day or two, if the heat's off . . ."

"I ought to cut your fucking balls off. Except you don't have any. No cojones, Ron. Even a damn lettuce picker has more guts than you."

"Jack, we can work something out."

"You're a dead man," Reynolds said, ending the call. "Fucking dead," he added to the empty room.

He threw the phone away. It clattered in a corner. He took a step in one direction, then another, unable to select any course of action, even where he wanted to walk. Then he turned and moved behind his desk, threw a row of books off the shelf onto the floor, and exposed a wall safe. He dialed the combination, opened the safe. Inside, among other valuables and secrets, there was a handgun. He pulled it out. Fully loaded. Spare clips in the safe.

He could do the job himself. Take the gun, drive to San Fernando right now, sneak unseen into Andrea's yard, get into her house. Shoot her dead. But the shot would draw the undercover cops. And he had no silencer. All right, so he would kill her some other way. Smother her, strangle her, drown her in the fucking toilet. A silent kill, then an escape into the shadows—

Bullshit.

He wasn't going to do any goddamn thing like that. He didn't even know how to do it. It wasn't part of his—how would Stenzel say it?—his *skills set*. Not one of his *core competencies*.

"Fuck," he snarled, tossing the gun back inside the safe and slamming the door. He left the books in disorder on the floor. He poured himself another Scotch from the minibar and downed it fast, hoping the burn of alcohol would calm him, but if anything, it made him hotter than before. The situation was insane. He knew her name and address. He ought to be able to stamp her out as casually as he would tread on a cigarette butt. Instead he couldn't get to her. She was closed off from him, protected by an unbreachable barrier. She might as well be in hiding on another continent. Yet she was so close—

He punched the oak-paneled wall. Pain flashed through his hand. He thought he might have broken it, but no, he could flex his fingers. The raw pulse of pain in his knuckles felt good somehow. Better than the Scotch had tasted. He didn't need Scotch. He needed pain.

Not his own pain, though. His own pain was never the answer.

He found his car keys and left through a side door, taking his Mustang coupe. He drove fast on the surface streets and reached Rebecca's condo in Costa Mesa. It was past one o'clock by now, and she was asleep, of course. At the front gate he buzzed her unit until she answered.

"Me," he said. "Open up."

She did, but only after she hesitated. He made a mental note of that. She would pay for hesitating.

She met him at her door. He pushed her inside and shut the door behind him.

"What's wrong?" she asked, seeing his face, and from her expression he knew he must look like a wild man.

He didn't answer. He pushed her down, and she fell on the floor in a confusion of long limbs and the tissuey folds of her nightgown.

"You bitches," he said.

She stared up, uncomprehending.

"Dumb fucking bitches, playing your games." He thought of Andrea. And Abby Sinclair, who'd walked out on him.

"Jack?" Rebecca whispered.

He struck her in the face. Her head snapped sideways and she groaned and there was blood on her mouth, and it was all good.

25

Abby left the station house and caught the Hollywood Freeway, speeding south into Orange County. The day's traffic had finally cleared, and the car could go all out. Putting the pedal to the floor relieved some of her tension, but not much.

Along the way, she stopped first at a large discount drugstore, then spent ten minutes in the bathroom of a fast-food joint. When she emerged, her hair had been moussed and slicked back, her pageboy do transformed into a tight skullcap. Tacky oversized earrings, maroon lipstick, and glue-on fingernail extensions completed her makeover.

She didn't think the bad guys at Andrea's house could have seen her. If they had, it couldn't have been more than a glimpse. She looked sufficiently different to pass unrecognized now.

One thing was for sure. She could change her appearance a lot more easily than the man with the scorpion tattoo could change his.

At midnight she arrived in Santa Ana and cruised down South Grande Avenue until she found Fast Eddie's.

Wyatt's info had been correct. The Scorpions did hang out here, or at least some biker club did. Choppers, all of them American-made and none boasting engines smaller than 900 cc's, were parked out back in the deadpan glare of a mercury-vapor streetlight. The bikes were unguarded, their owners apparently known in the community—known and feared.

Abby didn't leave her car in the lot. She didn't want

anyone seeing the Mazda and remembering it from
Andrea's neighborhood. Instead she motored down
another block and found a space at the curb, then
walked briskly to the bar, her purse in hand with the
gun inside.

Fast Eddie's was a clamorous hellhole. Some kind
of noxious hip-hop was banging out of the cheap
sound system. A woman who was high on more than
life gyrated on a pool table while some guys yelled
catcalls, and others shouted at her to get off the table
so they could play pool.

Those guys weren't Scorpions, though. The Scorpions were seated together in a corner of the bar, ignoring the bedlam.

She knew them at once, not from the tattoos, which
she couldn't make out at a distance, but from the air
of masculine camaraderie that defined any wolf pack.

There were two dozen of them occupying a nest of
corner tables. They wore their colors, sleeveless
leather jackets with scorpion insignia on the back. A
few female hangers-on, ranging in age from jailbait to
over-the-hill, petted and fondled and looked bored.
The men were loud and drunkenly obnoxious, their
blurry stares daring any patron to start something. It
was a safe bet that every one of them was packing
a gun.

Although Santa Ana was largely Hispanic, the Scorpions were all Anglos. Most gangs formed along racial
lines. Probably this one had originated as a way of
defending a slice of this miserable turf from the en-
croachment of immigrants.

Abby went up to the bar and got the attention of
the slow-moving, heavy-lidded bartender. He was wiping a glass with a hand towel that looked dirtier than
the dishware. On the wall behind him was a sign:
PARKING FOR HARLEYS ONLY—ALL OTHERS WILL BE
SHOT.

Fast Eddie's, it would appear, was not aiming to
reproduce the social atmosphere of the Algonquin
Round Table.

"What?" the bartender said. His lower lip was set in a permanent curl.

"Vodka rocks."

He grunted and poured. She slapped a bill on the counter and told him to keep the change, advice he accepted without gratitude.

Abby wasn't a believer in drinking on duty, but if she'd ordered anything nonalcoholic, she might have called attention to herself. She sipped the drink. The cheap vodka burned with a sour aftertaste.

Her barstool afforded a good view of the Scorpions' conclave in the mirror behind the bar. She watched the rowdy crew, her gaze moving from one man to the next, dismissing anyone without a tattoo on his neck.

She spotted him at the second of the three tables. She hadn't expected to feel anything when she saw him again, and her reaction surprised her. She felt a sudden jolt like a fist in the stomach. Her eyes watered. She brushed them dry with the back of her hand.

For just a moment she had been trapped in the bedroom again, taking fire from front and back, with no way out and only five bullets in her gun.

She shook off the memory. She took another sip of vodka, which wasn't tasting quite so bad now, and studied the man who'd tried to kill her.

He was in his midtwenties, muscular and hard-eyed, but his face was softer than it should have been, almost feminine in its contours. He reminded her a little of Leon Trotman, who had stalked the schoolteacher in Reseda until Abby put him back in jail.

She had nearly killed Leon. And she hadn't had anything personal against him.

She watched the biker as he listlessly downed a stein. He was flanked by two sidekicks. One of them looked sleepy, and the other one looked restless. His two partners in crime, she guessed.

The man she recognized was paying little attention to his pals. His eyes were downcast and worried. No doubt he was concerned about his future. He'd failed in his assignment. Abby didn't know the Scorpions' penalty for failure, but she doubted it was anything to look forward to.

The rest of the gang weren't shunning him, though. Either they were exceptionally loyal or they didn't know he'd screwed the pooch. The best guess was they didn't know about the assignment at all. The whole thing had probably been kept on the q.t.

Abby had spent much of the ride from L.A. reconstructing how the hit had been arranged. Reynolds had grown up in Santa Ana and had been the DA there. At some point, either in his youth or on the job, he'd come into contact with the Scorpions. Probably he'd done them some favors as a DA. In exchange, they would do his dirty work. Every successful leader needed operatives at the grassroots level, and not all the operatives were the fresh-faced variety she'd seen at the campaign office.

The three men she was looking at weren't old enough to have been in the gang when Reynolds was a district attorney, let alone when he was a kid. Most likely, his personal allegiance was to one or more of the older members, the ones in leadership positions now. In a sensitive matter it would be smart to limit the people who knew the details. Reynolds had probably approached one of the leaders in the bike shop, and that man in turn had arranged the hit with a phone call.

She nursed her vodka for a long time, brushing off occasional come-ons from other patrons and ignoring the bartender's perpetual scowl. She was patient. The man with the tattoo was drinking a lot of beer, and as her dad used to say, *You don't buy beer. You only rent it.*

Around one o'clock the guy finally left the table to use the can. Abby vacated her barstool and followed him into the alcove where the restrooms were located. She pretended to use the pay phone while keeping an eye on the door to the men's room.

After only a minute, he emerged. She doubted he'd

had time to wash his hands. Drunk, homicidal—and unhygienic. This guy had it all.

She stepped away from the phone, timing the move so he collided with her from behind.

"I'm sorry," she said. "Didn't see you there."

"Should watch where you're going," he growled.

He started to walk on.

"I wasn't thinking," Abby said. "Guess I've had too much to drink."

This piqued his interest. An intoxicated woman was an easy lay, or so all males assumed. He turned to look at her. His glance rested only briefly on her face before checking her more important assets.

"My name's Sandi," she said. "Sandi with an *i.*"

She'd made up the name on the spot. It wasn't one of her aliases, and she had no fake ID in her purse to back it up, but she didn't expect to be showing anyone her creds tonight.

He burped. A real charmer. "Dylan," he said.

"That's a cool tattoo."

His hand went to his neck, tracing the insectile shape. "More'n a tattoo," he said. "It's a . . ." He searched for the word. "You know, insignia."

"You mean, like a sign?"

"Sign, yeah. It's a logo. Our trademark."

"Whose trademark?"

He shook his head, pissed off at her ignorance. "Shit, you live around here. You've gotta know."

"I live in Mission Viejo." A safe suburban town to the south.

"Mission fucking Viejo?" He hawked up a gob and spit in the general direction of a potted plant. "What the fuck you doing here?"

She showed him a provocative smile. "Looking for adventure."

He considered this, his narrowed eyes coldly thoughtful. "You might find more'n you bargained for."

"That so?"

"Yeah, it's so." He seemed to reach a decision, and

the decision was that he wasn't horny tonight. "Best skitter on home, Li'l Bo Peep. Ain't none of your sheep around here. You're way out of your element."

He took a step away.

"It's not the first time," she said.

The words stopped him. He gave her a grudging glance. "You been here before?"

"Not in this place. But I've been . . . around."

"Have you, now?" He found this amusing. "Like, where?"

"Like, all over. Up and down this part of the coast. Venice, Long Beach, Oceanside. I've hit some hot spots in San Diego, too."

He shrugged. "So you're some rich bitch who goes slumming."

"I'm not rich."

"You ain't poor, neither. College?"

She was hardly going to admit to having a psych degree. "Two years."

"That's two years more'n I got."

"You didn't miss anything. It was boring." She let a tone of seductive languor steal into her voice. "Of course, I'm easily bored."

"No, you ain't."

"Aren't I?"

"Nah. If you was, you would've offed yourself by now. 'Cause you're the most boring goddamned cunt I ever met." He snorted laughter. "Mission Viejo. Fuck."

He swaggered off, and she was left alone and frustrated. She'd sent out every sexual signal in her repertoire, and he'd blown her off. She had to assume he had other things on his mind. The alternative was that she was losing her allure, a hypothesis too far-fetched to entertain.

She returned to the bar and ordered another vodka. In the mirror she saw Dylan rejoin his buddies, his expression more sour than before.

Her best bet now was to tail him when he left the bar, which would probably be around closing time.

She would leave shortly before two and watch the parking lot from her car.

Tailing a motorcycle would be tough. The chopper could cut through traffic in ways no car could match. There was a good chance she would lose him.

Damn. She was so close, but she hadn't gotten him to bite.

But maybe there was still a chance. She saw Dylan's nervous-looking friend pointing at her and nudging. Apparently he'd seen them talking in the alcove, and he was prodding Dylan to go for it. Dylan brushed off the advice, but the other guy was persistent. Abby silently encouraged him. Peer pressure could be a potent force.

She watched the pantomime show in the mirror. From Dylan's body language, she could tell that his resistance was breaking down. He had gone from arms crossed—a defensive posture—to arms open.

The friend's voice rose above the general din. "Fuck it, man, she's *hot!*" Abby almost smiled, even if the compliment did emanate from a sociopathic scumbag. Then she remembered that if Dylan and his crew had been better shots, she wouldn't be so hot right now. She would be cold, morgue cold.

She felt another twist in her gut and found herself taking a bigger swallow of vodka.

In the mirror, Dylan rose from his seat. His friend's final line of argument seemed to have closed the deal. The biker came toward the bar, carrying his beer.

She looked away from the mirror and nursed her drink until he sat down on the barstool beside her. Then she glanced at him.

"That wasn't very nice," she said coolly. "What you said about me back there."

"Yeah. Well—I'm feeling kinda snarky tonight."

"Any particular reason?"

"Bad day at the office."

"What sort of work do you do?"

"The sort I don't like to talk about." He gulped a swig of beer. "You ain't Mex, are you?"

"What?"

"Dark hair, brown eyes. You a Latin?"

"Anglo."

"Good thing."

Yeah, Dylan was a real catch. "So, that matters?"

"Fuck, yeah, it matters. Goddamn taco benders are taking over this town. Before you know it, they'll be all over Mission Viejo, too. You just wait."

"What have you got against Mexicans?" she asked, her voice neutral.

He regarded her as if she were mentally defective. "What do I got against 'em? Well, they're fucking scum, to start with. And illegal. Not one of 'em has a green card. They take work away from Americans, too."

"Most of those jobs aren't so great."

"You wait. Before long, goddamn border jumpers'll be taking everybody's job. Like yours, maybe. What do you do?"

"Secretarial work."

"One of them strawberry pickers could do that job, at least one that can read and write and speak English. And he'd do it cheaper than you. Then you're out on your butt with not so much as a thank-you for your years of loyal service."

"Something like that happen to you?"

"Not me. I got a skill, see. I'm a mechanic. I know my way around an engine. Those campesino assholes—half of 'em ain't never even *driven* a damn car."

"You're safe, then."

"Not hardly. I can't charge what I used to. Wetbacks come in and lower the pay scale for everybody. You got an American who was trimming trees for fifteen bucks an hour. Speedy Gonzales shows up and says he'll do it for half that much. American is either out of work or he has to cut his pay to compete. Then he can't spend so much on getting his car fixed when it breaks down, so I gotta charge less if I want to get his business."

"You've thought about this a lot."

"When your livelihood's at stake, you got to think about it. And find ways to bring in extra money." He turned thoughtful.

"You mean, doing some repair work on the side?"

"Repair work. Yeah. That's a good way to put it. Fixing things."

"Cars," she prompted.

"Problems," he said. "People got problems, I fix 'em. Until today I always got it done. Today everything went to shit."

"People understand when you make a mistake."

"I dunno. With some people, it's all about results. You get the results, or you don't. And if you don't . . ."

"If you don't?"

He showed her a crooked smile. "You're screwed, blued, and tattooed."

"You've already got the tattoo."

"Yeah, you're right about that, Sandi from Mission Viejo." He looked her over. "How old are you?"

"Excuse me?"

"I'm twenty-six. You gotta be, what, thirty?"

At least he'd underestimated. "Something like that. Why do you ask?"

"I don't usually go for older women."

She reminded herself of all the reasons why she couldn't splash her drink in his face. "You don't?"

"Nah. Guys who're into that—they got, like, a mother complex, you know?"

"I'm *not* old enough to be your mother."

"Yeah, I know. You got a nice body, too. Work out, I bet."

"Every day."

"I can tell. You get all buff, and you come to dumps like this to meet guys like me."

"Pretty much."

"Scary hobby."

"I guess I need a certain amount of stimulation to stay interested in things. You know what I mean?"

"Not really."

"I need the rush. I need to put it on the line sometimes. You ever feel like that?"

Dylan got it. He nodded, his grinning mouth flecked with suds. "Baby, all the time."

"What gives you a rush?"

"You tell me first. Tell me what turns you on."

"Places like this."

"This?" He snorted. "This is a shit hole."

"That's why I like it. It's not safe."

"No, it ain't." He showed her a wolfish leer. "Getting less safe all the time."

She managed to hold eye contact without barfing. "That's why I'm liking it better all the time. So what's *your* poison?"

"What I did today," he said slowly.

He got off on killing. Great. "What did you do today?" she asked with bland innocence.

He shook his head, remembering that the topic was off-limits. "Nothing."

"So you won't share?"

He cast around for something safe to say. "I like to ride. Got a Harley Low Rider."

"That's a good bike."

"Better'n good." He stared into the depths of the mirror. "Way I got her customized, she's a thing of fucking beauty. Sweeter'n a woman, for sure."

"I don't know about that."

"I do. Woman's good for a couple hours, tops. My bike can go all night long."

"You ride all night?"

"Sometimes. When I can't sleep, I take her out on the freeway or down to the coast highway and fly, fly, fly."

"Sounds like fun."

He turned to her. "You ever ride a Harley?"

"Can't say I have."

He got off the barstool and drained his beer. "Come on, then. You want adventure, I got the ticket."

26

He gave her his helmet and rode without one, and she clung to his back as he cut through the streets to the freeway and howled up the on-ramp, whipping from lane to lane, everything blurred and spinning in a rush of speed and noise. The engine roared, throbbing like a racing heart, and the wind blew into her face while his sleeveless jacket beat against her throat, and the tattoo on his neck strobed in the passing headlights. She held on tightly to him, knowing that if she let go, she would be blown out of her seat and smashed on the road. He was drunk and angry and reckless, driving like a madman, and Abby was aware of the danger but accepted it without fear. She wasn't going to die in a drunk-driving accident; it would be too mundane.

He flew south on the freeway for miles, down to San Clemente, then doubled back and took an exit. On South Standard Avenue, he pulled into the parking lot of a dingy apartment building and killed the engine.

"Come on in," he said. They were the first words he'd spoken in nearly an hour. He led her up a flight of bowed wooden steps and unlocked his door.

Everything was proceeding as planned. Once inside his apartment, she would ask for a drink. He would pour glasses for both of them. While he was distracted, she would lace his beverage with one of the little white pills in her purse. The pills were Rohypnol, sometimes known as the date rape drug—a medication illegal in the U.S., but obtainable by those with connections.

The newer version of the drug turned blue when it dissolved, making it harder to conceal in liquids, but Abby's stash was the original variety, which dissolved clear.

The sedative would take effect within twenty minutes, knocking him out. The trick would be to keep him talking until the narcotic had spread through his bloodstream, but that was no big problem. If there was one thing Abby was good at, it was talk.

She would have to be careful, of course. During the ride she'd shifted her hold on his waist once or twice. She'd felt the handgun in the side pocket of his jacket.

She followed him in. He flipped a wall switch that turned on a pair of lamps flanking a futon. The apartment was sparsely furnished, dirty, and old. There were the usual accoutrements. A TV with what looked like a bootleg cable hookup. A stereo system that no doubt bothered the neighbors when it was cranked up to top volume, but the neighbors, of course, would be too intimidated to complain. A card table and folding chairs that served as a dinette set.

A doorway led into a kitchen that looked small and carried the stale odor of grease even at a distance. There must be a bathroom somewhere, and there might be a bedroom, too, unless the futon served as his bed.

"Nice place," she said.

"Yeah, it's a regular Taj Mahal." He showed her a crooked grin. "I'm going to fuck your lights out—you know that?"

"I kind of figured that was the idea," she said mildly, and then he grabbed her.

It happened so fast she had no time to react. His big arms were around her waist, and he was crushing her against his chest, his mouth on hers, his tongue probing, while his hands slid to her buttocks and squeezed hard.

She broke away from the kiss, gasping. "Hey, let's cool it, Dylan. Let's—"

"Shut up."

He pivoted sideways, carrying her with him, and she noticed for the first time how strong he was, strong enough to lift her off her feet and throw her down on the futon, and then he was on top of her, a huge, hungry smile on his face. But what she focused on was the scorpion, purple and swollen, clinging to the side of his neck. It repulsed her.

"You like adventure, bitch?" His hands were already working the button fly on his jeans. "You got a special one coming tonight."

Her purse was on the floor, dropped when he tossed her on the futon, and out of reach.

"This isn't the way I want it," she said.

"Tough shit."

"A girl likes a little foreplay—"

"I *know* what you like, and I got it right here, ten inches of it. I could be a fucking porn star. Give it a feel. Go on, feel me."

Reluctantly she extended her arm beneath his belly and felt what he had down there, a grotesque, monstrous thing, like a length of rope uncoiling from the bristles of his crotch.

"It ain't even waked up yet," he said proudly. "You wait till it's full-grown."

She was not anticipating that development with relish. Already she could feel it expanding with a stiff pressure that made her want to gag.

"Gonna do you good, woman," Dylan whispered. "When I get done, you won't never want no other man. They're all pygmies compared to me."

Pygmies, Abby thought, *but mental giants.*

She couldn't allow this to go much further. There had been a few times in her career when she'd no choice but to do the nasty with a man she was investigating, but those cases had been rare, and none of those men, despite their assorted mental problems, had been anywhere near as disgusting as young Dylan, with his insect tattoo and his hoselike appendage.

Besides, the bastard had tried to kill her a few hours

ago, and she was damned if she would help him get his rocks off now.

She let her hand slip a little lower, cupping his balls, caressing them to increase their sensitivity.

"That feels all right," Dylan said.

"Yeah?" she whispered. "How does *this* feel?"

She made a fist, crushing his scrota. He blanched, breath whistling out of him in a gasp.

She released his crotch, and with both hands she grabbed him by the neck, digging her thumbs into the carotid sheaths. There was a nice medical term for this procedure—sanguineous strangulation, otherwise known as a blood choke. However you said it, it simply meant stopping the flow of blood to the brain.

Dylan's face flushed. She wrapped her legs around him, pinning his arms to his sides so he couldn't draw his weapon. Another second or two was all it would take.

His eyes rolled up in his head, and he nodded on her chest with a drawn-out groan as unconsciousness took him.

She disentangled herself from his slack limbs. "Sorry, Dylan," she said. "Maybe next time."

27

Dylan came back to himself slowly, with a pounding headache and a weak, hungover feeling. His arms and legs were sore, and there was a dull ache in his neck. He opened his eyes and saw a white ceiling with cobwebs in the corners. It took him a moment to realize that he was in his own apartment, stretched on his back on the futon, and *she* was watching him.

Sandi from Mission Viejo.

She knelt before the futon, a gun in her hand. Instinctively he searched for his own weapon. Gone.

"What's the matter, Dylan?" she asked. "Don't you recognize your own gun when you see it?"

He focused on the pistol she was holding. His piece. The Glock 9mm he carried on the street.

"What the fuck is this?" he asked, his voice thick, his throat raw and scratchy. "You robbing me or something?"

"No, Dylan. I'm not robbing you."

"What'd you do, knock me out?"

"Yes."

"Shit." He released a thin laugh. "Guess you really do like adventure, just like you said."

"I'm not in this for adventure. There are things you need to tell me."

"What kind of things?"

"About the Scorpions. About who arranged your assignment this afternoon. And where you stashed your gear afterward."

His eyes narrowed. "You a cop?"

"No."

"Some kind of PI?"

"Who I am isn't important. I want you to start talking."

"That's not gonna happen."

"Yes, it is. You're going to answer every question I ask."

"Or what? You'll shoot me?"

"I'll hurt you."

He lifted his head, experiencing a brief wave of vertigo.

"Sandi from Mission Viejo, or whoever the fuck you are—you are in way out of your depth."

"I'll be the judge of that."

"Let me give you the best advice you'll ever get. Walk away."

"You're the second person tonight to tell me that. I didn't listen the first time. I'm not listening now."

"You're not listening, and I'm not talking. Sounds like a goddamned stalemate to me."

"You'll talk."

"Just because you laid me out on this couch don't mean you've made me your bitch. I know how to keep my mouth shut. Now, why don't you put that gun down and we'll get back to that lovin' feeling?"

"You're an asshole," she said, and she leaned forward and smacked him hard across the jaw with the butt of the gun. Pain startled him. He dropped back on the futon, clutching his mouth, which was suddenly full of warm fluid and splintered chips. Gagging, he rolled sideways and spit out the mess, staining the carpet with blood and broken teeth.

The pain was no big deal, but the teeth really bothered him. He had a nice smile, and now she'd fucked it up.

"Cunt," he growled, the word coming out a little slurred.

She hit him again. This time she caught him on the nose, snapping his head sideways with a sharp crack and a spurt of blood and mucus.

"God*damn* it!" He held his nose while a shooting migraine worked its way deep into his forehead.

"Feeling talkative yet?"

He looked up at her. She wasn't kneeling anymore. She had stood up and was leaning over him, the gun poised for another blow. He calculated the odds of lunging for it, snatching it out of her hand. Even as he did, he saw her smile as if she had read his mind. The smile seemed to dare him to try it. He didn't have the nerve.

"Who the fuck are you working for?" he said. His voice sounded funny in his ears, like it was echoing around inside his head.

"I don't work for anybody. I'm a free agent."

"Yeah, well, you ever need a job, you can get one. How'd you like to shake down guys who're behind on their dues?" He started to laugh; he didn't know why. It just seemed funny to him. "Hired muscle. All ninety-eight pounds of you."

"I'm not in the mood for comedy, Dylan. I'm feeling very serious right now. I think you should start to feel the same."

"It's the old lady, right? The one in the Valley. She must've hired you."

"Nobody hired me. Tell me who arranged the hit. Who sent you to that address?"

"I think it was Santa Claus. He has this list, you know—who's been naughty and nice. Guess the old lady was one of the naughty ones."

She struck him again. The gun hooked him under the jaw and clacked his teeth together hard enough to rattle his head. Then she was bending in close with the muzzle of the gun pressed below the socket of his left eye.

"Who sent you?" she asked again.

Her face was inches from his. He stared into her brown eyes and saw something that scared him, something like craziness. All of a sudden he wasn't so sure he would be getting out of this.

"You know I can't talk about that," he said, trying for the first time to sound reasonable. "They'll kill me."

"They're not here. I am. Worry about me right now."

"Lady, you got my attention. But you don't know what they do to snitches."

"I have a pretty good idea. Let me make it easier for you. Whoever hired you—does he work out of the repair shop?"

"How'd you even know about that?"

"Give me a name."

Still he hesitated.

She pressed the gun deeper into his skin. "I'm going to find out eventually. When I do, they'll assume you told me. So you're up shit creek whether you say anything or not. If you talk, you get to live through tonight. If you don't talk, then you die right now."

Her eyes, blank and cold like the eyes of a shark, told him she wasn't kidding.

"Shanker," he whispered, feeling like Judas delivering his fatal kiss.

"He runs the shop?"

"Yeah, it's his outfit. Ron Shanker. He's been a made man in the gang for—I don't know, since before I was born."

"How'd he get in touch with you?"

"Phone call."

"This phone?" She gestured toward a phone on a table near the TV.

"No, he called my cell. Left a message."

"And how did you call him back?"

"From here."

"The landline?"

"Yeah." Dylan licked his lips and tasted blood. "I don't like to talk business over a cell. Too many ways the call can be intercepted. What difference does it make, anyway?"

"It's called evidence, Dylan. Records of those phone calls will link you with Shanker. But Shanker didn't decide to pull this job on his own. He was asked to do it. You know that, don't you?"

"I don't know shit about how it was set up. Shanker never tells us anything."

"Do you know who Jack Reynolds is?"

Dylan knew. Everybody in the Scorpions had heard rumors about Jack Reynolds. He kept his face expressionless, or so he hoped. "Never heard of him."

"He's your congressman."

"I don't follow politics too much."

"Reynolds is tight with your gang, isn't he? He's a player?"

"Telling you, I never heard—"

She drew back the gun, and although he hated himself for it, Dylan flinched. Flinched like a whipped dog. He couldn't believe she'd reduced him to that.

"Tell the truth," she said, and the terrible thing was that the words were spoken without anger, without any emotion at all, as if she was feeling nothing and would feel nothing even if she battered his face into a bloody mask.

"Okay, I hear things. Reynolds, you know, he used to be the DA around here, a long time ago, and I guess he got in with the Scorpions back then, and maybe he still uses us sometimes for some, you know, odd jobs, but nobody ever talks about it, not out in the open—I mean it's not like we ever say his name. . . ." He was talking too much. All of a sudden he couldn't stop talking.

"The job you did this afternoon was for Reynolds."

"I don't know about that. I just don't know. They don't tell me shit like that."

"Do you even know the name of the woman you were hired to kill?"

"Never gave me a name. Just an address."

"Where's the gun?"

"What?"

"The gun you shot up the house with."

"Threw it away."

"Not likely. It was an expensive piece. Too expensive to toss. Besides, you're not smart enough to toss it." The muzzle of her gun was teasing the orbit of his eye socket again. "Where is it?"

Dylan thought about telling her to fuck herself. She would probably shoot him, but hell, it would be quick, bullet in the eye, right through into the brain, lights out. Better than what he could expect from Shanker. Or from Reynolds, for Christ's sake. Word was, that guy was a straight maniac. He could save himself a world of hurt just by telling this cocksucking bitch to go fuck off.

"In my bedroom," he said. "Bureau. Top drawer."

She almost smiled. "I'm surprised this shit hole has a bedroom."

Unaccountably, Dylan was wounded. "You said it wasn't such a bad place."

"I lied. I do that a lot."

"So you got Shanker's name and the gun and, I guess, the phone records. I gave you everything you wanted, right?"

"You cooperated. Eventually."

"So what happens now?"

"That's a good question, Dylan. That's the first really intelligent thing you've said. What does happen now?" She hadn't removed the gun from his face, and that was a bad sign. "I guess I'll have to give all this helpful information and evidence to the authorities."

"Yeah. Except you don't work for no authorities, do you?"

"Sometimes they work for me—without knowing it."

"So you're gonna have me arrested. Is that the plan?" At the moment, being arrested didn't seem like such a bad deal.

"Well, that's the thing. See, if you're in custody, you'll talk. I've already discovered that it's not too hard to make you open up. I didn't even have to break any of your fingers." Her mouth stretched briefly into a grin that scared him. "You'll tell them all about me, which will put me right in the spotlight. I don't like the spotlight, Dylan."

He swallowed. "You don't?"

"I'm a very private person."

He was thinking fast, or trying to think, but it was hard, because all at once his mind was crowded with thoughts, a million thoughts, memories of the jobs he'd done, the people he'd killed, the wet smack of his bullets in their flesh.

"Maybe," he said, fighting to control the tremor in his voice, "maybe you can give me a couple hours to haul ass out of town. Then they won't pick me up. They'll get Shanker because of the phone numbers. But Shanker don't know nothing about you, so he can't blow your cover. That'll work out. Work out for both of us."

She seemed to consider it. Dylan allowed himself to feel a thrill of optimism. Then her eyes narrowed, and he knew she had never given it any thought.

"What makes you think I want things to work out for you?" she asked, her voice dangerously gentle.

Dylan was silent. He had no answer to that.

He was in trouble, real trouble, the worst trouble of his life. This woman was a hard case. She was crazy, and she could blow him the fuck away without thinking twice about it.

She removed the gun from his face, but he took no comfort from that fact. Her expression was unchanged, and the coldness in her eyes was deeper than before.

As he watched, she took a pillow from the futon and wrapped it around the gun. He knew what that was for. To muffle the shot. She didn't want his neighbors to hear it. She wanted to kill him and get away clean.

The pillow made it fully real—what was about to happen to him. His heart shuddered with an electric jolt. He felt his hands trembling and willed them to stop, but they wouldn't stop. His stomach was sour, his bowels dangerously loose.

He had always figured he would go down fighting. Die like a man. But he couldn't seem to control his body anymore. He couldn't even muster the physical coordination to get off the futon. He couldn't do a damn thing.

"Hold on, okay?" he breathed. "Just hold on."

"The world isn't going to miss you, Dylan. I can pretty much guarantee that."

"You don't want to do this."

"I think I do." Her tone was flat, matter-of-fact.

"What I did in the Valley—it was a job, okay? Just a job."

Her gaze drilled through him. He felt his pants getting wet and knew he had crapped in his shorts, and they would find him that way, and they would laugh.

"We're both pros, you know?" He had to find a way to reach her. "I was doing a job. Like you."

Something flickered beneath her surface calm. "I'm not like you."

"Don't do this. Please?" He heard the terrible whining quality in his voice, and it sickened him.

"Quiet, Dylan."

"Don't do it. God, please, don't fucking kill me."

"Quiet," she said again, her voice so low as to be nearly inaudible. "Quiet now."

28

Reynolds awoke in darkness, which resolved itself into the office at his home. Vaguely he was surprised to find himself there. Then he remembered the time he'd spent with Rebecca, and how he'd left her curled on the floor and shaking, her midsection and thighs and upper arms purple with bruises. Having released his frustration, he'd felt calm, almost sleepy, as he drove home. He hadn't bothered going upstairs. He had retreated into his office for another Scotch, consumed it in the dark, and nodded off behind his desk.

The luminous clock at his desk read three thirteen a.m. And a phone was ringing.

His cell. He'd flung it into a corner after hearing from Shanker.

Maybe Shanker was calling back. Maybe he'd found a way to get the job done, after all.

He left his chair and searched the darkness until he retrieved the phone, then pressed TALK.

"Yeah?" he said, hearing both anger and desperate optimism in his voice.

"How's it hanging, Jack?"

It wasn't Shanker. It was Abby Sinclair.

He blinked. "Do you know what time it is?" The question was absurd—of course she knew—but it was the only thing he could think of to say.

"It's coming up on three fifteen. Gee, I really hope I didn't wake you."

"What the fuck do you want?"

"To do you a favor. Well, not so much a favor as

an act of reciprocal generosity. The old mutual back-scratching, first popularized by our primate ancestors."

There was something funny about her voice. She was speaking too fast, her words racing, her voice jumpy. Like she was on drugs or something. Or rattled, maybe.

Yes. He thought that was it.

Sinclair was scared.

"You're not making much sense," he said quietly, allowing all emotion to drain from his voice, setting his composure as a contrast to her panic.

"Sorry. Sometimes I start communicating in my own private language, you know. Like James Joyce, only without the artistry. Or the accent."

"What are you driving at?"

"What I'm driving at, Jack, is a bargain. A hard bargain, but one that will be beneficial to us both."

"Go on."

"Not over the phone. Some things need to be discussed face-to-face. I want a meeting. Tomorrow. You can fit me into your schedule, I'm sure. Get Moneypenny to arrange it. You know, your standoffish secretary."

"She's not my secretary. She's my constituent services coordinator."

"Well, I'm not a constituent, but I can do you a service—in exchange for certain considerations."

"There's nothing you can do for me."

"Wrongo, Jacko. I can do plenty. Are you going to meet with me or not?"

"We can meet privately in the morning—"

"Privacy isn't what I had in mind. No offense, Congressman, but I trust you about as much as—well, as any other politician. Especially after that stunt you pulled a few hours ago. You know, the jackbooted thugs goose-stepping through Andrea's bungalow like it was Poland circa nineteen thirty-six."

"Nineteen thirty-nine," Reynolds corrected automatically.

"Point is, I know what you're capable of."

He doubted that. He really did.

Of course he wasn't surprised that she'd heard about the attack on Andrea's house. It had been a top news story. And she wouldn't have needed much imagination to peg him as the one responsible.

But something more than that must have happened. Something that was testing the limits of her self-control.

"Are you sure you're all right, Miss Sinclair?" he asked.

"No. I'm not all right. I am, in the words of a recent acquaintance of mine, screwed, blued, and tattooed. I'm in a jam. It's only going to get worse. But you're going to help me out of it."

"What kind of jam?"

"The kind I could go to jail for. Which is all you're going to hear about it, because it's irrelevant. What's relevant is that I can solve your problems along with my own."

"And how can we do that?"

"Are we going to meet or not? I want people around. I want a crowd."

"I'm hosting a barbecue at my house for some of my more well-heeled constituents. It starts at noon. There should be at least two hundred guests. Is that enough of a crowd for you?"

"It'll do."

"Good. I'll have my campaign manager, Mr. Stenzel, put you on the guest list."

"Not under my real name. Any media going to be there?"

"One or two stringers, maybe."

"Have him put me on the media list under the name Wanda Klein. I'm with, uh, *Gold Coast Magazine.*"

"You'll need a press pass to get by security."

"That's not a problem."

"You still haven't told me how you can help me."

"Haven't I?" He heard her draw a deep, frightened breath. "Okay, then, Jack. How's this? I can give you

Andrea Lowry. I can deliver her right into your hands."

Click, and the call was over.

Reynolds stared into the darkness. Then slowly he began to laugh.

29

Abby lay in bed, awake but unwilling to rise and face the daylight beyond her bedroom window. She wasn't sure how much sleep she'd gotten—three or four hours, maybe. Not good sleep, either, but the restless, troubled kind. Last night she'd been too exhausted even to shed her clothes, spotted with blood from Dylan's broken nose. She was still wearing them now. They felt pasted on, a second layer of skin.

Finally she swung out of bed. She was thinking about running the shower and making it hot, very hot, when her cell phone rang.

"Hell," she muttered, not in a conversational mood. She picked up her purse and found her cell. "Abby Sinclair."

"We need to talk." It was Tess.

Abby managed a smile. "Miss me already?"

Tess didn't acknowledge the remark. Apparently she wasn't in the mood for banter, either. "There's a park on the bluffs in Santa Monica. You know the one I mean?"

"Palisades Park."

"Meet me there at Ocean Avenue and Wilshire Boulevard. Half hour."

"I'm not sure I can—"

Tess had already hung up.

"—make it that soon," Abby finished, speaking only to herself. She checked the clock: eight forty-five. Early for a phone call. Her friend at the FBI was pretty revved up about something. Three guesses what it was.

She got out a clean outfit, not bothering with the

shower. She stripped, then studied herself in the mirror. The bruises from her dustup with Leon Trotman were still visible, along with a couple of new contusions, courtesy of Dylan. No cuts, no scrapes. None of the blood on her clothes was hers.

That's how you know if you've had a good night, Abby thought. *If none of the blood is yours.*

It was what she'd always told herself. Now she knew it was a lie. Last night had not been good. Not good at all.

Tess drove to Palisades Park in her Bureau car, wondering how she was supposed to feel.

Scared, she decided. Scared of what she might be about to learn.

She wasn't quite sure why the prospect frightened her. Abby had never been a friend in a true sense. More like a sometime ally, whose deepest motives were hidden, whose agenda was purely her own.

But while Tess hadn't ever fully trusted Abby, she had thought she could count on her. No, that didn't make sense. Or maybe it did. She could count on Abby to do the right thing by her own standards, and though Abby's standards were more lax than her own, they were real and predictable. There were limits to what she would do. There were boundaries. Or so Tess had thought.

She might have been wrong.

The phone in her hotel room had started clamoring at five thirty. It was Hauser, calling to summon her to an emergency squad meeting at six a.m. She asked what had happened, but Hauser said only, "Get over here."

Even while she threw on clothes and retrieved her government-issue sedan from the hotel parking lot, she was fighting off an ugly suspicion at the back of her mind. But she didn't begin to believe it until she was seated in the conference room with twenty other agents, Crandall among them, while Hauser handed out crime scene photos taken by the Santa Ana PD.

"The victim's name was Dylan Garrick," Hauser said. "At about two thirty a.m. he was shot twice in the face at close range. Apparently the weapon was his own gun—a Glock nine, wrapped in a pillow to muffle the report. Even so, someone heard the shot and called it in. Police responded and found the door open—no indication of forced entry—and Garrick dead in the living room. Garrick was known to local authorities as a member of a biker club called the Scorpions. He had the gang logo tattooed on his neck, as you can see."

The insect design was clearly visible in several of the photos. A distinguishing mark if ever there was one.

"Assumption is that somebody offed him on gang-related business—someone he knew, since the door wasn't forced. In Santa Ana this is all pretty routine. But when they searched the place, they turned up a gun in the bedroom, H and K MK-23, with a military clip holding forty-five-caliber plus-P hollow points."

Tess flipped to photos of the gun in a bureau drawer.

"As you know, the crew who broke into Andrea Lowry's house were shooting forty-five plus-P JHPs. Our Santa Ana office was notified. We matched the gun to one of the weapons that left bullets in Andrea Lowry's drywall. Dylan Garrick was one of the shooters."

"They popped him because he screwed up the hit," someone offered. "Penalty for failure."

"That's what we're thinking."

It wasn't what Tess was thinking. She shifted in her chair.

Hauser noticed her restlessness. "Question, Agent McCallum?"

Actually, there was something she wanted to ask. "You said the gunshot was called in. Who made the call?"

"Anonymous female," Hauser said.

"Didn't they trace the call?"

"They did. To a pay phone down the street, which

suggests that our caller really did not want to be identified. Assuming the caller is a neighbor, she left the building to make the call. Muffled her voice, too—like she was talking through her hand."

"Why take all those precautions?"

Hauser shrugged. "The neighborhood's not one where there's a very good rapport between the police and the local citizenry. People don't want to get involved."

"Then why call it in at all?"

"Hell if I know. You have any ideas?"

None that she wanted to share.

Hauser finished his review of the facts by saying that Santa Ana police had already rounded up a number of Scorpions, including the pair who ran with Garrick. "And they picked up a guy who owns a cycle repair shop, name of Ronald Shanker, who runs the club. It's a good bet either Shanker zipped Garrick personally or he knows who did. So far nobody's talking."

"There any connection between the Scorpions and Reynolds?" asked a voice at the back of the room.

"I don't know the answer to that. It'll be up to you fine people to find out."

Tess wasn't sure she wanted to find out. But of course she had to know. She had to know everything.

And the first thing she needed to learn was Abby's whereabouts last night.

She arrived at Palisades Park and slipped the sedan into a space at the curb, then waited on the lawn, flicking glances at her wristwatch. Abby was late. If she failed to show up, it would be as good as an admission of guilt.

"You're looking a little squirrelly, Tess." The voice made her jump. Abby, behind her. The woman had some kind of knack for sneaking up on people.

"You're late," Tess said.

"Got here ASAP. I'm surprised you even know about this place."

Tess led her farther from the street, away from passersby. "I came here during the Mobius case to get away from people and think things through. I'd been working a crime scene across the street at the MiraMist."

"Oh, right. Mobius killed somebody in that hotel."

"Yes. And I ended up staying there the next time I was in town. In fact, I'm staying there now."

"Then I guess it's true. There really is no such thing as bad publicity." They had reached the walkway at the edge of the bluff, overlooking the coast highway and the beach. "I assume there's an urgent reason for calling me here at this ungodly hour?"

Tess wasn't quite ready to get into that. "Did I wake you? I thought you'd be the type to get up early."

"Usually I am. But I guess the shoot-out at the OK Corral left me a little keyed up. I was up half the night. Hey, that reminds me of a joke. You hear about the agnostic, dyslexic insomniac? He lies awake at night wondering if there's a dog."

She paused for a laugh. Tess didn't oblige.

"Tough room," Abby said.

"So is that the only reason you're tired?" Tess asked.

"Do I need another one?"

"Where were you last night, Abby?"

"With you, at the Boiler Room. Remember?"

"I mean, where did you go after you left the diner?"

"Home."

"Really?"

"Really. Where else would I go?"

That is the question, Tess thought. "I'm wondering if you didn't try to hunt down the shooters."

"Hey, didn't we already have this conversation? And didn't I tell you I'd love to find the bastards, but I don't know where to look?"

"Yes. You said all that."

"So what is this, *Groundhog Day*?"

Tess frowned. "What?"

"Bill Murray, Andie MacDowell, Punxsutawney Phil, same day over and over . . ."

Tess shook her head, uncomprehending.

Abby shrugged. "I forgot. You're not a movie fan."

"I don't have time for movies."

"Everybody has time for movies. Movies are what life is all about."

"I'll keep that in mind. Now I—"

"By the way, did it ever occur to you that Bill Murray's two most famous movies both feature rodents? Gopher in *Caddyshack,* groundhog in *Groundhog Day.*"

"That's very interesting, but—"

"If I were his agent, I would insist that he never do another movie without a rodent in it."

"Abby—"

"He could do a remake of *Fantasia*, maybe. That one had Mickey Mouse."

"So I recall. Now—"

"Or *The Green Mile.* Or *Of Mice and Men.* That's a classic. Speaking of classics, last time we worked together you told me you'd never seen *The Godfather.* That still true?"

Tess had lost control of the conversation, as she always did with Abby. "Haven't gotten around to it."

"Big mistake. Suppose you get killed in the line of duty. Your last thought will be, 'Darn it, I never saw *The Godfather.*' "

"I seriously doubt that."

"It's the things we never did that we regret most."

Tess tried to regain the initiative. "How about you, Abby? What are *your* regrets?"

"Well, I never learned to tap-dance. Or was it lap dance? I always get those two confused."

"Nothing more . . . immediate?"

"Is this the part where I confess my sins and you prescribe forty Hail Marys?"

"It's the part where I ask you again about your whereabouts last night."

Abby released a theatrical sigh. "I was home alone. Like Macaulay Culkin, which is another movie reference you're not going to get."

"Alone. So no one can back you up on that?"

"I share my condo with a collection of stuffed animals, but they're not talking. Why do I need an alibi?"

"Last night one of the shooters from Andrea's house was killed."

Tess watched Abby's reaction. She saw what might have been surprise, or only a very good simulation of it.

"You're not just saying that to make me feel better, I hope," Abby said.

"This isn't something to joke about."

"No, it's something to celebrate. Where did it happen?"

"At the victim's apartment in Santa Ana."

"He was no victim."

Tess gave her a sharp look. "He was, in this case."

"How do you know he was one of the hit men?"

"The Bureau has an RA in Santa Ana. A resident agency. Satellite office."

"I know the lingo."

"Since Reynolds's home base is Orange County, and we assumed he was connected to the home invasion, we told the Santa Ana office to be alert for any activity that could be tied to the case. They heard about the killing from the local PD."

"Don't tell me. *PD* stands for *police department*."

"The Santa Ana office had the victim's gun tested against some rounds dug out of Andrea's walls. They made a ballistics match."

"So this is good news. Just link this guy to Reynolds, and case closed."

"We don't think it'll be that easy. The shooter was probably working through an intermediary. He belonged to a biker gang called the Scorpions. Ever hear of them?"

"Nope."

"They're centered in Santa Ana."

"Reynolds's brownshirts?"

"Could be—although there's no known connection."

"He may have just been discreet." Abby smiled. "Well, I appreciate the heads-up."

"It's more than a heads-up, Abby."

"You don't seriously think I squashed this Scorpion?"

"So you didn't fire the shot that killed him?"

"Yes, I did. I mean no. No, I didn't. Oh, God, you've gotten me so confused—"

Tess ground her teeth. "Very funny."

"Look, I understand your concern. This guy came perilously close to nailing my ass. That burns me. I don't like spending my Friday nights dead. It's bad enough there's never anything good on TV."

"Can we stick to the subject?" Tess interrupted.

"The subject is me and my absence of guilt. Yes, I had motive. But I didn't have opportunity."

"If you'd had the opportunity, would you have shot him?"

"I make it a practice never to answer hypotheticals."

"Answer this one."

Abby took a moment to think about it. In a low voice she said, "Maybe."

"You would kill an unarmed man in cold blood?"

"Blood's warm, not cold. I've never understood that expression."

"You'd be willing to kill," Tess pressed, "rather than turn him in to the police? To get street justice instead of the real thing?"

"Sometimes street justice *is* the real thing."

"I'm sorry you said that."

"I'm sorry you asked."

Tess turned away. "I'm heading down to the crime scene. I intend to investigate further."

Abby simulated a shiver. "Watch out, bad guys. Inspector McCallum is on the job."

"If there's anything you need to tell me, now is the time."

Abby gave her a bland stare. "I'm afraid I don't have any true confessions for you."

"So if I were to examine your hand, I wouldn't find GSR?"

"Is that a trick question? Of course you would. I fired Andrea's gun during the shoot-out. I've showered since then, but there are probably still some traces of unburned particulate."

It was a good answer. Tess had to accept it. "All right. Well, I have to get to Santa Ana."

"Ever been there?"

"No."

"One recent survey rated it the most economically and socially challenged metropolitan area in the United States. Take that, Flint, Michigan."

Tess shook her head slowly. "I just don't know if I can trust you."

"Google the survey and read it for yourself."

"I mean about Dylan Garrick."

"Is that the guy's name? Feels weird to put a name on him. Makes him more of a person."

"He *was* a person."

"A bad person." Abby's eyes were hard. "I'm not shedding any tears for some lowlife who tried to whack me."

"I can see that. You aren't lying to me about this, Abby—are you?"

Abby smiled. "Tess . . . you know I never lie."

30

You know I never lie.

Abby ordinarily had no qualms about lying. She did it all the time. It was an integral part of her job. In a certain sense, it *was* her job—pretending to be someone she wasn't.

But she didn't like lying to Tess. It felt like a betrayal. Abby had been on the wrong side of betrayal once or twice. She didn't like putting Tess in that position. But she had no choice.

The lie, of course, had been only a stopgap measure. It would buy her time, but not much. Tess wouldn't take long to find out that Dylan Garrick had left Fast Eddie's in the company of a woman matching Abby's description. Once Tess knew about that, things would get ugly.

Tess was a sort-of friend now. Soon she would be an enemy, and no sort-of about it. A dangerous enemy.

As she'd told Reynolds last night, she was in a jam. Still, she had a possible way out. It entailed risk, naturally. She wasn't afraid of risk. Desperate times, desperate measures, all that jazz.

She drove back to her condo and rode the elevator to the tenth floor. It took her half an hour to manufacture a press pass for the congressman's barbecue. There was nothing very complicated about it. She used a graphics program to paste her photo below the word *MEDIA*. The name *Wanda Klein*, along with Wanda's particulars, was printed beside the photo. *Hair: brown. Eyes: brown. Height: 5'7". Weight: 125 lbs.* She cheated on the date of birth, shaving three years off her age.

She added a long string of random digits that served as her ID number, and left a blank line for Wanda's signature.

The reverse side of the tag was taken up with a lot of authentic-sounding legalese about rights and liabilities, along with a phone number that supposedly could be called to verify Wanda's fake identification number. Abby wasn't expecting anyone to call the number, which was good, since it actually belonged to a Thai restaurant down the street.

She printed out the designs, glued them to the front and back of an old luggage tag, signed Wanda's name, and laminated the tag with a gizmo she'd picked up at an office supply outlet. The faux press pass slipped into the clear plastic pouch formerly used for the luggage tag. The pouch had prepunched holes, through which she threaded an extra-long shoelace. With the shoelace knotted behind her neck, and the tag dangling over her sternum, she would be a bona fide member of the Fourth Estate. Or as bona fide as she was ever likely to be, anyway.

The barbecue didn't start until noon. She had extra time before she had to head down to Newport, and she knew how she wanted to use it.

She had to talk to Andrea again.

At ten a.m. the phone in the kitchen rang. Andrea had reattached the phone jack after the media left, and so far she hadn't heard from them. Now it seemed her luck had run out. Well, she would let it ring. She wouldn't answer.

This strategy worked until she had counted fifteen rings, at which point she went into the kitchen with a sigh.

"Yes?" she said, prepared to hang up instantly if it was a member of the press.

"Ms. Lowry, this is Abigail Bannister at Williams-Sonoma. The item you ordered has just come in."

She recognized Abby's voice immediately, even before she registered the name. Obviously some kind of subterfuge was in play. "The item . . . ?" she said cautiously.

"Your garlic genius. You can pick it up at our store in the Beverly Center at your convenience."

"My garlic genius." The term meant nothing to Andrea. "I see."

"I hope we'll see you soon." Abby put a subtle emphasis on the last word.

Andrea got the message. "Yes, I'll be right over. Thank you."

She hung up and stood in the kitchen, frozen in place. The ruse Abby had employed—there had to be a reason for it. And the only reason Andrea could think of was that the phone was tapped.

She didn't think Jack Reynolds could tap her phone. Even a congressman's powers didn't extend that far.

But the FBI could do it.

They couldn't be eavesdropping on her. Could they?

And if they were, did it mean they knew more than they'd let on?

They might know who she really was. They might know everything.

And if they had tapped her phone, what else might they have done? They had been all over her house. They could have installed hidden cameras. They could be watching her right now.

A shiver ran through her. For a moment she was back in the hospital. People monitoring her twenty-four hours a day. No privacy. And no way out.

She'd thought she had escaped all that. Maybe she'd been wrong. Maybe there was never any escape. Not for her, not ever.

No. She refused to think like that. Those thoughts were dangerous. They would lead her back into insanity. They would twist her mind into chaos.

Nobody was watching her or listening. Nobody.

She found her purse and left the house through the carport door. When she motored down the street, she kept her gaze on the rearview mirror, alert for anyone who might be following.

31

"Where were you last night, Jack?"

Reynolds looked up from his morning coffee, which he had brewed at the unusually late hour of ten a.m. after a restless sleep, to see the unsmiling face of his wife.

"Went for a drive," he said evenly.

"You go for a lot of drives."

"It's how I relax. You know that."

"Yes. I know that. It's what you've always told me."

He didn't answer. He was scanning the *Orange County Register* for news on the incident in San Fernando. He'd already checked the *L.A. Times* and found no new information, only a rehash of the details televised on the late local news.

The *Register*'s story was given even less prominence, since the attack had taken place outside Orange County. The brief item appeared to be a patchwork of wire service reports augmented by a few local touches—chiefly references to the growing trend of home invasions in the region. There was nothing new.

"Why didn't you come up to bed after your drive?"

He was surprised Nora was still in the room. He'd assumed she'd already left the breakfast nook. They never took their meals together anymore.

"I fell asleep in my office," he said.

"Were you drinking?"

"I may have had a nip."

"You've been taking your share of nips lately."

"Campaign season. It's tiring."

"You know you're a shoo-in to get reelected."

"Still takes a lot out of me."

"Yes, hours of schmoozing. I know how much of a strain that is on you."

He disliked sarcasm. It implied that he was not being taken seriously. He put a sharper edge on his voice. "I guess it's easy for you. That's why you need your triple dose of Xanax to get through the day."

"I'm not on Xanax anymore."

"What is it now? Valium?"

"At least I have a prescription for what I take. I don't think any doctor prescribes a pint of Scotch as a cure-all."

"I could probably find one who would."

He started to fold the paper, then noticed an item near the home-invasion story. A member of the biker club known as the Scorpions had been found in his Santa Ana apartment, dead of "multiple gunshot wounds." The man's name was Dylan Garrick.

Reynolds didn't know any Garrick. But then, he knew almost none of the younger Scorpions. His contacts were with the old guard, the men he'd known when they were boys growing up with him.

Interesting that a Scorpion would be killed on the night of the failed hit on Andrea. If Garrick had something to do with the hit, he might have been aced as a penalty for failure.

"You know, Jack, if you find campaigning so stressful, perhaps you should give it up."

He was astonished that Nora was still present, still talking. This was turning into the lengthiest conversation he'd had with his wife in the past month.

"I'm not giving anything up," he said with a prickle of rage. "I earned everything I've got, and I intend to keep it."

"Even if it's driving you to drink?"

He got up, leaving his coffee half finished. "You don't understand me."

"I suppose not."

"Take your pills and get dressed. We have company coming."

He walked out of the breakfast nook and climbed the spiral staircase to his bedroom, where he slipped off yesterday's clothes, then showered and changed.

Give it up, she'd said. Give up his job, his position. Give up everything that made him who he was.

In a couple of hours he would have two hundred of Orange County's wealthiest power brokers gathered in his backyard for hot dogs, burgers, and potato salad. They weren't coming because they liked him. They were coming because they needed him. They needed his pull, his influence, his ability to do favors and cut through bureaucratic obstacles. Secretly they might despise him—most of them probably did—but they would show up anyway, wearing broad smiles and offering firm handshakes. They were his courtiers, fawning and kowtowing, laughing at his jokes, grateful for his hospitality, eager to please.

And Nora wanted him to abandon all this—and do what? Practice law? Sit on corporate boards? Play golf and watch his life go by?

Never. He would never give it up. He would do whatever was necessary to preserve his place in the system. He'd proved it many times—most recently when he'd ordered the elimination of Andrea Lowry.

He would prove it again soon, when he met with Abby Sinclair.

His cell phone rang. He answered and heard Rebecca's voice.

"I'm not coming to the barbecue, Jack."

Both of the women in his life were giving him trouble today. "Why the hell not?"

"Because of what you did to me last night."

He barely remembered doing anything. He'd driven to her place, had a little fun with her, worked out his aggressions. "What are you talking about?"

"I'm all bruised."

"You know I like it rough."

"Yes . . . I know what you like." Her voice was a whisper. "This is different. I'm *all* bruised, Jack. I'm black-and-blue all over. You really *hurt* me."

"How's your face?"

"My face?"

"You know, the thing that looks back at you from the mirror. Any bruises there?"

"No."

He always took care to avoid the face. "So what's the problem? You know what they say: Clothes cover a multitude of sins."

"My arms and legs—"

"Wear long pants and a long-sleeved shirt."

"It's August. It's eighty-five degrees outside."

"So it's eighty-five fucking degrees. Big deal. Break out your winter clothes."

"It's *summer*."

"I fucking *know* it's summer. People wear long sleeves in summer. No one is going to notice. Your problem is you think everybody's focused on you. People don't give a shit about anybody but themselves."

"Jack, you left me on the floor. I could hardly move—"

"I had some issues that were eating at me. I got a little out of control. It won't happen again." This was as close to apologizing as he would come. Somewhere he had picked up the motto of tough old John Wayne, who had an airport in Orange County named after him. *Never apologize and never explain; it's a sign of weakness.*

Rebecca's voice hardened. "I'm not coming, Jack. I don't want to see you today."

"You don't want to *see* me? The people at the barbecue are my constituents. They know you. They expect you to be here. And you *will* be here."

"Tell them I came down with something. Goodbye, Jack."

"You hang up the phone, and you'll regret it."

He said the words very softly, without melodrama, the way any serious threat should be delivered.

She stayed on the line. "I'm not coming," she said again, but with less certainty.

"You're going to put on your long-sleeved shirt and

your long pants and whatever else you need to look pretty, and you're going to be here with a smile on your face, telling my constituents how good it is to see them, and remembering all their names."

"And if I don't?"

"You think I hurt you last night. You don't know what hurt is."

Silence for a moment. "I'm not afraid of you," she said finally.

"Yes, you are. Now get dressed and haul your ass over here. I haven't got time for this bullshit. I have real problems to contend with."

He ended the call and stuffed the phone into his pants pocket.

Bruises. Jesus.

So he'd gotten her a little marked up. It wasn't like he'd broken any bones. Bruises would heal. In a few days, a week or two at most, she'd be wearing her summer clothes again.

Unless he decided to pound on her some more, teach her a lesson for her disloyalty, her lack of respect.

Maybe he would. But he had other lessons to teach first, starting with Andrea Lowry.

And after her, Abby Sinclair.

32

Andrea had never been inside the Beverly Center. Shopping malls were always so bright and so crowded, and years of darkness and isolation had left her afraid of places like that.

The drive there took thirty-five minutes. She left her car in a self-parking area and rode a dizzying series of escalators that climbed the outside of the building, enclosed in Plexiglas tubes. Were there FBI people somewhere behind her on the escalators? If so, she couldn't spot them when she glanced over her shoulder.

A map of the mall showed her the way to Williams-Sonoma, a store she had never visited in her life. As she entered, she caught sight of Abby browsing in the kitchenware section. In what she hoped was a casual manner, she sidled up next to Abby and pretended to look at a ridiculously overpriced toaster.

Abby spoke in a low voice without looking at her. "Thanks for coming."

"What's this about?"

"I'll tell you later."

"Is somebody watching me? Or listening—"

"We'll get into that. Right now I want you to pick up the item at the counter. It's already paid for, and it's in your name. Then go up to the food court on level eight and meet me in the ladies' room."

Andrea swallowed. "Okay." She almost moved away, then hesitated. "What exactly is a garlic genius?"

"It's this little handheld metal doohickey that

minces garlic cloves. No household should be without one."

Andrea found it easier to obey than to ask any more questions. She accepted the package from the sales-clerk and carried her shopping bag out of the store. Abby, she noticed, was already gone.

On the eighth floor, near a food court called Café L.A., she found the ladies' room. It was empty except for Abby, who handed her a cell phone as soon as she entered.

"Keep this turned on and with you at all times. It's how I can contact you and speak freely."

"So . . . someone *is* listening to my calls?"

"Yes."

"And watching my house? Following me?"

"Yes."

"Who? The FBI?"

"That's right."

"Oh, God. They know who I am." It was not quite a question.

"I'm afraid they do." Abby glanced at the door. "There are two agents tailing you now. I saw them window-shopping near Williams-Sonoma when I left."

"I didn't see anybody."

"You're not trained to see them. The good news is, they're both male."

"How is that good news?"

"If there was a woman on the detail, she might come in here. Our gentlemen friends will probably be discreet enough to stay outside." Abby gave her a discerning look. "You seem pretty frazzled. How are you holding up?"

"Not too well. I hardly slept at all, and when I did, I had these terrible dreams. I dreamed the men were breaking in again, with ski masks and guns, and you weren't there to protect me. . . ." She ran a hand through her hair, pulling distractedly at the locks.

"You don't need to worry about that now," Abby said. "No one's going to get into the house again. Not with the FBI looking out for you."

"Looking out for me." Andrea almost laughed. "Yes, sure. Until they decide to arrest me for using a false identity."

"You won't go to prison for that. And although the FBI may be somewhat interested in you, they're a lot more interested in Congressman Reynolds."

Andrea felt a rush of blood from her head. She held on to a sink to steady herself. "But they can't know. . . . They can't. . . ."

"They do."

"How can they? Nobody knows. I never told. . . ."

"Don't worry about that now. They know about it, and so do I. But you need to tell me something about your relationship with Reynolds."

"What?"

Before Abby could answer, the door opened and a woman walked in. The two of them busied themselves at the sinks, taking an inordinate amount of time to soap up and rinse off their hands before drying them. Finally the woman left. Abby picked up the conversation as if there had been no interruption.

"Any significant detail. Something that only you and he would know."

"Why do you need to know that?"

"Don't ask for whys and wherefores. I'm asking you to trust me. Which I guess you do, or you wouldn't be here."

"Yes. I do trust you." Andrea realized this was true. It was the first time in twenty years that she had trusted anyone. The thought seemed to lighten her burden just a little. "All right. When he and I were . . . dating, we used to meet a lot of times on his boat."

"Where was the boat?"

"In the marina at Newport Beach."

"What was the name of it?"

"*The Mariner.* It was an old boat he bought second-hand, and he used to call it the ancient *Mariner.* Funny how I remember that. I haven't thought of it in a long time."

For a moment the old days came back to her, the

liaisons at the marina, hours of intimacy in the cramped quarters belowdecks, then the quiet time afterward when, in darkness, they would share a drink under the stars and watch the water ripple against the mossy pylons of the dock.

She caught Abby watching her with sympathy. "We always have nostalgia," Abby said in a low voice, "even for the things we regret."

Andrea nodded.

"Thanks for the info," Abby added more briskly. "Now get a bite to eat at the food court. Otherwise your friends may wonder why you came up here. Then go home and stay put. And keep that phone close to you. I'll be calling later."

"You have some kind of plan, don't you?"

"I always have a plan." Abby hesitated. "In this case, I may need you to act fast."

"To do what?"

"To get away from the watchful eyes of the federal bureaucracy. Don't worry. It's easier than it sounds."

"I don't understand."

"You will, eventually. In the meantime you'll just have to go on trusting me, if you can."

"I can. It's just . . ."

"Just what?"

"I've done such bad things. I'm not sure I deserve your help."

"We've all done bad things. I know I have."

Andrea met her eyes. "Have you ever killed anyone?"

Abby didn't flinch. "Yes."

"Did they deserve it?"

"Yes."

"Well, that makes it all right, then."

"I'd like to think so."

Andrea looked away. "The ones I killed . . . they didn't deserve . . ."

"I know."

"What I did—it's something you go to hell for. I think about that sometimes. Being in hell."

"Seems to me you're already there."

"I'm only punishing myself, that's all."

"That can be the worst kind of punishment."

"I don't know. I'm not sure it's enough. I don't know if anything can ever be enough."

A beat of silence passed between them. "Andrea," Abby said quietly, "can I ask you something? You could've told the world about Jack Reynolds, ruined him, ended his career. But you never did."

"No, I didn't."

"Why not?"

"He got to me while I was in the hospital. He was the DA, and he used his credentials to get in and talk to me alone."

"And he threatened you?"

"No. What did he have to threaten me with? I'd already lost everything."

"Then what . . . ?"

"He told me—he told me he still loved me." Her voice broke on the last words. "He told me he'd been wrong to break up with me. That he'd been planning to take me back—until everything happened."

"Did you believe him?"

She heard the skepticism in Abby's question. "I know what you're asking. How could I be so naive?"

"Something like that."

"Well, I *did* believe him. He said he forgave me for the children. He said it was all right. He said I hadn't been myself when I did it. And that I shouldn't blame myself or think of it as a sin."

"I see."

"He's the only one who said anything like that. To everyone else I was the devil incarnate. Medea, the witch. But he told me it was all right. And they were *his* children. He's the last person who should ever have forgiven me—but he did."

"Yes." Abby's voice was very low. "He did."

"It wasn't just talk. He helped me, too. He arranged it so I was declared incompetent to stand trial. If I'd been put on trial, I would have been sent to prison for life. As it was, I went into the hospital, and I was out in twelve years. And because he'd filed an intent not to prosecute, the case can't be reopened."

"Yes."

"I never would have survived prison. Do you know what they do in there to—to people who've killed children? He saved my life."

"I guess he did."

Andrea sighed. "I'm sure you think he was just manipulating me. That he didn't want me in a courtroom because I might say too much. But you're wrong."

"Am I? Then why did he send those thugs into your house yesterday?"

She knew the answer to that. "Because I screwed up."

Abby looked at her. "You?"

"I started going to his events. I didn't think he would recognize me, not after all these years, with a wig and dark glasses. But he did. I broke the rules."

"What rules?"

"He promised to help me only if I gave my word I would never try to see him again."

"If you gave your word, why did you start . . . ?"

"Stalking him?" Andrea almost smiled.

"Attending his campaign rallies," Abby said diplomatically.

"I don't know. Something made me want to do it. It didn't make sense. It was like—like I couldn't stay away. Like I just *had* to see him." She was touching her hair again—a nervous habit, but one she'd never noticed before.

"Did you hope to get back together with him?" Abby asked.

A shudder coursed through her. "No. No, of course not. I knew that could never happen."

"Then . . . why?"

"I don't *know*, Abby. I just *don't.*"

"Okay, okay." Abby reached out to steady her. "Sorry I pushed. It's an occupational hazard for those of us with a psych degree. We keep trying to peel the onion."

Andrea wiped her eyes. "Peeling onions makes me cry."

"Yeah, I got that. But at least now you can mince garlic with no problem." This was a joke, but Andrea couldn't find the strength to smile. "Look," Abby said more seriously, "go home, lie down, close your eyes. Just keep that phone nearby and turned on."

"Okay. I still don't understand, though. I don't see what you could possibly need me for."

"It all comes back to you, Andrea. Everything comes back to you."

That was true, of course. Reynolds and the killers who invaded her home, and the FBI people watching her and tapping her phone, and Abby's involvement—all of it came back to her, and to what she had done twenty years ago, her ineradicable past, which she could never escape.

Abby seemed to catch her mood. She smiled. "Hey, no worries. I'm on the case. I'm handling everything."

"I wish I could be as confident as you are."

"It's a gift. Now get going. Those G-men must be getting antsy. And don't do anything to show you're onto them. Just act normal."

"Normal." This time Andrea did smile. "Yes, that's me."

She left the restroom, taking care not to look for the FBI men, as Abby had warned. But they were there, anyway. She knew it now, knew it even without seeing them.

They would always be there.

33

Tess arrived at the crime scene shortly before noon. The neighborhood was as unprepossessing as she'd expected. Crandall, in the passenger seat of the Bureau car, glanced up at the two-story apartment building in distaste.

"I lived in a place like this when I was starting my own business." His expression indicated that the memory wasn't a happy one.

"Didn't you start more than one business?"

"Three in all. No success with any of them. I guess I was meant to be a fed. It's in my genes."

"There are worse things to be."

"True. I could be a biker, like Dylan Garrick."

"You could be dead, like Dylan Garrick."

"That, too."

It was the most he'd said to her today. He still mistrusted her for keeping Abby's secrets. Tess couldn't really blame him, but he would have to work with her now. Hauser, trying to keep a low profile on MEDEA, hadn't wanted a swarm of L.A. agents descending on Santa Ana. He'd authorized only the two of them to check it out, while the rest of the squad worked the case from the field office in Westwood.

They climbed the stairs to Garrick's apartment, identifiable by the yellow crime scene tape across the door. Tess stripped away the tape and unlocked the door with a key she'd obtained from the Santa Ana resident agency.

From behind her on the landing, Crandall said,

"Carson wanted us to wait for him before we went in."

Carson was the supervisory agent who managed the RA. He'd been driving behind them when they left Civic Center Drive, but apparently they'd lost him along the way. Tess wasn't going to wait. "He'll be here soon enough. Let's look around on our own."

She pushed open the door and went in, trailed by Crandall. The first thing she saw was the bloody stain on the futon where Dylan Garrick's head had lain. There were spatter patterns on the wall. More dried blood was dimly visible on the soiled short-nap carpet. The body was gone, as were Garrick's handgun and the pillow used to muffle the two shots.

Criminalists had gone over the apartment, dusting for prints and bagging fibers and other trace evidence. Tess saw black ferric oxide on some surfaces, silver nitrate on others. The walls and larger objects in the room had been decorated in more elaborate shades, from gaudy Pinkwop and Redwop powders that were processed with a portable laser, to fluorescent greens and oranges that luminesced in ultraviolet light. Whoever dusted the place had been thorough. Tess wondered if Abby's prints had been among those collected.

In her career she had visited many crime scenes, enough of them to make the experience almost routine. But there was one she had never forgotten—the bedroom of the house she'd rented in a Denver suburb, where Paul Voorhees had been murdered by the serial killer Mobius.

Other shocks had shaken her life, but finding Paul was the one that lingered. She'd never felt the same about a murder scene. Other people could crack jokes and act casual in the presence of death. Not her. She stood in Dylan Garrick's apartment as she would stand in a church—hushed and solemn.

In one hand she carried a folder of crime scene photos from the morning conference. She slipped out a picture of the body and studied it, getting a better sense of how Garrick had been positioned. He'd been beaten before he was shot—pistol-whipped with his own firearm. The photo showed the damage to his face, including a broken nose that had left a trail of dried blood snaking down to his upper lip. The gun itself, dropped on the floor, had dried blood on the barrel.

Could Abby have hurt him that way? Cracked the gun across his face, crunching bone? Tess wanted to say no. Yet she couldn't forget Abby at the Boiler Room, carving her steak with grim enthusiasm, the knife gripped tight in her hand. She'd been riding a wave of rage and hate, and there was no telling how far she'd ridden it later that night.

Of course she'd denied everything. But she had no alibi. And although there was no obvious way for her to track down Garrick, she was resourceful. She could have figured something out. She could have come here.

If she had, she had come as Garrick's guest. The lock on the door had not been tampered with. Garrick had let her in—or come home with her. Typically, in her work with stalkers, Abby would arrange to meet the guy in some seemingly accidental way, ingratiate herself with him, gain access to his home. She wasn't above holding out the promise of sexual favors. She . . .

Tess looked more closely at the photo. "You see this?" she asked Crandall.

"What?"

"Garrick's pants. They're open. Unzipped."

Crandall shrugged. "Guys hang around with their pants open when they're alone. You know, for comfort. Not me," he added hastily, "but—some guys."

She barely heard him. She was thinking of Abby's MO. "Mmm."

"What does that mean?"

"It meant nothing. It was just *mmm.*"

Crandall started to ask something else. A voice from the doorway interrupted him.

"Crack the case yet?" It was Senior Supervisory Agent Dwight Carson, who'd finally arrived.

A tall, paunchy man testing the Bureau's weight limit, Carson was from somewhere down South originally, a fact he liked to advertise by putting a little extra corn pone in his voice when he remembered to. Tess found him friendly enough, but behind his geniality there was an agenda, of course. He had been left in the dark about MEDEA. He didn't know what the L.A. office was involved in. Naturally he wanted to know.

"Never seen this much interest in our friendly neighborhood Scorps before," he observed as he stepped inside. He called the bikers Scorps, apparently to save the effort of pronouncing the extra syllables.

"It's a zero-tolerance policy," Tess said mildly. "We're cracking down on premeditated homicides."

"Not really the Bureau's bailiwick."

"It is today."

"Evidently. Still seems like a lot of trouble to go to for a piece of"—he caught himself before cussing in front of a lady—"uh, piece of work like Dylan Garrick."

"Garrick is tied in to a home invasion in San Fernando."

"Sure, I know. Our office is the one that made the connection. But I can't see why VALSHOOT has so many people's panties in a twist."

VALSHOOT, short for Valley shooting, was the code name for the attack on Andrea Lowry's house. The incident could hardly have been code-named MEDEA without raising unwanted questions in Santa Ana.

"There are various considerations involved," Tess said, hoping this formulation would be sufficiently vague to discourage further curiosity.

It wasn't. "And one of those considerations required flying in Annie Oakley?"

"What?"

"No offense. That's what some of us call you around here."

"Annie Oakley." Tess shut her eyes. "Great."

"It's a compliment. Annie was a straight shooter and ahead of her time. One of the original women's libbers, you might say."

"Well, I guess it's better than Ma Barker."

"No one's gonna call you a barker," Carson said.

This was so cornball she would have laughed if she hadn't been in a room still smelling of cordite and blood. She steered their conversation in a more professional direction. "Can the shooter's height be determined by the angle of fire?"

Carson shook his head. "Crime scene people say the gunman was probably leaning over Garrick, bent low. Which means he could be any height."

He—or she, Tess thought.

"Both shots were fired at nearly point-blank range. No exit wounds. Coroner recovered the rounds inside the vic's head."

"You mean the autopsy's already been done?"

"It was put on a rush basis. Pretty fancy treatment for a dead gangbanger. I gather there was some pressure applied all the way from Washington." He gave Tess a shrewd look. "Though I don't know why D.C. would care so much."

"Neither do I," she said evenly.

"I'll just bet you don't."

It might have turned into a staring contest if Crandall hadn't cut in. "You were saying two rounds were recovered."

Carson looked away, conceding defeat—for now. "Right. Nine-millimeter hollow points. One of them was all mashed up and fragmented. Ricocheted around the skull cavity something fierce. The other's intact. Ballistics has already matched it to Garrick's gun."

Tess ran a finger through some Redwop powder on an end table. "I assume forensics picked up a lot of prints."

"Whole slew of them, but most probably belong to Garrick or the girls he brought up here. According to the neighbors there were quite a few. The prints sure as hell didn't get left by any housekeeper. Look at this rat's nest."

"How about the doorknob?" Crandall asked.

"Killer wiped it clean when leaving. He's a cool customer."

Tess thought wiping the knob was exactly the kind of precaution Abby would take.

"You want a guided tour?" Carson asked. He headed into the kitchen without waiting for their assents. "Lots of beer in the fridge, hard liquor in the cabinets. Nothing else in here but take-out containers and fast-food leftovers. No drugs on the premises. Garrick was busted for cocaine a few years ago, but lately he seems to have been staying clean."

"Not exactly turning his life around, though, was he?" Tess asked.

Carson led them down the hall. "He was still a stone-cold killer. Probably quit the coke because he couldn't afford a rep as a user. No one hires a hit man who's got an itchy nose."

They entered the bedroom. Carson waved a hand at a tall stack of magazines on the floor. "See those? Porn. And over here"—he directed their attention to homemade cabinets constructed of cinder blocks and planks—"a whole library's worth of X-rated videos. Agent McCallum, if you've ever wanted to catch Debra Banger in *Sperms of Endearment,* this is your chance."

"I'll pass."

"Other than the magazines, which you can bet he didn't buy for the articles, there's no reading matter on the premises. Not a book anywhere. This boy's interests were limited to drinking and fu—uh, fornicating."

"And killing," Tess said.

Carson opened a bureau. The drawer was empty. "You know about the gun he kept here. The MK-23.

It's at the crime lab now. There was a silencer with it, kind of banged up, and some other gear."

Crandall toed the pile of smut, looking thoughtful. "I'm surprised the killer didn't toss the residence and take the MK, if only to eliminate evidence linking Garrick to the San Fernando raid."

"Or just to get hold of an expensive piece of hardware," Tess added.

Carson nodded. "My theory is that the killer got spooked. You know he muffled the shots with the pillow. Tried to, anyway. First shot was probably quiet enough, but the pillow's stuffing was half blown away, and it wouldn't have silenced the second shot nearly as well. That report was louder than our friend expected. He knew someone in the building would hear it, so he amscrayed pronto."

That is possible, Tess thought. But it was also possible that Abby had deliberately left the gun in place so Garrick could be tied to the crime.

"And no one saw him leave?" Crandall asked.

"In this neighborhood, no one ever sees a thing."

"How about phone records?" Tess asked. "If we know who he was talking to within the last twenty-four hours—"

"Already got 'em. He had two phones, a landline and a cell. The cell received a call from another cellular phone yesterday afternoon. He called that number back from his landline a little later. Later still, he called the same number from his cell. That was at five forty-two p.m."

Five forty-two was right after the assailants fled the scene in San Fernando. "The first two calls involved preparations for the hit," Tess said. "The last one was his after-action report."

"So we assume. But there's a hitch." Carson smiled. "Isn't there always? The other cell was a clone."

A cloned cellular telephone was a unit programmed with someone else's ownership data. Tess knew it would be impossible to determine the actual caller.

"Do we at least know where the cloned phone was operating from?"

"Somewhere between McFadden and Edinger, near Harbor Boulevard. But that covers a lot of territory. And it's prime turf for the Scorps. Unless we find the cloned cell in someone's possession . . ."

Crandall looked unhappy. "It's probably already been destroyed or reprogrammed."

"Probably," Carson agreed. "These Scorps aren't so dumb. They do know how to cover their tracks."

Tess asked him what was happening now.

"We've rounded up most of Garrick's scumbag friends for Q and A. So far it's all Q and no A. They're shut up tighter than a nun's—well, they're not cooperating."

"You grilling anyone in particular?"

"Yeah. Shanker."

Tess remembered Hauser's mentioning him. "Ronald Shanker. He runs the club."

"His official title is president." Carson noted Tess's raised eyebrow. "Oh, yeah. They're organized, these guys. Got themselves a vice president, a secretary-treasurer, and a sergeant at arms."

"How corporate."

"They're essentially a business concern. Sell Ecstasy, coke, crystal meth. Stuff is manufactured in Latin America, and the Scorps do the distributing here in the States."

"Sounds lucrative."

"For the top membership, it is. The guys at the bottom don't get much of a cut."

"Are the gang members still being held?"

"Some are. Some aren't. They'll all be let go before long. Nothing to hold them on. Being a dirtbag isn't a crime. Though maybe it should be."

"How about Garrick's whereabouts before he was shot?"

"He was with his buddies. They were all hanging together last night. The guy who popped Dylan was probably chugging beers with him a couple hours earlier."

"Where did they hang out?"

"Bar, name of Fast Eddie's."

A bar. The kind of place where Dylan Garrick might have met someone. A female someone. "Did he leave the bar alone?" Tess asked.

"I told you, no one's talking."

"How about employees of Fast Eddie's?"

"We talked to the bartender. He's as tight-lipped as the rest of 'em. Word is, he's an honorary Scorp himself."

"And no one saw him come home?" Tess pressed.

"Folks in this building aren't too talkative, either, like I said. Besides, the guy was always coming and going at all hours. Believe me, we're following up every available angle. We've got this thing covered."

"I'm sure you do," Tess said, though she was pretty sure there was one angle they had missed. Her gaze panned the bedroom, and she noticed Crandall watching her with unusual concentration. The look on his face disturbed her. He seemed to be reading her thoughts.

"Now if you'll excuse me," Carson said, "I have to use the can."

Tess frowned. "Here?"

"Scene's already been processed. There's no harm in it."

Tess knew there wasn't any harm. But using Dylan Garrick's toilet seemed . . . disrespectful, somehow. What made it worse was that Carson grabbed one of Garrick's porn magazines for reading matter before disappearing into the bathroom.

Crandall tapped her on the arm. "Let's talk," he said quietly.

She didn't like the sound of that. "What do you think we've been doing?"

"Let's talk about something *else*. On the landing."

She followed him out of the apartment. He stood looking over the parking lot, not facing her.

"Something wrong, Rick?" she asked, keeping the tone light.

He still didn't look at her. "I know something funny went down at Andrea's house yesterday. Making me stay outside while you cleared the premises—that wasn't standard procedure. Was Abby in there? Did you send her away before I came in?"

She hesitated a long moment. "You don't want me to answer that."

"Goddamn it. I knew it had to be something like that." He finally turned to her. "She killed Dylan Garrick, didn't she?"

Tess gave him an honest answer. "I don't know who killed Garrick. Abby denies having anything to do with it."

"You already interrogated her?"

"I *asked* her," Tess corrected. "Not interrogated. Asked."

"That's why you disappeared from the field office after the briefing. You had to do a little briefing of your own."

"I didn't brief her. I asked her what she was up to last night."

"Is she alibied?"

"No. But she says she had no way of tracking down any of the assailants."

"And you believe her?"

"I'm not sure what I believe."

He thrust his hands into his pockets. "We cannot keep a lid on this, Tess. We have to tell the ADIC."

"No, we don't." She said it firmly, leaving no room for discussion.

"Then how about Hauser?"

"I'm not saying anything to anyone until I find out what happened."

"You can't keep covering for this woman."

"Just let me handle it, Rick."

"You've been handling it ever since the Rain Man. You're in really deep. I'm not sure you still have a professional perspective on the situation."

"Are you saying I've lost my ability to make sound judgments?"

"Where Abby Sinclair is concerned, quite possibly."

"She doesn't have any sort of hold on me. I just want to be careful, that's all. I'll keep you out of it. Carson can take you to the RA. You can talk to some of the people they've rounded up."

"And where will you be?"

"Running down some ideas of my own."

Crandall sighed. "It's getting harder and harder to back you up on this. What if she's gone rogue? What if someone else dies? The congressman, even?"

"There's no chance of that."

"How do you know? You can't say what she might do. We need to tell Michaelson and get it out in the open."

"It hasn't reached that point yet."

"I think it has."

She felt a flutter of dread. "You're not planning to go to the higher-ups on your own, are you, Rick?"

"No. I wouldn't do that." But he said it with less conviction than she'd hoped.

"Just let me handle it," she said again.

"Right. So far you're handling everything just great."

Crandall walked back inside. Tess stared after him. He wouldn't rat her out. She was almost sure of it.

But he would never again be her friend.

34

Abby waited in the restroom until she was sure Andrea had lured the FBI guys into the food court. She didn't want to be spotted by the feebs. It was always possible that one of them would remember her cameo appearance in the Rain Man case.

Besides, she really did have to pee. She had kind of a nervous bladder today. Nervous everything, in fact. She felt like she was hopped-up on some designer drug that had her thoughts racing and her body humming.

When enough time had passed, she left the ladies' room and returned to her car. She was driving the Mazda, since she didn't anticipate any undercover work, except the small deception necessary to get past security at Jack Reynolds's house. Her fake press pass was in the glove compartment, along with a camera, notebook, and pen—a journalist's tools of the trade, or so she assumed.

Reynolds's address was unlisted but easy enough to find in the Internet databases she used. He lived in a gated community in Newport Beach. Abby was relieved to find Wanda Klein listed in the gatehouse logbook.

The guard directed her down a long, sweeping curve of immaculately landscaped homes. Reynolds's house was the last one on the right. The barbecue was already under way; parked cars clogged the cul-de-sac and the courtyard driveway.

She found a space and parked, assembled her paraphernalia, and hiked to the front entrance, where a female staffer and two men in suits were posted. The men had the look of off-duty cops moonlighting as private security. She gave her name as Wanda Klein. The rent-a-cops confirmed that she was on the media list, then scanned her with a handheld metal detector. *Wanda gets wanded,* she thought. Having anticipated the screening, she'd left her gun in the car.

The staffer handed her a new name tag, which she was supposed to wear around her neck along with her press pass. "Now just wait here, please, while I get Mr. Stenzel."

"That's not necessary. I can find my way around."

"I'm afraid he insists on personally escorting reporters at events like this."

Great. Abby waited as Stenzel was paged. She wondered if Reynolds had told him to expect her.

Apparently he had. She saw Kipland Stenzel approaching at a fast clip, a false smile plastered on his face.

"Ms. Klein," he said, offering her a perfunctory handshake. "I'm glad you were able to make it. Any trouble finding the place?"

Abby matched his phony smile with one of her own. "I never have any trouble finding things. I'm a regular bloodhound."

With a certain deftness he had managed to pull her away from the cops so they could speak more privately. His expression altered instantly from a counterfeit smile to an entirely genuine scowl.

"I don't know what kind of scam you're running," he said quietly. "But please understand that you will not get away with it."

"What makes you think it's a scam?"

"Everything you do is a scam. You're a lying, manipulating little bitch."

Abby cocked her head, curious about this outburst. "Kip, are you mad at me for quitting on your boss?"

"My personal feelings have nothing to do with it. I just want you to be aware that I am looking out for the congressman's interests."

"Good for you. Now may we get going?"

"I have half a mind to throw you out and tell Jack you never showed up."

"That wouldn't be smart. I came here because I have something to say to your boss. Something he needs to hear, involving Bethany Willett."

Stenzel did a fairly good job of looking unfazed. "Who?"

"Maybe you know her as Andrea Lowry."

"I have no idea what you're referring to."

"I'm referring to the onetime illicit relationship between Ms. Lowry née Willett and the congressman."

"There was no relationship."

"I'm afraid there was, whether you know it or not. And maybe you don't. It was well before your time. What are you, like, fourteen years old?"

"Insults won't get you anywhere."

"How about threats? Either I meet with the congressman or I track down a real reporter and do my talking to him."

He gave her a shrewd look. "Your career depends on keeping a low profile. You're not going to get yourself in the headlines."

"I'm more than happy to be the anonymous source behind the scenes. Just think of me as Deep Throat." Abby frowned. "On second thought, I want a different nickname."

"It would be a serious mistake to go that route, Ms. Sinclair. The congressman is not somebody you want to cross."

"Why not? Will he send some of his motorcycle compadres after me? Or does he only use the Scorpions when getting reacquainted with old friends?"

"You're raving."

"I guess you won't mind my raving to the press. Here's the bottom line, Kip. You don't run this show. I do."

Stenzel hesitated, his face a tight mask. Then he turned to the two cops. "Did you run the metal detector over her?" He didn't wait for an answer. "Do it again. Slowly."

The cop with the wand frowned but did as he was told.

"Afraid I'm packing heat?" Abby asked Stenzel, smiling.

"I'm just taking every precaution . . . Ms. Klein."

"We can't be too careful where the congressman's safety is concerned."

"No. We can't."

The cop confirmed that she was clean.

Stenzel nodded curtly. "Come along."

Abby was right behind him. "Kipster, you couldn't lose me now."

35

Reynolds's house was a massive modernistic pile. Twenty-foot ceilings soared over marble floors. Walls of glass let in the abundant California sun.

"Nice place," Abby observed. "I'm surprised your boss can afford it on a public servant's salary."

Stenzel caught the implication. "If you'd done your homework, you'd know that Mrs. Reynolds is quite well-off."

"The boy from the barrio married money? I didn't catch that detail on his Web site. Maybe it doesn't go so well with his rags-to-riches story."

"The congressman and his wife have a wonderful marriage. They recently celebrated their twenty-fifth wedding anniversary."

"So I guess she didn't hold his indiscretions against him? Or more likely, she never found out."

"I find you tiresome, Ms. Sinclair."

"Yeah, I'm a real pain in the ass."

They passed a game room and a small but well-equipped gym. He led her through a solarium and into the backyard. The yard wasn't huge, most of the property having been taken up by the house, and the square footage available for Reynolds's guests was further diminished by a swimming pool that simulated a tropical lagoon, complete with waterfall. The guests were crowded around the pool, doing their best not to fall in while they picked at plates of food. Abby was reminded that she hadn't eaten today.

A knot of visitors had formed around a well-dressed woman of Reynolds's age, recognizable from her photos on the Web site and in the *L.A. Times* article. Nora, his wife. Nearby, Reynolds's assistant—his constituent services coordinator, Rebecca, or as Abby called her, Moneypenny—was chatting with an earnest man who seemed in need of a favor from the congressman. Rebecca seemed a little overdressed for a summer day; she was showing hardly any skin at all.

Stenzel proceeded to the far end of the yard. There the crowd parted to reveal His Excellency in front of a monstrous gas-powered grill. He wasn't actually flipping or serving burgers, and Abby was a little disappointed about that.

Reynolds was in his element, surrounded by well-wishers, the center of attention, radiating authority, accepting the adulation of the wealthy and influential. Then his gaze flickered in Abby's direction, registering her presence, and something in his eyes told her it was a pose. Reynolds was scared. His hold on power was threatened, and he could see it slipping away. Beneath the facade of self-assurance she read fear, desperation, vulnerability.

That was good. She could work with that.

"I was wondering if you would actually be here," he said quietly as Abby moved alongside him.

She smiled. "No, you weren't."

Reynolds glanced at Stenzel. "Take her to my office. I'll be inside in a minute."

Stenzel ushered her away. "Hold on a sec," Abby said. She grabbed a plate and loaded it with chicken and potato salad, then found some plastic cutlery and paper napkins. What the hell, the food was free and she was hungry. Plate in hand, she followed Stenzel past a garden of hydrangeas, sea grasses, and bird-of-paradise, and back inside the house. Down a short hallway was a small office with oak shelving and paneled walls. It occurred to Abby that being out of public view was perhaps not the best idea, under the circumstances.

"By the way, your rent-a-cops will remember me," she told Stenzel. "If for some reason I don't leave this party, there'll be an investigation, and you'll be the first one questioned."

"Are you always so dramatic?"

"Most of the time."

"If you're worried about your safety, I'd advise you to walk away from this situation right now."

"Sorry, Kip. No can do."

"I've given you fair warning."

"You've been more than fair," Abby agreed.

"Then I won't consider myself responsible when they zip you up in a body bag."

There had to be a great comeback to that, but off-hand Abby couldn't think of one.

Fortunately she didn't have to. Reynolds stepped through the doorway, shutting the door behind him.

Abby took a seat and started on a chicken wing. "Nice little get-together," she said. "Few hundred of your closest friends?"

"My biggest contributors. Which amounts to the same thing."

"Somehow I find that sad."

"You know what Harry Truman said. If you want a friend in Washington, buy a dog."

"That's the second Truman anecdote I've heard from you. Are you just wild about Harry?"

"All politicians admire Truman," Reynolds said as he rounded his desk and sat in a plush leather chair. "You know why?"

"Enlighten me."

"We like him because he was always underesti-mated. The party bosses thought they could control him. The pollsters thought he couldn't win in 'forty-eight. He was dismissed as a mediocrity. And now he's an icon."

"So he gives hope to all the other mediocrities in politics?"

"That's a cheap shot, Sinclair. I'm starting to lose my respect for you."

"You never had mine to begin with."

"What is it you wanted to say?"

Abby looked up from her lunch and focused her stare on Stenzel. "Privacy, please?"

He started to protest, but Reynolds cut him off. "Wait outside, Kip. Tell the folks I'll rejoin them in a minute."

Stenzel opened the door, then turned back. "She's not wearing a wire. I had security check her twice." So that was the reason for the do-over.

Reynolds nodded, and Stenzel was gone, the door closing after him. With his campaign manager out of the way, Reynolds seemed more relaxed. He rose and moved to a liquor cabinet. "Drink?" he asked, sounding almost cordial.

"If you can make a New Year's Rockin' Eve, I won't turn it down."

"What the hell is that?"

"My own invention. Splash of rum, splash of gin, splash of vodka, splash of tequila, splash of rye, and a soupçon of carrot juice."

"Sounds god-awful."

"It really is."

Reynolds poured himself a Scotch, fixing nothing for her. She contented herself with the chicken. It was a little overcooked, but you couldn't beat the price.

"Tell me what this is all about," Reynolds said as he resumed his seat.

"First of all, there was an attempt on Andrea Lowry's life yesterday afternoon."

He gave her his best poker face. "I don't know what you're talking about or how it could possibly have anything to do with me."

"Right. Then let me make it clearer." She dabbed her mouth with a napkin. "Andrea used to be known as Bethany Willett. You and she had an affair. It didn't end well."

"I've never known anyone by that name."

"Give it a rest, Jack. Andrea and I have become pals. She opened up to me, told me the whole story. All the sordid details, like your floating love nest, *The Mariner*. She told me how you would have your intimate moments belowdecks, then share a nightcap under the stars."

"This is all bullshit. If the woman said any of this, she's delusional."

"She's not delusional, and you know it. This has been your nightmare for the last twenty years. Your past coming back to hurt you. A couple of months ago, it finally happened. The woman you knew as Bethany started showing up at your campaign events. You didn't know what she was up to. Maybe she was planning to go public. Maybe she was thinking of blackmailing you. Maybe she wanted to assassinate you. You were terrified, but you couldn't raise your concerns with the police, not without risking the exposure of your relationship. And exposure would kill your career, which means almost as much to you as life itself. Hell, maybe more."

Reynolds was doing his best to look bored. "Let's not get carried away. The electorate isn't so squeamish about infidelity anymore. We've come a long way from Gary Hart and Donna Rice noodling each other on the good ship *Monkey Business*. These days, in some circles a little extramarital activity may even be seen as a plus."

"How about two dead babies? Are they a plus? Especially when they're your flesh and blood, and your mistress shot them to death before shooting herself? And then there's the part about how you kindly arranged to put Bethany in the nuthouse so she couldn't talk about it. This is not the sort of thing that looks good on the résumé of an Orange County family man and former crusading DA."

"You're making a lot of wild allegations—"

"Cut the crap. You were scared out of your gourd, so you tried to find Bethany. I'm guessing you put Stenzel on the job. He called the hospital where Bethany had been treated, but he couldn't get any info. At least I assume it was Stenzel who called. I don't think you'd be ballsy enough to call them yourself."

"Get to the point."

"Point is, you had no luck tracking her down. How could you? She was living under a new name. You got desperate, so you brought me in. You figured I might succeed where your flunky had, well, flunked. And I did. But I wouldn't give you her new name or her whereabouts. Somehow you found her, anyway."

"Who says I found her?"

"The jacketed hollow points that were dug out of her wall. I'm really not wearing a wire, Jack. This conversation will go a whole lot faster if you decide to be straight with me."

Reynolds stood up, Scotch in hand. He hadn't touched it before, but now he took a good swallow.

"You told me she had a schedule of my events," he said as he started pacing behind the desk.

"So?"

"We mail those out."

Abby got it. "Mailing list. Shit." She cursed herself for being dumb. Dumbness was the one unforgivable crime in her line of work, the original sin.

Having polished off the chicken, she assuaged her guilt with a forkful of potato salad.

"Okay," she said, her mouth full, "so you knew where she was, and you sent in the storm troopers. You didn't know what she had in mind, and the only way to be sure she wouldn't do something crazy was to have her killed."

Reynolds gulped more Scotch. "The woman is crazy. Unpredictable. I had to be proactive."

"Well, the best-laid plans of mice and men, et cetera. Andrea, née Bethany, is very much alive. And the police have taken an interest in her."

She used the word *police* advisedly. She had decided not to mention the involvement of the FBI. As a Washington insider, Reynolds might have contacts in the Bureau. It was best to let him think that only the local authorities were on the case.

"I'm sure she wants nothing to do with law enforcement," Reynolds said, though he didn't sound sure at all.

"You're right. But my guess is, they're looking into her past. They'll find out that her credit history goes back only eight years. Then they'll question her. And she'll talk. She'll have to talk."

She paused to let the comment sink in. Reynolds drained his glass and poured another.

"She'll talk," Abby went on, "unless you silence her first. But here's the rub—you can't get near her. Police protection, you know. That's the thing about a failed hit, Jack. It's twice as hard to get to the victim a second time. So it looks like you're royally fucked. Unless you let me help you."

"You can't help me," Reynolds said.

"Yes, I can. Andrea trusts me. I can take advantage of that fact for our mutual benefit, as I told you last night."

"By handing her over to me?"

"Exactly."

"Yesterday you quit on me because I didn't meet your high ethical standards. Now all of a sudden you're willing to deliver the woman?"

"Ethics is a luxury I can no longer afford."

"And why is that?"

"I need to get out of town. For a long time. Maybe for good. And I need to do it fast."

"Sounds like you're in trouble."

She looked down at her plate. Her voice was low. "I am."

"What a shame. Care to tell me about it?"

"Maybe you've heard what happened to Dylan Garrick."

"I may have read something about it in the newspaper." Reynolds narrowed his eyes. "Are you telling me you're the one who offed him?"

"Me? I'm just a simple Arizona girl making her way in the big city. But I was seen with him."

"You mean you tracked him down?"

"It's what I do."

"So you *did* kill him."

"Haven't said that." Abby set down her plate and

got up, facing him. "Whatever I may or may not have done, people are going to suspect the worst, and I'm not going to have any way of proving them wrong."

A moment passed while Reynolds stood motionless. Then he lifted his glass and took a slow, thoughtful sip. "All right, maybe I can believe you need to go on the run."

"And to do that, I need a sudden infusion of cash, courtesy of you. I need money, you need Andrea. We can work together and solve both our problems."

"If the police are watching Andrea, how can you possibly deliver her to me?"

"She trusts me, like I said."

"So what?"

"I can get her to leave the house and ditch her police escort. Once she does, she'll be all yours."

"You're bullshitting."

"No, I'm not, Jack. I can get her away from the police. And I can do it tonight."

He considered the idea. "Once I've got her, you get paid? Is that it?"

"I get paid up front."

"How much?"

"Fifty thousand dollars. In cash, obviously. I'm afraid I can't take a personal check."

"I don't have fifty grand in cash here in the house."

"But you can get it."

"It's Saturday afternoon. My bank is already closed."

"Make the manager open up."

"You think I keep fifty thousand dollars in my checking account?"

"It's your rich wife's account, more likely, but I'm sure you have privileges. Or maybe you can borrow it from your campaign fund. Cut yourself a check and run one less billboard ad. Or take out a loan and say it's for the campaign. I don't care, as long as you have it by six o'clock tonight."

"What if I pay you the fifty and then you renege on the deal?"

"I'll have Andrea close by. The way I'll work it, you'll know you've got her before I take off. You'll have her, and you won't be able to touch me. It's not as complicated as it sounds."

"Let's say we were to have this meeting at six. Where would it be?"

"Brayton Hotel, just like before. Only in the lobby this time. Oh, and Jack—I want *you* to make the drop-off. Not Kip or some other low-level player. I want you to get your hands dirty, just like me."

"How do I know you're not setting me up? This could be some kind of sting."

"Do I strike you as the type who works hand in glove with the police?"

"No. But I wouldn't have seen you as the type to sell out Bethany, either. It's pretty cold, Sinclair. You really expect me to believe you're capable of it?"

"Brass ovaries, remember? You don't survive in my line of work unless you're willing to pull the trigger."

"Like you did on Garrick?"

"No comment, Mr. Congressman."

Reynolds studied her. "Okay. We have a deal." He showed her an archly cynical smile. "You know, you're a lot smarter than I thought you were."

"Am I? Funny. You're exactly as smart as I thought you were." Abby picked up her plate and dumped it in a wastebasket. She headed for the door. "Thanks for the chow. Tell Stenzel I'll let myself out."

36

Kip Stenzel wondered why politicians never learned anything from Nixon. Despite the example of Watergate, they continued to wire their offices with electronic recording and eavesdropping equipment. His boss was no exception. In his desk he had installed a microphone and transmitter, which sent a signal to a receiver in a room down the hall. He recorded his phone calls and teleconferences with his staff in D.C., and he liked to have Stenzel available to listen in on ostensibly private conversations, as he was doing now.

The audio clarity was excellent. Stenzel heard every word of Reynolds's discussion with Abby Sinclair. Truthfully, he'd heard more than he'd wanted to know. It was advantageous to retain some degree of deniability.

He waited until he was sure Sinclair had gone before he emerged from hiding. When he entered the office, he found Reynolds standing by his desk, talking into the phone.

"Save your breath, Ron. I'm still not interested in any excuses. But if you want another chance to redeem yourself, there may be an opportunity."

Reynolds listened to the reply and sipped his drink. Scotch, of course. It was always Scotch, but under normal circumstances Stenzel's boss wouldn't have been drinking before the dinner hour, especially with fat-cat contributors in the backyard waiting to jawbone him.

"Okay," Reynolds said. "Then meet me tonight at five thirty, level one of the parking garage of the Brayton Hotel in downtown L.A. I want you driving your van. Come heavy, and come alone. You'll need duct tape and handcuffs. . . . Remember that lesson in loyalty I mentioned? Well, school is in session."

He set down the phone hard enough to shake the table, then looked at Stenzel. "You heard?"

"I heard."

"Things are getting complicated," Reynolds said.

Stenzel swallowed. "Maybe too complicated. Now might be a propitious time to back off, Jack."

"Back off? How am I supposed to do that?"

"Cut our losses, walk away. Sinclair can't prove we had anything to do with the attack on Andrea Lowry. Right now all they can get you on is some shit that happened twenty years ago."

"That's enough."

"If it comes out, it's not necessarily fatal. We can spin it. The woman's a head case, shot her own kids, went to a mental hospital."

"She knows enough to make her story credible. A million details. Like the boat we used to meet on. No way she could have known about that unless Bethany—I mean, Andrea—told her."

"I'm not saying we deny the affair. But it's the past. It's ancient history. We get Nora on board, have her stand by you, say all is forgiven. The voters figure if your wife says it's no big deal, who are they to care?"

Reynolds downed another gulp of Scotch. "You don't get it, Kip. She blames me for pushing her over the edge. She thinks I'm the one who drove her to shoot the kids."

"She's a freak. We can paint her—"

"No matter how we spin it, the media will play it their way. She bore my children out of wedlock and killed them when I broke her heart."

"I'm not saying we won't take a hit."

"A hit? This will fucking *destroy* me."

"I think you can recover."

"Easy for you to say. If I go down, you just find some up-and-comer to latch on to, and you're back in the game."

Stenzel stiffened. "I don't appreciate your questioning my loyalty, Jack." He waited for an apology, got none, and forged ahead. "Bottom line, we're not in too deep yet. The incident yesterday afternoon can't be tied to you. We're still only talking about a love affair that went south. If you take it to the next level, there's no going back."

"There's never been any going back. Andrea Lowry is a problem. The way you deal with problems is, you eliminate them."

"That may be how it's done on the streets—"

"Yeah, that's exactly how it's done on the streets. What kind of war do you think we're fighting? This isn't one of your fucking focus groups. This is armed combat. If you haven't got the stomach for it, then get out of the way."

"I have the stomach for whatever is necessary," Stenzel said quietly.

"Then shut the hell up about cutting our losses. We're not playing defense. We're on offense. We're going to have Andrea handed over to us tonight."

"According to Sinclair. You think her proposal is on the level?"

"Yes, I do."

"So you think she aced the biker?"

"Probably."

"I don't get that vibe from her. She's not a killer."

"Anybody is a killer, given the right circumstances. And she's a street fighter. Vigilante type. She could have offed Garrick. Definitely."

Stenzel thought about the woman's hard-ass attitude. It was possible, he decided. "Did you know this guy Garrick?"

"No. But the newspaper said he croaked last night—shot in the face. If Sinclair had something to do with it, or even if it only looks like she did, then she's not lying when she says she needs to get out of town."

"What was the phone call about?"

"Friend of mine. His particular talents are going to come in handy tonight."

Stenzel figured he understood the game plan. The friend, Ron, would remove Andrea after Reynolds learned her whereabouts. More outsourcing. He wasn't happy about it, but he knew the boss was in no mood for argument.

"So I take it you'll pay Sinclair the fifty and trust her to come up with Lowry?"

"Trust has nothing to do with it. We're not taking action only with regard to Andrea. We're going to snuff Sinclair, too."

Stenzel required a moment to absorb this information. Then he saw why Reynolds's friend would be stationed in the hotel garage. Sinclair was his target. She would be taken out when she tried to leave. Gunned down—or maybe snatched alive. Reynolds had said something about duct tape, handcuffs. Stenzel didn't know. He was way outside his comfort zone.

"Jack," he said softly, in his calmest, most reasonable tone, "I understand your desire to recover your investment, but—"

"The fifty thou? I'm not worried about that, goddamn it."

"Then I don't see the rationale for this move."

"The rationale, Kip, is that I don't trust Sinclair any more than you do. She may be planning to stiff me on the payment. She may have some other game in mind. She was pretty vague about the details of this handoff she's arranging."

"If you think it's a con, don't go."

"I don't know if it's a con. If it is, then I intend to get Sinclair. If she's on the level, then I intend to get Lowry—and Sinclair, too."

"There's something more going on here than covering your bases, Jack."

"Damn straight there's more. Sinclair betrayed me. She's not getting away with it. I don't take betrayal well. Just ask Joe Ferris."

The name meant nothing to Stenzel. "Who?"

"Never mind. He was before your time."

Stenzel was trying hard to focus, but he wasn't sure he could. It had been one thing to track down Andrea Lowry and provide her address. He hadn't had to concern himself with the end result. And he'd never even met Lowry. She was an abstraction. This was different. This was real.

"So what you're saying is"—he spoke slowly—"you plan to, uh, terminate both women?"

"Right, Kip. That's what I'm saying."

"It doubles the risk."

"It also doubles the reward."

Stenzel knew this was wrong. From a cost-benefit standpoint, there was no justification for this course of action. It was highly unwise.

"I don't see any percentage in eliminating Sinclair," he said. "Just let her go. She'll be out of town, and no one will ever find her."

"No one will find her," Reynolds agreed, "but not because she's out of town. What do I have on the schedule for tonight?"

"Nothing. Why?"

"I want to make sure my night is free." Reynolds smiled. "You didn't think I was just going to have Sinclair blipped, did you? Uh-uh. Andrea gets a bullet in the head. No hard feelings there. Sinclair is a different story. That bitch owes me a good time."

Stenzel felt his gut tighten. He had trouble forming words. "That's a serious error, Jack. You're not thinking strategically."

"Fuck strategy."

"You're already pushing the envelope. You want to stay as far away from the actual . . . resolution of the problem as possible."

"No, I don't. Let me tell you how it's going to go down."

"No, Jack."

"What do you mean, no?"

Stenzel turned away. "Whatever you have in mind, I don't want to know about it."

"You don't want to know about it? You don't want to know?" Reynolds flung his glass. It shattered against a wall. "You *need* to know. You're *going* to know."

"Okay, Jack." Stenzel's mouth was dry. "Okay."

Reynolds rounded the desk and stared him down. His mouth was twisted in an indecipherable shape that could have been a grimace or a smile. His eyes were narrowed and unblinking.

"My friend grabs Sinclair and takes her to Santa Ana. He runs a motorcycle repair shop. Lots of power tools."

With a distant part of his mind, Stenzel wondered if he had ever allowed himself to know, really know, that his employer was a sociopath. It should have been obvious. There had been more than enough hints—the mood swings from affability to rage, the inner coldness, the shameless manipulations. And on some level he had seen it. But he had never put his knowledge into words. He had never wanted to. Perhaps because he saw so much of himself in Jack Reynolds, or so much of Reynolds in him.

"Of course," Reynolds added, "the party won't get started till I arrive."

"You're saying you . . . want to watch?" Stenzel asked, holding his voice level.

"Not just watch. I'm a hands-on guy."

The images this statement suggested were more than Stenzel could stand. He tried one last time to get through. "Jack, this is not a good idea. This is one task you definitely want to delegate."

"Wrong. I want to get up close and personal. I want to look into her eyes. I want to break her. I want her to die knowing I won and she lost."

"Why?" Stenzel asked, hearing the inane pointlessness of the question even as he uttered it.

"Because I always win. Always. She should've remembered that. And you, too, Kip. You should remember it, too."

"I will, Jack."

"So we're together on this?"

"We're on the same page."

"Great." Reynolds clapped his hands, smiling—a real smile now, not a frightening parody. "Then let's get back outside. Can't keep my constituents waiting too long."

He left the office. Stenzel followed slowly, telling himself not to be afraid.

37

Fast Eddie's was essentially what Tess had expected, though at one p.m. it lacked the raucous atmosphere it would no doubt offer after dark. The pool tables were unused, and most of the chairs were unoccupied, with only a few all-day drinkers lounging in the corners. Behind the bar a large man was scowling at a wall-mounted TV set that was showing an auto race.

Tess approached the bar, aware that every eye in the establishment had turned in her direction—even the bartender's, though he did his best to look uninterested. She leaned on the bar and let him take his time coming over to her. She pegged him as an ex-con—it was hard to say how, but there was something about his physique, the prison-buffed muscles that had turned to fat, and the set of his jaw, as if he had learned to keep his feelings hidden from anyone in authority.

"You Eddie?" she asked.

"What?"

"Fast Eddie's is the name of this place. Is that you?"

"There's no Eddie. It's just a name. Because of the pool tables."

Tess didn't get it. "Pool tables?"

"Like in the movie. *The Hustler*, Paul Newman, you know?"

She didn't know. Was everybody in the state of California a movie nut? Maybe Abby was right. Maybe she ought to start renting tapes, or DVDs, or whatever.

"All right, then," she said, "so what's *your* name?"

"Don't got one."

"Everyone has a name."

"All I got is a nickname."

"What is it?"

"Biscuit."

She looked him over. He was well over six feet tall and had to weigh in at no less than 275 pounds. "Biscuit?" she said skeptically.

"Some joker said I was only a biscuit away from weighing three hundred. Name stuck."

"Fair enough. I'm Special Agent McCallum, FBI." She allowed him a glimpse of her creds. "I'd like to ask you a few questions."

"I already been asked a lot of questions."

"They took you down to the police station, right?"

He lifted his meaty shoulders. "It's not like I ain't been there before."

"And you didn't cooperate. I'm not surprised. Why would you say anything that would get one of your buddies in trouble?"

"I don't know what buddies you're talking about."

"No, I'm sure you don't know anything at all."

"That's right. Now, are you gonna buy something to drink, or are you just wasting my time?"

"I don't drink when I'm on duty."

"Then piss off." He started to move away.

There were a lot of ways she could handle this. Intimidation was one possibility, but she assumed that the interrogators at the police station had already given it their best shot. She decided to try sweet reason instead.

"I can't say I blame you," she said mildly.

He looked at her. "Blame me for what?"

"For keeping your mouth shut. The people who talked to you at the police station were working on the assumption that Dylan Garrick was killed by one of his fellow Scorpions. And you don't want to give them anything that would help them nail one of your friends."

"I don't got no friends."

"One of your customers, then. Your clientele."

"Clientele. Fuck, I ain't got no clientele, neither. What you think this is, a fucking hair salon?" He turned aside. "I'm telling you what I told the cops. I don't know shit about anything they was asking."

"I believe you."

"Then why the fuck are you still here?"

"Because I think you may know something important, only it's not what the police were interested in. See, I'm working on a different theory of the case. I don't think Dylan's hit was an inside job. I don't think the Scorpions had anything to do with it. I think it was somebody else."

This got his interest, just a little. "Another gang?"

"Not a gang. I think Dylan may have been shot by a woman he was with. A woman he picked up here last night."

"A woman? Some hooker, you mean?"

"The woman I have in mind is more of a vigilante. A private operator with an agenda of her own."

"This woman got a name?"

"She usually goes by Abby. She may have started a conversation with you."

"She the talkative type?"

Tess winced. "Very."

"We didn't get no talkative women in here last night."

"Last night she may not have been in the mood for talk. I think she may have been, well, stalking Dylan Garrick." It seemed odd to imagine Abby as a stalker, yet that was the only word for it.

"Is that so?" the bartender said.

"I could be wrong. Actually, I hope I am. Maybe you can help me find out one way or the other."

"I don't know why you think I'd want to help you do anything."

"Because, Biscuit, you and I are on the same side. You don't want your friends to go down for Dylan's murder. If I can prove somebody else did it, they're in the clear."

"You're feeding me a line of bullshit. They sent you in here to work on me some more because I wouldn't give them anything. It ain't gonna work. So fuck off."

"You're a difficult person to reason with."

"Figured that out, did you?"

"You think I'm running some kind of game on you. You're wrong. I'm not in tight with the local police or even the local feds. I'm in from out of state, and I'm pretty much on my own, just following up a hunch that nobody else needs to know about."

"So you're the Lone Ranger." He snorted. "Feds never work alone. They're like ants in a pantry. If you see one, you know there's got to be more."

"Ever hear of Mobius?" she asked.

He paused, confused by the change of topic. "Nutcase with the nerve gas, the one who had L.A. shittin' its trousers a few years ago?"

"That's right. How about the Rain Man?"

"Kidnapper, put women in the storm drains and let them drown. Yeah, I've heard of them both. I read the papers now and then. So what?"

"If you read the papers, you ought to remember that I was involved in both cases. I came in from out of state, just like I'm telling you. And I worked alone."

"Show me your ID again."

She reopened her black leather credential case to reveal her gold badge and, under plastic, her photo and signature, along with her personal agent number and the signature of the FBI director.

Biscuit hesitated, then reluctantly reached into his shirt pocket and brought out a pair of reading glasses, which he perched on his battered nose. He caught her glance and mumbled, "We're all getting older every day." He studied the credentials. "Fuck, what d'ya know. You *are* her. I didn't, you know, register the name before. They got you working this piece-of-shit case?"

"It's tied in to something bigger."

"Huh." He appraised her with new respect. It occurred to Tess that her supposedly legendary status in the greater L.A. area was finally working to her advantage. "So you *are* the fuckin' Lone Ranger. You took out Mobius and that rain guy all by yourself."

"That's right."

"Got a set of balls on you, don't you?"

Tess ignored the question, assuming it to be rhetorical. "So you know I'm telling you the truth when I say I'm working an angle nobody else has picked up on. I don't care what the police wanted to hear you say. They weren't asking you about any woman who left with Garrick last night, were they?"

"No."

"That's all I want to know about. Did you see Garrick leave?"

"Yeah. I saw him."

"Did he leave alone?"

"No."

"Who was he with?"

"You really think I'm gonna tell you?"

"I'm hoping."

"Well, keep on hoping, but it ain't going to happen. Shit, you think I want to see *my* name in the goddamn newspapers?"

"I'll keep you out of it."

"Yeah, right, you will. Until you write some fucking bestselling book about it or sell your story to cable TV. No way, darling."

Apparently her notoriety wasn't such an asset, after all. "Just tell me if he was with a man or a woman."

"Hey, all I know, it was one of them cross-dressers." Biscuit laughed. "Put that in your book, why don't you?"

He wouldn't talk. She had wasted her time. She handed him a card with her cell phone number. "If you change your mind," she said simply.

He flicked the card into a wastebasket. "I won't."

She started to walk away. His voice stopped her.

"Hey. I ask you something?"

She turned back to him. "Sure."

"When you whacked the bad guys—you feel good about it after? Like, was it a rush?"

"No. I only felt good that I survived."

"Yeah. That's how it was for me, too." She recognized this as an admission that he had killed at least once. She said nothing. "I just wondered. Because everybody else, you know, they say it's a trip. They say it's like getting high. And I always tell 'em I feel like that, too. But I don't. I thought maybe it was just me."

"It's not just you."

He nodded and turned his back on her. Tess wondered if she should ask again for his help. But it was useless. In the end, she was the enemy, no matter what they shared.

She asked herself if Abby, too, saw her as an enemy, to be manipulated and cajoled, but never trusted. Perhaps she did.

And perhaps, from her standpoint, she was right. Because Tess still intended to learn what Abby had done last night. She would find a way. Somehow.

And if her suspicions proved correct, she would take Abby down.

38

Shanker knelt in the rear compartment of his van, arranging a small arsenal of illegal firearms under a pile of blankets. No way he would need all this fire-power, but he didn't know exactly what the Man had in mind for tonight, and his orders were to come heavy. He was debating whether or not to include the sawed-off shotgun he'd taken from a dead Mexican twenty years ago, a prized possession and one he ordinarily wouldn't bring into combat, when his cell phone rang. He pulled it out of his pocket and answered impatiently, annoyed at the distraction. "Yeah?"

"Ron, can you talk?"

The voice he heard belonged to Marvin Bonerz, an ex-con who'd done six years in Soledad for murder in the second, but who was known to his associates as Biscuit.

"A little busy right now," Shanker said.

"But can you *talk?*"

Shanker realized he was being asked whether or not he was still in police custody. "I can talk. They cut me loose."

"Me, too."

"So what's up?"

"Just wanted to pass on some news. There was a fed in here a few minutes ago, trying to pump me. Lady fed, McCallum—you might have heard of her—"

"I haven't. What's your point? The feds are talking to everybody today. This isn't exactly a hot news item."

"Thing is, she's working the case from a different angle. She thinks the hit on Dylan wasn't gang related. She thinks the shooter was some woman Dylan picked up last night."

For some reason Shanker couldn't quite identify, this information piqued his interest. He pressed the phone closer to his ear. "What woman?"

"Some bimbo, dressed real trashy. He left with her. I didn't think nothing of it."

"Why would some whore at Fast Eddie's want to ice one of our guys?"

"I asked her the same thing. McCallum says the woman she's thinking of ain't no whore. She's, like, a vigilante. Some kind of private operator."

"Sounds like a load of bullshit."

"Yeah, I thought so, too. Except for one thing. The woman who went home with Dylan, she got hit on by a few other guys and gave them all the brush-off. Zero interest. I pegged her for a dyke. Then Dylan comes over to chat her up, and in five minutes they're outta here. Like she was waiting for him, maybe."

"Seems thin."

"Well, I just thought I'd let you know."

"Yeah, okay, thanks."

"I didn't really think it was this Abby, anyhow."

Shanker frowned. "What was that?"

"I said I didn't think she did it."

"You called her Abby."

"That's the name McCallum had for her."

Shanker shut his eyes. He remembered a conversation with the Man in the office of his shop yesterday afternoon.

I'll be teaching Abby a few lessons about loyalty.

On the phone, minutes ago, Reynolds had used the same words.

It was Abby he meant to take care of tonight. The same Abby—had to be—that the FBI woman was looking to nail for Garrick's murder.

"You there, Ron?" That was Biscuit. Shanker had forgotten about him.

"The FBI agent," Shanker said, "she was working this angle pretty hard, huh? So there's a bunch of feds out looking for this Abby right now?"

"Not a bunch. Just one. McCallum. She's working it alone."

"She can't be."

"She is. It's her style. She's famous, Ron. If you would ever read the newspapers—"

"I only read the sports." This wasn't true. Shanker read the comics page, too, but never admitted it. "You really think McCallum is flying solo?"

"Looks that way."

Shanker was thinking fast. If McCallum picked up Abby for questioning, then he and Reynolds wouldn't be able to get her tonight. And Abby had worked for the Man before quitting. Under interrogation, there was no telling what she might say, especially if she was facing a homicide rap for Dylan Garrick. If she named Reynolds as her employer, the congressman would be the next one questioned. That might be what McCallum was really after. If Reynolds was brought in, it wouldn't be long before the whole goddamned thing was out in the open.

But if McCallum didn't find Abby by six o'clock tonight, it would be too late. Abby would be gone for good. She wouldn't be talking to anybody.

"You got any way to get in touch with McCallum?" Shanker asked.

Biscuit sounded puzzled. "She left her card. I tossed it. But I can dig it out of the trash."

"Call her. Set up a meeting, just you and her. When she shows up, kill her."

On the other end of the line, Biscuit drew in a harsh breath. "Fuck, man. She's goddamned FBI."

"Yeah, so what? You never bagged a fed before?"

"I only ever killed anybody that one time, Ron, and you know it."

"Yeah, well, today you get to go again. Don't act like you got a choice about this. You signed on, Biscuit. You would've been dead in stir if our boys hadn't adopted you. Those Mexishit assholes were just waiting to take you down. You haven't forgotten, have you?"

"No."

"White man kills a *cholo* in a bar fight, ends up in jail with a bunch of other *cholos* breathing down his neck, and only the Scorpions could save him. Pull up your shirt, you'll see a prison tat on your goddamned flabby-tit hairless chest. You're in the crew. We looked out for you in Soledad, and now we're calling in the favor."

"Ron, a thing like this can bring down a world of hurt on all of us."

"A world of hurt is what you're gonna be in if you don't follow orders."

"Shit."

"It's no big deal to zipper a fed. They act like they're ten feet tall, but they bleed like anybody else. And this one's a woman. That makes it double easy."

"I'm not a killer."

"You are today."

"Can't you get somebody else?"

"It's you she made contact with. If you set up a meeting, it's you she'll be expecting. So you get to pull the trigger on her. Nothing fancy, just one round in the head. You can nail her before she knows what's happening. Okay?"

"Okay, Ron. Okay. Goddamn, I never thought I'd have to do this shit again."

"It's like riding a bicycle, Biscuit. It'll come right back to you. Just make sure you drop her before she gets a chance to drop you."

Shanker ended the call, hoping he'd made the right decision. When McCallum turned up dead, every law enforcement officer in southern Cal would be hauling in suspects. It would get ugly. The situation might spin out of control.

But maybe he could start to set things right in a few hours, when he met the Man at the hotel.

He decided he'd better bring that sawed-off shotgun, and whatever else he had left in his wall safe.

Shit, bring it all.

39

Tess had returned to the crime scene and was thinking of reinterviewing the tenants when her cell phone rang. Caller ID showed a number with a local area code.

"McCallum," she answered.

"It's me."

She heard the growly voice of the bartender from Fast Eddie's, the last person she'd expected to hear from.

"Hey, Biscuit," she said warily.

"I gave it some thought. Maybe I can help you out, after all."

"Okay. So did a woman hook up with Dylan last night?"

"Yeah. They left together."

"Can you describe her?"

"I'm no good at descriptions."

"How about if you look at some pictures?"

"Yeah. Yeah, I can do that. But not in the bar. The place is already starting to fill up. People can't see me talking to you, looking at a six-pack."

A photo six-pack, he meant. Police terminology for a cluster of mug shots shown to a witness or an informant. She wasn't surprised he knew the term.

"Is there someplace private we can meet?" she asked.

"There's an alley out back, behind Fast Eddie's."

"Would you be willing to meet me there?"

"Yeah, okay. I can't leave the bar now, though. There ain't nobody to cover for me. By three o'clock a couple of waitresses will be here. They can handle things while I step outside."

"I understand." Tess needed time, anyway. She didn't have any other photos to show him. "So three p.m. is okay?"

"Three, or a little after. In the alley."

His hedging on the time made her suspicious. "You're not going to stand me up, are you, Biscuit?"

"I bet you're not a lady who gets stood up too often."

"And I don't want to start now."

"I'll be there."

Tess drove to the resident agency on Civic Center Drive in downtown Santa Ana. She showed her ID at the door to the third-floor suite and brushed off an offer of assistance from a bored duty agent. In a back room she used a secure computer connection to access the California DMV database, where she found Abby's driver's license. She printed the photo, then trolled the database at random for female names, compiling five photos of other women who bore no resemblance to Abby. The six printouts would make a decent collection. If Biscuit selected Abby's picture out of the six, there would be no doubt that she had been to the bar.

Ordinarily the photos would go in the pockets of a display sheet, but Tess didn't have time for anything fancy. She dropped the printouts into a manila envelope from a supply cabinet, then did her best to clear the history of her searches from the PC.

The duty agent checked on her as she was finishing up. "You're certain I can't be of help?"

"I'm fine, thanks. Is Agent Crandall around?" Enough time had passed that she might be able to smooth things over.

"Crandall? No, he left. Went back to L.A."

Tess frowned. "He couldn't. I'm his ride."

"He hitched a ride with one of our guys who was heading up there about an hour ago."

"Oh."

"I've got his cell number if you need it."

"No, that's all right. I just thought . . . Never mind."

I just thought he would wait for me, she almost said.

Apparently he hadn't wanted to be in the same car with her during the long ride back to the L.A. office. Either that, or he hadn't trusted her to pick him up.

The Bureau car felt lonely and too big as she headed over to Fast Eddie's. She wasn't looking forward to the drive north.

She arrived at the bar shortly before three and parked near the alley. It offered privacy, all right. A little too much privacy, perhaps. On one side loomed the rear wall of the bar, on the other the windowless back side of a strip mall. She wasn't thrilled about the situation. There was a reason FBI agents normally worked in pairs.

She removed her SIG Sauer 9mm from its cross-draw holster and placed it in her jacket's side pocket. In Denver she customarily wore a trench coat with a special side pocket for her weapon, but L.A. in summer was too warm for the coat. Even so, she felt safer with the gun at her side. In an emergency she could draw from the hip faster than from the shoulder.

She entered the alley, carrying the envelope in her left hand, leaving her right arm unencumbered. As she walked, she let her right hand brush against the jacket, feeling the weight of the gun. It printed against the fabric, but she didn't care.

A few minutes after three, the back door of the bar opened, and the bartender appeared about five yards from her. Instead of coming forward, he just stood there in an angle of shadow thrown by the wall. It seemed odd that he would stay in the shadows. Maybe he was just afraid of being seen—but there was no one to see him.

And he was wearing a nylon jacket, unzipped. The day was warm. He didn't need a jacket any more than she did. She wore hers to conceal a weapon. He might be doing the same.

"Biscuit," she said.

"Hey." He sounded more affable than before, and that was another thing that bothered her.

Her senses were heightened. She was aware of details that would normally escape her notice. A scrap of plastic scudding along the alley floor. The chatter of a bird. The heat of the sun on her face as she walked toward him, and then the coolness of the shade.

Above all, his hands. The hands were what could get you killed.

His hands were empty and open, at his sides. He made no move to strike when she came within range.

"I have some photos for you to look at," she said.

It would have been natural if he'd moved out of the shade for more light, but he stayed put, as if he wanted the additional cover the building's shadow afforded. "Okay, no problem."

"Why'd you change your mind about helping me?"

"I thought about what you said. How we're on the same side. If some bitch offed Dylan, I want to help nail her for it."

This was plausible enough, but the way he said it wasn't convincing. It seemed rehearsed, mechanical.

And he was calm. Too calm. Like a man who had switched into the mode of an automaton, shutting down his feelings. A man who might be readying himself to kill.

"Well," she said, her voice level, "take a look."

She handed him the envelope. This was a moment of risk. He could grab her by the arm, grapple with her, try to get her in a choke hold.

But he merely took the envelope. He undid the flap, then shifted the envelope to his left hand and reached into his jacket.

She tensed. He saw her reaction and hesitated, smiling. "Need to get my glasses," he said. "Okay?"

His reading glasses. She'd forgotten.

"Okay," she said.

His hand went inside his jacket. Went low.

Last time he'd taken out the glasses, they had been in the vest pocket of his shirt.

He wasn't getting them out now.

She closed the distance between them and brought the flat of her palm down hard on his wrist, and something clattered on the ground. A gun. With a swipe of her foot she sent it spinning into the sunny part of the alley. She grabbed his hand and yanked his index finger back, cracking bone. His face twisted. He doubled over. Her knee caught him in the gut before she kicked his feet out from under him. He fell on the asphalt, and then she was kneeling on his back with her chrome-plated SIG Sauer in her hand, having drawn it without conscious intention, and she was saying very quietly, "Don't move."

She held the gun to his head while she patted him down. He was clean. The gun, now yards away, was the only weapon he'd been carrying.

"You're on my fucking kidney," Biscuit complained.

She dug her knee harder into his back. "Why'd you try to draw on me?"

"I wasn't, I swear."

"Answer the question."

He groaned. "I don't like feds."

"That's all?"

"That's all."

"Not much of a reason to kill somebody."

"Who says I was trying to kill you? I never drew down on you. You can't prove a fucking thing."

"I can prove you were in possession of a firearm. I make you as an ex-con, Biscuit. Owning a gun is a felony for you."

"It's not my gun."

"Doesn't matter whose it is. Doesn't matter if you just borrowed it. You're not allowed to even handle a firearm."

"Maybe I didn't. Maybe you planted it on me."

"Very original. I'm sure that'll hold up in court."

"You got any witnesses to say different? You got a partner to back you up? My word against yours."

The hell of it was, he wasn't wrong. As a veteran criminal he would know how to game the system. He would know more tricks than the public defender they assigned to him.

And if she took him in, he might not give her anything.

"I came here for information," she said. "Was there really a woman in the bar, or were you just feeding me a line?"

"There was a woman."

"You willing to ID her if her photo is in that envelope?"

"In exchange for what?"

"Getting back on my good side."

"You saying you'll let this go if I help you out?"

"I'm not saying anything, except that the only way you can help yourself in this situation is if you help me."

He thought about it. She gave him time. She even eased up on his back a little.

"Okay," he said finally.

Tess reached over and retrieved the envelope, then spilled its contents on the ground in front of his face. "Is she one of these?"

He blinked at the pictures.

"Gotta have my glasses," he said a little sheepishly.

She pressed the gun to his head. "I'll get them. Don't try anything."

"I already tried everything I'm gonna try."

She reached under him and pulled the glasses from his vest pocket, then flipped them open and perched them on his nose. One lens was cracked.

"Shit," he whined, "you busted 'em."

"I'm crying for you. Look at the pictures."

He squinted through the good lens, surveying the printouts. She waited, breath held.

"The third one," he said.

Tess pointed at the photo. "Her?"

"Yeah."

"You sure?"

"No doubt about it."

It was Abby.

Tess felt a sudden sinking sadness, as if something inside her had died. Only then did she realize how much she had wanted to be proved wrong.

"Are you sure you could see her well enough?" she pressed.

"I only got trouble with close-up stuff. I can see anything at arm's length or farther just fine. It was her."

"All right."

She got off him and gathered up the photos. He remained prone on the ground.

"So what happens now?" he asked.

"I'll let you off with a warning," Tess said.

"Appreciate that. For a fed, you're all right."

"Is that why you tried to kill me?"

"That wasn't personal."

She shook her head. "You're a disappointment, Biscuit. I thought you were a better man."

He crooked his neck to look up at her. His eyes were cold. "Ain't no such thing."

She didn't react fully to the encounter until she was back in the car. Then she began to shake all over as a wave of nausea rolled through her. She knew what it was—the combined effect of her adrenaline rush and the revelation about Abby. Of the two, she wasn't sure which hit her harder.

All along she'd been hoping her suspicions were groundless. Now she knew she had been right from the start. Abby had lied about hooking up with Dylan Garrick, which meant she had lied about everything else. She had left the bar with him. She had gone to his apartment. She had pistol-whipped him with his own gun, and then she had shot him in the face—shot him twice, first taking time to wrap the gun in a pillow to muffle the reports.

She had gone rogue. And she had to be stopped. Had to be taken off the street. Now. Today.

There was only one way to do it. Bring in the Bureau. The secrets Tess had been keeping for more than a year would have to come out. She didn't know what it would do to her career or her life, but she couldn't think about that now. Sometimes it was necessary to do the right thing. She had put off doing it for too long.

And Abby . . .

Abby would be put under arrest. If things went well, she would go quietly. If she resisted—well, Tess didn't want to consider that possibility.

For a last moment she hesitated. She didn't want to start a chain of events that would end with Abby either dead or in custody, facing a life sentence. There ought to be another way.

"I could talk to her," she murmured.

A cop-out. She had tried talking. She had asked Abby to open up last night at the Boiler Room, and again this morning at Palisades Park. Both times she'd been lied to. Abby was beyond help, perhaps beyond redemption.

But not beyond punishment.

Tess pulled into traffic, heading for the Santa Ana Freeway, which would take her north to L.A.

40

Abby couldn't say exactly what brought her to Vic Wyatt's apartment in Culver City at three thirty. She had a little time to kill before she had to sneak Andrea away from the FBI, but there was more to it than that. She knew Wyatt would be home—he was working the night watch this week and usually slept till midafternoon—and he was always up for a roll in the sack. But that wasn't it, either. Not entirely, anyway.

What she needed from him—well, she couldn't quite say. She needed something, though. Something more than sex, but of course the sex came first, as it always did between them. He greeted her at the door in his underwear, and without a word he led her into the bedroom, where a neighbor's TV, tuned to a game show, was audible through the thin wall, and he stripped her down with unsmiling efficiency and mounted her fast and hard as the bed creaked and a contestant played the lightning round. A lightning round was what it was for them, too, no foreplay, nothing complicated, none of the rococo contortionism on display in late-night movies and teenage fantasies, just a single-minded mission, carried out in a rush of sweat and heat, and concluding with a burst of applause from the studio audience.

Then they were done, and Abby lay beside him, strangely unsatisfied.

"You're wound up tight," Wyatt said.

"Yeah. I guess."

"I thought you would have climbed down off that adrenaline high by now."

"Maybe I like it. The adrenaline, I mean."

"Do you?"

"Ordinarily, yes."

"But not this time?"

"This time it's different. I'm kind of—I don't want to talk about it."

She did, of course. He waited.

"I'm in sort of a tight situation," she said.

"Tell me."

"Can't."

This was only partly true. She could tell him some of it, but she didn't think he would understand. She knew she would tell him, anyway.

He didn't coax or pressure her. He just reached out to stroke her hair, a slow, loving gesture that soothed her.

"Things are falling apart," she said. "I mean, not completely, but . . . enough."

"How?"

"I have to rely on myself. And I'm not sure I can."

"You always have before."

"Maybe not this time."

"What's different?"

"Me. I'm different. I'm losing it."

"Losing what?"

"Control."

"We all feel that way sometimes."

"Not me. I've never felt it. Not until now."

"What happened to get you thinking like this?"

"Nothing happened." An obvious lie. She could lie to Tess, but Wyatt knew her better. With him it was harder.

"Does it concern those bikers you were interested in?"

She didn't answer.

"Did you find them last night?"

"That's something I *really* can't talk about."

He propped himself up on one arm. "What did you do, Abby?"

"Got myself in a jam."

"That's pretty vague."

"It's as clear as I can afford to be."

"When did you start dealing in ambiguities?"

"I've always dealt in ambiguities. That's who I am. The woman of mystery. Not like you."

"I'm not mysterious?"

"You have procedures to follow. You have a manual. There's no manual that comes with my job."

"That's because you invented your job from scratch."

"Sometimes I wish I hadn't."

"What happened last night?"

She ignored the question. "You have rules and regs to keep you in line. I don't. All I've got is my own judgment."

"Isn't that the way you wanted it?"

"Yes. Except maybe my judgment isn't enough."

"You have good instincts, Abby."

"I have animal instincts. Fight or flight. Usually fight. Now I think . . ."

"Yes?"

"I think it's an instinct that may push me too far."

He withdrew his hand from her hair. She had become unconscious of his stroking, and noticed it again only once it had stopped.

"You're not going to give me any details," he said. It was not a question, merely the acknowledgment of a fact.

"I never do. Some things aren't good to share."

"If I make inquiries about the Scorpions in Santa Ana, what am I going to find out?"

"Don't make inquiries."

"If I do?"

"Don't." Her voice was hard.

There was silence between them. The TV next door was playing a commercial. The jingle vibrated through the wall, ridiculously cheerful.

"I'm worried about you," Wyatt said.

Abby closed her eyes. "Me, too."

At four thirty she left him. "Got an errand to run," she said lightly, but he wasn't fooled.

Wyatt kissed her. "Be careful."

"Always am."

"Not always," he whispered.

She couldn't argue with that. She left him at the door. When she looked back from the stairwell, he was gazing after her, as if watching her go for the last time.

It felt like a bad omen. She took the stairs quickly, relying on physical exercise to clear her mind and lift her mood.

Driving away, she called Andrea's cell number. The woman answered on the second ring. She'd been keeping the phone close, as instructed.

"Guess who," Abby said. She made herself smile. She was of the opinion that a smile could be sensed in a phone call. "Wait, don't answer that. Don't mention my name. What part of the house are you in?"

"The living room."

A microphone could have been planted there. It would pick up Andrea's end of the conversation. "Go into the bathroom and shut the door."

"Okay," Andrea said after a few moments.

"Turn on the water—the sink or the shower. And the fan, if there is one."

Another moment passed. Abby heard a hiss of background static, then Andrea's voice. "I've done it."

"All right. I don't think anyone can hear you now. So how's that garlic genius working out for you?"

"To tell you the truth, I haven't tried it. I don't have any garlic cloves in the house."

"Then how do you keep the vampires away? Anyway, your new toy will have to wait. We've got things to do. You ready for action?"

There was only a brief hesitation. "Ready."

"I want you to put on that wig you wore the last

time you went to one of Reynolds's campaign events. Your car got a pretty full tank?"

"Sure."

"Good. I'm on my way over to your neighborhood right now. When I get there, I'll call back. Then you'll get in your car and roll."

"Roll where?"

"I'll tell you later. First you have to lose your pursuit."

"I'm a little scared, Abby."

I'm a little scared, too, Abby thought, but what she said was, "Don't be. It's a cakewalk. You do trust me, right?"

"I trust you."

"Then just follow my lead—and enjoy the ride."

41

Tess arrived at the field office in Westwood at four thirty and parked in the underground garage. She showed her creds to the Protective Service staff who guarded the parking area, then took the elevator to the FBI suite, trying to decide what she was going to say and how she would say it.

Sugarcoating the story was impossible. She had made her own choices, and some of those choices had been bad. Now there was a price to pay.

The elevator hissed to a stop. The temporary key card issued to her was already in her hand. It let her into the reception area, then the suite of offices beyond.

She traversed the labyrinth of hallways to Michaelson's office. Distantly she was surprised she remembered where to find it. It had been a year and a half since Michaelson had offered her the post of deputy assistant director—DAD, in the Bureau's disconcerting acronym. It was an offer he had made only because of pressure from Washington. He had been openly relieved when she'd turned him down.

She wondered how things might have turned out if she'd accepted the opportunity. She would have been in on the reactivated MEDEA case from the start. She might have been able to keep Abby from getting involved. She might not be facing the end of her career today.

On the other hand, she might have killed Michaelson by now. Set him on fire or thrown him out the window or something. It was hard to say.

The thought raised a brief smile to her lips, but the smile vanished when she approached the ADIC's corner office. It was situated across the hall from the media office, where two media liaisons helped Michaelson stay in the news. They might be busy soon, and not in a good way. Or perhaps her misconduct could be kept entirely under wraps, another of the Bureau's many secrets.

She entered the anteroom and faced Michaelson's secretary.

"I'm Agent McCallum," she said. "I need to see the director."

"Do you have an appointment?"

"No, but—"

"It's usually advisable to schedule an appointment, especially on a Saturday."

Tess knew that Michaelson was always in on Saturdays. "Just tell him I have something important to speak to him about."

"He's in a meeting."

"It's urgent."

"I can't just interrupt—"

"Yes, you can. Buzz him, or I'll walk in there without an announcement." She would, too. What the hell? She couldn't get herself in any worse trouble than she was already in.

The secretary grimaced but yielded. She activated the intercom and informed her boss that SA McCallum requested a few minutes of his time.

Tess expected Michaelson to make her wait, if only as a power play. She was proved wrong when his voice came over the speaker, saying, "Send her in."

"Yes, sir." The secretary conceded defeat with a flick of her wrist toward the closed office door. "He'll see you."

Tess walked to the door. She had time to wonder why Michaelson had allowed her to come in without waiting. Then her hand was on the knob, and the hard reality of it reminded her of what she was about to do. Michaelson had been looking for a way to undermine her career for years—since the Mobius case, in fact. Now she would hand him the chance he'd been hoping for. She expected him to take full advantage of it. He would show no mercy. He would do his best to finish her.

She opened the door, then stopped, freezing just inside the threshold.

His office was much like hers in Denver, only larger, with an even more intimidating desk flanked by two American flags. And there was an I-love-me wall, of course. Michaelson's encounters with the great and the near great were lovingly documented in a photo mural that really did take up an entire wall.

The secretary hadn't lied when she said there was a meeting under way. The ADIC sat behind his desk. Two of the leather chairs facing the desk were occupied. Hauser was in one. Crandall was in the other.

She saw their faces. Cold fury on Michaelson's face. Disappointment on Hauser's. And Crandall—he looked away from her for a moment, then steadied himself and returned her gaze. She read defiance in his expression. His face said, *I did what I had to do.* Tess supposed it was true. She had counted on his loyalty, but in the end she'd given him nothing to be loyal to.

She turned to Michaelson. "I was coming here to tell you."

"You're a little late," he snapped.

She looked at Crandall. "Evidently I am."

Crandall's throat made a slow swallowing motion. "It was for your own good, Tess."

She wanted to dispute the point, but she couldn't, really. He hadn't known she was coming. He'd reached the same decision she had, just an hour or two sooner.

"You're in a great deal of trouble, McCallum." The nasal voice belonged to the ADIC, whose prominent proboscis had given him the informal sobriquet "the Nose."

"Please, Dick," she said easily, "call me Tess." She

sat on the leather couch, another item that was larger and costlier than the equivalent furnishing in her own office.

Hauser was watching her. "Agent Crandall has told us quite a story," he said carefully. "I'd like to believe he's misconstrued the situation."

"He hasn't."

"He says you've been working with a civilian, covering for her. He says this individual played a key role in the Rain Man case. And she's been directly involved in MEDEA."

"All true."

"And you chose to keep this to yourself."

"Until now, yes."

Hauser went on staring at her. His presence meant that Crandall had gone to him first, and then Hauser had brought him to the director. It made sense. A low-level agent like Crandall wouldn't get in to see the ADIC on his own.

"Was there something else you wanted to say, Agent Hauser?" she asked.

"I had a very high estimation of you."

She noted he'd used the past tense. "I'm sorry to let you down."

Hauser's voice was low. "You let us all down."

His quiet disappointment was harder to take than the Nose's more theatrical outrage. Tess said only, "I made some bad decisions."

"Bad decisions?" Michaelson half rose from his chair, then sat again, as if unable to decide what to do with his body. "Bad fucking decisions? Is that what you said?"

"I didn't say *fucking*."

"Jesus Christ." Michaelson slapped his desk, a hard percussive sound like a gunshot. "I'll tell you what you've done. Passing Bureau sensitive information to non-Bureau personnel, falsifying an official report, participation in a cover-up, unauthorized use of Bureau resources, misprision of a felony, misuse of Bureau property, cooperation with a known lawbreaker. That's just for starters.''

"Abby isn't a known lawbreaker.''

"You're saying this friend of yours has never broken the law?''

"I'm saying she's not known for it. She has no record. And she's not my friend.''

"Not anymore, apparently, or you wouldn't be here.''

"She never was my friend," Tess said quietly. This was possibly true. She wasn't sure. It didn't matter, anyway.

"If not, then why did you cover for her for the better part of two years? You're fucked, McCallum. Any way you slice it, you are over and done with.''

She looked at him and caught the glimmer of a brief, furtive, feral smile. Beneath his indignation he was secretly pleased. He'd been waiting for this moment for a long time.

Tess sighed. "I get the picture, Dick. It's serious.''

"*Serious* isn't the word. It's career-ending. I always knew you would flame out eventually.''

"At least I'm going out in style.''

"We'll see how much style you have left after OPR is through with you. And after ASU implements your punishment, which, let me assure you, will be maximally severe.'' ASU was the Administrative Services Division, responsible for imposing whatever disciplinary measures the Office of Professional Responsibility deemed appropriate. "A letter of censure isn't going to cut it. At a minimum, you're looking at suspension without pay. Then reassignment to some choice locale—a resident agency in North Dakota, maybe. And that's a best-case scenario. Personally, I intend to press for your termination—along with criminal charges.''

The last part was an empty threat. The Bureau would never put an SAC on trial. Too many embarrassing secrets would emerge. But termination was definitely a live option. The review would take time—investigations by the OPR always did—but in the end they would nail her. Tess had run a couple of OPR reviews herself, as every agent on a management track had to do, and she knew that the work was slow but thorough, and nobody was cut any slack.

"And it won't help you that you never came forward," Michaelson added. "You never did the right thing."

"I did the right thing by coming here today."

Michaelson snorted. "You came because you knew Crandall was going to talk, and you wanted to put your spin on the story before he did."

Tess smiled a little. It was typical of Michaelson to think that way. That was what he would have done. "Actually, I didn't think Rick would come here. I guess I . . ." She tried to find the right word. "I misjudged him."

Neutral though it was, the statement seemed to pain Crandall. She saw him wince.

"I'm sorry, Tess," Crandall said.

Michaelson waved off his words. "He has nothing to apologize for—except not reporting your misconduct sooner."

"You're right." Tess nodded. "He has no reason to apologize. He was only doing what he felt was correct."

She said it while looking at Crandall.

"None of this was his fault," she added. "It's mine. All mine. I take full responsibility."

"You fucking bet you do," Michaelson snarled. "Now I want to hear it, all of it, from the beginning."

"Hasn't Rick told you—"

"He's told what he knows, which is only bits and pieces. You're the one who has all the details. I want to hear them. From you. Right now."

"Of course. And you will." She leaned forward on the sofa. "But the most important thing is what I've learned today. It's why I'm here. It's why I had to give Abby up."

"And what's that?"

"She tracked down Dylan Garrick last night. Found him at the bar where the bikers hang out. She left with him. I got a positive ID from the bartender."

Michaelson sat back in his chair. "So Abby Sinclair killed Garrick?"

"I believe so, yes."

"Shot him, execution-style?"

"Yes."

"Why? To protect Andrea Lowry?"

"I don't think so."

"Why, then?"

Tess took a breath. "Abby was in the house when Garrick's crew entered. She's the one who fought them off, not Andrea."

"You were in the goddamned house, too. You must have seen her there."

"I saw her."

"She's the reason you got interested in MEDEA in the first place?" Michaelson was getting it now. "She's why you wanted to be on the squad. You *manipulated* me."

"That wasn't hard," Tess said with a smile, "Dick."

She knew he hated to be called Dick. She wasn't helping herself by baiting him.

Hauser cut in. "I don't follow. If Sinclair wasn't trying to protect Lowry, why did she hunt down Garrick?"

Tess shut her eyes. "She was pissed off. She nearly died in the firefight. I think she wanted . . . revenge."

"Oh, great." This time Michaelson did get up. "Just great. She's killing people for revenge. Maybe she'll go after the congressman next."

He said it without thinking, but there was a sudden coldness in the room.

"Shit," Michaelson added. "You don't think she would, do you?"

"I don't know," Tess said.

"You know *her*."

"Not really. I'm not sure anybody does. She keeps

secrets. She plays games. You never know what she's really thinking—or what she might do."

"You're saying she could go after Reynolds?" Hauser asked.

"It's not impossible."

"We'll make it impossible." Hauser stood up. "We'll get her off the streets."

"If you can find her," Tess said.

"We'll start with her home address."

Tess shook her head. "I doubt she'll be there. She probably expects us to be onto her by now. She's not going to sit around waiting to be three-oh-two'd." Form 302 was the Bureau's standard arrest form.

"I'll get a warrant," Hauser said. "Telephonic approval won't take long. Or I can plead exigent circumstances and make a warrantless entry. One way or the other, I'll muster a raid squad and hit her residence. If she's not there, we'll conduct a search. There may be something in her records to indicate where she is and what she's planning."

"I'd like to be in on that," Crandall said with a glance at Michaelson.

The ADIC acknowledged him with a vague gesture. "First do an indices check on Sinclair. See if her record is as clean as McCallum claims. Then you can join Agent Hauser's team at the residence."

"Yes, sir."

"Go. Both of you. Agent McCallum and I have a long discussion ahead of us. Maybe by the time we're done, you'll have Abby Sinclair in custody. And I promise you, once we've got her, she'll never see the light of day again."

These last words were aimed at Tess. She knew Michaelson meant it.

The door opened and closed, and then she was alone with the assistant director. He settled down behind his desk again and steepled his hands. His ferret eyes and hawk nose loomed over his tented fingers.

"Start talking," he said.

42

Abby waited until she was on the outskirts of San Fernando, cruising down Foothill Boulevard, before calling Andrea again. This time Andrea answered on the first ring. The hissing noise in the background indicated that she was in the bathroom again.

"It's go time," Abby said. "Get in your car and head southeast on Glenoaks Boulevard. You're wearing the wig, right?"

"Yes." There was a tremor in Andrea's voice.

"Steady now. No need for any opening-night jitters. I've done this kind of thing before."

"You have?"

"More times than I can count." This would have been true only if she couldn't count to zero. Normally she was the hunter, not the quarry. She'd never actually had to break free of surveillance. But how hard could it be?

She supposed she was about to find out.

"Keep the phone on," she added. "Let me know once you've gotten onto Glenoaks. Oh, and remember rule number one of countersurveillance. No looking over your shoulder. That's what the rearview mirror is for. If you start looking around in an obvious way, they'll know you're onto them."

"I wouldn't even know what to look for."

"That's fine. Just assume they're tracking you. They may be behind or ahead or on parallel streets—probably all of the above."

"Behind *and* ahead?"

"Most likely. They'll be bookending you. Standard procedure, if they have enough vehicles."

"Then how can I possibly get away?"

"Piece of cake. Just do as I say. I've got it all worked out."

A few minutes passed. Abby spent the time navigating to Glenoaks Boulevard, where she parked at the curb and watched the traffic stream by. Andrea's voice came over the phone again.

"Okay, I'm driving southeast on Glenoaks."

"Tell me the next cross street you pass."

"I'm coming up to it now. Corcoran Street."

That was approximately a half mile northwest of where Abby was parked. "Call out each cross street as you pass it. I'm going to pull in somewhere behind you as you pass Filmore Street. Remember, don't look for me."

"God, I hope I don't screw this up."

"You're handling the assignment like a pro." This was true. Andrea was doing better than Abby had expected.

She waited as Andrea announced each new street in turn: Vaughn, Eustace, Paxton, Montford. As she said, "Filmore," the Chevy Malibu swept past Abby in the slow lane. She let a few more cars drive by before she pulled away from the curb. Ahead, she could see the Chevy.

"Got you in sight. Everything's hunky-dory. Just keep going for a while."

"What do I do then?"

"Don't worry about the future. Be in the moment. Countersurveillance is a Zen thing."

The next few blocks went smoothly enough. Abby almost got caught at a stoplight at Van Nuys Boulevard but blew through it as the signal cycled from yellow to red. Last thing she needed was to be red-boarded right now.

She knew that the undercover Bureau cars must be all around her, keeping Andrea in a surveillance net.

She made no effort to identify them. For undercover work the Bureau could use anything from an ambulance to a VW Bug. The agents could be alone or in pairs, and could be of any description. She wouldn't catch them talking into their radios, because the microphone would be hidden in the windshield visor or held below the dash.

Though she liked to talk down the feebies, the truth was that they were good at shadowing a moving target. Even so, they didn't scare her. Not much, anyhow. They might be good, but she was better. She was always better. Better than everybody. This was her philosophy, and it had kept her alive so far.

Up ahead she saw the landmark she was looking for. "See that car wash? It's one of those drive-through deals. Turn in there and get on line. I'll be right behind you."

"We're getting our cars washed?"

"Yes, we are. I hope you brought some money. It costs seven ninety-five. And don't get the hot wax, please."

"Why not?"

"Trust me on this. You'll thank me later."

"What are we doing, Abby? This doesn't make sense."

"All will become clear, Grasshopper."

The Chevy turned obediently into the parking lot and joined a short line of drivers waiting to pay their money and take a ride through the car wash. Abby pulled in behind Andrea's car. She checked her rearview.

The only possible hitch in her otherwise flawless plan would be if one of the surveillance vehicles decided to join the line, also. She was betting that none would; following Andrea into the car wash would be too conspicuous.

Since no one pulled in behind Abby, it seemed her gamble had paid off. She inched forward as the line advanced. Ahead, she saw Andrea roll down her window and pay. Her car was guided forward onto the rails and towed into the tunnel, veiled by a mist of spray.

Abby paid next, then put her car in neutral as the towline engaged. She eased along the rails, the Chevy a blurred white shape two yards ahead.

She spoke into the cell phone again. "Okay, take off your wig and leave it on the seat. Get out and switch cars with me."

"Switch cars?"

"That's the plan. Ingenious in its simplicity, don't you think?"

"We'll get soaked."

"Small price to pay for freedom. Let's go. And hold on to your phone."

Abby didn't wait for an answer. She threw open her car door and stepped out. The car continued to crawl forward through the artificial downpour.

For a moment, in the windowless darkness, battered by rain, she flashed back to the Rain Man case—the storm drains under the city, where she and Tess had nearly drowned. But the memory was gone almost before it registered.

She ran toward the Chevy and met Andrea halfway. "Aren't you glad we didn't get the hot wax?" Abby shouted over the roar. She hoped she saw Andrea smile, but in the gloom she couldn't be sure.

Ahead, large foaming brushes were descending to wipe the Chevy. Abby ducked into the driver's seat and slammed the door before the nearest brush could swab her.

In the few seconds she had spent in the spray, she'd been thoroughly drenched. She cranked up the Chevy's heater to full blast.

Looking back, she saw the dim outline of her Mazda. Movement in the front seat. Andrea was behind the wheel.

"When you leave the car wash," Abby said into her phone, "head east on the surface streets. I'll tell you where to meet me once I shake off my pursuit."

"You sure this'll work?" Andrea asked.

"Abso-tively. These FBI people aren't as smart as they like to pretend."

She hoped this was true.

As the Chevy advanced into the hot-air blowers, Abby stuck the wig on her head and patted it down. Water from her sopping hair dribbled out from under the wig and tickled her neck.

There was really no reason why the plan should fail. The interior of the car wash was dark and misty and obscured by moving equipment. No one would have a clear view of the inside from any likely vantage point, nor would the feds be looking inside anyway. They would be waiting until the Chevy emerged. When it did, driven by a woman in a brown wig, they would take up the chase again. They would never even notice the red Mazda.

The blowers receded into the background, the towline uncoupled, and Abby shifted the Chevy into drive and started forward, not hurrying. She waited at the curb for a break in the traffic, then turned right and blended with the stream of vehicles on Glenoaks.

By now the trigger—the surveillance operative with the best view of the car wash—would have radioed the rest of his squad, who would be executing a follow. Standard procedure in FBI vehicular surveillance was a floating box formation, a constantly shifting arrangement of vehicles arrayed behind, in front of, and parallel to the target.

Only one vehicle at a time, known as the command vehicle, would maintain direct visual contact. The others would assume command periodically as the target executed turns. If Abby made a left turn, an outrider vehicle somewhere on her left would follow and take point in the pursuit. If she turned right, a right-side outrider would do the same. Should she flip a U, one of the vehicles behind her would turn onto a side street, make a quick turn, and fall in behind her as she passed by. Take a side street, and her surveillance would pace her on parallel streets.

The idea was for the feds to keep the target contained without giving themselves away. Five or six cars would be sufficient to pull it off, though there could be ten or more.

It wasn't easy to break containment, but it could be done. What was required was a series of maneuvers that would shake off her pursuers one or two at a time, carried out quickly enough that they had no time to regroup.

The assignment would have been easier at night, with darkness as cover, but on these long summer days the sun didn't set before eight p.m. She would have to make the best of it.

She took a few moments to adjust to the Chevy's handling. Every car had its own feel. This one rode pretty solid, with no rattles or squeaks. Tight suspension, decent traction, smooth steering.

When she was comfortable behind the wheel, she decided to make her move.

She cut right on Tuxford Street and took the on-ramp to the Golden State Freeway westbound, easing into the fast lane. The chase cars were behind her, she had no doubt. She sped west for two miles, gradually upping her speed, then abruptly cut across multiple lanes and shot down an off-ramp onto Osbourne Street. A slick maneuver, which might have lost the command vehicle, at least.

But she had to assume that other surveillance cars had managed to follow her or had been paralleling the freeway on surface streets. She hooked southeast onto Laurel Canyon Boulevard, a major thoroughfare, and accelerated, weaving through traffic and running yellow lights. As she flashed through the intersection of Laurel Canyon and Saticoy, she spun the steering wheel and whirled around in a screaming skid, then slammed on the emergency brake and floored the gas. The car nearly flipped over from centrifugal force but somehow stayed upright, now facing north. She popped the emergency brake, and the Chevy tore forward, racing north while outraged drivers blasted their horns.

She didn't know what they were so upset about. It was a standard bootleg turn. Moonshiners did it all the time.

The tactic must have shaken off a few more of the pursuit vehicles. Any cars ahead of her would never be able to turn around fast enough to catch up. Any cars following too closely behind her would have been all the way through the intersection before they could react. By the time they found a way to turn around, she would be far gone.

The only danger was that one or two cars might have been farther behind her. If so, they could have been warned in time to stay on her tail. It was doubtful, but she was taking no chances.

She sped north for a half mile, then cut onto a side street lined with bungalows and slammed the Chevy left at the first intersection, then right, right again, left, cutting down street after street in the grid work of residential blocks, until even she didn't know where she was.

Finally she pulled into an alley walled in by a double row of houses and parked behind a Dumpster, where the car wouldn't easily be seen from the street. She let her head fall back on the headrest.

No way the feds could have followed her this far. Even if one of the chase cars had stayed with her after the bootleg turn, her subsequent maneuvers would have shaken it off.

Though she was out of pocket for the moment, she wasn't home free. Already the surveillance team would be initiating a lost-command drill, retreating to the perimeter of the area where she was last seen in an effort to pick her up again when she started moving. But that was okay, because it was the Chevy Malibu they were looking for, and the Chevy wasn't going anywhere.

She took off the wig and left it on the seat. Carefully

she wiped the steering wheel, dashboard controls, and door handle to remove any prints. Then she left the car and took her cell phone out of her purse. She had never ended her call to Andrea.

"Still there?" she asked.

"I'm here."

"I lost our friends and ditched the car."

"Ditched the—"

"Not to worry. You'll pick it up later. Right now, though, I need you to pick *me* up."

"Where?"

She glanced at the nearest street signs and told Andrea the intersection. "You know where that is?"

"Not really."

"There's a Thomas Brothers map book in the Mazda's glove compartment. I'll be loitering on the street corner like a hooker, only better dressed."

"What's the plan, Abby? What are we doing?"

"It'll all be clear soon enough. You've trusted me this far. Okay?"

There was a beat of hesitation. "Okay."

"Don't sweat it. You're in good hands. The hard part is over." She ended the call and hoped Andrea believed her.

There was no reason why she should. It was a lie, after all.

The hard part hadn't even begun.

43

Tess was finishing off the recitation of her misdeeds, and enjoying it considerably less than her last visit to confession, when Michaelson's secretary interrupted to say that Hauser was on the line. Michaelson took the call on the speakerphone.

"We've got a problem," Hauser said. "One of my surveillance agents just called. Lowry has broken out of containment." Michaelson uttered an expletive, which Hauser ignored. "She couldn't have done it alone," he went on. "She had to have help."

Michaelson shot Tess a cold glance. "Your friend again?"

Tess frowned. "Stop calling her my friend."

Michaelson asked Hauser where he was now. "At Sinclair's condo in Westwood. She's not here. Her Mazda Miata's not in its assigned space."

"She's hooked up with Lowry," Michaelson said. "For all we know, the two of them could be conspiring to kill Reynolds together. Or maybe Sinclair's working with Reynolds to get Lowry."

"Abby wouldn't do anything like that," Tess protested.

"How the hell do you know? She's already killed Garrick. Now she's pulled Lowry away from surveillance. The goddamned situation is out of control."

Hauser's voice crackled over the speaker. "McCallum, you've been in contact with her. You know her cell phone number?"

Tess recited it from memory.

"We can track her by her cell," Hauser said. "She doesn't even need to be using it. As long as the phone is turned on, it'll send out periodic transmissions to check for signal availability."

"We'll need the cooperation of her cellular provider," Michaelson said.

"Those outfits usually offer assistance to law enforcement voluntarily. We can use her number to find out which provider she subscribes to. Hopefully we can obtain whatever real-time info they're getting."

"How accurately can we track her?"

"Depends on the phone and the carrier. Mainly the phone. Most cell phones have GPS chips built in. With GPS we can pinpoint her to within five feet."

"And if her phone doesn't have a chip?"

"Then its position can be triangulated from the signals received by the three nearest cell towers. It's just as fast, but not as precise. We can narrow down her location to a city block, maybe."

Michaelson nodded at the speakerphone as if he were addressing Hauser face-to-face. "All right, get going on this." The call ended, and Michaelson turned to Tess. "Looks like we're done for now. You can go."

"I want to stay. I want to be part of the takedown."

"You have to be joking."

"I know Abby. I can be helpful."

"Yes, you've been nothing but helpful so far. Get lost, McCallum."

"Richard, you can have me shitcanned later. Right now the only priority is to get Abby in lockup."

"And how is keeping her best friend on the case going to facilitate that outcome?"

Tess stood. "God*damn* it. I'm *not* her best friend. If I were, would I be here now? I'm trying to fix things."

"Too late."

"I'm the only one who has any experience in dealing with Abby. I've already supplied her cell phone number, which you can bet is unlisted. You may need my help again."

"The day I need your help, McCallum, is the day I give up my post. Now get out."

Tess bit back a reply. She was moving for the door

when Michaelson got another call from Hauser, again on speakerphone.

"We've ID'd her provider. They're cooperating. Bad news is, her cell isn't GPS-equipped. Good news is, they've got a signal, and they're feeding us her location on a real-time basis."

"Where is she?" Michaelson snapped.

"The 101 Freeway. Moving southeast out of the Valley into downtown L.A."

"And they can locate her to within a city block?"

"One or two blocks, yes. Hold on. They say she's off the freeway now, going southwest on a surface street. Could be on Flower or Grand."

"What the hell's she doing downtown?"

"No idea."

With extreme reluctance Michaelson looked at Tess. "Any idea why she'd be going there?"

Tess wished she had something brilliant to contribute, but all she could say was "No."

"She have an office there, maybe?"

"As far as I know, she works out of her home. She's not exactly the nine-to-five type."

Michaelson asked Hauser if a search of the condo had turned up anything relating to a downtown address. Hauser said the search was ongoing. So far nothing of value had been found.

"Well, she must have something there. Records, computer disks—did you get into her PC?"

"Got a tech working on it now. I'm not too confident, though."

"What does that mean?"

"I don't think this woman is stupid enough to leave anything for us to find. She's the kind who covers her tracks."

"Sounds about right," Tess said.

Michaelson told her to shut up. To Hauser he said, "We'll have to BOLO her Miata."

"There are a million of them in L.A. Hold on." Hauser was gone briefly, then returned. "They tell me she's stopped. Hasn't moved in three minutes."

"Where?"

"Central business district. Parameters are Flower Street and Hill Street to the north and south, Sixth Street and Fourth Street to the west and east."

Michaelson paced. "What's there? Bunch of office buildings, all closed for the night?"

"And the library, the Brayton Hotel, Pershing Square, a lot of smaller places. Plus she could be in one of the office towers, even if it is technically closed. Doing some sort of black-bag work, maybe."

"It's a lot of territory to cover." Michaelson rubbed his head. "Say we send in every available street agent. We comb the entire area, find her vehicle, and close in on her."

"If she spots us first, she'll take off."

"We cordon off the perimeter so she can't get away."

"Cordon off downtown L.A.? We don't have the manpower."

"Get LAPD involved," Michaelson yelled.

Hauser wasn't budging. "It'll take an hour just to work out the logistics."

"I have an idea." Tess spoke quietly, her calm voice drilling through the clutter. "Let me talk to her on the phone."

Michaelson stared at her. "And say what, exactly?"

"I'll tell her we need to meet. We've had meetings before. It shouldn't tip her off."

She expected Michaelson to dismiss the idea out of hand. It was a measure of his desperation that he did not. "You think," he said slowly, "you can get her to agree to a rendezvous?"

"It depends."

"On what?"

"On whether or not she still trusts me. She knows I was suspicious about Garrick's death."

"It's too risky," Hauser said over the speaker. "If she senses a trap, she'll make a break for it. We're better off taking her unawares."

Tess shook her head. "Deploy two hundred agents

to scour the business district, and there's a fair chance she'll see them before they see her. If she knows she's been made, she probably won't take the Mazda. She'll hot-wire something or find some other way out. Road-blocks won't stop her."

"As long as she's got her phone," Hauser said, "we can still track her."

"The phone will be the first thing to go. She's not stupid. That's the thing you both have to understand. She knows how to take care of herself."

Michaelson pursed his lips. "But she's not smart enough to see through you if you call?"

"I don't know."

He hesitated for a long moment. "Call her," he said finally. "And be convincing."

Tess took out her cell phone and punched in Abby's number. She counted four rings before the call was answered.

"Hey, Tess," Abby said without preamble, obviously having recognized the number on the caller ID screen. "I enjoyed our picnic in the park this morning."

Tess swallowed. "Actually, that's what I called to talk about."

"Another lecture?"

"I wanted to apologize."

"Really?"

"It was wrong of me to suspect you." She held her voice steady. "All the signs point to a gang hit."

"Or maybe I just set it up to look that way."

"Stop playing games, Abby. This is serious."

"Sorry. Winsome drollery is my nature. Apology accepted, no hard feelings, yada yada. Now if you'll excuse me—"

"There's more."

"More apologizing? I've hit the jackpot."

"Not more apologies, just more to talk about. Something's about to go down. We're thinking of making a move tonight. A big move."

"Gonna nail a major target? Give somebody a one-way ticket to the slammer?"

Tess shut her eyes. "That's the plan. But I need to ask you a few questions first."

"I'm a little busy now—"

"I don't want to discuss it over the phone, anyway. Can we meet? Just for a few minutes?"

"I'm nowhere near Westwood."

"Doesn't matter. I can come to you. Name a place—I'll be there."

"Okay, I'm at the central library. You can meet me in the main lobby."

"It'll take me about a half hour to get there."

"Longer than that, if you're coming from Westwood."

"I'm closer than Westwood." A lie, but she could hardly tell Abby she'd be using her red light to cut through traffic and shorten the trip. "Thirty, thirty-five minutes. What are you doing in the library, anyway?"

"Catching up on my reading, what else? See you in a few, soul sister."

Soul sister, Tess thought numbly.

She didn't feel anything like Abby's sister right now.

44

"Who was that?" Andrea asked. "Why did you say you were at the library?"

"It's not important." Abby slipped the phone back into her purse and kept walking. "Just a pal of mine, playing games."

She knew what was going on. By now Tess must have linked her to Dylan Garrick. Presumably she was looking to bring her in for questioning. Tess could determine Abby's general whereabouts with the cell phone's signal, but she wouldn't be able to zero in on her exact location. The library was across the street from the Brayton Hotel—close enough, Abby thought, for government work.

When Tess failed to find her, she and her fellow feds—Abby assumed she was working with her colleagues at this point—would search the area. They might find the Miata, but maybe not, or at least not right away. She'd made Andrea park in an alley near the Brayton rather than in the hotel's underground garage. The garage was too obvious a place to stash the car, and in a situation like this, when meeting a man like Reynolds, it was best never to be obvious.

Things were a little complicated, but she could handle it—or die trying.

She guided Andrea toward the hotel entrance, trying to think good thoughts.

There was no way for Michaelson to keep Tess off the arrest squad. She had to be in place in order to draw Abby into view.

"We'll settle matters when you get back," the ADIC growled.

"Great, Dick. Something for me to look forward to."

Tess took out the red ·Kojak light carried by all Bureau cars and mounted it on her dashboard, then made her way to Abby's condo building at high speed. The sun in her rearview mirror was a brassy ball of glare. Still more than two hours till sunset. By the time the sun went down, Abby would probably be in custody—and then she would rarely see the sun again.

The trip didn't take long. As it turned out, Abby lived only a few blocks from the federal building, a fact that struck Tess as somehow ironic. In the condominium tower's curving driveway she met up with Hauser and six other agents, among them Crandall. The rest of Hauser's people were still upstairs going through Abby's things.

Crandall and two men Tess didn't know crowded into her car, while Hauser and the other three took a second Bureau sedan. Ordinarily they would have worn raid jackets for an arrest, but in this case they wanted to keep a low profile once they arrived downtown. With red lights flashing, they cut down to Olympic and sped east, sticking to surface streets because the freeway was jammed.

By now everyone was miked up, and conversation between the two cars was possible on a scrambled tac frequency. In the backseat of Tess's car, someone had brought up a map of the library on his laptop. "There are three entrances to the main lobby—Fifth Street, Hope Street, Flower Street. If Sinclair tries to run, we won't know which exit to cover."

"We can cover them all," Tess said.

"No time," Hauser said over Tess's earpiece. "We're barely going to make it there on time as it is. And the damn library closes at six."

Crandall frowned. "You don't think she's setting us up, do you?"

"I don't think so," Tess said quietly. "But I can't be sure."

Hauser's voice grated in her ear. "She can't be sure. Terrific."

Abby sat Andrea down on a sofa near the registration desk in the lobby of the Brayton Hotel. Andrea gazed around, blinking at the expanse of Saltillo tile, the great potted palms and indoor koi pond.

When was the last time she'd ventured into a hotel, any hotel? Before her institutionalization, probably. That was twenty years ago.

"Okay, kiddo," Abby said. "Focus. This is where I reveal my master plan."

"Which is?"

"You're going to help me out. And with luck, I'm going to help you out. We're like two baboons picking nits off each other. You scratch my back. I scratch yours."

"I don't follow."

Abby didn't blame her. She wasn't sure she followed herself. She got like this in the minutes before a potentially explosive situation. She talked too much and made little sense. It could be disconcerting to others. Heck, it could be disconcerting to her.

With effort she pulled herself together. "Here's the thing. I'm going to sit over there." She pointed at a scattering of tables and armchairs almost dead center on the lobby floor. "You'll sit close, but out of sight. Behind that plant, I think."

"That's a tree. A palm tree."

"Tree, plant, whatever. It's green, it has chlorophyll, and it provides better cover than, say, carpet moss. Or Kate Moss, for that matter. From my table you'll be invisible, I think. Let's test it out."

She placed Andrea at the hidden table and inspected the result.

"It works. You're totally concealed. Unless the tree starts molting, we'll be fine."

"Trees don't molt."

"Even better."

"I still don't understand."

"You'll be eavesdropping on a conversation I'm about to have. At a certain point you'll emerge from the greenery and confront the other party. Shock value is what we're going for."

"Shock value," Andrea echoed blankly.

"Amazing how a little honest surprise can penetrate someone's defenses. See, look at this." Abby produced an item from her purse. "Microcassette recorder. Not as handy as a garlic genius, but you can't have everything. Normally I use it for dictation. Note to self, that kind of thing. Tonight I'm using it as a clandestine recording device. I'm going to get the conversation on tape."

"The conversation with . . . ?" Then Andrea understood. "Oh, no."

"Oh, yes."

"Not him."

"In the very flesh. He's coming here at six."

"But . . . why?"

"He thinks I'm planning to betray you to him." Abby held up a reassuring hand. "Just a ruse. There's no betrayal."

"Jack . . . coming here . . ."

"I told him I'd tell him where to find you. In exchange, I get a pile of money. But what Jack doesn't know is, I'm not all that materialistic. Money can't buy happiness, or at least not enough happiness to tempt me."

The information finally penetrated. "He expects you to deliver me to him?"

"Right."

"He'll be furious when he finds out you lied."

"Good. Anger is another way of lowering a person's defenses. Angry people tend to blurt things out. I'm hoping JR will do a lot of world-class blurting tonight."

"JR. That's funny." Andrea had a faraway look. "I

called him that once. He hated it. He didn't want to be a villain on a prime-time soap."

"But he ended up as one, anyway. A villain, that is. He hasn't made it to prime time yet."

"I still don't get it, Abby. What can he possibly say? You think he'll admit to sending those gunmen to my house?"

"That—and maybe some other things. All you need to do is listen. At the right moment, step out from behind the foliage and confront him."

"What's the right moment?"

"You'll know. Trust your instincts. Whenever it happens, it'll scare the bejesus out of him. He hasn't been up close and personal with you in twenty years. He's not expecting to see you now."

"But he wants me *dead*."

"I know it."

"If he sees me—"

"There's nothing he can do. Not here. Look around you. We're in a very public place. The lobby of a five-star hotel."

Andrea nodded slowly, not quite believing it. "What do you want me to say to him?"

"Anything you like."

"I don't have any idea—after all these years—my mind's a blank."

"It won't be. You'll find the words. You'll have plenty to say to the distinguished congressman, believe me."

Andrea looked away. "You should have told me what I was getting into."

"I was afraid you wouldn't come."

"I might not have."

"Well, you're here now. This will all work out for the best." Abby put a hand on her arm. "You still trust me, right?"

"I trust you." Andrea smiled, a startling sight on her pale, serious face. "You're completely crazy, of course, but I *do* trust you."

Abby smiled back. "Nicest thing I've heard all day."

The agent in the backseat of Tess's car was still reviewing files on his laptop. "There are security stations at the lobby entrances. Metal detectors. To go in armed, you'll have to show your Bureau ID."

Tess wasn't going to do that. "If I start flashing my creds, Abby will notice, and she'll know I'm carrying. That'll be enough to tip her off."

"Well, you can't be unarmed," Hauser said over the air.

"Sure I can. Remember, she can't bring a gun inside, either."

"How sure are you she can't sneak a weapon past security?"

Tess, who was quite certain Abby could outwit any library rent-a-cop, didn't answer directly. "She's not going to take me out, for God's sake."

"Even if she thinks you've betrayed her?" Hauser pressed. "She took out Garrick for shooting at her, and that was just business. With you, it's personal."

"She won't shoot me," Tess insisted, hoping she was right.

"We'll send a man after you to watch your back."

"Abby can make a Bureau agent without even trying. Anyone you send in will be spotted immediately. I'm going in alone."

"I think, Agent McCallum, you've forfeited the right to work solo in this organization."

"We don't have any choice about it. Either I go in alone or Abby will be spooked for sure."

"Maybe you want to be alone with her so you can pass on a warning."

"If I'd wanted to warn her, I could have phoned her at any time."

Hauser drew an audible breath. "All right. We'll play it your way. But you won't be making the arrest alone."

"You're right about that." Tess almost laughed. Taking down Abby single-handedly was the last thing she wanted to try. "I'll wear my radio under my jacket. When I want you to move, I'll use a code phrase. I'll say . . ."

"Yes?"

"I'll say *The Godfather*. She's always talking about that movie. You hear *The Godfather*, you move."

"The Godfather." Hauser grunted. "Let's just hope this doesn't end up like Sonny at the tollbooth."

Tess didn't get the reference and didn't particularly want to. It sounded bad.

This whole thing sounded bad. But it had to be done. She just kept telling herself that. It had to be done.

45

Showtime.

Abby reached into her purse and activated the tape recorder. Across the lobby, a familiar figure was entering through the main doors.

Standing, she caught Reynolds's eye. He strode forward, a briefcase in his hand. He was nicely attired—suit jacket and tie—looking every inch the gentleman, a fact that proved only how deceiving appearances could be.

Abby waited until he had arrived at the table before she sat down again. She signaled for him to do likewise.

"So where is she?" he asked, forgoing small talk.

"First things first. As Tom Cruise would say, show me the money."

"It's all there," Reynolds said, handing over the briefcase.

Abby put the case on her lap. "Must have been tough to get all this cash together so fast."

"I've faced bigger challenges."

She popped the latches and found herself staring at rubber-banded wads of hundred-dollar bills. She had never seen fifty thousand dollars in cash, and she found the sight strangely compelling.

Reynolds's voice roused her. "Now it's time for you to fulfill your end of the bargain."

"Hey, whatever happened to the fine art of conversation?"

"I'm not in the mood for pleasantries."

"See, Jack, that's your basic problem. You don't take time to stop and smell the roses. You're a driven man. You'll give yourself a heart attack if you're not careful."

"I'm touched by your concern. *Where the hell is she?*"

The library, built in the 1920s, was a massive pile of eccentric architecture complete with carved sphinxes and a rooftop pyramid. Tess entered via the Fifth Street door, passing through the metal detector without incident because her SIG Sauer had been left in the car.

She stepped into the main lobby, a large room with a mess of abstract shapes painted on the ceiling in vivid colors. A few customers were lined up at the checkout counter playing beat-the-clock. One of the clerks at the counter gave Tess a disapproving glance, as if daring her to head for the stacks at closing time.

Abby wasn't in the lobby. Still, she might be watching from somewhere nearby. There was no shortage of possibilities—the upper levels of the building, where books were kept; the adjacent yogurt shop and fast-food Chinese restaurant; the gift shop; hallways and alcoves. Abby could be anywhere.

"No sign of her yet," she said quietly in the direction of the mike clipped inside her jacket. She wasn't wearing an earpiece now, so if there was a response, she didn't hear it.

Abby ignored Reynolds's question. "Here's a funny thing, Jack. Something I noticed about our mutual friend, Andrea."

"I told you, I don't have time for any bullshit."

"Indulge me. She said something interesting to me this morning. She dreamed about men breaking into her house. Men wearing ski masks and carrying guns."

"So what?"

"Yesterday Andrea never saw the intruders. She

was hiding behind the bed. *I* got a look at them. *She* didn't. But in her dreams she saw them, ski masks and all."

"Someone told her about the masks. One of the cops, probably."

"Could be. But I noticed something else. When she talked about her dream, she kept touching her hair. The hair behind her ear. You know, where she has the scar."

"Is this going somewhere?"

"It must be a traumatic thing to shoot yourself. Almost as traumatic as killing your own babies. But she had no memory of it. She remembered only after she'd been in the hospital for a few years. By then she'd heard the story over and over. Memory is a funny thing. It's not as reliable as we like to believe. We can manufacture memories that seem completely real. Three people witness a car accident and have three different recollections. They aren't lying. Their minds have reconstructed the events according to different narratives. As long as the narrative is internally consistent, it will be accepted as the truth."

Reynolds glanced at his watch. "I'm not real big on psychological theories."

"I am. As I may have mentioned, I studied psychology. Analyzing people is a big part of what I do. Want to hear my analysis of Andrea?"

"No."

"Oh, Jack, you're such a tease. Of course you do."

Tess forced herself to sit quietly for a few minutes in the hope that Abby would show up, surprising her as she always did, appearing out of nowhere.

Nothing happened. Five minutes after six o'clock, as the lights upstairs were going off, she gave up.

"No show," she reported as she left the building.

She rejoined the other agents and took back her sidearm.

"Think she's onto you?" Hauser asked.

Tess nodded. "Yes."

"God*damn* it."

"Now what?" Crandall asked.

Hauser was frowning fiercely. "She must have seen us and taken off. Maybe she was watching this entrance and spotted us when we pulled up."

"Her cell phone is still signaling from this area," the agent with the laptop said.

"She probably dropped it in a trash can. She could be on a freeway by now, heading for Mexico."

Tess wasn't so sure. "Not necessarily. She may still be in the vicinity."

"Why would she blow off her meeting with you and still hang around?" Hauser asked.

"I don't know. Why did she come downtown in the first place? Maybe there's something she has to do here."

"If she's here, we'll find her." Hauser clapped his hands. "Pair up, fan out. Search every building that's open. The office towers are closed, so unless she got inside illegally, she's not in there. Focus on the restaurants, the hotel, and Pershing Square. Keep an eye open for a red Miata. Go."

Tess realized the others had paired off, leaving her with Crandall.

"Looks like it's you and me, Rick," she said quietly.

Crandall managed a shaky smile.

"Andrea thinks she remembers what happened twenty years ago," Abby said. "But she's fooling herself. On some level she knows it. She knows what really took place. She just doesn't *know* she knows."

Reynolds shifted in his seat. "Are you going to give me the information or not?"

"After she got out of the hospital, Andrea moved to Florida. She was almost happy there. But something brought her back to California. She doesn't even know what. She felt a pull, an attraction, she said. That was my first clue. It told me she needed to resolve things here. She put it off as long as she could, tried not to deal with it, but in the end she had to obey the dictates of the ol' subconscious. It's all very Freudian."

"Maybe she just prefers this climate."

"Nothing's ever that simple. Think about it, Jack. Why was she showing up at your campaign events? Why would she risk it? I asked her, and she had no explanation. She didn't know what motivated her. But I do. Maybe you do, too. Care to take a shot at it?"

"No," he said coldly.

"Fair enough. It's best to leave this kind of thing to the experts. Returning to California, then seeking you out—it was her way of trying to come to grips with what really happened. It was her subconscious mind prodding her to face the facts."

"The woman is a nut job. We already knew that."

"That's not what I'm saying. And I don't think 'nut job' is a term you'll find in any diagnostic manual. She isn't crazy. She never was."

"There are two dead babies that indicate otherwise."

"Not a good comeback, Jack. Too obvious. We both know what happened. Andrea was getting too possessive. She'd given birth to your children. She wanted to be married, the way you'd promised. Of course you never had any intention of leaving your wife. When you tried to break off your relationship, it only made her angrier. You were afraid of what she might do. A woman scorned—you know how it goes. She might talk to the media. Or to your wife. Ruin your reputation, make it impossible for you to run for Congress. You were on your way up, but she had the ability to take you down."

"This is such a load of crap," Reynolds said, but without conviction.

"So you decided to handle things the way you always do—by hiring some of your biker friends to do your dirty work. That's what they're for, isn't it? You sicced 'em on Andrea twenty years ago, the same way you sicced 'em on her yesterday afternoon. That's the trouble with sociopaths—so predictable. Always re-running the same game plan in their heads, over and over.

"They wore ski masks that night, too. They got into her house, and Andrea and her children were shot. I don't know in what order. Maybe they shot her first, then the kids. But I'm guessing they made her watch while they killed the kids before they turned the gun on her. Her own gun. You knew she had one, and you knew where she kept it. You told them to leave the gun with her so it would look like she shot herself."

"She *did* shoot herself."

"No, Jack. The men with ski masks shot her. She got a good look at them—right before they shot her in the side of the head, behind the ear."

"You got all this from a dream she told you about?"

"A dream and some head-scratching. Don't forget the head-scratching."

"For Christ's sake, it was murder-suicide. Everybody knows that."

"Murder, yes. Not suicide. Andrea never shot anybody. Those two kids—their blood isn't on her hands. It's on yours."

Reynolds leaned forward, his face taut. "I want what I came for, and I want it now."

"Ever think about them, Jack? Your two lost sons? They were *your* kids. Doesn't that matter to you? Doesn't it keep you up at night?"

"Nothing keeps me up at night."

"What's sad is I believe you. Do you even remember their names?"

"*Fuck* you."

"What were their names, Jack?"

"I don't have to listen to this bullshit." He started to rise.

She seized him by the arm. "Tell me their names."

He twisted free. "Go to hell, Sinclair."

"What were their *names*?"

"Brian and Gabriel."

The voice didn't belong to Reynolds.

Andrea had emerged from behind the palm fronds—shaking, her face empty of color, her eyes huge.

"Those were their names," she whispered, her gaze locked on Reynolds. "Brian and Gabriel."

He stared at her, trying to process what was happening.

"You did it." Andrea spoke in a monotone. "You had them killed."

"Goddamn it"—Reynolds glanced from her to Abby—"you're running a game on me!"

"It was you," Andrea said. "It wasn't me. It was never me."

"Shut up," Reynolds snapped.

"You killed my children!" Her voice rose in a sudden hoarse cry of pain.

Reynolds raised his hands, looking around nervously. "Keep it down. Jesus."

"You killed them, and you let me take the blame. The men in masks—three of them—they wore gloves. They came in without making a sound. You had a key to my house. Did you give them the key?"

"Shut up. . . ."

"They held me down. And the boys were crying, and then they weren't crying anymore. I've never heard a silence like that. And I wanted to scream, but I couldn't . . . and one of them put the gun to my head—it was still warm from being fired—I remember how warm the barrel was on my skin. I remember. . . ."

"You don't remember anything," Reynolds barked. "Your mind is playing tricks—"

"No. No! *No!* You're the one who plays tricks! You're the one! *You're the one!*"

People were looking in their direction. Reynolds glanced around, panic in his eyes. "Lower your goddamn voice—"

"You're the killer. You murdered your own children. Your own flesh and blood."

"I never wanted the goddamned children. You fucking *played* me, you lying little bitch. You *swore* you were on the pill."

"They were *your children*."

"*I never wanted them!* I didn't ask for them. If you'd had the abortion—"

"You always wanted them dead."

"Of course I wanted them dead. *They were in my fucking way*."

"You're an animal. An animal. You know what they do to animals like you?"

"I'm an animal, sure. And you're a cunt with legs. That's all you ever were to me."

"They put you down—animals like you. They *put you down*."

"You should have been dead twenty years ago."

She reached into her coat, and a gun came out, a shiny silver semiautomatic.

"You should be dead right now," Andrea said.

46

Tess and Crandall were checking out the crowded bistro down the street from the hotel, looking at every slender, dark-haired woman in the shadowy, buzzing hive, when Hauser's voice came over their radios.

"LAPD's responding to a nine-one-one from the Brayton. Some kind of disturbance, altercation between a man and a woman, and something about a gun."

"Shit," Crandall said.

Tess was already moving. She pushed her way out of the restaurant, nearly knocking over a waitress burdened by an overloaded tray, and then she was pounding down the sidewalk, Crandall not far behind.

Abby almost lunged for the gun, but instinct told her that if she did, Andrea would fire. At this range she couldn't miss.

Instead she said quietly, "Andrea. No."

Andrea held tight to the pistol and didn't answer.

Across the lobby someone saw the gun and screamed.

Distantly Abby wondered where Andrea had gotten the gun. The revolver from the kitchen had been confiscated by the authorities.

"You're not a killer," Abby said in the tone she would have used to soothe a skittish animal. "You know that now."

"I'm not." Andrea's words came through gritted teeth. "He is."

Abby's glance flicked to Reynolds. He stood unmoving, his face bare of expression. He wasn't looking at the gun. His gaze was locked on Andrea's face.

There was movement around the lobby, people ducking for cover, seeking exits or places to hide. If Reynolds had wanted anonymity in this meeting, he'd lost any hope of it now. He was on center stage, visible to everyone.

"I know what he is," Abby said. "You don't have to be like him."

"Keep quiet, Abby."

"Give me the gun."

"Keep quiet, I said!"

Andrea shrieked the words, their echo volleying across the tiled floor. A child in a remote corner of the lobby started to cry.

Abby braced herself, expecting the violence of Andrea's outburst to be punctuated by a blast from the gun. It didn't happen.

"We're leaving," Andrea said, her voice lower, almost normal.

Abby nodded. "That's a good idea. Let's just go."

"Not you and me. Me and him."

Reynolds narrowed his eyes. "I'm not going with you."

Andrea stepped forward and rammed the gun into the side of his neck, her face inches from his. "You are."

Reynolds's mouth worked slowly. "You goddamned crazy bitch."

"If I'm crazy, you made me that way. Now walk."

"Where?"

"Where's your car?"

"Hotel garage. Level two."

"To the elevator, then."

"What about the money?"

"Leave it."

"It's fifty thousand dollars."

"Leave it."

He moved toward the elevators, Andrea staying close to him. Abby trailed behind.

"Go away, Abby," Andrea said.

"This is a mistake." Abby tried to find the right words. "You don't need to do this. You can have justice now."

"I don't want justice. There is no justice. How could there be?"

"Then what's the point of this?"

"He's got to suffer."

"We can do that to him. The law can do it."

"Since when have you ever cared about the law?"

Abby had no answer to that.

They reached the elevator bank. The nearest doors parted as soon as Andrea pressed the DOWN button. The compartment was empty. She ushered Reynolds inside and pressed B-2.

Abby knew she ought to let them go. It might be suicide to follow. But the thing was, she'd always had this obstinate streak of responsibility. It would get her in trouble one of these days.

She stepped in before the doors closed.

Tess reached the hotel entrance and stopped running. The reflected sun gleamed off the glass doors, dazzling her. She squinted against the orange glare.

Whatever was going on inside, she had to enter the building the same way she would approach any other hostile environment. It had been years ago when she'd undergone her training in Hogan's Alley, the fake town used by Bureau recruits at Quantico, but it came back to her now.

"I take the lead. You cover me," she said to Crandall as he arrived at her side. His weapon was drawn and she was mildly surprised to find that hers was, too. "We clear the room in stages, staying close to the walls, never out in the open. Okay?"

"At least this time you're not leaving me in the backyard," Crandall said.

They went in together, moving fast across the tiled floor to a group of potted palms that offered cover. Tess scanned the lobby, saw people running here and there, clerks at the registration desk making frantic phone calls, security guards racing for the stairs.

This much activity wouldn't be going on if an armed confrontation was still in progress. She stepped into view and grabbed the first person who came sprinting past, a bellman.

"Where's the individual with the gun?"

"The woman? She took the guy into the elevator. They went down."

"What's below this level?"

"Parking garage. It's two stories."

"Was there one woman—or two?"

"Two. And the guy they took—someone said they recognized him from TV."

"Who is he?"

"A congressman, they said. From around here, I think."

Tess let him go.

"*Two* women," Crandall said.

She nodded. "Yes. Two." She turned away. "Damn it, Abby. Damn it to hell."

"I told you to go away," Andrea said as the elevator descended.

Abby faced her. "I'm not leaving you."

"You should. You don't know what I might do. I might kill you, too. I might kill both of you, then myself."

In the brassy lights of the elevator car, Reynolds's skin was shiny with sweat.

"Why would you do that?" Abby asked.

"I don't know why. Why does anybody do anything? Nothing happens for a reason. Nothing makes any sense."

"You aren't yourself, Andrea."

"So who am I?" Andrea released a brief, disconcerting little laugh. "Tell me that, Abby. Who am I?"

The elevator doors opened on level two of the underground garage.

"Out," Andrea said.

The order was unnecessary. Reynolds was already stepping out of the compartment, the gun still riding his neck.

Abby had several options. She could draw her gun from her purse, but if she did, Andrea would kill Reynolds, and Abby would have to kill or wound her. Or she could jump Andrea and wrest the gun away. She was a trained fighter, and Andrea was not. But the struggle would leave Reynolds unattended, and there was a chance he was armed, as well. If he was, he wouldn't miss an opportunity to take out both women.

The remaining option was to talk Andrea down. It hadn't worked so far, but it still seemed to be her best move.

"Why don't you let me take it from here?" she asked softly.

Andrea didn't answer. To Reynolds she said, "Which way is your car?"

"Over there. End of the line. The blue Mustang coupe."

"Walk."

Reynolds hesitated. "You're not going to kill me."

"I'm not?"

"If you were, you'd have done it by now."

"You think so?"

"I know you. You can't pull the trigger." He studied her and nodded. "You won't."

Andrea snapped her arm down and fired once into Reynolds's thigh.

Reynolds didn't scream. He merely dropped to a kneeling position, his pants leg blooming with a maroon flower of blood.

Andrea pivoted, faster than Abby could have expected, and pointed the gun at her. "Don't try to stop me."

Abby slowly released her hand from the clasp of her purse.

"I'll kill you both," Andrea said. "I'll kill anybody. I swear I will. A person can only take *so much*." She swung the gun toward Reynolds again. "Get up."

"You shot me," Reynolds said, as if this were new information.

"Get up!"

He struggled to his feet. His pants leg clung to his skin, some of the material actually blown inward by the gunshot, glued to the wound.

"Walk to your car."

With pain, Reynolds obeyed. Abby started to follow. Andrea waved her off with the pistol.

"No farther."

"I can't let you go," Abby said.

"You don't have a choice."

"Andrea—"

"You're not part of this, Abby. You never were. It's me and him. That's all it's ever been." Andrea's voice hardened. "If you follow, I'll shoot you."

Abby stayed where she was. She watched as Reynolds led Andrea to the Mustang.

"Keys," Andrea said.

"They're in my side pocket."

"Just get them."

He reached into his pocket, fumbled briefly, and produced a key ring.

"Open the passenger door and get in. Then slide over. You're driving. I'm sitting next to you."

"I'm losing blood. I might pass out at the wheel."

"If you do, we'll both die. We're probably going to die together, anyway. Isn't that the way it should be, Jack?"

Reynolds looked back at Abby, yards away, his glance a silent plea.

Abby shook her head. She couldn't help him. Andrea was in control of this situation. Andrea, who had been in control of nothing in her life for the past twenty years.

Reynolds slipped into the car, groaning as he maneuvered into the driver's seat. Andrea slid in beside him, shutting the door.

The headlights and engine came on, and the Mustang backed out of its slot and sped away.

47

The garage had two levels, as the bellman had said. "We have to split up," Tess told Crandall. "You take level two. I'll take level one. Use the stairs—elevator's too dangerous. If she's waiting outside the elevator, she can shoot you when the doors open, and you've got no cover."

"When you say *she*, do you mean . . . ?"

"I don't know. It could be either one of them. They're working together, obviously. I wouldn't have believed it, but . . . ." She shook her head. "Get going. Take those stairs."

She pointed to the nearest stairwell. Crandall ran off. Tess thumbed her radio's transmit button and told Hauser she needed backup. "And get on the phone to the main desk—tell them to hold off using their security guards in the parking garage. We don't need extra bodies down there."

Extra bodies—perhaps not the best way of putting it.

She reconnoitered the lobby and located another stairwell. It was better to use two different approaches to the garage. That way she and Crandall were covering more territory. If the women decided to double back, using the stairs, there was more chance of intercepting them.

She ran to the stairwell. The lobby was a scene of utter confusion. People were racing all around her, some yelling into cell phones, others calling for family members they'd lost track of. She had the impression that security was evacuating the building, or at least the ground level. That was okay. It would keep the guards out of the garage, anyway.

She opened the stairwell door and went in, beaming her pocket flash down the shaft.

Abby was down there somewhere. Abby and Andrea.

Two felons. Two killers.

And the two of them had to be stopped.

Reynolds had been scared there for a few minutes. He could admit that much. For a moment he'd been certain the crazy bitch would pull the trigger and cut him down.

Death as such didn't scare him. Everybody died. But to die in a hotel lobby, shot by his ex-lover in a scandal that would ruin his reputation forever, to be remembered only as a DA turned congressman who'd diddled a legal secretary and gotten his brains blown out—that prospect terrified him. Life and death were unimportant, but pride mattered.

Now the fear had left him, and even the throbbing pain in his leg seemed distant and unimportant. He saw a way clear of this mess. A way to save himself and make everything right.

"I can't believe you're kidnapping me," he said, pitching his voice loud.

Andrea was silent. He risked saying more.

"My Mustang is pretty distinctive. The police will be able to spot it."

"I don't care about the police."

"We'll be lucky if we even get out of the hotel garage," he said, again too loudly.

"Stop shouting."

"It's the gunshot. My ears are still ringing. I can't hear myself think."

He steered the car forward between the ranks of concrete pylons under the glare of fluorescent lights. He'd done what he could. Now it depended on Shanker.

Reynolds had done more than retrieve his keys

when he'd reached into his pocket. He'd touched his cell phone and activated the speed dial. If he'd done it correctly, he should have placed a call to Shanker, who was sitting in his van on level one of the garage, waiting for Reynolds's signal.

If Shanker had heard the few words he'd just spoken, he ought to be able to figure out what was going on—and to do something about it.

All that was needed was a momentary distraction. Reynolds leaned forward in the driver's seat and felt the comforting weight of the gun under his jacket, the gun he had taken from the wall safe in his home office before driving to L.A.

He had only to get the pistol out of Andrea's hands, or pin her down so she couldn't fire. Then with her gun or with his own, he could take her out. One bullet to the head, and that would be the end of Andrea, formerly Bethany, the mother of two of his children, and the bane of his life.

And the beauty of it was, no one would blame him. The angry altercation in the lobby would actually work to his advantage. He had multiple witnesses to testify that the woman had been behaving in an irrational and violent manner, that she had held a gun on him and marched him into an elevator. He had the wound in his thigh to prove she was serious.

He was a victim, for God's sake. Andrea Lowry was a crazy woman with a history of mental illness, institutionalization, and violence. She had been stalking him. She had finally tracked him down in the Brayton—he could invent a convincing reason for being there. Fortunately he'd been able to defend himself.

She wouldn't be around to tell her side of the story. Only Abby remained to be dealt with, and she was already in trouble with the law, or so she claimed. Even if her story had been bullshit, there was a fair chance he could get to her before she could do him any harm. When both women were out of the way, there would be no one to refute his version of events.

He could make it work. Hell, he could come out of

this a hero. The crusading DA would now be a fighting congressman who'd taken on a stalker and won. He might be able to parlay this into a run for the Senate. And for a senator from California, a slot on a presidential ticket was not an impossibility.

Or he might just be getting light-headed from blood loss. But one thing was certain. If he had a chance to finish Andrea, he would take it. He would do the job his hired thugs had botched twenty years ago. He would kill the bitch at last.

The Man was in trouble. That much was obvious.

Shanker put the van into gear and barreled up a spiraling concrete ramp.

The voices on the phone had been faint and slightly garbled, but he'd made out enough to know that Reynolds was being forced to drive out of the hotel garage, and that he had been shot or at least shot at, and that the shooter was a woman.

Abby, of course. It had to be. The bitch had pulled off another double cross.

But this one would be her last.

Reynolds was pulling close to the exit ramp when he saw the gray blur of Shanker's van in his rearview mirror. The van was gaining fast.

Things were about to get interesting.

He tightened his grip on the wheel. A trickle of perspiration oozed down his neck. It was cold, as cold as the muzzle of the pistol still pressed against his skin.

"What's the matter, Jack?" Andrea was looking at him with a suspicious, quizzical eye. "What's going on?"

He didn't have to answer. Shanker answered for him.

The van swung out from behind the car, pulling alongside like a wall of gray metal looming out of nowhere.

Andrea saw it. Her mouth opened in the beginning of a shout.

With a scream of tires, the van veered sideways, slamming solidly into the Mustang's front end.

Instinctively Reynolds hit the brakes.

Too late.

The Mustang folded up against the van's back side, rocking Reynolds and his passenger in their seats.

Neither of them was strapped in. Reynolds hit the steering wheel as the air bag deployed, smacking him in the face and retracting instantly. He was dazed momentarily but shook it off and spun in his seat to face Andrea. The passenger-side air bag had crumpled in her lap, and the gun once held to his head was dangling from limp fingers.

He grabbed for it. She snapped alert and threw a clawing hand at his face, but he wedged himself closer, ignoring the shout of pain from his leg, and wrapped his fingers around the hand holding the gun.

Their eyes met, and he saw hopelessness and resignation in hers, submission before a superior adversary, acquiescence to the essential injustice of the world.

That was when he knew he had won. Prizing the pistol out of her grip was only an afterthought to his triumph. He pulled it free and jammed his forefinger between the trigger guard and the trigger, the barrel arrowed at her face.

To Andrea it was all strangely familiar, the gun in her face and the certainty of death—but really there was nothing strange about it, because she had died like this once before, hadn't she? The memory was suddenly keen and sharp—the explosion behind her ear, the rush of white light that surprised her because it wasn't darkness.

And her last thought—*Jack did this.*

That thought came back to her now, and with it came a surge of furious indignation at this man who had already taken everything from her, and who dared to take even more.

She twisted away from him as the gun went off, a

purplish blast clouding her vision, the shot missing her and tearing through the headrest of the passenger seat.

"Fuck you, Jack!" She heard a crazy woman screaming and realized it was her. "Fuck you!"

She lashed out with her fists. She beat him in the face. The gun lurched toward her but she batted it away and flailed at him, and one of her swinging blows caught him in the thigh where the bullet had struck.

Then he was the one screaming.

His cries brought her back to herself. She had to get out of this car. She had to get away.

She flung open the door and clambered out into the ugly fluorescent glow, the word *ugly* beating like a flap of wings in her mind—this basement world, like catacombs, an ugly place to die, all concrete and shadows.

She fell on the floor—more concrete—and threw herself upright, staggering toward the nearest row of columns, where cars were parked, and beyond the cars there was a door marked STAIRS, an escape route, if she could get there, but she couldn't, of course. Reynolds would kill her first, gun her down.

She heard the crack of a gunshot. Another. Another. But she wasn't hit. Somehow she was alive.

She stumbled between the pillars, half running, half crawling, her legs not working right, and by some inexplicable miracle she reached the shelter of a parked car and scurried behind it as the gun rang out again and again.

From her position of relative safety she risked a glance back, and then she understood. It wasn't Reynolds who was shooting.

Abby was there, gun in hand, crouching behind another column yards away, snapping off shots at the Mustang.

This probably made some kind of sense, but Andrea couldn't put it together, and she had no time to think about it.

She ran for the door to the stairs.

                              *   *   *

Abby had pounded up two flights of stairs and was running for the garage exit, meaning to retrieve her Miata from the alley, when she heard the crash.

It had to be Reynolds's car. He'd wrecked it somehow. And she had no doubt he would use the diversion to gain the upper hand.

She hadn't been far from the collision. She'd reached it in time to see Andrea emerge. When Reynolds leaned out, Abby snapped off a series of rounds, not expecting to hit him, just laying down covering fire so Andrea could escape.

It had worked. Reynolds had ducked back inside the car, and Andrea was gone, and everything was hunky-dory.

From the wrecked van, a volley of shots.

Okay, not so hunky-dory, after all.

Abby threw herself flat on the concrete and rolled to a new position. Evidently the van driver hadn't been an innocent victim in all this. He was one of Reynolds's buddies, trying to protect his boss by taking her out.

For the second time in two days she was in a gunfight. It irked her. Variety was one of the perks of her job, but this case wasn't offering her any.

Her revolver had used all six shots. She dumped the empties and speed-loaded another six. There was a second speed loader in her purse if she needed it. She figured she would.

Reynolds was edging out of the Mustang again, the gun leading him. She took aim this time—couldn't afford to waste any more shots—and fired once. He twisted away, disappearing into the vehicle's interior. She thought she might have scored a hit on his shoulder or arm.

More gunfire from the van. Sounded like only one gun, which meant only one bad guy inside. He had the advantage, though. As long as she was pinned down, he and Reynolds could pop caps in her direction until one of the shots connected.

She risked a peek at the van and saw that the gunman had ventured out of the vehicle. Time to go on offense. She fired off three more shots, repelling the driver back inside the van, then sprinted out from behind the pillar and dived under the Mustang. It was a good bet that in the dim light and the confusion of battle the van driver hadn't seen where she went.

Beneath the car she crawled forward on elbows and knees. Oil leaked from the chassis, forming a viscid pool on the concrete.

Movement from the van. It rocked gently on its springs. A pair of leather sneakers came into view.

The driver was out of his vehicle again, edging sideways along the Mustang.

That was a mistake.

Abby gripped the .38 in both hands and fired twice at his feet. He went down. Even as he hit the ground she dumped the spent shells from her revolver and speed-loaded her last six rounds.

A shot burned past her, her wounded enemy firing blindly under the car. She squeezed off three rounds and blew the gun out of his hand, which was not a hand any longer but a gushing stump. He howled like an animal and fell abruptly silent, unconscious or dead. No threat either way.

But Reynolds was still a threat. Directly above her, in the Mustang—

In time with that thought, a bullet punched through the chassis, plowing into the concrete and kicking up splinters of stone.

Son of a bitch was firing straight down through the floor of his car.

She rolled sideways, dodging three more shots that punctured the bottom of the Mustang, then fired upward into what she thought was the front passenger compartment, hoping for a lucky hit, but luck wasn't with her, and his gun boomed back, targeting the spot where the shots had originated, and missed her—but only just—as she flipped to one side. She squeezed off two more shots, and the hammer made a dry click.

Out of ammo. No more speed loaders in her purse. Not that it mattered, since her purse was gone anyway, lost in her rapid maneuvers beneath the Mustang.

Reynolds hadn't run out. He fired again and again, and above the roar of the shots she heard him yelling, a long incoherent shout of rage.

Andrea's gun was an automatic. Maybe fourteen rounds in the clip. And Reynolds was probably carrying a gun of his own. Too much firepower. She couldn't dodge every shot.

She propelled herself out from under the car, sliding on a slick of blood from the van driver, and found his gun, the one he'd dropped when she blew his hand off his wrist.

She spun in a crouch and fired at the Mustang, gouging a hole in the side window, and Reynolds, in silhouette, dipped quickly as if hit.

She waited, expecting him to pop up and return fire.

He didn't. Maybe he was hit worse than she'd thought. She wasn't in a hurry to find out, though. He could be playing possum. Never trust a politician— that was her motto.

Movement in the car. It shivered on its springs, rocking gently, and something fell out of the far side, something heavy and ungainly.

Reynolds, blindly seeking escape.

He drove himself to his feet and stumbled away, one shoulder crooked at an impossible angle, his legs trembling with the strain of holding him upright. Behind him leaked a long ragged trail of blood.

Abby jumped onto the hood of the Mustang and tackled him. He went down hard, the gun still in his hand. She ripped it free and pitched it into the shadows, then pressed her weapon to the back of his head.

For a moment the garage disappeared, and the ruined vehicles, and she was facing Dylan Garrick again.

"Don't do it," a man's voice said, and it might have been Reynolds or Garrick, she couldn't say. "Please. Don't."

She felt her finger tighten on the trigger. Just a little

more pressure, a few ounces' worth, and she would expel this man from the world.

But she didn't fire. She took a long, slow breath and let her grip relax.

"Quiet, Jack," she said softly. "Quiet, now."

Beneath her, Reynolds was whimpering. In pain, maybe, or in humiliation. She knew he didn't like to lose.

Well, he'd lost now. Lost everything.

Behind her, a clatter of rapid footsteps. Beam of a pocket flash impaling her in its glare.

"Drop your weapon! You're under arrest! *Drop your weapon!*"

Slowly, Abby smiled. She tossed the gun aside and stood up, raising her hands.

"Hey, Tess," she said. "Long time no see."

48

Stenzel's desk phone rang in the emptiness of campaign headquarters. No one was here on a Saturday night. Even the lowliest volunteers had some kind of life. Only Stenzel had shown up, not because he had work to do—although there was always work to do—but because he couldn't relax until he knew that the operation at the Brayton Hotel had gone smoothly.

He picked up the phone on the first ring, hoping it was Jack calling to say everything was taken care of.

It wasn't Jack. It was a newspaper reporter from the *L.A. Times,* a pain in the ass like all of them, but someone whose calls Stenzel had no choice but to take.

"I'm kind of tied up right now, Charlie," Stenzel said, in no mood for the usual pleasantries, off-the-record remarks, deep-background quotes, and other bullshit. "Whatever this is, maybe it can wait till tomorrow."

"I'll make it quick. Just want to know if you have any comment about the situation."

"What situation?"

"At the Brayton."

Stenzel had occasionally encountered the expression *His heart skipped a beat.* He had never taken it literally until this moment.

"I don't know what you're referring to," he said.

"I'm referring to the fact that your boss was reportedly seen in the lobby of the Brayton Hotel in downtown L.A. earlier tonight, in a heated discussion with a woman, or maybe two women—the reports are unclear—and some people say this woman or women kidnapped him at gunpoint, and now I'm hearing that arrests have been made. And the FBI is all over it. That situation."

"This is the first I'm hearing about it. You sure you're not putting me on?"

"No joke, Kip."

"It can't have been Jack. Why would Jack—I mean, Congressman Reynolds—why would the congressman be at the Brayton Hotel, anyway?"

"You tell me."

"The whole thing sounds like some crazy mix-up. You're not running with this, are you?"

"Shouldn't I?"

"You'll look pretty foolish when you have to retract the story."

"Maybe you can put me in touch with the congressman, and he can straighten things out."

"The congressman isn't here at the moment."

"Where is he?"

"I'm not sure."

"You may want to track him down."

"I'm sure he has no involvement in any of the events you've described. And I'm sure you won't be printing rumor and innuendo in a reputable paper like the *Times*."

"Is that your only comment?"

"I don't have any comment. This entire conversation is off the record."

He ended the call, stifling the reporter's protests. He noticed he had stood up at some point during the conversation, and he sat down slowly, knowing there was a chair somewhere behind him.

There was no way to be sure of exactly what had happened at the Brayton Hotel tonight. But it was reasonably clear that Reynolds's plans had been compromised. The woman in the lobby must have been Abby Sinclair, or if there were two women, then maybe one of them was Abby and the other was Andrea Lowry. That much was evident. Now arrests had been made, and the FBI was involved.

The FBI, for God's sake.

"Shit," Stenzel said, intoning the word softly as a sober assessment of his circumstances.

People often talked about virtues. Stenzel was perfectly willing to listen to such talk and to write speeches incorporating such talk and to include questions about virtue in public-opinion surveys he commissioned. He did not, however, actually believe in any virtues—with a single exception. There was one virtue he both preached and practiced, and it was the virtue of flexibility.

It was time to show some flexibility now.

He felt a little bit sorry for what he was about to do. But he had learned from Jack Reynolds and learned well, and one lesson of Jack's, reiterated many times, was the famous witticism attributed to Harry Truman. *If you want a friend in Washington, buy a dog.*

Stenzel dialed 411 and asked for the number of the Federal Bureau of Investigation in Los Angeles. He needed to initiate a dialogue—ASAP.

49

"You're in a great deal of trouble, Ms. Sinclair."

Abby lifted an eyebrow. "You think?"

Assistant Director Michaelson leaned back in his chair in the interrogation room. Abby would have liked to lean back also, but her movements were restricted by the manacle securing her left wrist to a steel eyelet in the table.

"You were apprehended," Michaelson said, "while holding a gun to the head of a United States congressman."

"Who'd been shooting at me."

"Because you tried to kidnap him. You and Andrea Lowry."

Abby glanced from Michaelson to the only other person in the room—Tess, seated across from her. "Oh, come on."

Tess offered no response.

"We have witnesses," Michaelson said. "People in the hotel who saw you and Lowry forcibly escort Congressman Reynolds from the lobby."

"Those witnesses must also have told you that I wasn't the one holding a gun on him."

"It doesn't matter who was holding the gun. You aided and abetted Andrea Lowry's escape from FBI surveillance. You orchestrated a meeting with the congressman. Then you and Lowry abducted him."

"You're wrong about that last part. But two out of three ain't bad."

Michaelson seemed to sense an opening. "So you admit to helping Lowry evade surveillance?"

"I more than helped. I pulled it off solo. I was driving Andrea's car."

Abby was aware that the meeting was being recorded by hidden cameras, and that her admission could most definitely be used against her. But she saw no point in lying. She was in a locked room in the FBI suite of the federal building, under suspicion of multiple homicides. It was time to test the old adage and see if the truth really would set her free.

"And you admit to setting up the meeting with Reynolds?"

"Correct-amundo. But not to kidnap him. That was Andrea's idea—and in her defense, she wasn't thinking clearly at the time."

Tess spoke up for the first time since the interrogation began. "If you weren't there to harm Reynolds, what was the reason for the meeting?"

Abby shrugged. "Therapy."

"Come again?" Tess asked.

"Well, therapy was one reason. Getting Reynolds to incriminate himself was another."

Michaelson frowned. "I'm not following you, Ms. Sinclair."

"Why does that not come as a surprise? Okay, here's the story. Reynolds is the bad guy. He was behind the attack on Andrea's house yesterday. He was also behind the murder of Andrea's children twenty years ago. She didn't do it. His thugs did. They put a bullet in her to make it look like suicide."

Sometime during this explanation Michaelson had folded his arms across his chest, his body language radiating disbelief. "And you know all this—how? Clairvoyance?"

"I'm not clairvoyant—just unusually perceptive. And way smarter than, say, you."

"Are you, now?"

"Oh, yeah. Not that I'm bragging. Because, let's face it, if I wanted to brag, I wouldn't be comparing myself—"

Tess cut her off. "Abby."

The low warning tone wasn't lost on her. Abby smiled. "Pissing off the boss man isn't such a good idea?"

"You ought to be taking these proceedings more seriously, Ms. Sinclair," Michaelson warned.

"I never take anything seriously. It's all part of my elusive je ne sais quoi. Anyway, to answer your question, I knew the truth about Andrea's past because of a conversation I had with her this morning."

Michaelson folded his arms tighter, as if trying to hug himself to death. "You're lying. You were never in contact with Andrea Lowry after the attack on Friday, which means you had no opportunity—"

"Oh, spare me. I met her in the ladies' room of the Beverly Center while your idiot surveillance squad stood around window-shopping outside. The garlic genius she picked up there—I bought it. Incidentally, is there any way I can get remuneration for that? Put it on the Bureau's tab?"

Michaelson ignored the question. "Even if you did talk with Lowry, how can anything she told you possibly relate to the meeting with Congressman Reynolds?"

"I needed him to admit what he'd done. I wanted Andrea there to hear it—and to participate. The plan was for Reynolds to say too much, reveal that he'd sent his brownshirts after Andrea twenty years ago. I was hoping if Andrea heard this, she'd have a breakthrough. She'd remember what really happened that night. Not the phony, reconstructed memories the shrinks pounded into her, but the truth."

"And did she?" Tess asked, sounding just the tiniest bit intrigued.

"She did. Big-time. It was, if I say so myself, a thing of beauty to behold. Up to a point."

Michaelson still hadn't released himself from his death grip. "What point?"

"The point when she pulled a pistol out of her pocket." Abby shook her head. "Wow, try saying *that* three times fast."

"You're claiming you didn't know she was armed?"

"How could I? You guys confiscated her revolver, right? She never said anything about a second gun."

Michaelson finally unfolded his arms, but only to tent his fingers in front of his face, another sign of resistance. "So you didn't anticipate that she would abduct the congressman?"

"Nope. I didn't see that one coming. A rare lapse of prescience on my part."

Michaelson spoke through his fingers. "But you accompanied her when she left the lobby with Reynolds."

"I was trying to talk her down."

"And I suppose you expect us to take your word for that."

"Not at all. It's on tape. I recorded everything that happened."

"And where is this tape?"

"In my purse."

"And where's that?"

"I lost it when I was scrambling around under Reynolds's car. One of the crime scene guys must've found it."

"I wouldn't know."

Abby felt her first flutter of anxiety. All along she'd assumed the purse would turn up. "They *have* to have found it. I mean, it's a regular-size purse with a micro-cassette recorder inside, and my wallet and ID. . . ."

"Anything else?"

"Probably some condoms."

Michaelson's eyes narrowed. "Condoms?"

"Be prepared. That's my motto."

"You and the Boy Scouts," Tess said.

"Do they carry condoms, too?"

Michaelson stood abruptly. "Ms. Sinclair, this narrative you've shared with us is all very interesting, but in the absence of proof it really doesn't amount to much."

"Andrea will vouch for me."

"The statement of your accomplice isn't likely to carry much weight."

"Then find my purse and play the tape."

"And will the tape also clear you in the murder of Dylan Garrick?"

She'd been expecting them to bring that up. She expelled a breath. "No."

Tess straightened in her chair. "You met with Garrick when he left the bar. I have a witness."

"Probably the bartender, right? That's who I would've pumped for info."

From the way Tess's eyes flickered, Abby knew she'd guessed right. "The identity of the witness is unimportant," Tess said. "What matters is that you left with Garrick, and he was shot later that night. When I asked you about it this morning, you lied to me."

"I lie all the time, Tess. It's a major part of my lifestyle. You ought to know that by now."

Michaelson had turned away. Tess was handling this phase of the interrogation. "I don't know why you would lie about Garrick unless you have something to hide."

"I *did* have something to hide. I was in his apartment. I held him at gunpoint, using his own gun."

Tess's face hardened into an expression of contempt. "And you pistol-whipped him."

"Yes."

"And wrapped the gun in a pillow."

"Yes."

"And then you shot him."

"No."

"Why did you wrap up the gun, if not to muffle a shot?"

"I wanted him to think I was going to shoot him."

"But you didn't?"

"Again, *N-O*."

"So who did?"

"No idea."

"You were trying to scare him as part of an interrogation. Is that what you're saying?"

Abby hesitated. "Not exactly."

"What, then?"

"The interrogation was already over. I wanted to scare him just because—well, because he scared me. He put me through two or three minutes of hell in Andrea's house, and I wanted to return the favor."

"So you're telling us Dylan Garrick was alive and conscious when you left?"

"He was alive. Not conscious. I KO'd him with the butt of the gun."

"Why?"

"Because I wanted to toss his place, and I didn't want him tiptoeing up behind me."

"You searched his apartment?"

"Sure did. Found the gun he used at Andrea's, and a slightly damaged silencer tube, and some other stuff. It was in his bureau in the bedroom, just like he told me."

"And then?"

"Then I turned out the lights so I wouldn't be seen leaving, and I sneaked out. Found a pay phone a mile away and called in a shots-fired to nine-one-one. Muffled my voice so I couldn't be identified on tape."

"Why report shots fired if there were none?"

"I figured it was the best way to get a fast response."

"Why call the police at all?"

"So they would find his gear, link him to the shooting in San Fernando. Come on, Tess, you know how I work."

"Yes," Tess said quietly, "I know how you work."

"Not sure I'm liking the mother-superior tone. I was trying to help out. I even left the door unlocked to make it easier for the cops to get in."

"When they got in, they didn't find Dylan Garrick unconscious. They found him dead."

"I know. I was watching."

Michaelson turned to face her. "Watching?"

"After I called nine-one-one, I doubled back and parked a few blocks away. Then I found a vantage point where I could observe the action. I wanted to make sure the cops checked out the whole apartment and found the gun in the bedroom. That was the only link to the assault on Andrea. Instead I saw them call for a morgue wagon. I saw Dylan carried out in a body bag. That's when I knew there was a problem."

"A problem," Michaelson said coldly, "because you shot him."

"No, dickwad. A problem because *somebody else* shot him, but I would be linked to the crime. People saw me leave the bar with Dylan. Tess here already suspected me of having vengeance in mind—"

"Because you *did* have vengeance in mind," Tess snapped.

"I didn't shoot Dylan."

"No, I'm sure the thought never even crossed your mind."

"It crossed my mind." Abby took a breath. "I thought about killing him. I wanted to. And . . . I came close. When I put the pillow around the gun, I wasn't *just* trying to scare him. I was . . . thinking about it. How easy it would be."

"And you yielded to that temptation," Michaelson said. "Come on, be straight with us. I understand what you were feeling. I can sympathize. You'd hardly be human if you didn't hate the man."

This was the ADIC's ham-fisted way of trying to establish rapport with the suspect. Abby could see why this bozo didn't do fieldwork. Any halfway intelligent street criminal would see through him like Plexiglas.

"Don't give me the touchy-feely routine, please," she said. "I cry real easy, and I don't want us to get all *Oprah* and start exchanging hugs."

Michaelson backed off, frustrated. Tess took over again. "If you left Garrick alive, how did he end up dead?"

"Obviously someone else decided to do the job. I guess I'd made it easy. I left the door unlocked, lights off, Dylan unconscious with his gun on the floor where I'd put it, and the pillow right next to it."

"In other words," Michaelson said with heavy sarcasm, "someone just happened to walk in there, saw Garrick unconscious, and whacked him?"

Abby wrinkled her nose. "Don't say 'whacked.' Too *Sopranos*."

"It's a rather large coincidence, wouldn't you say?"

"Not necessarily. Dylan was pretty nervous. He'd screwed up royal. Disappointed Reynolds—and other folks, too. It's not too surprising someone would take him out."

"Someone like you."

Abby sighed. She definitely was not getting through to this guy. "No, someone like one of his fellow gang members, enforcing discipline, imposing the penalty for failure. Maybe someone who was watching the apartment and waiting for Dylan's girlfriend—namely me—to leave. When I did, this other guy comes upstairs, finds the door open, sees Dylan asleep, or so it appears. In the dark the intruder wouldn't see the bruises or the blood. He moves closer, finds the gun on the floor. Realizes he can do the job with Dylan's own piece. Fires twice through the pillow. Then runs."

"All this takes place while you're off providentially making a phone call to nine-one-one?"

"I'm not sure how much providence had to do with it, but yeah."

"Why would the shooter run?" Tess asked. "Why wouldn't he search the apartment like you did, take the evidence tying Dylan to the San Fernando raid?"

"I'm guessing that was his plan. But maybe the second shot was too loud. Or he might have heard the sirens of the cop cars responding to my call."

Michaelson folded his arms again. A bad sign. "That's an interesting series of suppositions."

"Thank you."

"But entirely unnecessary. We don't need a mystery gunman on a grassy knoll. We have you."

"I never mentioned a grassy knoll."

"Are you listening, Ms. Sinclair? *We have you.* You're looking very, very good for the murder of Dylan Garrick."

Abby gave up on Michaelson and looked at Tess for support. "You know that's not my style."

Tess took a long moment to respond. "Honestly, Abby, I don't know what to think about you anymore."

Silence in the room, broken finally when Abby heard herself say words she had never spoken before. "Maybe I'd better call a lawyer."

Michaelson gestured for Tess to rise. "There'll be time for that later."

"Hey. I'm supposed to get a phone call. It's in the Constitution, or the Declaration of Independence, or some old document under glass."

Tess walked out of the room without answering.

"It could be the Magna Carta," Abby added helpfully. "You might check there. You hear me? I *want* a lawyer."

Michaelson gave Abby a dismissive backward glance. "Later," he said.

The door shut behind him, and she was alone.

50

Abby didn't know how long she was left in the interrogation room. Time had a funny way of not passing when there were no windows and no clocks. Even her wristwatch had been taken. From beyond the closed door she heard activity in the hall, which seemed to flow in cycles, brief periods of commotion interspersed with long intervals of quiet. After a while the quiet times seemed to become longer. She had the impression that it was late. They had brought her in at eight o'clock and interrogated her for more than an hour. By now it must be well past midnight. She wondered if she had been forgotten.

"Hey," she said loudly. "Anybody home?"

No answer. She spent some time making faces at the corner of the ceiling where she believed a hidden camera would be installed. She half hoped somebody would come in and tell her to cut it out. No one came. Maybe no one was watching.

Her left wrist remained manacled to the table. Although it constrained her movement, she was able to perform some simple exercises to work her biceps and hamstrings. Just because she was a prisoner in a federal facility didn't mean she intended to get out of shape.

At some point she became aware of being hungry. The roast chicken and potato salad she'd swiped at Reynolds's barbecue had been the last meal she'd eaten. How long ago was that? More than twelve hours, certainly. If she'd been smart, she would have grabbed an early dinner rather than a quickie with Wyatt.

Then again, it might be the last quickie she would have for a while. Did they allow conjugal visits in federal prison? Didn't matter; she wasn't married. She had no husband to visit her. Ordinarily that thought wouldn't have bothered her, but for some reason it chewed at her like acid tonight.

She was all alone. She had no one to come to her aid. She'd built a life based on isolation and secrecy, and now she was facing its downside.

"Anybody out there?" she yelled again. No response.

She tried to take stock of her situation. Things weren't all bad. Her purse, with the tape recorder inside, would probably turn up. Unless that prick Michaelson didn't want it to turn up. He could make it disappear. Such things happened. But she couldn't start speculating that way. She couldn't operate on the premise of a government conspiracy that would conceal evidence just to nail her. Not because conspiracies were impossible, but because that line of thinking would make her crazy.

She had to stick to the simple facts. Fact one, she was innocent. True, she might *look* guilty as hell, but she wasn't. Fact two, the feds had already been suspicious of Reynolds. They would press him hard. Of course, what Reynolds said wouldn't necessarily help her, even if he told the unvarnished truth. After all, she'd told him she had to get out of town because she was in trouble with the law. Her story had been a lie designed to sell the idea that she would betray Andrea, but unfortunately it also fitted neatly into the scenario the feds had written for her.

And the tape recording, even if it turned up, wouldn't clear her in Dylan Garrick's murder. She wasn't sure what would exonerate her, short of a confession from the real killer.

She winced. *The real killer*—it sounded like something O.J. would say. And she wasn't one of your multimillionaire celebrity defendants. She couldn't afford a Dream Team of lying lawyers.

Heck, she wasn't even sure there would be a trial. Maybe they would just lock her up in Guantánamo Bay and leave her there to rot.

There was that incipient paranoia again. She really shouldn't watch so many Oliver Stone movies.

It could be any time of night now. One a.m., three a.m., later. No way to know. The sun could be rising, and she wouldn't be aware of it. In here, there was no sun. That might be the worst thing about being locked up for life. She would so rarely see the sun or feel the air on her skin. Her world would be a concrete cell barely larger than a closet. She wasn't worried about the other inmates—she could fend for herself in any company—but to be caged for life, trapped within walls like that guy in the Edgar Allan Poe story, the one who was bricked up alive . . .

She realized she had leaped ahead to her incarceration as if it were a sure thing. Maybe it was.

The prospect seemed astonishing and unreal. She'd broken the law often enough in her career, but she'd never expected to be caught. Oh, sure, she could imagine herself on the run from the law—leaving the country, living abroad under an assumed name. She even had foreign accounts available for such a contingency. But never had she seriously imagined herself in lockup. Probably she'd always assumed the authorities would be too slow or too clueless to catch her. For the most part, her assumption had been valid.

But Tess had been up to the challenge, hadn't she?

Abby shook her head. Never should have teamed up with a *federale*. But as the man said after diving naked into a briar patch, it seemed like a good idea at the time.

She studied the cuff on her wrist. If she'd had her set of picklocks, she could've made short work of it. Even a safety pin or a scrap of wire would do. She scanned the floor, vaguely hopeful of finding some usable item.

Then she smiled at herself. Even if she did pick the lock, what was she going to do? Slip out of a high-security federal high-rise unobserved? Steal a gun and shoot her way out?

Besides, there was probably somebody watching her, even now. She thought about giving the finger to the hidden camera, if it was really where she thought it was, but didn't bother.

She was tired. She rested her head in the crook of her arm and closed her eyes. This was probably a mistake. She knew that law enforcement agents often judged a suspect guilty if he or she fell asleep in custody. An innocent person was presumed to be fueled with so much indignation and righteous anger that sleep was impossible. Only the guilty dozed off.

She didn't care. Hell, everybody was guilty of something.

Abby slept.

51

Abby's stomach was strongly advising her that it was breakfast time when the door finally opened and Tess came in.

"Thought you folks forgot about me."

Tess smiled a little—a tight, nervous smile. "We didn't forget." She took out a handcuff key and released Abby from the manacle.

"So what's it gonna be?" Abby asked. "Lethal injection or firing squad?"

"Come with me."

Abby stood up, massaging her wrist, though it wasn't really sore. It just seemed like the right thing to do. "Come where?"

"The director wants to see you."

"J. Edgar himself, back from the dead?"

"The ADIC. Michaelson."

"About what?"

"I don't know."

"Come on, girlfriend, level."

"I really *don't* know, Abby. They pulled me off the case after I arrested you. I was in the interrogation room with Michaelson only because he thought you might talk more freely with me present."

Abby shot her a cool glance. " 'Cause we're such good buds."

"That was probably the idea. Anyway, I haven't been privy to any new developments in the investigation. I have no idea what's going on."

Tess led her out of the room and down a series of hallways. Abby tried to ignore her hunger and fatigue, and the fear that had been growing inside her since her arrest.

"You know," she said as they rounded a corner, "at some point I really am entitled to see a lawyer."

Tess nodded. "I'm aware of that. Most of the sworn agents in the Bureau have law degrees. We're all very much aware of your rights."

"Then how come I spent the night in solitary? I mean, I assume it was the whole night. What time is it?"

"Seven a.m. To be honest, I think they were trying to figure out what to do."

"With me?"

"With *us*. This is a delicate situation. You have to appreciate that."

"Oh, I'm very appreciative. My sore ass is especially grateful. Not to mention my empty tummy. What makes the situation so delicate, anyhow? You're guilty of misconduct, and I'm a menace to public safety. It's open-and-shut."

"I'm sure that's how Michaelson sees it."

"But . . . ?"

"I don't know if Washington has the same perspective. Especially given the way the story is playing in the media."

"How is it playing?"

"To our advantage—I hope."

They reached a corner office and entered the anteroom, where Tess started to announce herself. Michaelson's secretary cut her off. "Yes, he's expecting you both. Go right in." Abby noted that the woman regarded them both with an unmistakable look of disapproval. She expected to be seeing a lot more of that look in the months ahead.

She followed Tess into the assistant director's inner office. Michaelson was lodged behind his desk, apparently talking to himself, a worrisome sign in a man in his position. Then—mystery solved—Abby saw a woman seated on the sofa opposite the desk.

She rose to greet the new arrivals. Abby was mildly shocked to recognize Nora Reynolds.

Nora seemed to recognize her, as well. "Do I know you?" she asked.

"You may have seen me at the barbecue yesterday. I'd, uh, arranged to talk with your husband there."

"Oh, yes, of course." Nora showed the practiced smile of a political spouse. "Working undercover, I imagine?"

"Something like that."

"Well, I hope you tried the food."

"It was excellent, thanks." Abby didn't think this was the right time to mention that the chicken had been overcooked.

Tess evidently had never met Mrs. Reynolds. "You're Congressman Reynolds's wife?" she asked.

Nora smiled again—a genuine smile this time. "Not for long. I wanted to meet you, Special Agent McCallum. I wanted to shake your hand."

"Shake *my* hand?"

Nora already had Tess's fingers in an unbreakable clasp. "You *got* the son of a bitch. It was more than I was able to do."

Tess's expression changed. She had understood something. "You're the insider we were working with."

"I am."

"But . . . how?"

"A few weeks ago I overheard my husband making a phone call. He was trying to track down someone named Bethany Willett. The name sounded familiar to me. I ran an Internet search and discovered that she was a key figure in an old murder case. The MEDEA case. I remembered it from the news coverage."

"Must have been quite a surprise," Abby said, drawing a cool glance from Mrs. Reynolds.

"Indeed. I spoke to a personal friend in the FBI. He got me involved in the investigation. I was to observe from inside."

"You must have known," Tess said, "that whatever you found out might incriminate your husband."

"I wanted him incriminated. I wanted out of our marriage."

"Because your husband had broken the law?"

"Because my husband is a sadist. And an increasingly violent sadist. He had become quite demanding in his, mmm, intimate conduct. I wouldn't cooperate with him, so he stopped approaching me. I was reasonably sure he was going elsewhere. He had found someone who would go along with his . . . tastes."

"I see," Tess said quietly.

"When I learned he was somehow involved in the MEDEA case—well, I just couldn't stand to be with him any longer. I wanted to see him brought to justice. That's why I was keeping tabs on my husband. Unfortunately, I don't think I learned anything useful."

"Don't sell yourself short, Nora," Michaelson said patronizingly. To her credit, she ignored him.

"As it turns out, my testimony isn't needed, anyway. We have enough evidence to put my husband away for years." She turned her smile on Tess. "And I have you to thank for it."

"Me?"

"You're the hero. Everyone knows it. It's in all the papers and all over TV. They say you saved the day single-handedly."

Tess fidgeted. "Not exactly."

"She's just being modest," Abby said.

Tess shot her a glare.

Nora didn't notice. "Well, I'll leave you to your meeting. I stayed around only to express my gratitude. Thank you again."

She clasped Tess's hand a second time, then left the room, forgetting to say good-bye to Abby.

Tess looked after her. Abby said quietly, "I guess the media coverage *is* advantageous—for one of us."

"If you think—" Tess began, but Michaelson interrupted.

"Be seated, both of you."

Tess took the space on the sofa vacated by Mrs. Reynolds. Abby sat next to her, feeling like a little girl in the principal's office. Only, in this case, she was facing the prospect of twenty or thirty years of detention.

Michaelson focused on her, ignoring Tess for the moment. "First of all, Ms. Sinclair, you'll be pleased to know that your purse was recovered at the crime scene."

"I'll be even more pleased if my tape recorder was inside."

"It was. The tape has been played. It does substantiate your version of events with regard to Congressman Reynolds's appearance at the hotel, and his subsequent abduction."

"Would it be wrong for me to say I told you so?"

Michaelson regarded her without friendliness. "It would be ill-advised."

"Just asking."

"The tape has been brought to the attention of the congressman, who is recuperating from his gunshot wounds at California Hospital. He is, by the way, expected to make a full recovery."

Abby blew out an exaggerated *whew*. "That's a relief. I don't know how our democratic republic would manage without him."

"It will have to try. Reynolds will not be returning to Congress. He will, in fact, be spending the next decade in a federal prison."

"For ordering the murders of Andrea and her children?"

"And for ordering the hit on Andrea last Friday."

"He didn't confess to that on the tape."

"He didn't have to. We have two very good sources. One is the driver of the van, Mr. Ronald Shanker, who is also recovering at the same hospital. Recovering from wounds you inflicted, Ms. Sinclair."

"In self-defense."

"I understand that. He's permanently lost the use of his right hand, by the way."

"I hope he's a lefty."

"He isn't."

"He is now. So who is this Shanker guy? One of Reynolds's Scorpion pals?"

"As a matter of fact, he's the president of the Santa Ana chapter of the club."

"I wouldn't have expected a guy like that to turn state's evidence."

"Fortunately we were able to apply pressure to Mr. Shanker. The congressman's campaign manager has proved most helpful in that regard. I believe you've met Mr. Stenzel."

Good old Kip. Abby almost smiled at the predictability of it. "Yeah. He's a weasel. I'm not surprised you turned him."

"We didn't have to turn him. *He* called *us*. He was very eager to talk. The information he supplied is what persuaded Shanker to deal. And the combined effect of Stenzel's and Shanker's statements, plus the tape recording, motivated the congressman to make a deal of his own."

"So all the dominoes fell in a neat row." Abby tried to see ahead to the conclusion. "And the result is . . . no trial? For any of them?"

"No trials. Reynolds and Shanker are going away for a while. Stenzel escapes with probation."

"It figures he'd land on his feet. Weasels always do."

Tess spoke up beside her. "That's cats. Cats land on their feet."

"Weasels, too," Abby said. "It's a little-known fact. How about Andrea Lowry? Is there a courtroom in her future?"

Michaelson shifted in his seat. "She is certainly guilty of kidnapping and assault with a deadly weapon. She doesn't even contest it. But there are extenuating circumstances."

"I'll say."

"She's been released, and no charges are pending."

"Well, it seems like everything is all wrapped up.

Except I can't help wondering about a little detail I like to call . . . me. Where's yours truly in all this? Still facing a murder rap for Dylan Garrick?"

Michaelson got up and moved to the windows, which provided a nice view of the city in the morning light. "You didn't kill Garrick. We already have the killer in custody."

Abby let out another sigh of relief, with no need to exaggerate it this time. "Let me guess. Shanker."

"Very good. You get a gold star."

"I don't deserve it. It's obvious. If Shanker was running the Santa Ana organization, he'd be held responsible for the screwup at Andrea's house. He would've been sucking heavy heat from Reynolds. He blamed Dylan for the failure of the operation, so it only makes sense that he would go after Dylan. And he would do it personally. No middleman. No more delegating."

"That's essentially the line of thought we followed." Michaelson studied her coldly. "You have a good head for these things."

"Next you'll be recruiting me for the Bureau."

"I wouldn't hold your breath waiting for that offer."

"I'm not really cut out for the cubicle farm, anyway." She was starting to enjoy herself, but then Tess had to ruin it.

"I don't get it," Tess said. "Why would Shanker confess to killing Garrick? We had nothing on him for that crime."

Abby turned to her, irritated. "Tess, that kind of question is called looking a gift horse in the mouth."

"At first, naturally, he wouldn't own up to it," Michaelson said, "even though, for all the reasons you suggested, we were starting to think he was the likely suspect. So we got creative. We'd heard your story about what happened to Dylan Garrick. We used it against Shanker. Told him there was a witness. We described everything Shanker had done, from finding the door unlocked to picking up the gun and the pillow on the floor. By the time we were through, he must have thought we had a hidden camera in Garrick's apartment. It broke him. When he started talking, he wouldn't stop." He turned his gaze on Tess. "He even informed us about ordering a hit on Agent McCallum, to be carried out by the bartender she interviewed."

Abby was surprised. "Tess, have you ever come to L.A. *without* someone trying to kill you?"

Tess ignored her. To Michaelson she said, "It was nothing. The guy put some moves on me, and I busted his chops for it."

"A detail you omitted when you related the encounter to me."

"I made a deal with him. He ID'd Abby from a six-pack, and I forgot about his momentary misjudgment. Now, if you want to bring him in on the basis of Shanker's testimony, which I had nothing to do with . . ."

Michaelson nodded. "We're trying, believe me. After Shanker was taken, word got out to the rest of the club. All the Scorpions have crawled under rocks for the moment."

"Excuse me," Abby cut in. "Not that I'm uninterested in the fate of the homicidal barkeep, but am I getting the right impression here? Am I off the hook?"

The sigh that escaped from Michaelson's lips was a profound expression of frustration. "Ms. Sinclair, there are a dozen things for which we could prosecute you. None of them would be as sensational as homicide, but the sum total would be more than enough to put you away in a maximum-security facility for many years. However . . ."

"I like that word 'however.' "

"However," he repeated, "to put you on trial would mean opening up the details of this case to the public, and since the major players have already plea-bargained, we're not sure a trial would really be in anyone's best interest."

"Certainly not mine," Abby agreed.

Tess was watching him. "You're not telling us everything, Richard. There's a reason you don't want to go public, and I think I know what it is."

"I'm sure you do. You must have had your publicity mill in D.C. working overtime."

"You know I didn't have anything to do with that."

Abby was getting lost. "To do with what? A little backstory for the exposition-impaired, please?"

"The story has generated national interest," Michaelson said. "A sitting congressman, a twenty-year-old murder case that was notorious in its day, a shoot-out in a downtown parking garage . . ."

"It's page one everywhere," Tess added.

Abby frowned. "They haven't mentioned me, have they?"

Michaelson shook his head. "Your name has been kept out of it. Actually, there's only one person whose name keeps coming up."

"I had nothing to do with it," Tess said again.

"Well, regardless of how it happened, the spin on the story is that Tess McCallum, already famous for her earlier exploits in Los Angeles, foiled the abduction and took Andrea and the congressman into custody—all on her own."

"Nice work, Tess," Abby said warmly.

Tess regarded her with a sour look. "Shut up."

"Witnesses saw a second woman with Reynolds in the hotel lobby. The second woman, we are told, was Agent McCallum, undercover. It was apparently Agent McCallum who pursued the congressman and shot it out with him and Mr. Shanker in the garage. It was Agent McCallum who made the arrest. Another triumph for you, Tess—though of course," Michaelson added, "you weren't responsible for leaking any of these details."

"The leak originated in D.C. You said so yourself."

"You have friends in D.C."

"Not friends who could put that story in the pipeline."

"Perhaps you have a guardian angel. How nice for you. The bottom line—"

"The bottom line," Abby said, "is that you guys have got a story that makes the Bureau look all nice and shiny like a brand-new car, and you don't want to spoil it by revealing that some unlicensed civilian did the real heavy lifting."

Michaelson's distaste for her was becoming almost palpable. It exuded from his body like ectoplasm. "We are concerned with the Bureau's reputation, yes. And there are certain benefits to the positive publicity accruing to Agent McCallum—"

Tess got it. "You can't touch me, either. That's right, isn't it? You can't even discipline me without risking a media inquiry."

"No final determination has been made—"

"Don't use Bureauspeak on me. You can't suspend me, let alone fire me, let alone charge me with anything criminal. Not without opening the whole can of worms. And you know it."

Michaelson's eyes shut briefly, as if in anticipation of a headache. "You won't be punished. But you won't be going places, either. Any other agent who'd reaped a public-relations bonanza like this would be headed straight to upper management." He leaned in close to the sofa. "Not you, McCallum. You're going to stay in that cow town of yours for the rest of your career."

Tess stared back at him, a faint smile on her lips. "Believe it or not, Richard, that's just the way I want it."

He believed her. Abby could see it in the way he straightened too abruptly and turned awkwardly away. "Attach an administrative section to your report on MEDEA. For the director's eyes only. Leave nothing out. I want the full extent of your misconduct on the record—even if it never sees the light of day."

"Anything to oblige a friend." Tess got up.

Abby followed her lead. "I guess I'm free to go, huh, Dick?"

He winced at her use of the nickname. "You can go. But remember, Ms. Sinclair, you're not so low-profile anymore. We're aware of you and your activities. And we will be watching you."

"Remind me to shut my blinds."

She and Tess didn't speak again until they were out in the hall.

"Well," Abby said, "that worked out better than expected."

Tess looked at her, a confusion of emotions on her face. "Abby . . ."

Abby waved off whatever the next words might have been. "Sorry. I'm not in the mood for a heart-to-heart. I'm going to reclaim my belongings and get out of here."

"I did what I thought was right."

"That's the problem," Abby said quietly.

She walked off, leaving Tess behind.

52

Tess returned to the squad room, where she was, pre-dictably, the object of stares and the subject of whis-pered asides. She ignored them. Crandall was watching her with peculiar intensity. She ignored him, too. Hauser's secretary let her in to see the squad commander, who looked as if he hadn't slept all night. Then again, neither had she.

"I just wanted to say I'm clearing out," she told him. "And to say you did a good job on this case. I'm sorry if I made it more difficult."

Hauser looked up at her from his desk. "I know you're not being disciplined, Agent McCallum. I want to say . . . I still think you did the Bureau wrong. And I'll never respect you again."

He returned his gaze to the paperwork in front of him. After a moment she let herself out.

In the hall outside the squad room, Crandall caught up with her. "Hey, Tess. Heading home?"

She was surprised by the friendly tone. "Battered but unbowed."

"Said your good-byes to Hauser?"

"More like a good riddance, from his point of view. It appears I'm more of a persona non grata than ever." She smiled. "How about you, Rick? Will you ever respect me again?"

"I'm not as much of a hard-ass as Hauser. Tess, if I'd known you were going to come clean to Michael-son, I never would've—"

"How could you have known? Even I didn't know what I was going to do until I did it."

"I still feel bad about it."

"You shouldn't."

"I do. But I've taken steps to redeem myself."

"What steps?" She studied him, an idea forming. "Rick, are you the media's anonymous source?"

"Me? What kind of media contacts do I have in L.A.?"

"The leak didn't originate in L.A. It came out of D.C.—where Ralston Crandall is currently posted as deputy director."

"Let's not bring my father into this."

"The question is, did *you* bring him into it?"

"I'm not going to lie to you, Tess." He left that statement hanging enigmatically in the air, then clapped her on the shoulder and added, "Have a safe trip. And stay in touch, okay?"

Crandall went back inside the squad room, and Tess was left thinking that, despite it all, she still had one ally in this town.

53

By nine in the morning Andrea had run out of ways to distract herself. Watching television was out of the question. She'd made the mistake of turning on the TV and had caught part of a report on the arrest of Congressman Reynolds, which included a garbled recap of what the newscaster called "the Medea child murders of twenty years ago." Radio was even worse. The call-in talk shows were a fever swamp of speculation by the uninformed and the self-styled experts, none of whom understood a thing.

She couldn't sleep with the constant noise and couldn't concentrate enough to read or work a crossword puzzle. All she could do was pace the house and occasionally sneak a glance through the curtains. The crowd of journalists and curiosity seekers surrounding her house never grew smaller. If anything, it had increased in numbers as the story spread.

After the attack on her home, there had been three or four TV news vans and a few other reporters. Now the vans lined the streets—representing not only the local TV channels but national cable outlets. Every news radio station had sent somebody, as had every newspaper within five hundred miles, it seemed. Not to mention half the population of the Valley, who apparently had nothing better to do on Sunday morning than stand outside her house. Enterprising vendors had already set up carts selling hot dogs and tamales, and somebody had printed T-shirts with her picture on them from twenty years ago.

What did they all want from her—the journalists

and the spectators tramping on her lawn and snapping photos of her porch? Well, the answer was obvious enough. They wanted a comment, a statement, or, failing that, a sighting, a few seconds of footage to run on their next newscast or a blurred image to print on the newspaper's front page.

She knew better than to give it to them. They would not be satisfied with only one statement or one appearance. They would want more, always more.

Of course, it might be in her interest to cooperate. She could tell her side of the story, get the truth out to the public after two decades of lies. But she couldn't be so pragmatic about it. The simple fact was, she hated the press. They had hounded her for years. They had forced her to change her name and live in hiding. She would give them nothing now. They could go to hell.

Her phone rang again. She was so tired of that sound. And yet—she blinked in surprise—her phone couldn't be ringing, could it? Hours ago she had unhooked it from the wall.

It was her cell phone, then—the one Abby had given her. And only Abby knew the number.

She found the phone amid the items she'd brought home from the downtown hospital where she had been examined for injuries suffered in the car crash. There had been nothing serious, only a few scrapes and bruises. She had endured a long interrogation by a nice young man named Crandall and, much to her astonishment, had been released with no charges filed.

On the eighth or ninth ring she answered. "Hello," she said tentatively, ready to end the call if a reporter had somehow gotten hold of the number.

"Hey, kiddo. How's tricks?"

"Abby. Where are you?"

"Eating a late and much needed breakfast at a yogurt shop in Westwood. It's within walking distance of the federal building, which is good since my Mazda is still in an alley downtown. Unless it's been towed by now."

"I was afraid you were in trouble. They said something about pressing charges against you."

"They were bluffing. You know these Eliot Ness types. All talk, no action. I hear they let you go, too."

"Yes. Though I'm still not sure why. I abducted Jack Reynolds. I *shot* him."

"You weren't yourself."

"I know. I was acting crazy. I don't even know what I intended to do. I mean, I thought I was going to kill him, really *kill* him, but if that's all I wanted, why did I bother to make him go anywhere? I could have killed him at any time. It doesn't make sense."

"Want my take on it?"

"Even if I said no, it wouldn't stop you."

"True enough. I think you were conflicted. Part of you wanted revenge on Jack. Another part wasn't willing to pull the trigger. So you compromised. You put off taking any final action."

"I would have had to choose eventually."

"You weren't thinking that far ahead. And if you had chosen, you would have made the right choice."

"You believe that?"

"I really do."

"Well, I hope you're right. You probably are. You've been right about most things. But I wouldn't have thought that kind of explanation would get me very far with the authorities. There was no way I expected to be released. I'm still thinking they'll show up at any minute and take me back into custody."

"They won't. What you're not taking into consideration is a little thing called extenuating circumstances. To prosecute, they have to be reasonably assured of a conviction. Now, what jury is going to convict you after hearing the tape I made?"

"I suppose that's true. I have to admit, though, that I was prepared for the worst."

"Well, that makes two of us. But you know what they say. Always prepare for the worst, and most of the time you'll be pleasantly surprised."

"They advised me not to say anything about you if I talk to the press."

"That's a good idea. But you're not going to talk to the press, anyway, are you?"

"Of course not."

"Didn't think so. You weren't too eager to be interviewed the night I pulled that stunt to get into your house."

"I held a gun on you. I'm sorry."

"All in a day's work. So who are you going to be from now on?"

"What?"

"Andrea . . . or Bethany?"

"I don't know. I suppose it doesn't matter."

"No, it doesn't. What matters is how you feel."

"How I feel?" Andrea closed her eyes. "Well, I'm encircled by those jackals from the press. There are television vans parked up and down the street. People won't stop ringing my doorbell. I think they'd climb in a window if I left one open. I had to disconnect my phone. Every time I turn on the TV or radio I see pictures of myself from twenty years ago. I can't even think of looking at a newspaper. I've become a celebrity again. Only this time I'm not Medea anymore. This time no one is saying I killed my babies. They know I didn't. And I know I didn't. I know I never killed anyone."

"So how *do* you feel?"

"Free, Abby," Andrea whispered. "I feel free."

54

After finishing her breakfast, Abby hiked from Westwood Village to the Wilshire Royal, where she found Vince and Gerry on duty at the front desk. They were both properly outraged by the search of her condo last night. She told them not to worry about it. "Just a minor misunderstanding," she said lightly. They pretended to believe her, the same way they pretended to believe she was a sales rep. Denial could be a beautiful thing.

She checked the garage and found her Hyundai still in its reserved space. Later she could bum a ride off Wyatt and pick up her Mazda. At least for now she had her backup car.

The elevator took her to the tenth floor. She opened up her condo after stripping off the crime scene ribbon festooned on the door.

The place was a mess, of course. The feds had not been gentle when searching the premises. Every drawer had been opened, the contents strewn on the floor. For some unaccountable reason her sizable collection of CDs had been scattered. The clothes formerly hanging in her bedroom closet had been cast around like rags. Her computer was gone, taken to a crime lab for analysis, though she'd been given assurances that it would be speedily returned.

The search had never posed any threat to her. She wasn't careless enough to leave incriminating information in her home. Sensitive material—ID kits, client lists, illegal weapons and eavesdropping devices—was kept in Santa Monica in a storage locker she'd registered under an assumed name. Electronic data of a private nature were stored on a secure Internet site. No one could find the site by examining her PC; a sophisticated program permanently erased all records of her online activity with every shutdown.

She'd worked too many cases where a stalker had stashed incriminating photos under his bed or left damaging e-mails on his computer's hard drive. She wasn't going to make the same mistake.

Still, the impossibility of finding anything to use against her hadn't stopped the *federales* from trying.

With a sigh, she set to work cleaning up the mess. She had succeeded in reorganizing her music collection when the intercom buzzed.

"Yes?" she said.

Gerry answered. "An agent from the FBI is here to speak with you." He made no effort to conceal his disapproval of the visitor.

Abby frowned. Just what she needed. Another feeb to make her life hell.

"Send him up," she said in resignation.

She placed the last few CDs back on the shelf before the doorbell rang. When she opened the door, Tess was there.

"Oh," Abby said. "It's you."

"It's me."

"You're looking well."

"Cut the crap, Abby. May I come in or not?"

"Make yourself at home." She gestured at the disaster that was her living room. "Your fellow jackbooted thugs already have."

Tess entered and stood awkwardly amid the disorder. "I'm sorry about that."

"Yeah, I'm sure you're real broken up. It wasn't too long ago that you thought I was good for Dylan Garrick's murder." Abby knelt and began gathering up her smaller but still considerable collection of DVDs.

Tess spread her hands helplessly. "What else was I supposed to think? Everything pointed to you."

"Tess, if you would watch more TV, you'd know it's never the most obvious suspect."

"Well, forgive me for taking the evidence at face value."

"You could have tried taking *me* at face value."

"You were lying."

Abby started putting the DVDs in alphabetical order. "Not about anything important. I told you I didn't kill Garrick. That part was true."

"You should have told me the rest."

"Couldn't risk it. You might not have believed me."

"Maybe I would have. I never wanted to think you were capable of murder."

"And yet you thought it, anyway. You're always underestimating me. But I can't entirely blame you. Sometimes I underestimate myself."

"Now, *that* I don't believe."

"You should." Abby arranged the first third of her DVD library, from *A* to *H*, on the shelf. "Remember how, in the Boiler Room, you asked whether my conscience was enough to keep me in line?"

"I remember."

"Well, it was a fair question. In fact, I started wondering the same thing after Friday night. Wondering if maybe I'd become too much of a desperado. Whether I need somebody to ride herd on me. Whether I'm getting out of control." She put titles starting with *I* through *P* on the shelf. "I came pretty close to shooting Dylan Garrick. Closer than I admitted to you."

Tess took a step forward. "How close?"

"I wasn't sure. What I knew was that something he said changed my mind. It was just a little thing. He said we were both pros. He said the hit on Andrea was just a job for him—a job like mine."

Tess nodded, understanding. "He said you were the same."

"Right." The DVDs with titles from *Q* through *Z* were added to the shelf. She really did have a *Z*. Two of them, in fact—*Zoolander* and *Zulu*. "He said we were the same. And suddenly I . . . well, I didn't want it to be true."

"If he hadn't said those words . . ."

"Would I have gone through with it?" She turned to face Tess. "That's the question I kept asking myself the next day. And I didn't know the answer. And it scared me. It made me doubt if I could really go on—or if I even *ought* to go on. You know the old Nietzsche thing, about how when you fight monsters, you risk becoming a monster yourself? That's what worried me. I thought maybe I'd crossed the line. But I didn't. And I won't."

"How can you be sure?"

"Because last night I had the opportunity to shoot Jack Reynolds in the head. I wanted to. I mean, I *really* wanted to. But I didn't do it. I'm still in control. I'm still me."

"Then you're okay with yourself?"

"Yeah. But I'm not okay with *you*." Abby knelt and started stacking books in neat piles. "I'm not blaming you. Your response was predictable. But that's the problem. I *know* you. I know you'll put what you see as your duty above any personal loyalty."

Tess took a moment before asking, "Is that wrong?"

"I don't know. It's not my way. And it complicated my life a lot, and nearly got me killed."

She went on stacking books, not trying to organize them, just needing something to do.

"So what are you saying?" Tess asked. "You can't trust me?"

"Yes. And no. I *can* trust you to always do the right thing—as you see it. I *can't* trust you to see eye to eye with me on what the right thing is." She looked up from the fourth pile of books. "Which means we're not going to be working together anymore."

"I hadn't expected us to."

"And it means—we're not friends, Tess."

"What are we, then? Enemies?"

"Not yet. But if you ever come back to my town and get mixed up in my business again—we will be."

"I hope that day never comes."

"Me, too." Abby let the words settle into the silence of the room. Then more brightly she added, "So, are you flying back to your nest in the Rockies?"

Tess hesitated, then knelt beside her and started stacking books herself. "On my way to the airport. Michaelson even arranged a driver."

Abby wrinkled her nose at the mention of Michaelson. "He's a piece of work, huh?"

Tess grunted. "There's definitely something to be said for working alone."

"You've gotta watch that guy. He's still gunning for you. Probably now more than ever. He'll sink your career if he gets half a chance."

"I know." Tess paused to examine one of the books, which was, Abby noticed, a sex manual, and a darn good one. Tess added it to the pile without comment. "And he's still rising in the ranks. Could be the director someday."

"Remind me to move to Mexico if that happens."

Tess smiled. "I might be moving there with you."

Abby found herself smiling, too. "I have to say, I've enjoyed our two little outings."

"I can't say I have. Sorry to put it that way, but—"

Abby waved off the apology. "I'd be disappointed if you said anything else. It would be disturbingly out of character."

Tess sighed. "Well, as much fun as this is, I'd better get to the airport."

They rose together. Tess walked to the door and stepped into the hall, then turned, her face serious again.

"I don't plan on coming back to L.A. But I don't always have a choice about where I go—or the cases I work. You know that."

"I know."

"It's not impossible we'll cross paths again. And Abby, if that day ever comes—I'll be ready."

Abby met her gaze. "So will I," she said, and slowly she closed the door.

Author's Note

Tess and Abby, the two heroines of *Mortal Faults,* teamed up (reluctantly, as always) in my most recent book *Dangerous Games,* and also appeared separately in two earlier novels. Tess McCallum stars in *Next Victim,* and Abby Sinclair in *The Shadow Hunter.*

My gratitude goes out to all the people who helped me with *Mortal Faults,* including Tracy Bernstein, executive editor at New American Library, whose careful reading of the manuscript resulted in many improvements; Doug Grad, formerly of NAL, who first suggested pairing off two of my characters; copy editor Michele Alpern, who caught and corrected many mistakes; my agent, Jane Dystel of Dystel & Goderich Literary Management, who helped define and shape the story in its early stages; and Miriam Goderich, also of DGLM, who likewise supplied feedback and suggestions that turned a vague idea into a workable plot. I'd also like to thank my friends in Florida, Sherry and Cullenthia, for their support, and Lisa DuMond for supplying me with the "brass ovaries" line. That's one I wouldn't have thought of on my own.

Readers are invited to visit me at michaelprescott. net, where you'll find information on my other seven books, as well as interviews, essays, and an e-mail address.

About the Author

Michael Prescott is the *New York Times* bestselling author of several novels. You can contact him at his Web site at www.michaelprescott.net.